RESOLUTIONS

DISCPLACED BOOK 3

STEPHEN DRAKE

THE DISPLACED SERIES:

Displaced

Civilization

Resolutions

Dedicated to Linda and Susan; for without their help and support, this work would not have been possible.

A special thank you goes to Paula Shene, K.J. Simmill, and J.C. Stone. Excellent authors all, in their own right, for their friendship, suggestions, help, and for taking the time from their busy lives to read my work. Words fail to convey my deep appreciation for them.

I would also like to thank:

Shihan Samuel H. Hyatt, Sr. for his technical assistance, instruction, and friendship.

Shodan Kenny Evansen for his friendship, instruction, and fabulous artwork.

Author's Note: Since the publication of the first two books in this series, I've had several questions from my readers. This book was written to answer those questions and to move the story along.

For as long as I can remember, I've heard people refer to my father as everything from Saint to Demon. To be sure, at any given time, he could be all that and more, but he was just a man, with all the faults and failings that go with being human. Most people forget that all-important fact.

— ANDREW MURDOCK, *THE REAL KEVIN MURDOCK: A DIARY*

M urdock was tending his fire atop the *Stairs of Mount Oomah*, as he referred to the series of plateaus, when something silver went streaking past, far overhead. Long after it had disappeared, he heard the deafening roar split the night. Beron had just given notice to him, and he was to pass on the notice to everyone who could perceive his thoughts. The newest arrivals were on their way.

Oh… joy, Murdock thought. *Has it been five years already? We haven't recovered from the last bunch of invaders.*

"If anyone is interested, we're about to have more invaders," he flashed to his tribe.

"I was wondering what that was," Declan replied. *"How long before it lands?"*

"I have no idea how many orbits it'll take before velocity is reduced enough to allow planetfall. If it follows the same procedures as the last one, it'll be at least two days after landing before anyone disembarks."

"How many are on this one?"

Murdock did a quick mental calculation. *"Another two thousand people, supposedly."*

Murdock guessed it was two hours before sunup when the approaching ship circled the area several times before it hung motionless in the sky. The maneuver had awakened him, putting him in a foul mood. A mood that was worse than the one he was in when he was notified.

"It'll be landing soon", he flashed to the others. *"Probably at sunup."*

Irene Harris, MD, Annie Cooper, LPN, and Roy White, EMT, were sitting out on the roof of the medical facility when Irene and Annie received the message. They both stood with excited expectation and looked up at the quickly lightening pre-dawn sky at what appeared to be a dark hole ... and it was getting larger.

Declan Griffen was saddling his new mount in preparation to continuing toward home, when Murdock's latest message reached him. He stopped handling the tack to calm the skittish beast, and looked up to see the huge hole in the sky, and whistled.

"Dancer, either that is one huge ship or a meteor is coming," he said to the mount, as he watched it descend.

Murdock levitated off the step and across the open plain, to the top of the next step, where he saw the colossal ship descend. When it was a few thousand feet up, the ship separated into several and formed a circle before continuing its descent. Then Murdock heard the booming separation explosion. He counted eleven ships. *Why eleven? Two thousand should fit in ten pods. What's in the extra pod?*

Just at full sunup, all eleven ships touched down on the bluish-green, grass-covered plain with rolling hills surrounding it. They weren't far from the empty landing pods he had placed below the second step. From his vantage point, he could see the enormous circle they formed. Each lander looked to be the same size as the previous pod that had landed five years ago and was set aside not far from the stream that ran down each of the steps. They were several miles from the river and the medical facility.

"*Did you want to meet the newcomers?*" Murdock flashed to his wife, Mei Lee.

"*Yes, and so does Emily. We're hitching up Donder to the cart,*" she replied.

He wondered, *Why did the deer that Heather and Alvin tamed end up with those particular names? It had to be Heather or Emily.*

"*Be careful,*" he flashed. "*The landing was noisier than usual since there are eleven pods this time. It'll draw attention from Elizabeth Reyes' group, and others.*"

"*We're planning on crossing the plain off the top step, a few miles from the river.*"

"*The new pods are off the second step, close to the stream, so make a direct course toward there. I'm close to the landing site now. Bring*

3

plenty of hides. I'm thinking of making camp close to the step and the stream, for safety."

"Head to the stream under the second step," Murdock flashed to Declan. *"Our wives are on their way."*

"I know," Declan replied. *"Em let me know. I should be there in four or five hours. I'll let Irene and Annie know where we are. I'm sure they're gonna want to meet the newbies."*

"Well, be careful. I'm sure our enemies know another ship is down, and they will come around to see what they can do to further complicate an already complex situation."

"Are you always so... negative?"

"I'm not being negative. Just realistic. With all we've been through, there are some that would like us to... go away. If any of them show up, I'm planning to defend me and mine. Is that okay with you?"

"Hey, I'm on your side, brother. I don't like to admit it, but you're right more often than not. I'll see you when I get there."

I've only known Declan for three or four years, but I like having him around. He makes me laugh. Murdock smiled.

By the time Declan arrived at the campsite, it was late afternoon and Murdock had several poles stacked and was lashing them together at the top.

"Greetings, brother. I come bearing gifts." Declan held up four large fish, already cleaned and ready to cook.

Murdock smiled. "You know what to do with them, don't you? If you start them now, they may be cooked by the time the wives and kids get here. I'm expecting them any time now."

Declan nodded and started cooking the fish.

"I've been thinking—"

"Uh-oh, we're all in trouble now!"

Murdock became stone-faced and tried not to chuckle. "Like I was saying, I'm thinking we need to keep some sort of record of who arrives, who dies, who's born..."

4

"That would work out pretty good... if we had miles of paper and gallons of ink."

"Ever thought of clay as a medium?"

Declan's mouth opened, shut, then opened again and nothing came out.

"Wow, I left you speechless. Who would've thought *that* was possible?"

"I was thinking about that before I learned to fire clay. Since then, I haven't given it much thought. I guess I could do it. It would take skill to write legibly and to keep it that way through the firing. But yeah, I think it would work."

"See what you can do. Our wives are here. Time to get the tipis assembled."

It was shortly after sunset, both lodges were assembled, and the two families were sitting around the campfire eating the fish.

"When do you think the *newbies* will be up and about?" Declan asked while finishing his fish.

"The procedure I observed, when you and Em arrived, was during the third day, after landing, there should be signs of life. Can you hit anything with that yet?" Murdock indicated Declan's bow.

Declan chuckled. "The safest place seems to be in front of me."

"He does fair," Emily corrected, "if he has time to practice. He's been practicing some, but not like he should."

She was untying the front of her buckskin dress and pulled out an arm. It briefly exposed her milk-filled breast before she held little Gordon to her nipple.

Declan smiled. "Greedy little guy, ain'tcha?" He grinned at his son, caressing the infant's cheek.

"No different than his father," Emily quipped which caused everyone to laugh.

"So, what's the plan?" Mei Lee asked once the laughter quieted.

"Tomorrow, I'm planning on marking out a barrier line to keep these idiots—I mean *invaders*, corralled," Murdock said.

"Why do they need to be corralled?" Emily asked.

"There are two thousand people, who don't understand what this place is like or how to defend themselves against the dangers here.

"Remember how weak you all were, when you disembarked. I'm sure they will be weak also. Do you think they should just be allowed to wander off on their own? Besides, a barrier works both ways. Keeping them corralled and safe, and keeping anything, or anyone, out that might endanger them."

"At some point, though, they'll be released?" Emily said.

"Yes, they will be loosed upon our world, for good or ill. I want my family out of their reach when they are."

"Are we going to have a guard tonight?" Declan said.

"Why wouldn't we? We have Liz Reyes' group, who are belligerent toward us. We have Raymond Tutt, Ted Wagner, and their bunch of pirates and thieves. And we have Keith Rogers and his group of *Lotus Eaters*. About the only group we haven't managed to honk-off are Markus Lantz and the farmers in his group. We're away from home and the protections that go with it. You go and rest. I'll take the first watch. I need to plan things with Beron so we have some backup."

Vernon Parker, Sebastian Heartly, Elizabeth Reyes, and three others, from their group, were laying on their bellies, looking over the cliff-edge at the landed pods.

"Where did those women we were following go?" Reyes whispered to Heartly.

"We lost them shortly after we saw them in the distance," Heartly whispered back. "One of them looked familiar."

Reyes frowned, trying to think. "That was Mei… something. She's Murdock's woman, or so I believed a couple of years ago. She came around once when the doc was attacked."

"Ah," Heartly nodded, "that's where I saw her before."

Reyes motioned Heartly to move back as she moved back from the cliff. Heartly passed on the signal to the man next to him. He motioned to Parker and all the way down the line. Reyes stopped fifty yards away from the cliff edge, as did the rest of their party.

"Make camp here," she said. "I want two of you to mount a guard while the rest of us sleep. I doubt anything will happen with the pods for a while yet. The winters haven't been kind to us over the past five years. We've lost the majority of our people, and we're in dire need of an infusion of new blood. It's imperative we make a case for our group to the newcomers."

"We all understand that, Liz," Heartly whispered, while another man got a small fire started.

Reyes smiled at Heartly. "You know, Bass," Reyes said as she moved closer to him and slipped her hands around his waist, "just because I let you grope and snuggle with me doesn't give you permission to use familiar terms in front of others." She grabbed his genitals. "I could have these removed, you know? I don't think you'd like that," she said, with sugar in her voice.

Heartly cleared his throat. "Sorry, Elizabeth."

"*Ma'am* is better." She gave his genitals a squeeze.

"Um… yes… *ma'am*, I understand."

Markus Lantz, Kathy Watkins, and Heather Stevens crept into the medical facility compound just before sundown.

"Hello?" Heather yelled when she entered. "Is anyone here?"

"What do you need—Heather!" Annie Cooper ran over and hugged her. "Is there an emergency?" She looked over Heather and the two guests.

Heather took a deep breath. "No, no emergency. This is Mark Lantz and Kathy Watkins. They're the leaders of our group, the one down from this plateau. We've come because of the new arrivals. Are you gonna go meet them?" She looked at Annie with begging eyes.

"As a matter of fact, I do have to go to do medical assessments and give my personal okey-dokey. Why do you ask?"

"Our group needs wood and metal workers. We lost a couple of them last winter to exposure. Do you think we can go with you to meet them?"

"Well, you can go with me, but I don't know how close you'll be able to get for a day or two. If you remember... well, maybe you don't. When we arrived and disembarked the pod, Murdock was only there for two full days, maybe a little more. That's as long as I'm planning to stay there, unless things change that requires me to stay longer. But you're free to travel with me, there and back."

"I know it's a big intrusion, but can we rest here until we leave? We didn't come prepared for a long trip. We really don't have what we need for a trip into the wild. If you say no, we'll understand."

Irene Harris came out of the house. "What's going on, Annie? Your dinner is getting cold. How are ya, Heather?"

"Hey, Doc, all of us are fine," Heather yelled.

"They need a place to sleep until tomorrow," Annie said. "They're going with me to see the new arrivals."

"You make it sound like a trip to the zoo." Harris chuckled.

"*You mean, it isn't?*" Annie flashed to Irene. "*I hope Kevin can corral the beasties.*"

"Sure, bring them in," Irene said. "I'll get Roy-Boy to rustle up something for them to eat." She turned and entered the house.

"*You know he hates it when you call him that,*" Annie flashed, and motioned for the rest to follow Irene as she brought up the rear.

Murdock was standing a few paces from the campfire, gazing out into the night.

"You know what I have in mind," he flashed to Beron. *"Will you help?"*

Murdock knew the huge bear was lying atop the step above the camp, keeping a watch of a different type. He also knew Bridget was lying next to him, as usual, her focus directed to the human children, whom she adored.

"We will help all we able." Beron replied. *"You know all need is ask. Bridget guard families."* Beron paused. *"Why use food for travel?"*

A picture of the deer popped into Murdock's mind. *"They are what humans call draft animals. They are stronger than humans and can pull for a longer time. I appreciate that you remain invisible to them. Seeing you would frighten them and cause disruption."*

If there was such a thing as shrugging while communicating telepathically, that was what Murdock perceived.

"We remain hidden from you kind at these events," Beron flashed.

When Murdock woke Declan for his watch, he had gathered more wood for the fire, enough to last through the night.

"I'm going to get things set at the landing," Murdock whispered. "I'm counting on you to see to it that camp is struck and our families are transported. Bridget is watching and will help. Not that I'm expecting any trouble, but you never know."

"What about you?" Declan said.

"Beron is going with me, so, I'll be fine," Murdock said as he slipped off into the darkness.

Murdock was above the landing site, atop the plateau that was across the stream from the landing area, gathering poles needed to mark the barrier, when he heard a strange noise coming from the trees. He checked the breeze and found it blowing into his face, so he froze amongst the saplings.

As he readied himself with his bow, he could hear snuffling and grunting sounds headed his way. He crouched as the creature broke into the open. *A wild boar... sort of. It must weigh five hundred pounds, and what a tusker! That head almost looks like a warthog. It may be a cross between a warthog and a razorback.*

The boar stared at him, stomped the ground and snorted before continuing to forage. As it turned, Murdock drew back and let an arrow fly. The beast dropped.

"*Destroyer,*" Beron flashed. "*Stray. Difficult control and confine.*"

"*This is a destroyer?*" Murdock replied. "*I should have known. They eat anything they can find, leaving little, if any. It never occurred to me.*"

"*Why you take?*" Beron flashed.

"*Where humans come from, they are good to eat. Many have tamed them.*"

"*Strange, you kind.*"

A few hours later, Murdock levitated the processed porcine and two dozen one- to two-inch diameter poles off of the ridge above the landing site. As he did, he saw Declan and their families heading his way.

"Where did you get the tusker?" Declan asked as he dismounted.

"Up there." Murdock indicated the ridge he had just descended. "Get it cooking while I place the poles, and then I'll help with resetting camp."

After the poles were set, marking off a three-hundred-square-yard area with the pods inside, Murdock helped to get the tipis set up again. There wasn't much left for him to do, as his family, and Declan's, had worked together to get the tasks accomplished.

It's amazing what can happen when everyone works together.

"Raise the pig," Murdock told Declan. "Slow cook it and turn it so it's not dry. What do you think of trying to trap some young ones and tame them?"

"We'd have to make an enclosure to keep them in and predators out," Declan said, "but I don't see why we couldn't try to tame them. I'm sure the older kids could do quite a bit of the raising. It would secure another food source for us."

"Hey, Murdock!" Annie Cooper yelled, from a distance.

Murdock turned and saw her. Heather, Kathy Watkins, and Mark Lantz were further away.

"What's going on, Annie?" Murdock flashed.

"They need help. Not too bright to venture out unprepared."

"What kind of help?"

"They need replacement craftsmen, metal and wood mostly."

"If they're not armed, bring them in."

Annie retreated to talk to the trio, and then all four proceeded into the camp.

"Not too bright venturing out unarmed and ill-prepared," Murdock said, as the four entered the camp proper. "Heather, you know better."

Heather moved over to Murdock and gave him a hug. "I know, but someone *insisted* we didn't need them," she whispered in his ear. "They refused to travel with me if I were armed."

"Is that true, Lantz? Did you refuse to travel with Heather if she were armed?" Murdock scowled at him.

"This is not that hostile of a place," Lantz said. "Weapons are not needed most of the time." Lantz said dismissively.

"How would you like to walk home alone? I know the dangers, and I go everywhere armed. You are a fool!"

Lantz backed up a step or two. "Are you saying you won't help us?"

"I don't suffer fools," Murdock snapped, "but you're worse! You're an imbecile *and* a fool. Anyone who would ever listen to you is asking to end up as dinner. I told you about the cougar. Did you or your people take care of it? There are also wolves and pirates. What was your plan if you ran across one? Push Heather out in front of you so you can run?"

Lantz took a couple more steps back.

"You can take your stupid ass right on back to where you came from. I'll have a powwow with Heather, and then decide for myself."

"But... but... I don't know the way home."

Murdock arched his back, let his head hang back, and exhaled loudly. "Maybe, sometime in the last five years, you should've gotten outside your house for more than five minutes." He stomped over to Lantz and grabbed his upper arm, instinctively digging in his fingers to separate the bicep and tricep muscles, to reduce the amount of resistance Lantz could affect. He dragged the taller man to the first pole. "See pole? Follow pole, that way," Murdock said condescendingly. "When you get to the cliff, you can do everyone a favor and jump off. Or you can turn left and go to the river. At the river, you can drown yourself, or turn right and follow the path home. If you ever endanger Heather or Alvin—or anyone else, for that matter—I'll show you, firsthand, what the wolves can do!" He shoved Lantz back, causing him to stumble. "Now get your dumb ass home! You see what I have to put up with?" He entered the camp. "And people wonder why I am the way I am. And you, young lady!" He scowled at Heather. "You should've never left the house without something, anything. I thought I taught you better than that."

"Lantz wasn't going to give her the annual allowance of flour if she didn't guide him unarmed," Annie said.

"Why you?" Murdock asked Heather.

12

"Because no one else knows where the medical facility is. I knew because Declan told me on one of his visits."

"So, you and Alvin don't live with the rest?"

"No, we moved about a mile toward the stream so we could do what we needed with the deer. Built our own place and have been improving it. We're both still expected to help with the harvest for our bag of flour."

"As well they should," Watkins said, then seeing the glare from Murdock, decided silence would be the better option.

Murdock turned his attention back to Heather. "What happens if you need help?"

She shrugged. "Deal with it ourselves, mostly."

"But if *they* need help, you better show up fast, right?"

"That's about the size of it."

"Do they use your mounts?"

"Most of the time they just take an animal they need for plowing or whatever."

"Payments?"

Heather shook her head.

"And why should there be any payment?" Watkins said. "None of us get paid. Labor is donated for the good of the community."

"You need to move your operation across from the medical facility," Murdock said. "Let them see the value of you being there. Think about it and discuss it with Alvin. How's that pig coming along?" he asked Declan.

"You have another issue to deal with." Annie pointed discreetly toward the landing pods.

Murdock turned to see one of the pods opening its ramp. He stood there, sucking saliva through his teeth as if he had something stuck between them.

"I'm not in the mood for this."

Curtis Griffen held up his arm to block the sunshine from his light-sensitive eyes as he made his way down the transport pod's ramp. The meal inside the pod was insufficient for him, and his rubbery legs protested. *I hate that feeling.*

Once his eyes adjusted to the sunshine, after he'd reached the bottom of the ramp, he thought he could make out something. *Are those... Indians? With a couple wigwams, no less. Am I hallucinating? Maybe I'm still in stasis and this is just a dream... or a nightmare.*

A few seconds later, as everyone moved toward a figure walking toward them, he could see two men and three women wearing buckskins, and two women dressed much as the rest of the newcomers, just more worn, almost threadbare. The man coming toward them was short and appeared to be well-armed. From what Curtis could see, a bow, arrows, and two machetes. *He walks with authority and a purpose. Danger!*

"I am Murdock," the man said, "and I have been here for ten years. If any of you think they know more than I do about this place, then speak up. I'll be more than happy not to think about you when winter comes and you're starving and freezing. If you look that way," he pointed at the sticks poking up from the ground, "you'll see sticks. Stay away from them. There is a barrier there for the safety of all concerned. If you look toward the stream," he pointed the other way, "you'll see a cliff face. Don't go up there. If you look behind me, you'll see another cliff face. You can go up there if you want to, but not the one behind it. Off toward the poles is the river. Once I've released you, you are free to go that way. There are lots of fish in the river. This planet has various wildlife. There are deer, wolves, and mountain lions. Deer being the most plentiful. There are also bears, but don't hunt, bother, or molest them. All the wildlife is bigger than you'd expect."

"Why should we do anything you say?" someone asked. "Who appointed you Lord over us?"

Murdock grinned mirthlessly. "You can do whatever you

want, but when you end up dead, you'll have no one to blame but yourselves. Going contrary to what I said will get you killed, so you go right ahead. It won't bother me in the least. I'm not here to babysit a bunch of whiny tenderfoots. I'm here to give you all a fighting chance to survive, but you can do what you want. I'll not waste my time with any of you. I don't suffer fools."

"He sounds harsh," whispered a woman standing close to Curtis.

He frowned at her.

"What's your problem?" she asked in a surly tone.

"Shut up. I'm tryin' ta listen." Curtis answered.

"How rude can you get?" the woman asked rhetorically.

"I know some of you might think I'm harsh," Murdock said, "but I'm not as harsh as nature. This isn't a vacationers' campground. Survival is harsh, and you might as well get used to it. You don't have a lot of choices. You will only be as safe as you want to be, but that will take a lot of work, from you, to accomplish."

"Where is our equipment? Did you steal it?" a man said, from the middle of the crowd.

"Why would I do that? If you listened to your briefing, it said your equipment was under the pod, unless they changed it from when I arrived. If you can't find it, then get back in the pod, close the ramp, and never come out. You're just too *stupid* to survive. If I took your stuff, wouldn't that make you more dependent on me? Believe me, that's the last thing I want. I have my own children to worry about. I don't need more little babies. There are some here already that would kill you for what you're carrying, but that isn't me. Now then, all those who think they're qualified to lead this group, go over to the stream. Everyone else stays at this end."

Murdock waited while the group separated into two groups. He drank from his waterskin while he waited.

"Now, I want you to be honest with yourself," Murdock said to the remaining, when the sorting was complete. "If you absolutely and unequivocally, don't want to lead, then come forward. That would include those who feel you're totally unqualified, or have trouble giving orders to others."

The waiting continued while they thought about it for some time. Five people came forward.

"You five remain. The rest of you can go over to the stream."

Murdock sized them up. He looked at the smallest of the five, who were still taller than he was.

"What's your name?" he asked the smallest man.

"Charles. Charles Benteen."

"Are you any relation to Frederick Benteen?"

"Not that I'm aware of. I don't know who that is." Benteen answered softly with a confused look on his face.

Soft-spoken, shortest man, doesn't want to lead. "Well, Chuck, you're it. You're in charge of this... this herd. Come over here by me."

Benteen ambled toward Murdock, hesitating at the poles that marked the barrier.

"Why did you pick me? I don't want to lead. I'm not qualified to lead myself, let alone two hundred." Benteen protested.

"That's why I picked you. I'll explain it later, after they empty the other pods and I pick the leaders. For now, you need to get all the gear in the compartments on the ground, and get everyone outfitted similar to me. Get the waterskins handed out, two to a person, and get them filled, hopefully without muddying the stream. If the other pods open, separate yourselves and don't tell them anything about this conversation."

Benteen nodded and started back beyond the barrier.

"Oh, and Chuck, if I call for you, don't make me wait and don't make me come looking for you."

Benteen blanched. Once he was on the pod side of the barrier, Murdock went back to his campsite to wait.

———

"Why did you pick that guy?" Declan said, when Murdock had returned.

"Because he didn't want it." Murdock poked the roasting porker, then took out his six-inch knife and cut off a piece. "I'm trying to prevent those with megalomania from gaining power over these tenderfoots." He took a bite of the pork. "That's good stuff," he said, around the mouthful of meat.

"Thanks." Declan smiled.

Everyone at the campsite cut their own piece of pork.

"What about Watkins?" Heather hesitated to take a piece of the meat.

"Heather, what kind of a leader is she?" Murdock glared at Watkins.

"She mainly keeps the women in line and agrees with Lantz." Heather kept her gaze forward and didn't look toward Watkins. "I think they have something going between them, though."

"If you stand there holding that meat, it will get cold and greasy." Murdock took another bite. "I suppose she can have some, but only because I know you and you feel guilty eating in front of her. It's not because she deserves anything from us."

2

"Every decision has its upside and its downside. The key is to make the best decisions you can with the facts available at any given time. Refusing to decide is, of itself, a decision."

— KEVIN MURDOCK, COLLECTED SAYINGS

An hour after the first newcomers disembarked from their pod, the ramp of the second pod opened. Murdock was waiting at the barrier when the inhabitants exited.

After eating, Declan had gathered a large amount of clay, with Andy's help, from the stream bank, and was now cleaning it of larger bits of debris that would hinder the manufacture of high-quality clay. Mei Lee helped by emptying the cart and getting it set closer to the barrier so Declan could use it as a bench. The younger children, Rosa Lea, Maureen, and Roslynn, were playing near Emily and little Gordon, staying out from underfoot.

When Declan started making the frames, he was interrupted

18

by Sebastian Heartly, Elizabeth Reyes, and the rest of their troop getting close to the camp fringes.

"What're you doing here?" Declan growled.

Annie joined him.

"Relax, Declan," Bass Heartly said. "We aren't here to cause any trouble."

"Where's Murdock?" Reyes asked dismissively as she pushed her way forward. "We have business here, so go fetch him."

"What's the nature of that *business*?" Annie asked the shorter, Hispanic woman. "He's busy, at present, so you can tell me and I'll see to it he gets the message."

Reyes chuckled. "My business with him is *my* business. I don't deal with underlings. Is that pork you're cooking?" She pushed Annie aside and strode into the camp with her five followers.

"That's close enough, Elizabeth." Mei Lee had approached from behind Declan and Annie, and no one had noticed the short Asian woman. "You're not barging into our camp, uninvited!" Her bow was at the ready.

"And who'll stop me? You? There are enough of us to take over your camp."

One man stepped forward. Mei Lee shot him in the leg and nocked another arrow before anyone could react. Another man reached for his machete, but before it cleared the scabbard, she shot him in the arm. Everyone not injured rushed her. She used her bow as a staff, laying out Bass Heartly with a strike aside his head. Another man grabbed the bow from behind, lifting Mei Lee off the ground. She kicked Reyes in the solar plexus. While Reyes gasped for air, Declan and Annie jumped in and tried to subdue the remaining men.

"*Bridget?*" Mei Lee flashed.

Reyes and her followers dropped to the ground, unconscious.

STEPHEN DRAKE

When Reyes awoke, she saw the sky and Murdock bending over her.

"What?" Reyes said, after a long silence. "Did you take advantage of me while I was unconscious?" She glared at Murdock, who remained silent, scowling at her. "Where are my men?" she said, after looking around. "Are you going to answer me or just stare?"

"What're you doing here?" Murdock asked impatiently.

"I've come to get replacements. I'm allowed, aren't I?"

"You're allowed to come to the newbies and ask if any want to join your group. However, you may not come into *my* camp and try to take it over for yourself."

"Your *minions* attacked a *peaceful* party," Reyes said.

"My *wife* did as I would expect her to. Besides, there's nothing *peaceful* about your party. Be thankful I was busy. If it would've been me, you wouldn't be explaining yourself. We'd be burying you."

"That sounds like you. Two years ago, we marked you a bandit. You're someone to be eliminated at any opportunity. You, and any who follows you, are a plague upon those who live here."

Murdock laughed. "Well, here I am. Eliminate me."

"That's just your style. You won't face a man, but an unarmed woman is all you can handle!"

Murdock pulled out his eighteen-inch machete. "Would this be big enough for you?"

Reyes stared at him for a few seconds. "You'd like that, wouldn't you? It would give you a reason to kill me and claim self-defense."

"I don't understand your anger with me." Murdock replaced the machete.

"You stranded us in the middle of nowhere! You let us all freeze and starve!"

"*You* chose the place for your encampment. I tried to help you get started. It's not my fault if you didn't learn or do the

20

work required." Murdock looked at her with mock compassion. "I told you early on I wouldn't do the work for you. So now you feel justified in attacking my family." He shook his head. "You *think* I owe you something. You *think* I owe you survival. You have a right for a *chance* to survive. Survival isn't guaranteed. I gave you your chance to survive, so it's not my fault you squandered it." He turned to leave.

"Is that it, then? You're going to turn your back on us... again!"

Murdock stopped. "Liz, go home. Take your men and *go home*." He didn't turn around. "Take this as my *last* friendly gesture. I *won't* recommend your group to any of the newcomers, so *go home!*" he growled, through clenched teeth.

Reyes stood to protest, but didn't see Murdock anywhere. When she turned around, she saw her men staring at her, their wounds dressed and treated.

"Get on your feet! He can't do this to us. I refuse to let that be the last word on the matter."

"Um... Elizabeth," Heartly whispered, "I think you need to let this go. If you don't, then we'll all end up dead. Murdock wasn't speaking from anger. He was serious."

"How did it go with Reyes?" Mei Lee asked Murdock, once he returned.

"Not well." He exhaled loudly. "I let her and her men go. I told them to go home, and I told her I'll not recommend any newbies go to her group." He shrugged.

"What was her reaction?"

"I don't know yet. I left after telling her to go home. Whatever her reaction is, we all need to be on our toes." He looked to the pods. "It's time for me to give my spiel... again."

Mei Lee watched her husband plod back to the barrier. She could see how the stress of the situation was wearing on him.

21

He's exhausted. After ten years of fighting with others, he's getting worn out.

"We need to be on our toes," Mei Lee flashed to all that could hear her thoughts. *"Reyes and her cohorts are now an unknown element. We have to be ready for any repercussions."*

"What is the threat level?" Irene Harris asked.

"Assume their group is the highest possible threat to all of us," Murdock replied.

Before Murdock started his spiel again, he called for Benteen.

"Line up your people. I want them to give their name to my associate," he motioned toward Declan, "and then our medico will assess them." He pointed at Annie. "If they get out of line, my people have my permission to take them down... hard. Get me?"

Benteen nodded and ran off to corral the rest of his pod-mates, and got them cued close to Declan, with himself at the head of the line.

"Next!" Declan motioned the first person in the cue, forward. "Name?"

"Charles Benteen."

"You're the leader, yeah?" Declan asked as he scribed Benteen's name onto the clay tablet with the chisel-shaped stick.

"So I'm told," Benteen whispered.

"I want you to go over there and see Annie. If she clears you, come back to help keep your fellows in line. Try not to upset her. She doesn't like hurting anyone, but she will, quicker than you can imagine. Next," Declan called to the next person in line.

Things progressed quietly for the first fifty of the first pod.

"Name?" Declan said, without looking up.

"Curtis Griffen."

"Middle initial?" Declan's heart pounded.

"D."

"*I have a problem,*" Declan flashed to Annie. "*This may be my brother, but he doesn't recognize me.*"

"*You have changed,*" Emily replied. "*You've filled out nicely.*"

"*I'll hold him aside for Mei Lee,*" Annie flashed back.

"Go see Annie. Next."

While Curtis was walking to Annie's position, which was away from the rest, for patient privacy, Annie flashed Mei Lee about the situation. By the time Annie finished with Curtis' exam, Mei Lee came over to him.

"Come with me," she said.

"Why?" Curtis balked. "I din't do nothin'!"

"Shut your pie-hole!" Mei Lee said. "Nobody said you did. Just do what you're told. You'll have your chance to lodge any complaints." She herded Curtis to where Kathy Watkins was sitting. "Sit here and wait for my husband."

"What's goin' on?" Curtis asked Watkins, after Mei Lee left.

"How the hell would I know? I think these people are all crazy."

Curtis shrugged. "I woul'n't know. Jus' got here."

"No shit, Sherlock! I was here before you exited the pod!"

"I was just tryin' ta conversate. No need to get pissy."

"Can you move over? A mile or two should be sufficient."

Curtis gave up trying to talk to Watkins, and lay back, closing his eyes to avoid further conversation with her.

"Hey, Cee Dee, want to help me process more clay?" Declan tapped the bottom of Curtis' foot with his own.

He had run out of clay after the third pod, and needed more.

"Huh?" Curtis tried to focus. He had fallen asleep, and hearing the pet name his brother used to use caused him confusion. "How d'ya know what m'brother used to call me?" he said, groggily, as he got to his feet.

"How *is* that worthless brother of yours? Seen him lately?"

"Not for a while. Don' know what happened to him."

"How are your sisters?" Declan dug clay and put it on a hide.

Curtis scowled. "How d'ya know so damn much about me?"

Declan chuckled. "I know you didn't stop sucking your thumb until you were six."

Curtis grabbed the much more substantial Declan and tried to shake him, which was ineffective, as he was too weak to do much.

"You tell me right now how you know so much about me!" He tried to be stern.

"Or what, little brother? What do you think you can do? You're weak as a kitten."

Curtis moved backward. "What'd you call me?"

"You heard me. I said you were weak as a kitten."

"No, before that."

Declan laughed. "Have I changed so much? You used to call me Dee Cee, and I called you Cee Dee. You called me Dee Cee because you knew I hated my middle name. I still do."

Curtis stood back, eyes wide. "Declan?"

Declan held out his arms, palm up. "That's me! Now, let's get this done." He turned to his task of collecting clay.

Both brothers dragged the hide loaded with clay back to the cart bed, where Declan was doing his scribe work.

"Go get some pork. It'll help you get over the grogginess." Declan smiled.

"*He is my brother,*" Declan flashed.

———

It stunned Curtis. *I haven't seen my brother in years, and now here he is.* He walked over to the fire. As he got closer, a huge woman came over. *She's six-six, at least, and built like a tank.*

"Hello, Curtis," she said, sweetly. "I'm Emily, your sister-in-law." She pulled a six-inch knife and sliced through the cooked pork, then handed him the knife. "Use the knife to stick the meat and eat it that way, or you can use your fingers. We don't carry plates when we're out and about." She smiled at him.

"Uh... thanks, Emily. I'm a little stunned by all this."

"That's understandable, given the circumstances." Emily chuckled. "When you're more emotionally steady, I'll introduce you to your nieces and nephew."

Nieces? Nephew? I can't believe Declan landed anyone, let alone someone so large and so nice. I always thought he'd end up with a skinny screecher. He chuckled before biting into the meat.

Once Declan was back with wet clay, the line proceeded.

"Are you okay?" Murdock asked his friend, bending in to make their conversation private.

"I'll be fine," Declan said, between the individuals filing past.

"Andrew?"

Declan looked up and saw an older man, maybe late fifties, coming toward Murdock.

"Andy Murdock! It is you!"

The man grabbed Murdock's hand and pumped it. "You old so and so! I thought you were dead! That's what they told me, at any rate. And yet here you are!"

With difficulty, and without injuring the man, Murdock extricated his hand.

"I'm sorry, sir, but you have me mistaken for someone else. I don't recognize you."

"You're not Andrew James Murdock? Sorry, but you look exactly like him!"

"Andrew James Murdock was my father," Murdock said.

The old man smiled. "That explains it! I'm Zeke. Zeke Jakes. I guess you'd call me a good friend and confidant of

Andrew's." He stepped back and offered his hand again to Murdock.

He warily shook Zeke's hand. "You knew Andrew well?"

Zeke leaned in. "I knew him better than you did, and I know things you will want to know. When this all calms down, find me and we'll talk."

"Give Declan here your name, get checked out medically, and then come find me."

"Sure, I can do that. It'll be nice to sit and talk to someone that knew Andrew toward the end."

"Mei Lee, please keep track of an old guy. Name is Zeke." Murdock flashed. *I need to ask all kinds of questions, and I hope Zeke has the answers.*

Declan ran into several snags while scribing the names. More than once, he ran out of clay and had to collect more. He had to take several breaks to wait for the scribed tablets to dry enough to remove the frames and not have the tablets fall apart.

By the end of the first day, he had only gotten through half the newcomers, having to stop because of the failing light. Murdock had gotten the ten initial leaders picked. There were ten new arrivals that did not revive, in the ninth and tenth pods, and he got them buried, away from the pods and the stream.

"I'm whupped." Declan sat close to the fire. "I haven't written for that long in years. I must be getting old."

Everyone laughed.

"You certainly look much older than you did this morning," Murdock said.

"Is there more pork left?" Declan flexed his fingers. "I sure could eat more of that!"

Emily got up to cut some pork for Declan, and gave it to him.

"Thanks, Em. You're the best."

"Is this a bad time to bring up my group's request?" Kathy Watkins said, in a surly tone.

"I think it should wait until we know the skills available, don't you?" Murdock replied. "We don't even have all their names yet. Is there something so pressing you can't wait another day or two? Even if you find replacements, those meeting your requirements, you will have to take it slow going home, or give them another day to build up their strength. Besides, once we find them, you have to *convince* them to join you. I'll not force anyone to go where I or anyone else thinks they need to go."

Even though Murdock had slept hard until Declan woke him, he greeted the day tired and testy. Declan—feeling the same— Andy, and Curtis managed to get more clay and get things set for finishing the lists of newcomers after breakfast.

Declan was looking forward to finishing the list. *I don't know why I want to be done with it. I'll be home, but then I must fire all the tablets and hope none break. It'll take weeks to fire them all, even with Curtis' help. I know I have to talk to him and try to convince him to come home with me and Emily. I can't lose him again.*

Murdock spent his time trying to get everyone outfitted. The leaders he'd selected had failed to outfit anyone properly. He also had to teach them how to collect water without getting dirt into their waterskins and without muddying the water in the process. He only had limited success in his instructions.

By late afternoon, Declan had just started the list from the last pod. As soon as he had the leader's name, Murdock called all the leaders to a meeting away from the rest. Declan kept working.

"Name?" he asked, with impatience.

He had asked the same thing, the same way, for almost two days. He glanced up at the cue and figured he was in the last fifty.

"Angelica Griffen," a deep, sultry voice replied.

"I need you to go over there and get checked out by Annie, and then come directly back here," Declan said, without looking up.

He was glad for the mental training Beron and Murdock had given, so his thoughts were his own. He wanted to surprise everyone at their camp with yet another family member.

When Angelica returned, he was almost finished creating the lists.

"Have a seat on the other side of this cart. I'm almost finished," He watched her surreptitiously while she complied. *I need to calm myself. I'm getting too anxious.*

"So, why did you pick us to lead?" Johann Spitzer said, once all the leaders had gathered away from the rest.

"Mostly, because you don't want it," Murdock said. "The previous pods held elections for their leaders, and those elections led to tyrannies with a lot of pain for everyone. I'm trying to prevent that from happening to you."

"Well, you know we'll be replaced as soon as they hold an election," Parker Sheetzen said, "either by pod or as a complete group."

"Possible," Murdock said, "even probable, but that won't change anything. I will still seek you all out and hold you accountable. In the last two landings, we had several rapes, bullying, and murders, with no one stopping any of it. They all thought it wasn't any of their concern, so they stayed out of it. However, if all you want is to behave like a pack of wolves, then go ahead, but don't be surprised if someone treats you as such. I had in mind something... more. Something with some semblance of being civilized."

"How come the others acted that way with their fellows?" Georgia Nyree said.

"Some were spoiled brats, some were bullies, and some were

just power hungry. Out here, it doesn't matter what you did before. What matters is what you do now. I don't expect anyone to know everything. I do expect humans to behave better than the animals they claim to be superior to."

"So what are we to do now?" Sanittie Laust said.

"Gee... I don't know," Murdock said sarcastically. "It's now late spring or early summer and you have until winter begins to get sheltered, warm, and fed, you and your charges. So what do you think you should be doing?"

When no one answered, Murdock said, "Don't you think you should figure out who amongst your people are hunters, builders, farmers, and a thousand other occupations? If you have no experts, would hobbyists work? Are you going to need weapons? You need to keep one thing in mind, always. There are animals here that would love a human for a meal, four-legged and two-legged animals. I want all of you, at your first opportunity, to walk to the river. It's that way." He pointed toward the river. "And when you see the speed and volume of the water, keep in mind it freezes solid each winter."

The entity had been awake a short time and was reluctant to exert control over its host. It had sensed its enemy nearby, along with its fellow entities. There were fewer of its fellows than it had expected, but it was unconcerned with the losses.

It opened a passive connection to the host's visual cortex, allowing it to receive the images the host saw. As the host turned its head to take in all within view, the entity stimulated the second-sight part of the host's visual perceptions and saw the two figures, cloaked in black robes, invisible to the host's usual visual perception. It also saw the red-tinted psychic barrier that closed off the pods and the humans from the greater local environment. This action lasted only a fraction of a second, but it risked the entity being perceived by its enemy and its host.

29

As a precaution, the entity erased any memory of what the host saw.

The entity had decided to seek its fellows when the hosts were resting, during their period of inactivity and low luminosity, when the hosts were the most unaware of the entity's presence.

Murdock had dismissed the meeting of the leaders about an hour before sundown. He was irritable and tired from a lack of sleep and from dealing with these intruders. *I know I'm not a people-person.* He splashed water from the stream onto his face to wash away the strange taint he felt from dealing with the newcomers.

"Kevin, I have someone for you to meet," Declan said, from behind him.

Once Murdock stood and turned to face Declan, he saw a familiar female.

Angelica saw the expression on Murdock's face go from startled confusion, to hurt, and then to anger in a fraction of a second as the stream water ran down his face.

Declan, this is a mistake, she thought. *I don't know why, but I know this is a mistake.*

"This is my sister, Angelica," Declan said, in an upbeat tone.

Angelica could see the anger directed at Declan, and then she saw Murdock's lower lip quiver, a burning glare in his eyes. He turned and strode to his lodge and shut the flap.

As Murdock passed her, Mei Lee stood with a puzzled look.

She turned toward Declan. "Declan, what—"

Standing before her was the spitting image of Rose. Not the Rose she knew with the scars, but the one she'd briefly met when she'd first arrived. Her mouth hung agape.

"Mei Lee, this is my little sister, Angelica," Declan said. "Angelica, this is Mei Lee Murdock."

Angelica smiled sweetly and extended her hand to the small Asian woman. "Nice to meet you, Mei Lee."

Oh, my god. She looks and sounds just like her. "Nice to meet you, Angelica." Mei Lee took the offered hand and shook it, and flashed a brief smile.

Declan received a cold glare.

Declan looked back, confusion on his face.

"I don't think Murdock likes me," Angelica said to Declan.

"Sorry about that. It wasn't you, Angel. I'm certain of that. He's probably just tired."

"You know, you owe her an apology," flashed to Murdock's mind, from Mei Lee.

"I know. I was taken by surprise when I was tired. I thought I was losing my hold on reality when I turned and saw her."

"I understand. I, too, was taken aback when I saw her. She is the spitting image of Rose. She even sounds like her."

"I thought I was seeing a ghost. She looked the way Rose did when we first arrived. I knew about finding his brother, but not his sister."

"No one did. Declan, thinking he was being clever, hid it well." Mei Lee's anger came through her thought transmissions.

"Don't be too cross with him. He was just excited."

"He's shared with us enough to know our feelings for Rose. He should've given us a heads-up at least, so we would be prepared."

"She is his sister. I think he doesn't notice the similarities since he hadn't seen Rose in several years. I think he's missed his brother and

31

sister for a long time. Having them both here now brings out his excitement."

"Are you making excuses for him?"

Heather Stevens and Kathy Watkins were sitting together close to the fire when Murdock stormed past.

"This looks interesting." Kathy smirked.

"What's that supposed to mean?" Heather said.

"Looks to be trouble in paradise, to me." Watkins was still smirking.

Heather shook her head. "You disgust me. You're just looking for grist to feed your rumor mill. These people are my friends. I've lived with them for some time before coming to your group. They all have their issues, but they're good people and don't deserve your innuendos and lies."

"Sounds like you're more comfortable with their company than ours." Watkins glared at her. "Keep in mind, we took you in, gave you a place with us. Should I take this conversation into account when it comes time to dole out the flour and grain?"

"You've reminded us of that at every opportunity. Maybe I need to keep your threats in mind when you come around looking for my and Alvin's help, or when you want to borrow one of our animals." Heather glared back at Watkins as she stood. "You have a right to your opinion, but you needn't be such a bitch about it. We also have the right to ignore you and your requests."

She stepped over to the fire, turning her back to Watkins.

Murdock exited the tipi two hours after sunset. As he approached the fire, he clapped twice to get everyone's attention.

"I would like Curtis and Angelica to come forward," he said, once he reached the fire.

It didn't take them long to join him.

"As most of you know, our brother Declan has found his Earth brother and sister. As Declan is my brother, so is Curtis. And Angelica is my sister. I was married to their sister Rose. As she was family, so are they. I look forward to the day they are fully trusted and accepted as family to all of us."

"What's that supposed to mean?" flashed to Murdock's mind, from Declan.

"You know what it means. When you first arrived, I accepted you as a brother-in-law. Now you are more than that. You're one of the most trusted people here. They both need to prove themselves to be worthy of joining our tribe."

"But I wanted to bring them home and keep them safe from the abuses that are sure to be inflicted by the other new arrivals," Declan flashed.

Murdock marveled at how even Declan's thoughts came across as whiney at times.

"You can't keep them safe, as you well know. This planet isn't safe. You're free to take them home with you, as long as you take responsibility for their conduct and their training. In the future, should they join our tribe, they will become full members, just as Irene, Annie, you, and Em did, and will, thus, be held accountable for their own actions."

Ted Wagner was lying just inside the tree line, close to the river. He had been watching the granite building that was against the ridge to the next level up. *Twenty-foot walls of granite* he thought as he lay watching for signs of life, *narrow doorway into the compound, two-story house, possibly a water filtration system on the roof. It had to have been built by Murdock or with his help. It needs to be conquered or destroyed.*

"What do you think, Ted?" Harvey Stoddard whispered.

"I think we need to wait and see who's inside. It would be foolish to take over the building if Murdock is in there."

"Before the wall that confined us was constructed, that wasn't there. Murdock has been operating longer than that building has existed. You're not scared of Murdock, are you?" Stoddard looked at Wagner sideways.

"I wouldn't say I fear him," Wagner said, with more conviction than he felt. "What does it gain us if we die trying to improve our situation? Imprisoning us was wrong. We're just trying to survive any way we can. Besides, you didn't feel the effects of Murdock's anger." Wagner rubbed his chest absentmindedly, as he always did when he remembered the confrontation with Murdock.

Stoddard snickered. "Maybe you shoulda made sure Murdock was dead before you took his stuff and the women."

Wagner shot a glare at Stoddard. "If I would've hit you in the head like I did him, what little brains you have would be splattered all over the place."

3

People always assumed my father was raised to be a killer. He was raised to be a hunter. There is a difference between hunting and killing. Some understand the difference. Some never will.

— ANDREW MURDOCK, THE REAL KEVIN
MURDOCK: A DIARY

The next morning, Charles Benteen was the first of the new arrivals to exit his pod. What greeted him was Murdock, standing alone. He saw no tipis, no cart, no draft animals, and none of the other people who had greeted them a few days prior.

"Where'd everyone go?" Benteen walked toward the shorter man.

"My family and friends are going about our business. You need to wake the rest of the leaders," Murdock responded hastily.

Benteen, shocked at Murdock's attitude, roused the rest of the leaders. It took time to get them all gathered and facing Murdock.

"As you can see, my friends and family have better things to do," Murdock said loud enough for all to hear. "You are, therefore, on your own. If you're going to kill each other, at least have the courtesy to wait until I'm out of sight." Murdock turned to leave.

"Wait!" called Erycca Valdez, leader of the third pod.

Murdock stopped.

"What are we supposed to do? How will we live?"

Murdock's shoulders slumped and he turned around. "Haven't you been paying attention? You build fires to keep warm and cook food. You build houses to live in. You do whatever it takes to survive."

"Where are we supposed to find food?" Erycca asked innocently.

"You hunt and fish, or gather grain, or gather wild vegetables, or any combination thereof. How many hunters, fishermen, woodsmen, or survivalists do your groups have?"

"Um... we don't know," said Parker Sheetzen, leader of the sixth pod.

"You don't know?" Murdock crooked his finger in Sheetzen's direction. "Why don't you go find out?" he whispered, once Sheetzen was close.

Sheetzen made as if he would go do it, and then stopped.

"Yesterday would have been a good time!" Murdock shook his head at Sheetzen's back as he ran. "You were all supposed to figure out the skills of your people. Did any of you do it, or did you think I was kidding?"

Blank faces and downcast eyes met his gaze.

With the butt-end of his spear, Murdock made two parallel wavy lines in the dirt. "This is the river." He drew a single wavy line. "This is the stream, the one over there." He stuck the spear point in the dirt close to the single line. "You are here. You can get a few fish from the stream, but I'd recommend going to the river. Don't go alone, and be sure to take someone that knows how to harvest them.

"On the other side of the river are trees. You know, for building shelter. But I wouldn't go there."

"Why not?" Benteen said.

"That side of the river is home to two different groups. One is a bunch of cut-throats. The other group is what I call *Lotus Eaters*. They'll either help you, enslave you, or they'll ignore you. Neither group is one I'd recommend. Just off this plateau, down-river, are a group of farmers. They may help some of you, but there's a price to pay for their help. I'm not here to tell you what to do. You can go anywhere you choose, as long as you stay off the plateau second up from here, and off that plateau over there." Murdock pointed to the cliff across the stream. "I've been here for ten years, so you can believe what you will. But I'd say your best chance for survival is downriver from the farmers. I'd stay here for a few more days, though, to build up your strength and get the lay of the land, so to speak. Whatever you decide, don't venture out alone and don't pollute the water."

Sheetzen came hurrying back. "There are several hunters and fishermen." He panted. "Exactly how many, I don't know, but we have some."

"Well, that's something, anyway," Murdock said. "There are deer and fish here, and there are also wolves and cougars. The wildlife will take care of you, one way or the other. Either you'll learn to survive, or they'll remove any sign of your existence."

"You don't like us very much, do you?" said Georgia Nyree, leader of the tenth pod.

"It's not a matter of liking you or not. From my perspective, you're all interlopers and tenderfoots. I don't know you well enough to say if I like you or not. I've given you a few things you need to do, but most won't believe me and will insist on doing things your own way. So why would I invest any time or emotion in someone who, most likely, won't be around this time next year?"

Everyone stared after Murdock, mouths agape, as he strode over the rolling hills toward the river.

"We're on our way to you," Murdock flashed to Irene Harris, who was inside the medical complex. *"We have three new arrivals—"*

"You better hurry and get here!" flashed Harris. *"We're under attack!"*

"Who's attacking?" Murdock picked up his pace to a ground-covering trot.

"I don't know for certain. It appears to be the Pirates or the Lotus Eaters. Luckily, I'd closed the wooden portcullis when you warned of Reyes's anger. There are steel arrows coming over the wall, and one has hit Roy. Nothing major, but we're barricaded inside the residence with the ladders pulled up."

Murdock sped up to his mile-eating run. *"Stay undercover. I'll be there as soon as I can!"*

He peered ahead to see his family upriver from his track, far enough that none could see his passage.

"Harris is under attack," Murdock flashed to his family.

"Do you need help?" replied Declan and Mei Lee.

"Declan, ride hard and get there as soon as you can. Mei Lee, guard the rest of the family. I'll be there in a few minutes."

Declan, riding Dancer, stopped long enough for the rest to catch up to him. He leaned over to kiss his wife, who was driving the cart being pulled by Donder.

"Stay safe," he flashed to Emily. *"And keep the rest of the family safe."* He reined up his mount and rode off.

"What's going on?" Kathy Watkins said. "You roust us in the middle of the night to break camp and walk to the river. Now, Declan rides off. And where is Murdock?"

"Madam, kindly shut your trap," Zeke said. Since the wee hours of the morning, he'd walked next to her. "I've had to listen to you run your mouth, and, frankly I'm tired of hearing you. It's obvious that there's an emergency somewhere."

"Does this happen often?" Curtis asked Emily, as he trotted

next to the cart carrying the hides for the tipis, the younger children, and the leftover pork.

"Rarely, but your brother is well-versed in what he needs to do." Emily said, trying to remain positive.

"I can see by the look of ya that ya be worried," Curtis said.

"Only a fool wouldn't be concerned," Emily replied. "Out here, anything can happen at any time."

Mei Lee prepared her bow and further extended her lead of the group. *You better be careful, Kevin. I'm not done with you, yet.*

When Murdock caught sight of the walls of the medical facility, he could see several men with bows, firing over the walls, and he sped up. When he jumped the river, he landed close to one man, his spear at the ready. He struck the man as he passed, with the butt-end. He ran around the area, dropping the aggressors with non-fatal strikes to the head with the blunt end of his spear.

Once everyone was down, holding their aching heads, he stopped in front of Wagner.

"Obviously, you've learned nothing from our last encounter," Murdock grinned, trying hard to slow his breathing. "What is the meaning of this attack?"

"The meaning should be obvious," Wagner said dismissively.

"So I take it you and the rest of this crew are... intellectually deficient. Well, that answers that." Murdock chuckled.

"We value strength! The weak have always been the prey of the strong!"

"You were attacking a medical facility manned by two people, both medically trained, and you couldn't manage it. So who is the stronger?"

"We would have, eventually, if you hadn't stuck your nose into our business."

"Just so happens that this facility *is* my business! I built it and I watch over it. How strong are you if I can stop your attack?

One against, what," Murdock glanced around, "ten men? By your logic, I should be in command of your entire crew!" He heard the scrape of a blade against scabbard. "If you continue to draw that weapon, I'll be forced to defend myself." He stared at Wagner.

Murdock heard the blade clear the scabbard. He turned his body and threw his spear. The spear hit the man in the shoulder of the arm holding the twelve-inch machete. The man screamed and dropped the knife as he hit the ground. Murdock turned to face Wagner, his own twelve-incher in hand.

"Anyone else?" Murdock looked around at the rest of the attackers.

"Need any help?" Declan said, from atop his mount, bow in hand with an arrow nocked.

"Nope, I can handle this bunch, but thanks for asking," Murdock replied, without turning to look at Declan.

"What are you going to do with us?" Wagner said, defeat in his tone.

Murdock looked up in the air. "Let me see, you were behind a wall to keep everyone else safe from your predations, but that didn't work. You tried to kill me and stole everything I had. I warned you the last time I saw you, Wagner. I should kill you here and now."

"What goes on here?" a man yelled, from the trees. "Drop your weapons!"

Murdock chuckled. "No, I don't think so. Be warned, I'm not in the best of moods, so attacking me will be... detrimental to your well-being."

"Why are you holding those men?" the voice said, from the cover of the trees.

"He attacked us for no reason!" Wagner said. "We were just hunting, and he attacked us!"

"They were attacking the medical facility. I stopped them."

"Is Doc Harris and Roy okay?" the voice said.

"From the information I received, they injured Roy, but I don't know to what extent."

"What do you intend to do with them?"

"I haven't decided, yet."

"How are we to know the truth of this matter?"

"Send one of your men to check with Doctor Harris. I'll wait."

Murdock heard someone run toward the medical facility. Then heard someone walk toward him.

"Aren't you Clem Adams?" Declan said, as the man cleared cover.

He nodded.

"It's been a while since I've seen you."

"By rights, I should take you and Murdock into custody," Adams said to Declan.

"Good luck with that," Murdock said, with a surly tone. "I'm not in the mood!"

"I said I *should*. However, since these... people attacked Doc Harris and Roy, I'm inclined to let it slide."

"Adams, what would your people do with this bunch?" Murdock said.

"I can't speak for everyone, but I'm sure it would be something nasty. Strip them and tie them to a tree for the wolves, would be my guess. The more the wolves get to eat, the less they attack us."

Murdock heard running feet and whispering behind him.

"My man says Roy was injured, a metal arrow in the shoulder. But Doc is fine. Roy is one of ours." Adams walked toward Wagner, a scowl on the bigger man's face. "If you want us to deal with them, we will!"

Wagner blanched as he looked between two angry men.

"I think, since they admire strength so much, that all of them should strip. I want them as bare as the day they were born. Declan, come down and collect their weapons and clothing."

41

"Is that all you'll do to them?" Adams said. "I'm surprised you're being so lenient."

"I also need to know which hand is their dominant one," Murdock boomed, as he put away his twelve-inch machete and picked up one of the captured bows.

As Mei Lee, Zeke, Emily, and the rest of the group arrived at the medical facility, Declan, leading Dancer, and Murdock approached the compound. They all were met by Doctor Harris.

"Welcome. Welcome to our home," Harris greeted everyone.

"Are you okay, Irene?" Annie asked.

"I'm fine, but poor Roy-Boy caught an arrow in the shoulder. He'll be out of commission for a while, though. I had to do surgery to remove it without tearing up his shoulder."

"Irene, this is my brother, Curtis," Declan said, "and my sister, Angelica."

Each shook hands with the doctor.

"You look none the worse for wear," Irene said to Watkins. "Wasn't Lantz with you?"

"He got sent home," Murdock said. "He wanted to be stupid and endanger Heather, so I sent him packing."

"Looks like you brought the whole fam damily, Declan," Harris said, as Emily and all three kids entered the compound. "Mei Lee, nice to see you. And you three sure have grown! Who is this?" she said, when Zeke presented himself.

"*Ezekiel* Jakes, madam, at your service." He grinned, and then kissed the back of her hand.

Irene blushed.

By sundown, Murdock and his extended family had set up their tipis inside the walled compound. Annie had checked on Roy White, who was recovering from surgery on his shoulder.

"Who was it that attacked us?" Doctor Harris asked as she joined everyone else around the fire.

"Wagner and his group were the attackers," Murdock said. "I explained that they should… refrain from further attacks."

Declan chuckled. "You certainly explained it to them."

"What does that even mean?" Harris said.

"Believe it or not, we had help from a small group of Lotus Eaters," Declan said.

"It was a small group going to the river," Murdock said. "They heard the uproar and called a halt to the argument we were having with Wagner. When they heard what Wagner had done, and that Roy was injured, they became temporary allies." He grinned.

Curtis, Angelica, and Zeke appeared confusion.

"I don't understand," Zeke said. "Lotus Eaters… as in the Odyssey?"

Murdock grinned. "It's what we call the group that's located not far from here. Like those in the Odyssey, they're apathetic to the concerns of the rest of us and live pretty much isolated. Emily used to be their leader. Declan spent some time with them, as does Roy White. They have some *strange* ideas and can be dangerous."

"They have the notion," Annie approached the fire, "that once you've been accepted into their group, you are theirs. For as long as you live. They threaten, every so often, to reclaim Emily and Declan."

"I washed my hands of them some time ago," Emily said, angered by the memory. "I have no interest in returning. My place is with my husband and my tribe."

"I tried, some time ago, to get them to be more… sociable," Murdock said. "I tried to get them to trade with the other two groups in the area, but it did no good. I'd recommend no one to their group."

"What other two groups?" Zeke said.

"Further away from the river and on this plateau are a group of miners. Or they used to be. Now, they're a bunch of cut-throats and thieves. They feel that if you're not strong enough to protect what you have, they're free to kill you and take it from you."

"They almost succeeded in killing Murdock and stealing Annie and me," Heather said, "along with everything we had with us. It was scary for me to see the level of violence they were capable of."

"And you let them live?" Zeke said, incredulous.

"Everyone is eager to have someone killed," Murdock muttered, "as long as they don't have to be the one to do it. They live because no one else will do what they all wanted me to do. They now control most of the metal workers that had arrived on the last ship."

"The other group," Heather said, "lives just off this plateau, downriver. They're mostly farmers. I live outside of their group, with Alvin Jones. We farm a little, but mostly we tame the deer we can catch."

"That was a nice story for the newbies," Harris said, "but I want to know what you mean by you *explained it to them*. How can we remain safe here?"

Declan laughed. "Murdock had them strip, and then we used their arrows against them."

"How did you *use* them?" Harris said, losing patience.

"I nailed them to a tree by putting an arrow through their dominant hand," Murdock said. "And then, since I had their attention, told them to reconsider attacking you again."

"What? Is there a reason you can't be more specific?" Harris said.

"I told them that if I find them again, doing what they are in the habit of doing, I'll remove their dominant hand—"

"And the time after that, they'll lose their other hand," Declan said. "And then their feet. That way, they'll know how many more chances they have."

"Why didn't you kill them?" Zeke said. "You know they'll continue to be a problem."

Murdock shrugged.

"Did you tell the leaders where to go?" Watkins said. "I know I didn't get the chance to recruit any for our group."

"I directed them to consider going downriver from your group," Murdock replied. "I'm fairly certain that some will build their homes closer to your group."

"What makes you think so?" Watkins said.

"People who are new congregate with those that have been successful. Out of almost two thousand people, I would expect some to be farmers. Those who feel they have no skills for survival would want to join your group. It's easier."

"What do you people do for entertainment?" Zeke said. "I'm just trying to lighten the mood some," he added, after the harsh looks he received.

"Entertainment is a low priority," Murdock said. "You asked for a reason, what is it?"

"Well, I have few skills to offer for your hospitality," Zeke said to everyone. "I can recite a poem if you'd like."

Murdock bowed his head and motioned for him to continue.

Zeke stood and cleared his throat. "The only poem that seems to come to mind, given the circumstances, is *The Shooting of Dan McGrew* by Robert W. Service." He cleared his throat again and started his recitation.

Murdock sat and listened as the older man started the poem, his clear baritone sounding more like a musical instrument than a speaking voice. He noticed that everyone remained quiet and listened intently. Zeke was putting himself into the poem, speaking dramatically.

When the recitation got to the point of describing the miner, Murdock blushed and was thankful for the darkness when everyone turned to look at him. Their gaze remained on him through the piano playing part of the poem. Irene and Annie wiped away tears at the intense loneliness Zeke had conveyed.

Everyone jumped when he clapped at the part about gunfire. Murdock chuckled to himself at the sly way he finished the poem. Everyone gave a raucous applause and Zeke took his bows.

Once the recitation was over, Murdock moved to the closed portcullis and sat on a wood round. As he stared out into the darkness, he heard Declan approach.

"You okay?" Declan said, his voice conveying his concern.

"I'm fine," Murdock shifted, "just tired."

"Mei Lee and Em are getting the kids bedded down. Are we going to have a watch? We're relatively secure here and I don't think Wagner or any of his bunch will try anything."

"Is this a bad time?" Zeke approached the two men.

"Is there ever a good time?" Murdock said.

"I need to go kiss the kids g'night," Declan said, voice shaky.

"No. Stay, Declan. What is it you wish to convey, Zeke?" Murdock allowed everyone in his tribe to perceive the conversation with Zeke.

Zeke looked around, trying to decide who should or could hear what he had to say.

"I can trust everyone here except for Watkins, Curtis, and Angelica with any information you may have. How is it you knew Andrew?"

"First off, I'd like to apologize for not being able to inform you before today. Andrew tasked me to pass on this information in the event of his passing. I had intended to intercept you after he died, but they picked me up before I could."

"No need to apologize for that. Please continue."

"Andrew James Murdock, the man you knew as your father, was a dear friend. I met him my first year of college. He was a strange bird, to some, since he kept to himself. When I first met him, he was consumed with some genetics project. I thought it was for his doctorate at first, but later found out it was more. Andy was afflicted with some genetic abnormalities, nothing that was apparent, but it sufficed to cause him concern. He knew these abnormalities would shorten his life, and he worried he wouldn't finish in time."

"Finish… a cure?" Declan said.

"There was no cure for Andy. The only cure was to prevent the alignment of certain genes from taking place. You, Murdock, were the cure he sought."

Murdock tried to remain stoic, but the shock caused him to grind his teeth and frown.

"Andy was not what he seemed. He had no mother. He was cloned, which at that time was illegal. But his cloning was imperfect and the genetic anomalies presented themselves. Some anomalies made him more intelligent than the average person— his I.Q. was, I suspect, well over one-sixty. Other anomalies caused his body to fall short, be more frail than average. For you, he wanted intelligence *and* a sound body. He wanted you to live a life he never could."

"So Murdock is some sort of superman?" Declan said, skeptically.

"To some, he would seem to be. I prefer *future*-man, myself. He can retain most everything he sees, reads, or learns. Because Andy was frail, he sacrificed height for increased muscle, co-ordination, and stamina, a hyper-efficient immune system, increased cross-section on all bones, and an increase in musculature. He is where I would hope mankind would be in a hundred thousand years."

47

"What does his immune system have to do with anything?" Declan said.

Zeke got a far-away look in his eyes. "I'd say he could walk through a sealed room containing the most virulent strains of viruses known to mankind, and at worst, only make him sick for a day or two. No permanent damage at all. If a mosquito carrying typhoid would bite him, his system would probably manufacture something to kill the virus and re-infect the mosquito to eliminate the bacterium completely and pass on the cure to whomever the mosquito bit next."

"That would be impossible," Murdock said. "Mosquitoes don't like me. I've never been bitten by one."

"That's just an example," Zeke said. "The alpha, the donor of your genetic material—which wasn't Andy—was quite tall. A hundred years before our time, a six-foot man wasn't considered tall, but wasn't considered short either. In our time, that same six-foot-tall man is considered short for a man. There are a few women who are shorter, but not many, and getting fewer all the time."

"He *is* the shortest man here," Declan said.

"Were there any men shorter than you on your pod?" Zeke asked Murdock.

"No. There was one close to my height, though."

"Doc Harris did say you were thick-headed," Declan said.

"No, I said he had a thick skull." Harris walked up to the men. "Are any of his immunity traits inheritable?"

"I don't know." Zeke shrugged. "Why do you ask?"

"Well, Chunnie had been sick, from what I have no idea, but little Andy has never been sick, that I'm aware of."

"Chun Hua isn't related to me, genetically," Murdock said to Zeke.

"Quite possible then, I'd say," Zeke replied. "How is your vision at night?"

"Why?" Murdock asked guardedly.

"It was one thing that vexed Andy. He was trying to develop

48

the eyes to be more like a dog's in low-light. I was just curious if he succeeded. I'm sure you can see further than most as well?"

Murdock fidgeted. *I'm getting uncomfortable. Feel like someone's medical experiment.*

"I'd say he succeeded," Murdock muttered.

"Hearing?" Zeke said.

Murdock thought for a second. "I've heard Declan and Emily talking in their cabin during the winter nights when it's quiet."

"And where were you?"

"In my cabin."

Declan was dumbstruck. "That's more than a hundred yards, and through the logs, no less!"

"I'm feeling like Frankenstein's monster," Murdock mumbled. "If that isn't all, I think it needs to keep for a while. Let me digest what you've told me so far."

"I think that would be best," Harris replied.

"I'm sorry," Zeke said. "I was attempting to impart information I felt you had a right to know. I wasn't trying to imply that you're some sort of monster."

"It seems to me that Andrew succeeded in his endeavors in a short amount of time," Murdock said. "How was it possible?"

"As with most things scientific, he worked at it, he got lucky, and stumbled on things by accident," Zeke whispered.

He, Declan, and Harris drifted back to the others.

Irene Harris felt sorry for Murdock. *I always knew in my gut that he was odd. I had no idea just how odd. What I wouldn't give for the equipment needed to study his genetics and to test his capabilities. It would take more than a lifetime to glean anything useful from that study.*

"Doctor Jakes," Irene intertwined her arm in Zeke's, "since you seem to know a lot about Kevin, what level of education does he have? He's always seemed to be... more educated than he portrays."

Zeke eyes widened and he pulled away from Harris to look at her. "What did you call him?"

"I called him Kevin. Kevin Murdock. That's his name."

Zeke looked down.

"Why are *you* upset?" Harris said.

"I did a lot of research on the Murdock family, and nowhere is there a Kevin." Zeke gave a sad smile. "My middle name is Kevin."

Harris jerked back. "He was named after you?"

"Apparently. And to clarify, I'm no doctor, not in any form. I always thought of myself as a researcher of genealogies."

"I find it odd that Kevin would be named after you in lieu of some familial name."

"Not really. Andy was my friend... I'd say best friend. He had no friends or family, other than me, as the alpha had died before I'd met him. We used to sit and talk for hours and drink whiskey."

"Your Andy drank? I wonder if Kevin has that proclivity."

"Actually, Andy never drank. I took care of the drinking part of our relationship."

It had been several hours since Murdock left, before the temporary—that's the way they saw themselves—leaders of the newcomers had come together around a small fire close to where Murdock had gathered them. Each sat, eating the bland gruel that someone had prepared.

"So has anyone decided where to go with their people?" Charles Benteen, leader of the first pod, said around a mouthful of the thin gruel.

"Some of us have talked," said Georgia Nyree, leader of the tenth pod, "and we think it would be smart to break up all the groups so that each group has the same number of the essential occupations.

"For example, we all know the survivalists will be the most essential for a while. They will have to train some of our people so we can all at least feed our people. An equal number for each group would be the only fair way to proceed."

Several of the leaders nodded.

"Georgia, your idea might work," said Johann Spitzer, leader of the second pod, "if the skill levels were equal. If not, then one group would have the advantage."

Several of the small group raised their voices in support of Spitzer's argument.

"Oh, Jesus Christ!" Benteen stood. "Time!" He made the letter "T" with both hands. "Time out! Time freaking out. I just wanted to know if any of you had decided on where to go. We're in deep doo-doo if we can't even make a simple decision without starting an argument."

4

The family is the tribe. The tribe is the family. There is no separation of the two. There is only the tribe. All others are outsiders.

— KEVIN MURDOCK, COLLECTED SAYINGS

It took a few minutes for the leaders to quiet down, and Benteen was losing patience.

"We need to quit arguing and make some kind of decision as to where we're going," he said. "Otherwise, we'll accomplish nothing. Speaking for myself, I believe Murdock. About winter, anyway. I know I don't want to be out in it when it arrives."

"What do you suggest?" said Dean Zelmiss, leader of the fourth pod.

"I plan on trying to get a large enough team together to at least go to the river, but I'm hoping to persuade a couple of the outdoorsmen to run point."

"Do you know where you'll end up?" said Sanittie Laust, leader of the ninth pod.

"Hopefully not inside some beastie," Zelmiss said.

Everyone laughed.

"This is serious," Benteen replied. "This isn't some colossal joke! We need to find food and shelter for everyone before winter. Murdock has accomplished it. What I have in mind is a settlement that will ensure a better chance to make it."

"Based on what I heard from Murdock, there should be plenty of resources if we can exploit them," said Bart Oldkampo, leader of the fifth pod, frowning. "I agree that, as Murdock told us, we'll need weapons, ranged weapons, to utilize the food resources. Any ideas?"

"The only idea I have is to find someone who knows what weapons we need and how to make them," Benteen said.

The others nodded.

"I'm concerned with medical personnel," said Camden Shultz, leader of the seventh pod. "There are a few medics here already, thankfully, but do we have more? If so, how many, and what type of practice did they have?"

"I'm concerned with the prior arrivals," said Xavier Alderman, leader of the eighth pod. "How are we going to be received by them? We're new here, and they have all survived at least five years. They could harbor animosity toward us."

For a few minutes, there was silence as the thoughts expressed were contemplated.

Christopher Gundersen had been listening to the row that had ensued amongst the leaders. *Well, Gunny, what are you going to do.*

He was never a marine, but he enjoyed referring to himself with the time-honored nickname for Gunnery Sergeant as a play on his last name.

Are you going to play it safe? He rubbed his rumbling stomach. *The gruel isn't sitting well with me. I need something, anything, more substantial. I know I can make it here.* He wandered back to the pods. *I've survived before with less. But here, there is nothing to scrounge.*

He had always found what he needed by scrounging through

other people's trash and things they left behind. He had been the one that transferred the hot coals from Murdock's fire after he'd left. He had looked over the rest of the campsite and had found nothing left behind by Murdock or any of his people.

This won't be like living on the streets of Minneapolis. There are no firearms here. At least, not yet. I wish I had a pizza. He sat with his back to one of the landing struts. The thought of a pizza made his stomach grumble again. *Maybe I need to look into joining the group that the others referred to as Pirates.* He had never been good with his hands, and he had no idea how to make a fire or make any weapons. *The Pirates had to have made weapons by now. How could they survive without weapons of some sort? I know I can turn my hand to anything if I try. Murdock was right. It won't matter too much what we knew or did before. This is a new start. I have to make the best of it. Besides, working for the Pirates doesn't make me a pirate.* He closed his eyes and promised himself that he would draw a line for avoiding some of the nastier aspects that could come up with Pirates.

He fell asleep with his hand resting on the hilt of his twelve-inch machete.

The next morning, Murdock woke early and revived the fire. He was joined shortly after by Declan's family and little Andy.

"What's the agenda for today?" Declan tried to stretch the sleep from his muscles.

"I'm thinking you escort everyone home while I escort Heather and Watkins to their home," Murdock said. "I want to have a discussion with Heather and Alvin."

"Where am I going?" Zeke stretched and groaned as he joined the group.

Murdock furrowed his brow. "Where do you want to go?" He added wood to the fire. "What skills do you have?"

Zeke frowned. "I guess I have no skills for surviving out here."

"He can stay here for a while," Irene said. "With Roy-Boy down, we could use a hand around here."

Murdock frowned at her.

"I know," Irene said, "but he needs to be somewhere, and with us would be as good a place as any."

"I've been thinking," Mei Lee said, as she, Chun Hua, and Rosa Lea joined, "Andy, Chun Hua, and Rosa need an education—"

"Do we have to?" Chun Hua looked pleadingly at her father.

Murdock looked at Andy, who avoided his father's gaze.

Murdock tapped the rocks of the fire-ring with a stick. "I think they're well educated for survival, and I agree that they need to be better educated in the finer things of life—"

Andy and Chun Hua groaned. Rosa Lea said nothing, but glared at her father.

"And... it would give Zeke a way to earn his keep," Murdock said. "The question is, is he willing?" He looked at Zeke.

"I'm honored you would entrust your children's education to me," Zeke said. "I am, however, at a loss as to the details."

"We must discuss it further, but I think it's doable," Murdock replied. "It'll be a few years before the farmers have children old enough to take advantage of extra schooling."

"What's it going to cost us?" Watkins asked, with a surly tone.

"What I'm thinking," Murdock said, "is several centrally located one-room buildings to act as school houses, with Zeke traveling to those buildings once or twice a week to conduct classes. The parents whose children are in school will provide what he needs. Since my children are older, he can start anytime. I have to figure out the logistics of travel, both his and the kids', to be the most efficient. And the safest."

After breakfast, Murdock, Zeke, and Heather gathered outside the medical facility to bid farewell to Murdock's tribe.

"*You be careful, Kevin,*" Mei Lee flashed to Murdock.

"*I will. You also need to be careful. There is still the threat from Reyes and her group. I know Bridget will escort you and keep you safe, but I want you to be on your toes.*"

"See that our families arrive safely," Murdock said to Declan. "You won't be alone, but keep a sharp lookout."

"I will." Declan reined his mount around and took up his position at the lead.

"Are *we* leaving?" Watkins said. "You've said your goodbyes. It's not like you'll be gone long."

"You can take off now since you're in such a big rush," Murdock said, matching Watkins' surliness. "We'll catch up... maybe."

"I'm not leaving alone," Watkins said. "You want me to leave without protection?"

"Why not? Isn't that what you and Lantz did coming here with Heather? Not so smart when your ass is on the line, is it."

Half of the day later, Murdock, Heather, and Watkins were standing on the cliff above the farmers' settlement. Murdock and Heather had arrived earlier than Watkins. Heather, being used to Murdock's pace, had kept up with him with ease. Watkins, however, had trouble.

"It's... about time... you stopped." Watkins panted, bent over with her hands on her knees. "What was... your hurry?"

Murdock scowled at her. "I have things I need to get done. I don't have all day to escort you. You need to tell Lantz to move his settlement back a bit. Since this is the easiest descent point, anyone passing downriver is forced to walk through your settlement. If he has a toll in mind for those going further downriver, then maybe I need to raze a few of your buildings to clear a path." Murdock guided Heather toward the stream a few paces, and motioned for Watkins to start down.

"You aren't coming?" Watkins said, when she was only a few steps down the zigzag path.

"What concern is that of yours?" Murdock snapped. "I'll see that Heather gets home safely. Busybodies!" He shook his head as he led Heather toward the stream while following the ridge.

"There's no easy way down," Heather said, after a half-hour of hiking the edge of the ridge.

"You let me worry about that," Murdock replied. "Will Alvin be at your place?"

"He should be. Since I've been gone, he's had to do all the chores himself."

When they had traveled about a mile from the river, they stopped and peered over the edge of the step.

"If he's there, he's inside your soddy," Murdock said. "Close your eyes."

Once Heather's eyes were closed, Murdock levitated himself and Heather off the step.

"This way," Heather said, after her feet were once again on the ground.

She led him into the hovel. A quick scan of the interior showed Murdock that Alvin wasn't there and that the pair had lived a simple life.

"Can I get you anything?" Heather stirred the coals in the fireplace, causing sparks to dance around the hearth.

"I'm good," Murdock removed his waterskin and set it on the small table made from a wood round.

He popped a bit of smoked venison into his mouth.

"What did you have in mind?" Heather asked as she sat across from him. "You said something about me and Alvin moving up the step, closer to the medical facility. There's nothing there, so what did you have in mind?"

"What I had in mind was you getting away from people who

like putting you at risk. I'm not trying to coerce you. Just giving you an option."

"An option for what?" Alvin Jones entered his small lodging.

"Alvin, glad you're here," Heather said.

"An option for you and Heather to be... freer. Or feel like it, anyway," Murdock felt claustrophobic in the tiny sod house with three adults inside.

"Murdock was pissed that Lantz and Watkins insisted that I lead them, unarmed. After a few questions, it came out how we're being taken advantage of by Lantz." Heather giggled. "You know how Watkins is. Every time I said something, she'd insert her opinions. She dug her own grave with her tongue!"

Alvin eyed Murdock. "Why would you offer to help us?"

"So far, my tribe has had a satisfactory relationship with you and Heather." Murdock paced around the room. "I wish that to continue. Also, Heather has long been a good friend to my tribe, and I wish *that* to continue also. My idea is to have you two move your operation close to the medical facility. With Roy White injured in the attack, Harris and Annie could use help with chores for now, and later, defense."

"Attack? What attack?" Alvin said.

"Heather didn't mention that the medical facility was attacked just before we got there."

"What?" Alvin looked to Heather, with wide eyes. "Who was it?"

"Wagner and a few of his followers," Murdock said.

"Why would he do that? What was he going to get out of it?"

"Who knows? Their kind doesn't need a *logical* reason," Murdock spewed.

"Wagner tried to kill Murdock. He stole all his equipment and kidnapped me and Annie. That was before we were together."

"Oh." Alvin returned his attention to Murdock, inhaling and then exhaling. "We have little here, but it's something we built without help from anyone. It's not something I'm willing to abandon on a whim. You're asking a lot from us."

"I understand. Think about it. I need to spend time at the medical facility doing some... *security* upgrades. If you accept my offer, just go to the medical facility. I'll hear about it and will come to help you build a new home." Murdock left the hovel, and Heather followed.

"We'll discuss your proposition and give it all due consideration," Heather said, after exiting the soddy.

"That's all I can expect." Murdock grinned. "Whatever you decide, be well and take care."

Murdock walked toward the stream.

Shortly after leaving the medical facility, Mei Lee climbed the face of the second step, with Curtis and Angelica behind her, Emily driving the cart with the younger children and all the equipment, Andy and Chun Hua following the cart, and Declan riding drag.

"How come the rest ain't followin'?" Curtis said, when they were halfway up the face. He had stopped and looked back.

"No need to worry about them," Mei Lee said, irritated. "They're well-versed in navigating this obstacle. Just pay attention to what you're doing and keep going. They'll catch up."

At the top, Mei Lee kept going. After about a mile, Curtis looked behind them and saw that the others were there. Far back, but there. As the miles clicked by, Curtis kept checking and found that the others weren't far behind and had made up the distance. At what Mei Lee perceived as midday, they all stopped.

Declan handed out pieces of the pork to everyone, while Emily fed little Gordon.

"How's your water?" Declan whispered, as he gave Curtis and Angelica their meat. "If you need to refill any, do it before we move on."

"Why are you whisperin'?" Curtis said. "I don't see anyone else around."

"Just because you see nothing, doesn't mean threats aren't there. Out here, you need to keep your wits about you and look everywhere. We make no unnecessary noise if we can help it."

"Usually, if you see something dangerous, it's already too late," Mei Lee said. "Until Murdock assesses your fighting skills, if we run into trouble, I want you to run away. Do it as fast as you can."

"Run? Run where?" Curtis said, with a confused look on his face.

"Anywhere!" Mei Lee replied. "What part of *away* don't you understand? Away from the trouble. You run and keep on running until you're far enough away to make chasing you undesirable." She turned her attention to Declan. "I want to move away from the river until we are atop the next step. What do you think?"

Declan thought for a second. "I think it would be safer. I'd say a mile or two should be sufficient."

Mei Lee nodded. "I want to get home before dark, but camping—"

"Why move away from the river?" Curtis said, overloud.

Declan grabbed Curtis' upper arm and turned him away from Mei Lee. "You don't get a vote yet," he hissed. "Mei Lee and Murdock have been here for ten years. It's best to do as they do. If they want your opinion, they'll ask for it. Do not anger them unnecessarily."

"It's my life an' I have a right ta express my opinion! Besides, I don' take no orders from some sawed-off, scrawny, bit..."

His diatribe ran out of steam when he realized Mei Lee was standing close enough to hear.

"Continue!" Mei Lee glared at Curtis. "I want to hear more!" she said, and no one said anything further. "I say I can knock you out and there's nothing you can do to stop it," she said angrily. "Ready?" she asked after a short pause.

Declan got out of the way. Curtis was standing, tall and lanky, looking at her with a condescending smirk. Mei Lee jumped up, and then he felt a jolt of pain as she executed a front kick to his bladder. Then the other foot slammed into his solar plexus with another front kick, knocking the wind out of him. At the apex of her jump, she executed a round-house kick to the side of his neck, knocking Curtis unconscious. Mei Lee and Curtis hit the ground at the same time, Mei Lee landing gracefully on her feet, and Curtis falling like a chopped tree.

"I think that should let everyone know who's in charge here," she said. "When he comes to, we'll be moving on. And you, Declan, need to do a better job of informing your guests."

Raymond Tutt was shocked when he saw Ted Wagner wiggle under the wall. Ted was naked and was protective of his right hand, which was covered in mud. Harvey Stoddard was also naked and favoring his left hand.

"Ted, what happened?" Tutt said.

Wagner ignored him and disappeared into the mine.

They were all clothed and armed when they left. Tutt stared at those entering their compound and following the rest into the mine. As the last one past him, he followed.

By the time Tutt had caught up with Wagner, they were in the lower portions of the mine, in the bathing area.

"I don't appreciate being ignored, Ted."

"Sorry, boss. We've been running and walking for the better part of a day and a half."

Tutt noticed Wagner was trying to keep his right hand hidden. "What happened to your hand? I notice that everyone returning with you has a hand injury, so don't give me your usual placating rhetoric. I want answers!"

Wagner said nothing.

"I thought we agreed that you weren't to aggravate the situation with Murdock," Tutt said, when he grew tired of waiting for an answer. "What did you do this time?"

"We shot a few arrows over a walled enclosure."

"You were attacking someone that Murdock was protecting... and you got caught. Was anyone injured?"

Wagner shrugged.

"You were sent to find deer and see what all the noise was from a few days ago. You weren't supposed to draw attention to yourself or attack Murdock. I don't want to give him a reason to come here again. And what happened to your clothes and weapons?"

Wagner took a deep breath and let it out slowly. "Our clothes and weapons were confiscated, at Murdock's orders, by a few of Rogers' men. I have no idea what they did with them. We didn't see any deer, and the noise was the new arrivals—two thousand more newbies, if my math is correct."

Tutt rubbed his forehead with his hand and exhaled audibly. "What am I supposed to do with you? Am I supposed to just let you ignore any orders you want? Your actions have seriously impacted our readiness by reducing our available men-at-arms by a third. You have lost valuable weapons and clothing, and now someone has to either try to retrieve what you lost or replace it."

"I can't stomach Murdock or those under his protection! He stole from me and I will repay him for it."

Tutt chuckled. "Didn't you steal from him first and try to kill him?"

"Yeah. So? Don't you think he should've had the good manners to stay dead?"

"Shut it!" Tutt thought about back-handing Wagner across the face, but decided against it... for now. "You are my second-in-command, but that position comes with some expectations. I expect you to follow my orders. You expect me to have your back, but when you go against my orders, backing you becomes problematic for me. You didn't follow directions and put us all at risk! Luckily you're no longer prepared to continue your... vendetta against Murdock. Now I have to go around behind you and try to get the things you lost."

Wagner tried to burn a hole through Tutt's back as he walked away.

"Wha' happened?" Curtis said, as he came around.

His face was damp and Declan was kneeling close to him.

"I warned you," Declan whispered. "Murdock and Mei Lee have the experience to live here. I can also live here now because of them, their training. This isn't what you're used to, so a word to the wise should be sufficient."

"Why din't ya defend me, *brother*?" Curtis spat. "You shoulda come ta my defense."

"If I thought you were correct, I would have. But you were wrong. Mei Lee's responsibility is to see all of us safely home. What you did put us all in jeopardy."

Declan stood and offered a hand to Curtis, which Curtis slapped away and got to his feet unaided.

"Just shut up and do as you're told. I used to take you down when we were kids, and I'll do it again if I have to. Don't force me to." Declan re-mounted Donder. "Hurry it up. We're falling behind." He reined up his mount.

Mei Lee, you and I are going to tangle, Curtis trotted after Declan. *And you, brother, have to learn that blood is thicker than water!*

63

It was late in the day when Zeke and Annie exited the medical facility to look for firewood.

"Might I inquire, what is Irene's status?" Zeke said, after they'd wandered around.

Annie looked at him with a raised brow. "Why?"

"No particular reason. I'm just curious. I don't want to assume, and Mister White does live here."

"Roy, for lack of a better explanation, prefers the company of a woman living in the big cave with the Lotus Eaters. He works with us and lives here a few days out of fourteen until winter. He has no other ties to us. What's your interest in Irene?"

"Other than she is a striking woman, I was asking if she's married, spoken for, maybe seeing someone."

Annie noticed he was turning a little red around his neck and ears.

She chuckled. "No, as far as I know, she isn't married or seeing someone. I'd suggest you ask her if you want to know more."

"*Ahem...* I'll take your suggestion under advisement," Zeke reached for some wood."

It didn't take long for the pair to gather two loads of wood.

"How's it going?" Murdock said, from behind Annie and Zeke as they were walking back to the compound.

Zeke jumped and dumped most of the wood he was carrying.

"Hello, Kevin." Annie smirked at Zeke's mishap. "How was your trip downriver?"

"It was rather pleasant, actually. We'll talk about that later. When you two are finished gathering wood, I need to have a private discussion with Zeke."

"You can have him after he deposits the load he has now outside the residence."

"I don't want to interfere with any work he needs to do."

"It'll be fine. Besides, it has to be important for you to request him—at least it must be to you."

"*Beron and I need to talk privately with Zeke,*" Murdock flashed to Annie. "*We'll be at the private little cave.*"

"*Understood. You want him conscious or unconscious?*"

"*Beron will handle Zeke's level of consciousness. I'll lead him to the area.*"

"*You need to find out what his intentions are toward Irene. I think he has designs on her.*"

Murdock chuckled. "*Good! She needs someone, but I'll not interfere with her decisions. She's an adult and can make those decisions for herself. I'm not her father, and you should respect her enough to allow her to decide.*"

"*I do, but I'm also protective of her.*"

"Come with me, please," Murdock said, when Zeke returned empty-handed.

"Sure." Zeke shrugged. "I take it this is a good time to talk?" He followed Murdock toward the cliff face and away from the river.

It didn't take too long for Murdock and Zeke to reach the wedge-shaped indent in the cliff.

"Just relax, Zeke," Murdock said, as Zeke fell asleep while standing, and caught Zeke, as he fell, and levitated him into the small cave that had been meant for Declan and Emily.

When Zeke roused, he darted his gazed around and jerked his head left and right. Murdock was in the darkened cave, tending the fire, which was the only light. He could hear water falling into a pool somewhere close behind him.

"Where are we?" Zeke said.

"We're somewhere safe and secure. It's a private place."

"If it's just you and me, then why do I feel like there's someone else here?" Zeke looked around.

"I didn't say we were alone, but we are safe. This may sound strange, but I need to ask if you're willing to share your thoughts with me."

"I *have* shared my thoughts with you... freely." Zeke shook his head with a questioning look. "So I don't understand what you mean."

"If you could, would you share everything inside your mind with me?" Murdock said.

"You mean, like telepathy?" Zeke chuckled with disbelief. "Yes, if it were possible! I've nothing to hide." Zeke fell over sideways, asleep.

Murdock sat before the fire and closed his eyes and cleared his mind.

———

Hours after Murdock and Zeke had entered the sharing state, they awakened. Zeke opened his eyes and saw Murdock sitting cross-legged, floating a few inches off the sand-covered floor.

Murdock inhaled loudly and opened his eyes. "How are you feeling?"

"Fine, I guess."

"You look puzzled."

"What was that?"

"What was what?"

"What was it I just experienced? What, or who, was the dark figure?"

"That was what I like to call the sharing state. It's a way to communicate telepathically."

Zeke made a face as if he were about to argue that there was no such thing as telepathy, but became confused and couldn't say anything.

Murdock sat quietly. He knew Zeke needed time to be introspective and come to grips with his own beliefs, which had just been shot down. Murdock recognized the look. He had seen it before, on Declan, Emily, Mei Lee, Annie, Irene, Rose, when everyone came out of their first sharing.

"Was that real?" Zeke whispered.

"What you have just experienced is between us. You are not to mention it to anyone except those of my tribe."

"Your... tribe?"

"My family. My family *is* my tribe."

"Annie and Irene are members of your family." Zeke nodded.

Murdock could tell that the light had finally turned on in Zeke's mind.

"But who was the dark, cloaked figure?"

"That was a being that had a hand in making this place. They are powerful, and they are my *personal* friends."

"They made this cave?"

"This planet."

Zeke fell asleep again.

———

When he awoke, he and Murdock were back at the cleft in the ridge.

"You've been given a gift," Murdock said, once Zeke was alert. "You've been allowed to remember all that has transpired, but you're not to talk to anyone about it, including my children. They're too young to understand. The adults of my tribe are aware of what you've been shown and what I learned. It means we trust you... to a point. We'll be watching you and getting to know you. Once we all agree that you can be trusted with more, more will be given."

"So I take it I know more than the rest of the newcomers?"

"You know more than everyone, other than my family. That includes those of the previous pod. So take it for what it is and don't look into things too closely. We are wary of outsiders."

"I can understand that and you have no reason to distrust me, but you'll see that for yourself soon enough."

The pair entered the walled medical facility.

5

Surprising someone is not always the smartest thing to do. If you don't know them, then you're asking for trouble. You never know what others have been through and how it affected them. I've seen the nicest people become not so nice when startled.

— KEVIN MURDOCK, COLLECTED SAYINGS

A few days after Zeke's sharing, the normal routine at the medical facility was disrupted. Annie and Zeke were outside the facility, gathering firewood.

"I would like to talk to Murdock," Raymond Tutt yelled out, from a distance. "I come for peace, not trouble."

"Tutt is here to talk to you," Murdock heard inside his mind, from Annie.

"What do you want, Tutt?" Murdock asked testily as he stormed past Annie, who was standing defiantly with her hand on the hilt of her twelve-incher. He glanced at Zeke as he passed. *"Take Zeke inside and close up the facility,"* he flashed to Annie.

"I come for peace, not trouble," Tutt repeated, as Murdock approached. "I would like the weapons and clothing returned that were taken from my men."

"Why ask me? I don't have them and they're not here." Murdock stopped some distance away from Tutt and the two men with him, glaring at them all.

Tutt handed his weapons to one of the other men and inched toward Murdock, hands raised.

"I've come to apologize for my men. I'd given them specific orders to avoid antagonizing you, but Wagner had other ideas I wasn't aware of. I hope there were no major injuries."

"This facility is to provide medical treatment to any who require it. Wagner screwed up when he attacked. The medicos are re-evaluating their *open door* policy." Murdock scowled, and Tutt stopped moving toward him. "As far as Wagner goes, he's had his warnings."

Tutt stopped. "That may be true, but I wanted you to know I didn't authorize the attack."

"To me, it doesn't matter much if you authorized the attack or not. Wagner is part of your crew, so I hold all of your people responsible."

"I just don't want you to feel the need to come to the mine." Tutt smiled sheepishly.

Murdock clenched his jaw. "*If* I come to the mine again, it will be to take possession of it. Do you understand?"

Annie and Zeke entered the medical facility enclosure through the new entryway, which was now closer to the river. Zeke carried the wood inside while Annie levitated the colossal stone into its place, closing off the entire compound to the outside world.

For the last two nights, and without any help, Murdock had extended the compound wall, the one that held the portcullis, across the entire side by fifteen feet and had placed slats of stone across the gap. As Annie looked up, she remained confused about the need to slat the roof over the tunnel.

"It's slatted so you can shoot through the gaps from above," Murdock had said.

But to her mind, those trapped inside the tunnel could still shoot through the gaps.

Annie walked through the opened portcullis, and after closing it, climbed the ladder that allowed those inside the compound to access the newly extended section. She saw that Murdock had been working on the top of the outermost wall before Tutt's interruption. It held long, three-foot-high stones, with others placed atop them. The effect made the outer wall look like pictures of castles she had seen when she was a child.

As she walked across the length of the tunnel, she found that she could see a great distance across the river as well as down-river. As she walked back toward the ladder, she noticed that Tutt and his men were moving downriver and toward the river bank.

"It appears as though Murdock is almost finished with the upgrades," Zeke said, from behind her.

"Looks like it," Annie replied. "I'm a nurse, not an engineer, so the reasoning behind the slats and the scalloping on the outer edge escapes me."

"The slats allow anyone up here to shoot arrows through the slats at anyone or anything trapped inside by the portcullis and the outer door."

"But can't they shoot up through the slats?"

"They could, but the odds of anyone accomplishing that are slim. It's far easier for us to shoot through the slats because we can stick our arrows into the gaps before releasing. Anyone inside the tunnel will be fifteen feet away from those gaps, and thus have to be steady-shots to make it through the gaps. Do you understand archery?"

"Some. Why?"

"One of the principles that archers and other shooters have to keep in mind is the closer a target is, the easier it is to hit. If your aim is off a little on a close target, you can still hit it, but if it's further away, the error in aiming compounds itself. The longer a projectile is in flight, the more natural forces act on it. It slows and it drops. If you shoot an arrow at a target ten yards away, you have a large margin of error and can still hit the target. But if you're shooting at the same target at a hundred yards, the smallest error can cause a miss, and a crosswind can send an arrow off target by feet. Then there is the archer's paradox. Most people are unaware that arrows flex when they're first released, and depending on the type of riser, will bend around the riser. The further they go, the more they steady down and stop flexing. Here," Zeke pointed to the slats, "the gap is small compared to the distance. I doubt most arrows would stop flexing before they entered the gap. The arrow shaft would most likely strike the edge of the slat and be deflected. If we're up here shooting down, the flex becomes inconsequential. The arrow is into the gap before it's released. Zeke pointed to the outer wall. "The gaps that line the wall are crenels, or wheelers, and are there to allow us to shoot out and then duck behind the taller parts for cover. The taller parts are merlons. The whole effect is called crenellation."

Annie stood there, mouth agape, looking at him. "That was the most in-depth explanation of a simple question I've ever heard."

She slapped him on his shoulder and they both laughed.

Charles Benteen was pacing around the small group of newcomers. It had been three days since Murdock left them, and he was anxious to get started. He had managed to convince fifty of the newcomers to follow him to reconnoiter the possibilities for their permanent settlement. Most were unskilled or had a limited skillset, but one, a Dirk Benson, was supposedly an outdoorsman and hunter before coming here, and Benteen was hopeful he would lead them to an area that would provide them the needed resources.

As Benson started off, everyone else picked up the few tools Benteen had thought they would need. It took the group most of the day to reach the river.

"I'd make camp here," Benson said to Benteen, as the pair walked along the riverbank. "It's been a long walk and everyone needs to rest up for tomorrow. Any idea of where you want to go from here?"

Benteen looked upriver for a while, and then downriver. "I'd say downriver. According to Murdock, there's a settlement just off this plateau. I want to be downriver from that settlement."

"How far? You know, the people of that settlement may resent our presence."

"I'm sure that the people downriver from here have staked out their claim to the land they want. I want to be about a mile downriver from that point."

"Why? Why don't we settle here or close to the edge of this plateau?"

"Murdock informed us that this area has the medical facility as well as some... unsavory characters. Establishing our settlement on this plateau may diminish the available resources to the point that we would be in direct competition with the others who are here already. I feel we would lose that competition. They understand this place better than we do."

"Well, I'm just leading you, so I don't care where we go. I'll get the others started on fires and gathering fish."

As Chris Gundersen strolled around the campsite, he watched a few of the others trying to get a fire started, after some direction from Benson.

This is the river. I need to cross somewhere around here to find the Pirates. I'm excited about the possibility of joining a group that's already established. Besides, who doesn't like the idea of joining pirates?

Gundersen's head snapped around when someone grabbed his upper arm.

"You're needed at the river." Benson released his grip. "We need fish caught, skinned, gutted, and cooked."

"But I have no idea how to do any of that." Gundersen's eyes were downcast.

"Well, then, you'll learn," Benson chuckled as he gave Gundersen a shove in the direction of the river.

I don't understand why I should gather fish. Gunderson trudged toward the river. *I'm not planning on being with these people long enough for it to matter.*

When he got to the riverbank, he saw several people standing in the water, trying to stab fish with their twelve-inch machetes, while others were gathering firewood. He chuckled to himself as a couple reached too far into the deeper water and fell in. There were, however, several fish on the bank.

"You can start by cleaning the ones we've already caught," Benson said, jovially, from behind him.

"I've never cleaned fish before," Gundersen looked at Benson.

Benson pulled out his twelve-incher and grabbed one of the flopping fish. "Then it's high time you learned." He knelt and began showing Gunderson how to clean the catch.

Shortly after dark, everyone sat around two campfires, eating.

"I think we need two from each ring to stand guard while the rest sleep," Benson said, between bites.

"Why?" Benteen said. "I'm not trying to argue, just trying to understand," he added, when Benson stopped chewing and glared at him.

"While we were traveling here, I was paying attention to

tracks," Benson replied. "I've seen an abundance of deer sign, or what I assume is deer—even though they would be the size of elk—and bear tracks. The bear sign and the humans are what concern me. The bears appear to be large and heavy, and humans are, by far, the more dangerous. The guards will raise an alarm if an intruder should venture into our camp."

Benteen nodded.

"I know we don't have the ranged weapons we'll need, but being awake and armed with the eighteen-inch machetes should allow us to defend ourselves. I'll sleep better, knowing someone will wake me if something happens."

Someone got to their feet with some fish and was about to put it in the fire.

"What are you doing?" Benson snapped. "If you're finished, then store the rest. We aren't wasting anything."

"How and where are we supposed to store it?"

"I don't care how you do it. Just know food is not to be wasted. If I see it, you'll miss a meal." Benson glared around to everyone.

"I'm sure that won't be necessary," Benteen said.

"It's my job to get you to your more permanent camp. Until that happens, you're all going to follow my instructions. If not, then I'll leave you to your own devices."

Everyone nodded, eyes downcast.

"Here you go." Annie handed Murdock a plate of food.

He accepted it and sat looking out over the new wall.

"What are you looking at?" Annie flashed.

"I've been keeping an eye out for Heather and Alvin." Murdock chewed. *"I was hoping they would take me up on my offer. I'd feel better knowing they were here to help defend this place."*

"Surely we can defend ourselves if we have to, especially since you updated our defenses."

Murdock looked at her. "Annie, you are a hell of a nurse, but you can't hit the floor with your hat."

"Well, then, I'm glad I don't wear a hat." She smirked. "With Zeke here, I'm sure we'll be fine."

"You're more optimistic than I would be in your position. Zeke has no idea how to defend himself or how to shoot. He's not prepared for this place. Not physically, not emotionally."

"I thought you liked him."

"I do. But my liking him has nothing to do with his ability to survive here. You of all people should know that. Defenses are to slow down attackers. Their losses are what deter them. Can you do what's necessary?"

"I'd like to think so," Annie said, after thinking about it.

Murdock stiffened.

"What is it?" Annie asked.

"Some of the new arrivals are at the river."

Annie went to the wall and stared downriver. "I don't see anything."

"Neither can I. But I *can* see their camp fire, though."

I should leave, Gundersen thought. *Cleaning the fish wasn't too bad, and learning to make a fire can be helpful. At least I'm further along to being able to live here. But what about the Pirates?* His blood ran with excitement at the thought of joining the group. *Are you sure they'll accept you? What happens if they try to kill you on-sight? How does one become a pirate without being on an ocean?*

"How's it going?" said a voice from behind him.

He jumped. "Nothing is wandering around out there, as far as I can tell." He turned to see Benson looking at him with a grin.

"You probably won't see anything, but you may be able to hear and smell them," Benson whispered.

"All I can hear is the fires crackling and some footsteps, mine and the others. All I can smell is myself and the smoke."

75

"Focus your ears toward the river. Can you hear the water running?"

Gundersen noticed that Benson had closed his eyes and turned his head toward the river.

"I don't hear nothin' from the river," Gunderson said, after trying half-heartedly.

"You don't hear anything." Benson chuckled. "How old are you, kid?"

"I ain't no kid! I'm old enough."

Benson looked him up and down, and then cuffed him close to his right ear. Gundersen glared at the older man.

"Now that I have your attention, we're going to play a little game. I'm going off into the dark. If you hear me, you're good. If you don't, I'll cuff you again."

"I didn't *say* I'd play your game." Gundersen rubbed the side of his head.

"I'm sorry if I gave you the impression you had a choice." Benson grinned.

Gundersen blinked and Benson disappeared into the dark.

I should just go get some sleep, Gundersen strained his ears to hear any movement that would give Benson away. *This guy will just wake me up by cuffing me if I lay down.* He jumped. *Was that him? I thought I heard something in the grass… off that way.* He turned in the direction he heard the noise come from, and leaped up with his hand on the hilt of his twelve-incher. *What was that? Was that Benson?* He turned in a different direction. He tilted his head and tried to force his ears to pick up any noise.

After a little while, Gundersen turned around and saw Benson standing inches from him. The shock caused him to jump back just as Benson cuffed him again, hard enough to turn his face away.

"What's your name, kid?" Benson said.

"Chris… Gundersen." He rubbed the side of his face.

"Well, Chris, you have a lot to learn. You're standing guard, but you do realize that anything coming into the camp isn't going to announce itself?"

Gundersen nodded.

"To make your guarding worthwhile, you need to learn to listen. I want you to sit and listen for the river."

"Now?"

"Why not? You have somewhere else to be?"

"But I'm tired and want to sleep."

"So go ahead. You'll sleep soundly and won't hear anything that's hungry for Chris Gundersen. You'll die without so much as a whimper. I didn't know you wanted to die."

Gundersen thought for a second. "I don't *want* to die. I don't know how to do what you asked."

"So sit, close your eyes and open your ears." Gundersen sat and closed his eyes. "Now do you hear the fires?"

"Yes."

"That's something. Do you hear the others sleeping?"

Gundersen listened and could pick out several variations of slow, heavy breathing.

"Yes," he breathed.

"Do you hear the other guards wandering around?"

Gundersen could hear three of the four guards that should have been up, keeping watch.

"Only three," he whispered.

"Where is the missing guard?"

Gundersen frowned as he tried to locate the missing guard. He knew where the guard should be and tried to listen in that direction. It took a few seconds, and then he heard him.

"He's peeing, a little further out."

"Good. Now do you hear the river running?"

Gundersen refocused his hearing toward the river, frowning as he tried to have his ears reach out for any sound from that direction. Finally, he nodded.

"I can hear the river and the deer on the other side, drinking."

"Excellent," Benson whispered with excitement, and held out his hand. "I'm Dirk Benson. You can call me *Mister* Benson, Chris." He gave a friendly grin.

Gundersen shook the offered hand.

"Now go get some sleep. I'll teach you more tomorrow."

———

"What now, boss?" said Timothy Daniels, who sat close to the campfire.

"I don't know, Tiny." Raymond Tutt chuckled at the thought of the nickname.

Tiny was anything but.

He stands at least six-foot-eight and has to tip the scales at 270 or 280.

Raymond had been sitting quietly for an hour. "Since Rogers refused to return the bows and clothing confiscated from Wagner, I'm at a loss as to our next move."

"They did give us back three of the bows," Blandean Marchand said, "so it wasn't a total loss."

"Rogers is keeping four and is planning on giving three to White and the rest inside the medical facility," Tutt said, "as reparation for the injury he sustained at the hands of that *idiot*, Wagner." All three men looked at the three bows and quivers of arrows. "We're running out of men to use the weapons we have."

"Wagner and those that attacked the facility should be fine... eventually," Marchand whispered at the fire.

"Maybe we can get more men from somewhere else," Daniels whispered back.

"Do we know where everyone from our pod went?" Tutt asked, after several minutes of silence. "I know there were one hundred fifty, or thereabouts, of us that left the pod and headed here. Do we know where the rest went? I mean, it was fifty people, or close to it."

Daniels and Marchand stared blankly at Tutt.

"I take your blank looks as a no. Since we need people, maybe they're willing to join us? Or we join them? There needs to be a sharing of resources, in my opinion. What do you think?"

"I think we need to check it out before we head home," Daniels said.

"It won't matter much," Marchand replied. "Wagner is going to have a fit since he wasn't consulted."

Tutt frowned. "Wagner isn't in charge! I am! We leave tomorrow to look for them."

"I'm going to check on Heather and Alvin," Murdock flashed to his tribe, as he made ready to leave the medical facility. *"I suspect that Lantz might try to prevent them from leaving. I'll be heading home once I'm satisfied that they can leave if they want to."*

"You made the offer, and you may want to leave it alone," Mei Lee flashed back, *"otherwise they may feel pressured. They need to decide this for themselves."*

"The other reason is the first newbies may be heading down to Lantz's area. I'll feel better once they're past Lantz's area unmolested," Murdock started off at a trot.

He hadn't gone more than a few miles when he came upon Tutt and his men.

"What are you still doing here!" He stormed toward Tutt. "I'd thought you'd have gone back to your hidey-hole."

"We go where we want," Tutt replied. "Where we go is *our* business!"

Murdock's vision was obstructed for a second as he passed through the trees. When the intruders came into view again, his brain didn't register that one of the men was missing.

He said, "If you're here to cause more trouble—"

A giant man stepped out from behind a tree and grabbed Murdock by the throat as he stormed passed. Murdock dropped his spear and delivered a double tiger-paw strike on either side of the man's arm, just above the elbow, numbing the bigger man's arm. Murdock moved the man's arm to the side. The other hand hit him with a vertical-fist in his solar plexus. Murdock's knee then slammed into the bigger man's leg, just above the knee joint and on the outside of his leg, numbing it and felling the bigger man like a tree. With the bigger man lying face up on the ground, Murdock kicked him in the side of his head, rendering him unconscious. He then reached out and his spear leaped into his hand. It all happened in fractions of a second, from start to finish. Tutt and Marchand stood dumbstruck. It had all happened in a blink of an eye. Murdock spun the spear as he prepared to strike the finishing blow.

"Wait!" Tutt said.

"Why should I?" Murdock scowled as he paused before the final spear thrust. "He *is* one of yours, and *you* failed to control him. Why should he be spared?"

"To be frank, he isn't all that bright." Tutt shrugged. "He thought you were going to attack me and he did what he thought was needed to protect me."

Murdock relaxed a little, but his spear was still poised to strike. "Where were you going?"

"We're going to seek out others from our pod, but we were going to cross the river before heading upriver. We were going to give you and the medical facility a wide berth, but now we may need to stop and have Daniels there," Tutt indicated the fallen man, "checked for permanent damage."

Murdock relaxed completely and moved away from Daniels. As he did, Marchand hurried over to Daniels to try to revive him.

"You and your people, are getting on my last nerve!" Murdock readjusted his equipment. "My patience with you is quickly wearing thin. Do I need to make an example of you?" He glared at Tutt. "I will if you keep insisting."

"Come on, Bones!"

Gundersen heard Benson's voice, and then felt a soft kick on the bottom of his foot.

"We're burning daylight!"

Gundersen slowly opened his eyes and saw others breaking camp. *It isn't even sunup yet. How can we be burning daylight if there is no daylight?* He took a draw on his waterskin.

"I feel like I just went ta sleep. Why'd you wake me so early?"

"We'll be breaking camp soon and you need to get ready to move, unless you want to be out here alone. You need to eat if you have anything left from last night."

"I don't. I ate it all last night." Gundersen stretched his tortured muscles again.

"Here.," Benson offered Gundersen fish. "Seriously, how old are you, Chris? You don't look a day over thirteen, but I suspect you're older than that." He stood relaxed, with his hand resting on the hilt of his twelve-incher.

"I'm fifteen, if it matters so much," Gundersen snapped.

"No need to get testy. I was just asking. I'm thinking I need an apprentice. I'm no Murdock, but you can learn a lot from me. Interested?"

Gundersen looked to Benson, his brow creased. "Wha' do ya expect from me?"

"I expect you to try, to do your damnedest, no matter what I ask. And I expect you to be respectful, trustworthy, and honest, with yourself and with me. I don't expect perfection, just an honest attempt at doing your best."

"What do I get out of such an arrangement?"

"Out here, there are three types of people. Friends, enemies, and those you can't tell if they're friends or not. What you get out of the arrangement is someone you *know* is a friend, someone that has your back, a pardner, if you will. Add to that, you gain

81

the skills you'll need to survive. I'm willing to teach if you're willing to learn."

"Can I think it over, or do you want an immediate answer?"

"I've agreed to lead these people to a place they should be able to survive. At some point, I'll be heading off in my own direction. You have until that day to give me a definitive answer.

"In the meantime, I'd like you to walk with me. Observe and learn as much as you can while I'm here, and ask whatever questions you may come up with."

"Why me?"

Benson smiled. "Mainly because you're young and inexperienced. You seem to be a good kid, and I'd feel better if you did manage to learn *something* from me. Now saddle up! We're moving out soon."

Gundersen got to his feet and watched the older man head downriver. *Saddle up? What does that even mean? We didn't ride here.*

"Did you see that?" Marchand asked Tutt, breathlessly, as he assisted Daniels toward the river.

"See what?" Tutt asked.

Both men were having a hard time getting Daniels to move.

"Tiny is the biggest guy I've seen here, and Murdock went through him like crap through a goose. And I thought he dropped his spear. How did it reappear in his hand?"

"Shit, Tiny, you need to go on a diet," Tutt said to his unconscious companion. "I don't know," he said to Marchand. "I was shocked that Tiny would try to take Murdock down like that, and Murdock looked like a whirling dervish, and then Tiny was down. I yelled *wait* as soon as I realized what Tiny was doing. It wasn't to stop Murdock."

"You were almost too late. Why do I feel like we're dragging a tree?"

"I'm six-five, and you're what, six-three? And Tiny dwarfs us! So, yeah, we *are* dragging a tree."

Tutt and Marchand were knocked to the ground when Tiny became conscious and flailed his arms.

"What happened?" Daniels got to all fours.

"You knocked us to the ground." Marchand rolled over. "We were trying to get you to the river."

"No, not what I meant." Daniels shook his head, trying to clear the fog. "I remember grabbing Murdock by the neck, and then my lights went out." He panted.

"What the hell were you thinking?" Tutt got to his feet. "Don't ever grab Murdock like that again, unless I say different."

"Tutt saved your life, you know." Marchand sat next to his large companion. "Murdock had you under his spear and he was going to run you through, but Tutt stopped him."

"I thought Murdock was goin' to do somethin' to hurt you, Mister Ray. I figur'd I'd grab him first before he could. Sorry if it wasn't the right thing ta do." Daniels bowed his head as he sat on the ground.

Tutt walked over and squeezed Daniels shoulder. "It's okay, Tiny. I know why you did what you did. Just do us all a favor and don't do it again. At least, not with Murdock. How are you doing? Can you walk on your own now?"

Daniels nodded. "Think so. My chest hurts, though… a lot! Right there." He indicated the base of his sternum. "Hurts like hell ta breathe."

"I was going to cross the river here," Tutt said, "but I think we'll head upriver on this side instead. I want someone to look at you, to be sure you'll be okay. We'll just take it slow. We aren't in a big hurry."

Daniels stood and then flinched and favored his foot. "My arm is still tingling and my leg is numb. What the hell happened?"

"Murdock is what happened," Marchand said.

"No shit!" Tutt shook his head.

6

From the first gasp of air, life is a struggle. You have to kick, bite, scratch, and claw. No one is owed anything in life except the chance to survive. For some, that's not enough. They want a guarantee. The only guarantee you get is that, at some point, life will end.

— KEVIN MURDOCK, FAMILY CONVERSATIONS

It was late morning when Murdock reached the step that went down to Lantz's level. He had traveled with the river to his right, staying on the same side of the river as the medical facility. He had seen the people left behind, across the river, and now, he could see a bunch of them milling around at the top of the plateau. A chill went through him as he realized he was close to the place where Wagner had rolled his unconscious body off the plateau.

Murdock kept a close eye out as he levitated off the ledge and walked to the river. Once at the river, he could see several people congregated at the base of the path off of the ridge above, but he couldn't hear the obvious argument from all the angry gesturing, as the sound of rushing water from the river was drowning out the words. Since no one was looking in his direction, he levitated across the river and strolled to the arguing group.

"I don't know who you think you are, but you can't come traipsing through our village," Lantz growled.

"Murdock told us to come this way," Benteen spewed.

"Well, Murdock isn't here, now is he? And if he were, I'd tell him the same thing." Lantz poked his finger into Benteen's chest.

"And what would you tell me?" Murdock said, from behind a few of the crowd members.

Lantz paled and jumped back a step or two as Murdock pushed past the crowd.

"How did you get down here?" Lantz looked up the cliff face and back to Murdock.

"The *how* is immaterial. The fact is that I *am* down here. What kind of shit are you shoveling now, Lantz?"

"These... these *people* can't come traipsing through our village anytime they feel like it."

"Village?" Murdock gave a sarcastic smirk. "This conglomeration of sods is barely a camp. A far cry from any definition of a village. You must not have gotten the memo I sent you."

"Memo? What memo?" Lantz asked incredulously.

"So you don't talk to your underlings? Watkins had a message from me she was supposed to deliver. Did she?"

"Kathy Watkins is *not* my underling!" Lantz clenched and unclenched his fists as his face reddened.

"Huh! I thought she was, by the way she deferred to you. The same deference a servant would give to her master. Oh well, my apologies." Murdock placed his right hand on his chest and bowed, then turned to Benteen. "How many men do you have up there?" He glanced at the top of the ridge.

"We weren't intending to return, so we have twenty-five men up there, and another seventy-five coming in the next day or two. Why do you ask?"

"You are aware I'm standing here?" Lantz said.

"I was asking," Murdock said to Benteen, "because they obviously don't want you to go downriver from here. That means you'll have to fight to get past them. I haven't taken a census, but I doubt there are all that many here."

Benteen covered a smirk. "I'd have to ask for volunteers. I don't want to force anyone to fight if they're opposed to it, but I think we could launch an attack in," he looked up and closed his eyes, "oh, say two days at the earliest. Three days would be better."

"I'm standing here!" Lantz said.

"Okay. Take your men and go back up the ridge." Murdock turned back to Lantz as Benteen, Benson, and Gundersen started back up the winding path to the top of the ridge.

"So Lantz, you have three days before this... this *so-called* village is nothing but a memory. What are you going to do?"

"Do? What am *I* going to do?" Lantz sputtered.

"That's what I said. Is your hearing okay?"

"My hearing is fine. You, Murdock, have instigated a war! Whatever happens here is on your head."

Murdock jumped up on the roof of the nearest sod house. "Everyone gather 'round. Get everyone here." He waited for several minutes for the people to gather. "Lantz, your fearless leader, has determined that no one can pass through your... whatever *this* is." He indicated the collection of sods. "In his *infinite* wisdom, he has committed you all to fight the newcomers, who just want to pass through on their way downriver. If they were here to over-run your camp, I'd try to stop it. But they've indicated that all they want is to go on their way. Consequently, you are about to have the equivalent of your pod come through here. If you get in their way, they're prepared to kill you all. Should they fail, there's another eighteen hundred people to come after. Frankly, I doubt anyone can stop that many."

"So what are we to do?" called someone from the crowd.

"From my perspective, you can fight, or you can run. Is it really worth it to die for keeping newcomers from passing through?" As he looked out over the crowd, he saw Heather and Alvin leading their mounts.

"But what about the next time?" someone else said.

"First of all, you should've never built this close to the only trail up or down the ridge. Move your... *village* further away and build a wall with a gate. For now, though, I'd let the newcomers pass."

"But won't they rob us and take what little we have?" said the first person.

"If you refuse to let them through, they'll kill you all and take whatever they can find. So what are you out by letting them through? What you do is your business. It's your decision, not mine."

Murdock jumped down and sought out Heather and Alvin. He caught up to them close to the base of the cliff.

"At last!" Heather said, her face betraying her relief. "We've been here for two days trying to get up the ridge, but that ass-hat Lantz wouldn't let us."

"Why not?" Murdock frowned.

"He was giving us some tripe about reducing the resources the village requires. Alvin and I refused to leave our stock animals, so we were hoping you would come by when we didn't arrive at the medical facility."

"I almost didn't come. I didn't want to pressure you into anything. Right now, Lantz's charges are questioning his leadership. I'd go now, before they decide with him and against you."

"What about you?" Heather said.

"What about me?"

"What happens if they decide to come after you?"

Murdock frowned. "Everyone makes mistakes, and that will be one of *their* last. I'm not in the mood to suffer these fools, and so I will... *defend* myself."

———

"Gangway!" Benson said, as he reached the top of the ridge.

The rest of the people that had gathered began to back away.

"Make a hole, dammit! There's nothing to see here."

"But what's going on?" someone in the group said. "Are they going to let us pass?"

"You'll be told what's going on in due time." Benteen cleared the top of the ridge. "Me and Benson need to discuss the situation, so rest up. Eat and drink while you can."

He caught up with Benson and Gundersen, and the three of them separated from the rest.

"What the hell was that?" Benson asked Benteen, after they were seated.

Benteen chuckled. "That was a way for those idiots below to be made aware of the realities. Murdock was playing on their fears."

"That is all well and good for him," Benson said, "but it means we may have to back up his threats. You making a threat like that would be a different story."

"I couldn't make a threat like that without discussing it with everyone up here. I don't think they'll call us on the threat."

"And why's that?"

"From my understanding of the situation, they've been here for five years. Murdock has been here even longer. They *know* Murdock as someone not to be trifled with. They *know* he'll make good on the threat. "If we made the threat, they wouldn't have been intimidated since we're new here. They know we need them as much as they need us."

"What do you mean? They don't need us," Benson said.

"Sure they do. They've been here for five years. They've suffered losses and need an infusion of us newbies to bring their numbers up to something sustainable."

"What the hell?" Benson turned to peer toward the plateau's edge.

The other two looked also and saw two people mounted on deer, riding toward them. Each rider had two other pack animals following behind. All three men got to their feet and interposed themselves in the path of the riders. Benteen raised his open hand as the riders approached.

"Hey, there!" Benteen said, as the riders stopped.

"What do *you* want?" said the first rider, mounted on a buck.

"Just marveling at your mounts," Benteen replied. "Where did you get them?"

"We caught them," said the female rider, mounted on a doe. "We caught them and we broke them."

"Are your mounts deer?" Benteen said.

"Of course they are, you moron!" Benson replied. "They're huge! How did you ever catch them?"

The male rider chuckled. "The first one, we trapped. It was a small doe and was unable to jump the corral we built to trap 'em. As you can see, they're quite large and high jumpers. After that, with the help from one of these," he handed down a coiled, leather loop with weighted ends, "it got easier. But breakin' 'em is the hard part. Just like breakin' a horse. It ain't easy, but if you bring one dressed out, I think we can make a trade."

"What does he mean?" Gundersen whispered to Benson.

"He means, for food. Shot, skinned, and cut up." Benson answered softly.

"Where are you heading now?" Benteen said.

"The medical facility," replied the female rider.

"Are you sick?" Benson said.

The female rider chuckled. "Nope. Moving."

The male rider snapped his fingers a few times and reached for the weighted, coiled, leather. After securing it, he made a clicking sound, one familiar to all equestrians, and the pair rode on, upriver.

"Those are some really big deer," Gundersen said, as all three men watched the pair ride off.

Benteen replied, "Murdock did say the deer were large—"

"I know, but... damn!" Benson said.

While the three men stood watching the retreating riders,

Murdock came up behind them.

"Impressive, aren't they?"

The three men jumped.

"What's the verdict from below?" Benteen said, once he'd regained his wits.

"Unknown at this time. I'd let them stew a bit longer."

"How are we supposed to take one of those deer?" Benson was still watching the riders. "We have no range weapons."

"You can harvest them the same way I did. Ambush works well." Murdock looked Benson up and down. "You ever do any hunting before coming here?"

"Yeah, I have, but I used a rifle."

"Then you know how to track. That's a plus! The first one I took was with a spear—a pole with a machete attached to it. I found where they were traveling and ambushed it. It shouldn't be too hard for you, assuming you were any good at it. As I said, they are bigger than you'd expect, and the meat will go further than you'd think. I smoke a lot of my meat. It helps to preserve it."

"So how are we to get off this plateau?" Benson said, as he, Gundersen, and Benteen sat.

"The trail you've just traversed is the easiest way down. How far downriver were you planning to go?" Murdock sat and pulled out bits of dried meat and popped a couple into his mouth.

"I'd planned to go to the edge of the territory claimed by... Lantz?" Benteen said. "Lantz's group. I wanted to be close enough to possibly rely on them—a little, anyway—if things go south."

"There may be another way down, if you're willing to work for it." Murdock eyeballed the three men. "If you have enough rope, you could cross the river and rappel down."

"How would that help?" Benson said.

"You would avoid a confrontation with Lantz, and you would be in territory that, as far as I know, is unclaimed. Lantz sends people across the river to harvest wood for fires and other purposes. However, the last time I was in that area, I was recovering a body from cougars."

"Cougars?" Gundersen whispered.

"Yes, quite large ones, too." Murdock chuckled. "That's one of the reasons Lantz hasn't claimed that area and only sends men there if he has to."

"What resources are available there?" Benteen said.

"I have no idea," Murdock stretched his legs out in front of him. "Never explored that area. I was following a trail left by one of the previous pod's inhabitants when I found his body in a shallow cave, being eaten by the cougar's kits. That was, oh, three or four years ago. Anyway, I had warned Lantz at the time, and I guess he figured it wasn't worth the risk."

"So what's the advantage for us to occupy that area?"

"As far as I know, there is no *advantage*. It's just the chances you take. You want *guarantees* and I don't have any for you, other than you will die at some point, as everyone will. If you want to know about resources, then go there yourself and make your own determination. I was just offering an alternate way off this plateau."

Murdock got to his feet and moved toward the river.

Benteen, Benson, and Gundersen said nothing for a long time after Murdock left.

"Are we looking for a guarantee?" Benteen said. "I didn't think we were, but I could be wrong."

"No, we're looking to improve our odds, in my opinion," Benson said.

"So, what do you think about the alternative way off the plateau?" Benteen asked.

"I don't know," Benson said. "I'd have to look at the ridge across the river. From what I saw, when we went down the path into Lantz's… um…village, there are more trees across the river. We're going to need resources to make range weapons, and we won't find it where there are no trees. We'd be able to get water and fish from the river to tide us over until we can take a deer, and we wouldn't be encroaching on Lantz, except in the area he uses to get wood."

Benteen nodded. "I want you and Gundersen to check out the area across the river with a mind toward getting off the ridge from across the river.

"We have time, and we may as well check things out while we wait for the rest of our initial group. However, you need to be careful. We need information."

"So, you're saying, don't get killed." Benson got to his feet and chuckled.

"That would be a good idea," Benteen laughed.

Gundersen walked beside Benson, silently, as Benson investigated the ledge. He kicked the dirt at the top, knocking some rocks and dirt over the edge.

"See anything down there?" Benson peered into the thick woods.

"I don't see nothin' movin', if that's what ya mean. But cain't see much of anything from up here. Trees are too thick."

"Well, can't be helped. Give me the rope."

Gundersen dropped the rope he'd been carrying across his body, onto the ground.

"You do any climbing?" Benson strung out the rope.

"Nope. I have no idea what you're doin' or why." Gundersen studied Benson, with his hands on his knees.

"Well, this is not the recommended way to rappel down, but what can you do? This is going to be painful, but not as painful as falling."

Benson grabbed the trunk of a five-inch diameter tree and

shook it.

"This one is close enough and is alive. It should hold my weight," Benson said, more to himself than to Gundersen.

Benson took a turn around the tree trunk with one end of the rope, and then evened the leftover rope and tied a quick knot in the ends. He coiled the doubled rope and walked to the edge and tossed it over.

Gundersen saw that the rope was long enough to reach the bottom of the cliff with some extra.

"Pay attention, Christopher. You'll have to do this. Be warned that this is not the recommended way. It's painful, but it'll work. First off, you stand between the ropes and pass them behind you, crossing in the back. Then you step over the ends, like this, and pass both ropes between your legs. Bring them to your front, around your dominant leg, and hold it in your dominant hand. On your way down, you'll hold the rope at your hip or a little lower and behind. Now you back up to the edge, paying out the rope you need. Keep your feet against the vertical surface and lean back into the rope. Don't bend your knees. Trust your rope. You want to brace yourself against the surface." Benson demonstrated everything . "Take your time. Go slow and maintain control." He stepped off the edge and slowly lowered himself down the face of the ridge.

Gundersen stared after his mentor, mouth agape as Benson descended. It took him several minutes to reach the bottom, where he freed himself from the ropes.

What the hell am I doing? Gundersen assumed the position and duplicated Benson's movements. It wasn't long until he had his back to the ledge. *Trust your ropes. Lean into the rope and brace yourself against the surface.* He took a deep breath and let it out slowly. He stepped off the ledge and lowered himself. He was hurting were the ropes ran around his body. With each foot lowered, the more the friction was burning his skin through his clothes. It seemed to take forever, but he was finally down, and he hurried to remove the ropes.

Benson untied the knot at the ends and began pulling the rope toward him, coiling it as he did.

"I know it was a painful descent, but without any climbing equipment, it's the best that could be done," Benson handed the rope to Gundersen.

While Gundersen stowed the rope diagonally across his body, Benson pulled his eighteen-inch machete and glanced around.

"Pull your eighteen-incher and be ready for anything," Benson whispered, as he looked around.

Gundersen pulled on the rope a little to resettle it, and then fumbled with his eighteen-incher when he tried to pull it and got it tangled in the loops of rope, creating too much noise.

"Quietly!" Benson hissed.

"How're we gonna get back up?" Gundersen whispered.

"The same way Murdock did." Benson moved forward. "The river is that way. We cross it and go up the trail to the top of the ridge."

"That's another thing. Murdock didn't have any rope with him, so how did he get down here in the first place?"

Benson chuckled. "You can ask him when you see him again. I'm sure I have no clue."

Benson and Gundersen silently explored the forest for more than an hour. They heard nothing. They saw deer sign and cat sign, presumably cougars. When they decided to leave, they headed for the river. The pair hadn't taken more than a couple of steps, when they heard the distant yowl of a large cat. Both stopped and whipped around in the direction of the noise.

"I think we need to beat a hasty retreat," Benson said.

"Yeah, let's get across the damn river, ASAP." Gundersen agreed.

"Whatever you do, don't run. But let's not dilly-dally either."

It was several hours before Benteen saw Benson and Gundersen walking toward him. The sun had gone down, but it wasn't fully dark yet.

"What did you find?" Benteen said, as Benson and Gundersen sat at the fire.

Benteen was cooking fish and was fussing over it.

"Trees," Benson replied. "Lots of trees."

"Trees? Is that all?"

"We heard a large cat yowl, presumably a cougar. We did see deer sign as well."

"In your opinion, will it work for us?" Benteen said.

"Depends on what you mean," Benson replied. "There are plenty of trees to build fortifications and domiciles, if that's what you mean. The trees don't go clear to the river, so walking for water and fish will be the norm."

"Mmmm." Benteen removed the fish and indicated that Benson and Gundersen should help themselves. "That doesn't sound too bad. It's no more than I expected. So we can trust in what Murdock says?"

"I'd say that's a yes. He did say something about cougars being there, and even though we didn't see any, we heard at least one, but I think there are probably more. He didn't think there were any claims to that area and we didn't see anyone or any indications that someone has been there for any length of time."

"How did you know it was a cougar?" Benteen said.

"Have you ever *heard* a cougar before?"

"Not really, no."

"Well, I have, and I can tell you it's something you don't forget!"

Heather and Alvin rode side by side. When they crested a small rise, they could see a large group of people milling around the river.

"Looks like this could be trouble," Alvin said. "Where is the medical facility?"

"Further on and across the river," Heather replied. "I doubt they'll give us any grief." She indicated the newcomers ahead of them.

"I'm not that trusting, so if they start something, get across the river as fast as you can. It should slow them down some and allow you to ride hard for the medical facility. Don't stop until you get there, understand?"

Heather nodded. "I understand, but—"

"No buts! Do as you're told for once, without arguing."

Asshole. Heather clenched her jaws as she rode on in silence.

As the pair started into the crowd of people, most were awed and gave way in silence. Alvin glared at them.

"Excuse me," a man said, as they neared the center of the group. "Do you know where the rest of our group is?"

Alvin scowled and ignored the man.

"Downriver," Heather said. "Just keep going downriver."

The man reached out for Heather's leg as she passed. She had put the lead rope for the two pack animals under her thigh, away from the man, and had taken a turn of the reins around her saddle horn. She released the reins, grabbed a handful of the man's hair and twisted his head to the side, and pulled him toward her. When the back of his head hit her leg, she was bent down to him with her twelve-incher at his throat.

"A little helpful advice," Heather whispered to the man. "When you see riders, you signal and *back off* so they can pass you by, if that is their intent. If someone *wants* to talk to you, they'll come to you. You don't force them to ride through a crowd. It could make them... *nervous.* Do you understand?"

The man nodded and continued to walk beside Heather. He didn't have a choice. She had his hair and a machete to his throat. Heather maintained her control of the man until they were past the majority of the group, then she released him.

The man looked at them as they rode on, but Heather never took her eyes off him. She replaced her machete once they were through the group, and kneed her mount to a trot to catch up to Alvin.

"Was that really necessary?" Alvin said, once she was beside him.

"In my estimation, it was. He wasn't looking for information. Otherwise, he would have tried to talk to you. He thought I would be the easier target."

"I doubt he'll make that mistake again." Alvin chuckled. "Sorry for the way I spoke to you," he said, after a few moments of silence. "I guess I've gotten used to not having a lot of people around. I get nervous in crowds."

It was shortly after midday when Murdock returned to the medical facility. Once he arrived, Zeke and Annie asked him to tutor them on shooting the bows that had been delivered about an hour before his return.

"To get good with a bow," Murdock said, "you have to practice a couple hours a day, every day." He demonstrated the proper form and breathing. "Don't hold your breath and relax. You fire after you exhale." He drew back and let an arrow fly toward a deer hide he had suspended from a tree limb.

Annie and Zeke did their best to imitate his actions. Their arrows missed the massive hide. Annie's fell short and stuck in the ground. Zeke's went wide and stuck in a tree to the left of the target.

"Your arrows are going to be hard to come by, so retrieving them is essential. You have to draw the bow with your shoulder, not your arm."

It was getting close to sundown when Murdock called the practice session to a halt. Zeke had managed to hit the hide twice, and Annie hit it once.

"Understanding the dynamics of archery is a lot easier than putting them into practice," Zeke said, as he and Annie were retrieving their arrows.

"I found it to be a bit embarrassing," she said.

"Why? I didn't do much better than you."

"Murdock said I couldn't hit the floor with my hat. It's embarrassing to admit he was right."

"If we practice, we'll get better."

"I agree. It's hard to imagine we could get worse."

They both laughed, as they entered the compound.

───────

Murdock had sought out Irene Harris after the practice session. He found her watching from atop the slatted roof of the corridor.

"You need to practice as well," Murdock said.

"Not me. I'm a doctor, not Robin Hood." Irene giggled. "Leave my bow and quiver for Alvin or Heather. They'd be better at it than I would. When are they going to get here, anyway?"

Murdock sniggered. "They're on their way and will arrive when they get here. How's Roy doing?"

"Roy-boy is fine. He's getting stronger all the time. He'll be making his rounds again in a few days."

"How are *you* doing, Irene?"

"I'm fine." She looked away. "How else should I be? Why do you ask?"

"You've been around Roy for years, and now there's Zeke. I ask because of your... *issues* with men, and because I worry about you."

"No need to worry." Irene clucked and waved a hand toward Murdock. "It's been years since I've had an anxiety attack, or whatever it was." Her hands started to shake.

"If you say so, Irene. You are family and I do worry about you. It goes with the territory."

They both sat in silence for some time.

"Heather and Alvin are almost here." Murdock got up to leave. "I'll go meet them and do what I can to get them and their animals settled."

Tutt, Marchand, and Daniels had been walking all day, and had finally arrived outside of a compound. They found it by following a few men when they came to the river to fish.

"You two keep quiet," Tutt said. "Let me do the talking."

"Who are you and what do you want?" someone asked, from atop one of the twin guard towers that flanked the gate.

"Raymond Tutt and company, to speak to your leader," Tutt boomed.

"Speak? About what?" the guard called down.

"Mutual benefits."

The gate creaked when it opened. Three men came out, armed with staffs, followed by a short woman.

Tutt, Marchand, and Daniels stood with their arms extended letting the bows they carried dangle from their shoulders.

"I'm Elizabeth Reyes. What mutual benefit are you referring to?"

Tutt looked her up and down. *Nice looking. Well-proportioned, black hair, brown eyes. Looks like she's in her thirties.*

"We recently had an incident and have come to offer you three bows, with arrows, for trade."

"What do you want in trade for them?" Reyes narrowed her eyes.

"What do you have?"

"We could use the bows," Reyes said. "What's to stop us from killing you and just taking them?"

Tutt heard a noise from the guard towers and looked up to see arrows pointed at him.

"You could, I suppose, but then you'd miss out on an

99

opportunity."

"What opportunity?" Irritation crept into Reyes's tone.

"I'm the leader of a group of miners and metal workers. We have numerous items to offer, but we need deer hides. I wish to discuss the possibility of a trade deal. If you're not interested, then we'll just be on our way."

"What we need is people. Do you have any to spare? If so, then maybe we can dicker. We've suffered greatly under Murdock's lies of help and support."

"May we sit and discuss things? I'd like to hear more, as we, too, have suffered because of Murdock's interferences."

Reyes's face betrayed that she was considering his offer. "Come inside. Night falls and wolves may be about. We can talk and eat in relative safety." She turned and re-entered her compound.

Her men followed, as did Tutt, Marchand, and Daniels, with some trepidation.

"No weapons beyond this point," Reyes said, as the gate was bolted closed. The three men looked back at the gate.

"You'll get them back when you leave. Those under my care already know weapons aren't allowed further into the compound. So relax. If I wanted you dead, I could've done that without opening the gate." She smirked.

Reyes motioned to one of her men and he came over to her.

"Mister Heartly, take Raymond's men and get them something to eat and find a place for them to bunk. And get me and Raymond something to eat. We have much to discuss, so I will be... indisposed for the night."

Heartly looked at her with a raised brow. "All night?"

"That's what I said!" Just as quickly, her demeanor changed as she led Tutt to the cave close to the small waterfall. "Come, Raymond. The time has come to talk of many things. Of shoes, and ships, and sealing wax. Of cabbages and kings."

Tutt wore a puzzled expression as he followed her into the cave.

7

I've heard knowledge is power. I'd modify that statement to, practical knowledge is power. What does it profit an astrophysicist to be so smart if he can't figure out how to build a fire to cook his dinner?

— KEVIN MURDOCK, FAMILY CONVERSATIONS

Angelica Griffen sat with a dour expression, staring at her brother. "Curtis Daniel Griffen, why do you feel it's absolutely necessary to cause trouble?"

They were inside Declan's pottery workshop, which housed several kilns and work tables. Shelves lined most of the walls and held finished plates and various sized pots and cups.

"*I'm* causing trouble?" Curtis fired back angrily. "Our *elder brother* started it all!"

"Just how did he manage that? He's done what he could to see to it we're safe and fed. How is that causing problems?"

"He took an *outsider's* side against *family*. He failed to stand up for me with Mei Lee! He sided against us—his *blood*."

Angelica smirked. "I was there. I saw you being an *ass* toward someone you should have respected, and you got what you deserved. You wouldn't have talked to Mom or Dad that way. Hell, you wouldn't have talked to *Rose* that way."

"Why bring up Mom and Dad? Why bring Rose into this? They have nothing to do with anything here. This is between me and Declan. I respected Mom, Dad, and Rose. But this is *Declan*. He's not *deserving* of our respect. We know how big of a flake he's always been. Our *brother* and that bitch Mei Lee waited until we couldn't defend ourselves before they disrespected us."

"I haven't been disrespected!" Angelica said, "and neither have you. You should've learned by now to keep your racist comments to yourself."

Curtis stormed over to his younger sister. "What did you call me?" Curtis was seething with anger. "You think *I'm* a racist?"

"I didn't say you were a racist, but you did make a racist, and sexist, comment. Worse, you're blaming our brother for something *you* did. You're the one who is being disrespectful."

Curtis backhanded her just as the door opened.

"What are you doing!" Emily rushed over to Angelica's side and put herself between the siblings.

Curtis said nothing, but drew back to strike Emily with another backhand.

Emily could see the rage on Curtis's face as she caught his hand and squeezed. She turned his fingers toward the ground and bent them toward him, raising his straightened arm.

"Ow, ow, ow," he cried, dancing on the balls of his feet.

"This is called the waterfall," Emily said, calmly, and placed her free hand at his wrist, tilting it toward her. "From here, I can snap your wrist should I choose to." She grinned. "You shouldn't hit a woman. She may just have the skill to fight back." As she walked Curtis to the door, she spun him around and grabbed him by the collar and the seat of his pants. After a couple shuffle steps to gain momentum, she tossed him through the door.

Curtis tried to roll, and only made it halfway. As he lay on his back, he flexed and rubbed his wrist.

"What's going on here!" Mei Lee said.

Curtis turned to see the glare Mei Lee directed at him.

"He slapped his sister." Emily put herself between the door and Curtis.

"He didn't mean it!" Angelica cried from the doorway, unable to get around Emily's bulk.

Mei Lee's jaw muscles flexed. "Did you?"

"Whether I did or not is none of your business," Curtis spat. "It's a *family* matter, and you need to keep your nose out of it."

Declan stormed over to Curtis and backhanded him, the resounding slap heard by all present. Curtis fell to the ground.

"I agree, *brother*! It *is* a family matter, and I'll take care of it!"

Curtis looked up at his older brother with a grin as he rubbed his sore jaw. "You take *their* side again, *brother*? You side with *outsiders* against those you should be the most loyal to? You ain't no *brother* of mine!"

"Curtis, you have a strange view on loyalty. You hit our baby sister, and you *dare* to hit my wife?"

"I didn't hit the heifer!" Curtis got to his feet and squared off with Declan.

"Not from the lack of trying." Emily smirked.

"But since you want to take someone else's side against your own kin," Curtis said, "then so be it."

The brothers squared off with each other, slowly turning; waiting for the other to attack.

How the hell did things get to this point, Declan thought. *When I slapped Curtis I was upset. I was angry that he would hit Angel and then his try at slapping Em sent me over the edge.*

"You need to get your eyes checked, *brother*! Angelica is no longer a baby. She's an adult and can be held responsible for her own words!" He grinned.

Obviously, he's been looking forward to this. He saw Curtis tense

103

his legs a moment before he launched at Declan, who turned to let Curtis pass by, and as he did, lifted his right foot, catching Curtis's foot to send him sprawling.

Curtis slapped the ground and pushed to his feet, then turned to face Declan.

"The rest of you better stay out of this!" Curtis said.

"We have no intention of interfering." Mei Lee chuckled. "Declan is quite capable of taking care of this... minor correctional situation."

Curtis furrowed his brow into a scowl. Shuffled toward Declan and drew his right arm back for a haymaker. Declan ducked in, wrapped his arms around his brother's chest and back, bracing Curtis' right armpit on his shoulder. He clasped his hands at Curtis' neck and pressed his thumb into the pressure point where Curtis' neck met his collar bone.

"Ack—" Curtis winced at the pain at the base of his neck.

"Are we done?" Declan growled.

Curtis nodded and Declan released him cautiously. Curtis swung his arm and turned his neck to work out the kink, while watching Declan out of the corner of his eye. Curtis flashed his hand out and grabbed Declan by his leather shirt. Declan trapped his brother's hand against his chest as he stepped toward Curtis and turned, forcing Curtis's arm to straighten. A quick knife-hand strike to the pressure point just above the straightened elbow, and then Declan dragged him to the ground, face down. He re-grabbed the once-trapped hand and started to twist it, with Curtis's wrist resting on Declan's raised knee, while he pressed his knife-hand into the younger brother's shoulder joint.

"Declan! Please stop hurting him!" Angelica yelled from the shop doorway.

"Well, little brother?" Declan said. "I've been nice so far. Next time I have to take you down, I won't be so nice. Do you yield?"

"You're breaking my arm, you son-of-a-bitch! I'll get you for this!"

Declan leaned further into Curtis' shoulder. "Are you done?"

"Yes, damn it, I'm done!"

———

Declan, Mei Lee, Angelica, Curtis, and Emily all sat at the wooden table. Curtis had his hands tied in front of him, and his feet were secured to the bonds on his wrists.

"Okay, Curtis, I want to know what your problem is," Declan said.

Curtis scowled at his brother. "You flaked out on us. You left us alone—"

"I did no such thing," Declan said, in a calm tone. "I was taken after work."

"Yeah, right! Convenient." Curtis glowered at him. "We were counting on you and you let us down. First, Mom and Dad died. Then Rose disappeared. You went years later. We were waiting—"

"Clean out your ears, Curtis. I was taken after work that day. There was nothing I could do about it. No way to call you or—"

"A likely story! We waited for you for five years. Five years of not knowing what happened to our brother. Our brother, who had taken it upon himself to care for us, deserted us!"

One... two... three...

"Keep calm, husband," flashed into Declan's mind.

"I'm trying to," he replied.

Declan had started tapping his fingers on the table to the cadence of his internal counting.

"What's the matter, *brother*?" Curtis gave a sarcastic grin. "Cat got your tongue? Nothing to say for yourself?"

"What, if anything, can I say that you'd listen to?"

"Not a damn thing!"

"Where and when were you captured, Declan?" Mei Lee leaned on the table.

"Yes, Declan, tell us another lie."

That got Curtis a warning glare from Mei Lee.

"I was just coming out of work. It was... July 15th, three years after Rose disappeared." Declan focused on a spot in the center of the table.

His tapping had stopped.

"Is that what you remember, Angelica?" Mei Lee said.

"She doesn't remember that," Curtis replied.

Emily reached across the table and gripped Curtis's hair and did a quick pull. His head bobbed forward.

"Let her answer, or so help me, your face will kiss this table," Emily warned.

"Emily, if he disrupts us once more, take him outside and tie him to a tree," Mei Lee said. "We'll let the wolves have him."

"Oh, all right," Emily said, clearly disappointed.

"Well, Angelica?" Mei Lee said. "Do you remember?"

Angelica nodded, her eyes downcast.

"Was that when Declan disappeared?"

Again she nodded.

"Was it the same as when Rose disappeared?"

She nodded once more.

Mei Lee sat back, her face indicating she was deep in thought.

"This," she whispered "is the first time I've thought of those left behind. Everyone coming here had just disappeared, based on my own memories and those that have talked about it. Leaving friends and family not knowing what had happened." She indicated Curtis and Angelica. This really brings that loss home. To me, anyway."

Declan and Emily nodded.

"That being said, what are we going to do with the situation with Curtis?" Mei Lee said.

"Personally," Emily said, "I'd just as soon not have him around. He feels he is justified in slapping a woman. I believe he would do the same thing against anyone he perceives as weaker than he is. Mei Lee, any of the kids."

"I agree with you, Em." Mei Lee scowled at Curtis. "He already knows Emily, Declan, and I can defend ourselves. It's the kids I worry about. Declan?"

Declan refused to look at anyone and continued to stare at the center of the table. "He seems not to have grown up, and acts like an entitled ass and a bully. Maybe if I'd been there, I could have corrected that character flaw." He took a deep breath and slowly let it out. "I concur with Emily and Mei Lee."

Curtis looked at the others with bulging eyes.

"Do I get to say anything?" Angelica whispered.

Mei Lee looked around the table and saw Declan and Emily shrug. "Sure, go ahead. Speak your mind."

Angelica stood and squared her shoulders and took a deep breath. "Since I was the first injured party, and since I'm related to him, I think he needs to be... quarantined. Not confined in a prison or totally ignored, just kept away from the children."

"Ang?" Curtis said.

Angelica turned to face the younger of the brothers. "You have it coming. You were wrong to talk to Mei Lee the way you did on our trek, and you had no right to slap me. You really needed to be put in your place when you tried to slap Emily. She is family, you know.

"But I can't send you out into the wild alone, so I'll be going with you."

Everyone looked at Angelica and gasped. "What!"

Erycca Valdez, Bart Oldkampo, and Xavier Alderman, leaders of the third, fifth, and eighth pods, were standing at the base of the eleventh pod.

It had been fourteen days after landing, and those remaining at the landing site had finally gotten around to opening the eleventh pod. They'd already found and unloaded all the exterior storage compartments of all the pods. They held nothing but food—boxes and boxes of the bland, watery gruel that those remaining had been eating since their landing. Alderman had to stifle the urge to throw up at seeing the all-too-familiar boxes.

Through trial and error, they found that it took three people to open it. The button that would lower the access ramps on the other pods had been replaced by a small hidden compartment that held three DNA samplers. Valdez had been the first to let her curiosity get the better of her, and tried to open the silent pod. It took seven hours to figure out the combination.

Valdez, Alderman, and Oldkampo opened it and were the first to enter. Once inside, they found it to be crammed with medicines, medical equipment, and twenty submersible generators. The message that played, upon their entry told them what the pod contained and the most important feature—a digitized library.

All three were stunned into silence by what they'd found.

"Do we have a librarian?" Valdez said. "We need to do whatever we can to protect this pod."

"I have no idea," Oldkampo replied. "I agree that we need to protect the library, but what data is stored here? I don't know how to find out."

Alderman and Valdez had stared at him.

"What? I was never tech-oriented." He shrugged.

"I think we need to ask everyone left if there are any that can function as a librarian," Valdez said, as they watched the interior being unloaded.

"That's going to be a boring job," Alderman muttered.

"Maybe so," Valdez said, "but we need to know what knowledge is available in the data storage."

"Who was that old guy?" Oldkampo asked.

"Old guy? What old guy?" Valdez said.

"The one that left with Murdock. He had that... professorial look about him."

"What do you mean by old?" Valdez said.

"Oh, geez, he musta been mid-forties, at least."

"Wow! That is *old*." Alderman said. "I'm certain he'd be perfect for the job. For as long as he lives, anyway. He's too old to do much of anything else."

"Do we know if we have any medical people?" Valdez said. "There appears to be a lot of medical supplies. They should be in the care of the professionals."

"We'll ask tonight when everyone is around," Oldkampo said. "There should be."

Alderman frowned. "I think we need to notify the medical people that are already here, about the medical stuff. Maybe we need to send a runner to the medical facility Murdock mentioned."

"And where is that?" Valdez said. "I don't recall Murdock saying where the medical facility is located."

Alderman looked toward the river. "I think the medical facility is located near the edge of that plateau," he motioned toward the cliff that led up to the next plateau, "and close to the river."

"And what makes you think that?" Valdez said. "No one saw his family leave or knows what direction they went."

"When Murdock left, he was going toward the river, but it wasn't a straight line. He was angling toward the cliff. Besides, it makes some kind of sense if you think about it. If it was located downriver, he would've angled that way."

"What's to prevent him from walking one direction and then changing direction once he's out of sight?" Valdez shook her head and rolled her eyes when Alderman didn't answer. "Face it, Alderman. He could have gone anywhere once he was out of sight. You're just guessing."

"Maybe so. I guess the only ones who would know would be someone from Benteen's group."

Murdock was relaxing, sitting on a large round of wood in the yard, with Alvin and Heather, after completing the construction of their new cabin.

"Where are you off to now?" Heather handed out plates of cooked venison.

"Home." Murdock exhaled a deep breath. "I'm tired."

Alvin sat on another round. "We wish to thank you for your efforts on our behalf."

Murdock got to his feet and looked toward the pods. After setting his plate down, he trotted in that direction.

Alvin and Heather stared after him.

"No rest for the wicked." Alvin took a bite of the venison.

"That man is always busy," Heather said.

They could barely see Murdock in the distance, with someone else.

"Looks like we're gonna have visitors," she said.

"Do ya think I need to be armed?" Alvin asked.

"I doubt it. Murdock would stop anyone long before they could get close. Just eat."

Alvin re-adjusted his seating so he could toward Murdock, before resuming his meal.

Not long after, Murdock headed back toward them. Alvin, seeing someone accompanying Murdock, got to his feet and set his plate down on the round he'd been sitting on, and walked a few steps closer to Murdock.

"Expecting trouble?" Heather said.

"Not really, but if a stranger is coming here, I think it prudent to meet them on my feet and ready." Alvin waited for Murdock with a hand on the hilt of his twelve-incher.

"It's okay, Al, stand down," Murdock said, as he passed. "This is Mackenzie Braddock. She was selected to bring word about the contents of the eleventh pod."

He picked up his plate and motioned for Mackenzie to sit on the wood round, and then handed her his plate.

"How did she find us?" Alvin said.

"It was a gamble. They could only guess, and this one was brave enough to make the trek out here."

Heather looked the woman over. She was shorter than Murdock, but taller than herself. Not fat, but not thin either. She appeared to be well-muscled. She had long brown hair, in a ponytail, and hazel eyes. On her hip was the ubiquitous twelve-inch machete.

"I need to borrow a couple of your mounts," Murdock said to Alvin.

"Sure, not a problem" Alvin shrugged as he left to prep two of the pack animals.

Heather turned to look toward the medical facility, and saw two people moving toward her from that direction.

"That's Doc Harris and Zeke," Murdock said, from behind her. "That's why I need the mounts."

Heather nodded. "Provisions?"

"No, we won't be gone that long."

"When you get the time, would it be possible for me or Alvin, or both of us, to communicate the way you do with the others of your tribe?" Heather turned to look at Murdock.

"What makes you think there's some sort of communication?"

Heather frowned. "Please don't treat me like I'm stupid. I *know* there is. Otherwise, how would Harris know to come here? How would Annie call for help when she and I were taken? I've walked with you and Annie, and she seemed to know where we were going without you speaking. All I'm saying is, I want in on it."

Murdock frowned. "That was something you decided to forego when you chose not to join our tribe. However, I can see it would be to our benefit and yours, so you need to discuss it with Annie and Doctor Harris, and don't mention it to Alvin. For now, though, we need to go to the pod landing area."

Alvin handed Murdock the reins to two mounts just as Dr. Harris and Zeke arrived.

"Doctor Harris and Mackenzie can double-up, and Zeke will ride the remaining mount," Murdock said.

Harris swung up onto the mount and offered a hand to Mackenzie, swinging her up and behind. Both women settled in. Zeke was trying to swing himself up, but kept falling short.

"Lead yours over to a wood round and stand on the round to swing yourself up." Murdock tried to suppress a snicker.

"What about you?" Zeke stepped up onto a wood round.

"I prefer to walk," Murdock said, from the mount's head, where he held the animal steady for Zeke.

Once the three were mounted, they bid their farewells and headed off to the pod landing area. Murdock was leading the mounts since the others didn't know how to ride.

It took Murdock, Doctor Harris, Zeke, and Mackenzie Braddock a few hours to reach the landing area of the pods. They were greeted by Valdez, Alderman, and Oldkampo.

"So, what is it that warrants sending a runner?" Murdock was holding the head of both mounts while everyone dismounted.

Zeke, tried to gracefully dismount, but became crossed up and fell off, hitting the ground with a *thud*.

Murdock looked around the mount, at Zeke. "Will you quit playing around? Are you badly hurt?"

Zeke got to his feet and brushed himself off. "Is there such a thing as *goodly hurt*?" He chuckled.

"Ahem," Valdez cleared her throat. "We managed to get the eleventh pod opened." Valdez led the way toward the eleventh pod. Everyone else was following, along with the mounts. "Underneath, in the external storage, we found more boxes of the gruel, and we've removed them to other storage areas. What we found inside concerned us—me, Alderman, and Oldkampo."

"What was it that concerned you?" Murdock said.

They'd reached the bottom of the ramp, and he tied the mounts to a landing strut.

"I would like the doctor and Mister Jakes to enter the pod," Valdez said.

She, Alderman, and Oldkampo opened the ramp. Murdock, Harris, and Zeke leaned back.

"There's nothing overtly hostile in there," Valdez said. "It's just that the contents are of special interest to them. You're all free to enter, but it will get pretty crowded. There's limited free space to move around."

Zeke led the way up the ramp, and Harris followed him. Murdock went up the ramp as well, but stopped short of entry.

"*If there's any threat, let me know,*" Murdock flashed to Harris.

"*Will do,*" Harris flashed back as she disappeared inside the pod.

As Harris and Zeke cleared the top of the ramp, the internal lights flickered on.

"*OMG!*" Harris flashed to Murdock. "*The whole interior seems to be crammed full of medical equipment and drugs!*"

"*What kind of equipment?*"

"*Unknown,*" Harris responded. "*I'd have to unload and inventory everything to be certain of what we have.*"

"Looks to be just a bunch of medical stuff." Zeke wandered around the restricted space.

"Mister Jakes, check toward the front of the pod." Valdez poked her head into the pod, from the ramp. "You'll see a chair bolted down."

Zeke got turned around and squeezed past Harris. As he reached the chair, he saw an ancient keyboard and monitor attached to a small area that could have been a modified command deck. When he sat in the chair, a message flashed on the monitor.

"Unsecure. Ramp open!" flashed in red.

"Murdock, I want to close the ramp temporarily," Zeke called out. "There seems to be a computer system here that is complaining about the open ramp."

"The message we received when we first opened the pod said something about a digitized library system," Valdez said. "Since none of us were tech-savvy, we decided that maybe Mister Jakes might be."

Murdock nodded at Valdez. "Okay. Clearing the ramp," he called into the pod. *"If something goes wrong, flash me a message,"* he flashed to Harris.

"Will do."

The whine of the closing ramp started.

Zeke felt a slight breeze on his face as the ramp clicked closed.

"Ventilation system: starting..." came onto the screen. "Initializing first-time boot..." appeared right below it.

Zeke thought he could hear something speaking. When he investigated, he found a compartment that held a pair of haptic glasses with earpieces attached to the bows, and a haptic glove with contacts on the fingertips. He put on the glasses and put the earpieces into his ears.

"State your name," came through the earpieces, as the same message popped onto the screen.

"Ezekiel Jakes." He pulled on the glove.

Through the glasses, he could see an animated three-dimensional head appear in the air by the monitor. As Zeke turned his head, the animated head followed.

"Hello, Ezekiel Jakes. This is the Computerized Library System. You are now the system recognized librarian. Do you wish to add more librarians at this time?"

"No."

"Who are you talking to?" Harris moved behind Zeke, rested her hands on his shoulders and watched the screen over his shoulder.

"I'm talking to the computer," Zeke said, over his shoulder, tingling from Harris' touch.

"Unrecognized command," came through the earpiece.

He could see the text of all the messages on the screen.

"Command?" said the feminine voice, through the earpiece.

"Menu."

The computer read the menu options, with a highlight bar going down each item on the screen. Zeke saw what he was looking for close to the bottom of the list.

"Help," he said, and then, "Operations."

Over the next few minutes, Zeke watched and heard the video of the "Proper Operations" of the CLS. When it was completed, the screen reverted to the menu.

"Pause." Zeke turned to Harris. "I think I understand the system." He removed the glasses and replaced them in their proper compartment. "It only works if the ramp is closed, and it'll only work with librarians. Right now, that's only me, but I can add more of them."

"Can we open the ramp now?" Harris said. "I hadn't noticed before, but now I'm getting claustrophobic."

"Sure." Zeke shrugged. He got up and pressed the button to open the ramp.

———————

"What's the verdict?" Murdock asked Zeke, as he and Harris stepped off the ramp.

"The CLS is fairly easy to use, but it will take me some time to familiarize myself with it. I could spend weeks in there." His eyes glazed over.

"Would you speak English?" Murdock said. "CLS?"

"Computerized Library System. Apparently, this pod, once it's emptied, can be used as a library system. Or a teaching center, if you will. The particulars of its capabilities will take me some time to figure out."

"Is there a way to change who can open it?" Murdock said.

"There should be. But as I said, it'll take me a while to figure it all out. Why do you ask?"

"I'm asking because if we move it, we're going to need a way to lock and unlock it. Otherwise, someone will have to stay inside at all times."

Murdock turned to Valdez. "Is there a problem with us taking the pod?"

"Take it?" Valdez looked at him incredulously. "Take it where?"

"The plan is to move it over by the river and the medical facility. It will, of course, be available to those who wish to use it."

"How the hell are you going to move it?" Valdez asked. "It's too big to move without a lot of bodies to help, if then."

"We'll take care of that part. I'd say tonight, after everyone is asleep. No one sleeps outside, do they?"

"No. Everyone seems to sleep better inside the pods. With one empty pod, Benteen's, and both of the previous pods, we should be okay room-wise," Valdez said skeptically. "I don't see how you're going to manage to move it, but knock yourself out."

It was halfway through the night when everyone at the landing area was asleep. Zeke and Harris were inside the pod, working on the library computer, with the ramp closed.

Without giving it a second thought, Murdock levitated the craft and walked off toward the river and the medical facility, leading the mounts.

Everyone will be shocked in the morning. He smiled. *It'll really cook their noodles trying to figure out how the pod was moved.*

116

8

"Beware of Greeks bearing gifts."

> *— FROM VIRGIL'S AENEID, BOOK II, LINE 48:*
> *TIMEO DANAOS ET DONA FERENTES.*
> *TRANSLATION: I FEAR THE GRECIANS, EVEN*
> *WHEN THEY OFFER GIFTS.*

It was shortly before sunup when Alvin Jones exited his cabin. He was looking around and listening to the soft sounds of the rain just starting to fall. His gaze slowly panned toward the river and froze there.

"Heather, come out here!" he said. "You're not gonna believe this."

"What?" Heather hurried out onto the covered porch.

Alvin pointed toward the river and the medical facility.

"Huh!" Heather's mouth dropped open.

"How did that pod get here?" Alvin said.

"I discovered a while back, before we were together, not to question some things." Heather patted his arm. "It's here. That's a fact. Just accept it and move on."

"How can you say that?"

"I speak from experience. Want to go for a walk?"

"A walk? Where?"

"We can walk over to look at the pod. If you get a chance, you can ask Murdock how the pod got here."

"Will I get an answer?"

"Probably. But it won't be the answer you want, if I know Murdock."

Heather and Alvin had just arrived outside the pod, when the ramp opened and Harris came out.

"It's about time," Murdock said.

"I spent the night trying to ascertain what medical supplies are in this pod," Harris said, groggily. "And I'm more than a little bleary-eyed." It was then that she noticed Heather and Alvin.

"Where's Zeke?" Murdock said.

Harris chuckled. "He'll be out in a second. He's been geeking out on the CLS."

Zeke exited the pod, and without saying a word, pressed the button to close the ramp.

"What are you doing!" Murdock said, as the ramp was closing. "How are we going to remove the supplies? You needed to stay inside."

Zeke raised a finger in Murdock's direction. It was then that Murdock noticed the haptic glasses still on Zeke's face.

"Open the pod's bay door, Al," Zeke said.

To everyone's surprise, the ramp opened again. Zeke placed the glasses on top of his head and crossed his arms, grinning.

Then he scrunched his brow and looked around. "How did we get here?"

"I take it you've had some breakthroughs?" Murdock said.

"Um... a few. I've discovered that this pod is capable of using an external power source, instead of just using the solar panels on the top."

"An external power source?" Murdock said.

"There are two submersible generators inside, in crates."

"What good would that do? Come winter, the river will freeze solid. No running water means no juice, and undoubtedly damaging the generators."

"True, but the CLS shows how to convert a submersible to a wind-driven generator. It looks fairly easy to do, and it can be plugged into the pod, thus recharging the batteries all year long."

"I want to see the instructions before I can say how easy it is," Murdock said skeptically.

"I understand. I'd be skeptical, too." Zeke smirked , then looked past Murdock. "Who is that? I recognize Heather, but who is that with her?"

"That's Alvin, Heather's significant other. He's okay. A little standoffish, but that's to be expected." Murdock turned to greet the pair. "I was on my way to return your mounts, but since you're here." He handed the reins to Alvin. "Thanks for helping us out. It was appreciated."

Alvin accepted the reins and nodded. "How did *that* get here?" His gaze darted toward the pod.

"I moved it. This pod contains, among other things, a computerized library. Zeke here," Zeke raised his hand and smiled at the pair, "graciously volunteered to be the librarian."

"What's in the library?" Heather said.

"Digitized books, movies, pictures, and music," Zeke replied.

"Seriously!" Heather said. "What kind of music?"

Zeke shrugged. "I haven't been able to get a complete listing, but it appears to be every movie ever made, as well as pictures of all the great pieces of art, buildings, and other things, every book ever written, and all music ever produced. It's quite extensive… and what I would have expected."

"Why would you expect that?" Heather said.

"Well, if we're out here with no way to get home, a complete library would be a way to keep us from trying to get back to Earth."

"So you're saying it is a placation tool?"

"It can be. Amongst other things."

Murdock looked puzzled. "So what's the downside? I know there is one."

"We have no way to print or project anything. We have the haptic glasses and the monitor inside, and that's it. Don't even have any external speakers."

Murdock chuckled. "Maybe those things will come in later pod landings."

"One can always hope," Zeke said, wistfully. "One can always hope."

Gunderson woke when the rain started. He and Benson had managed to make a temporary shelter that kept them dry, and when he looked around, he noticed that Benson was already up and gone.

Probably went to get fish. Gunderson went to the small stores of kindling to get the fire restarted from the hot coals. He marveled at the amount of skill he had attained it the last twenty-one days. His tracking skills had improved, as well as his fire-making, fishing, shelter building, and cooking. He looked proudly at the flames that had re-immerged.

"Glad to see you're up and about." Benson entered the shelter, carrying a fish.

"It's funny. I used to sleep hard and complain about having to get up, at least until I was on the streets." Gunderson took the fish from Benson.

Benson nodded and squatted to warm his hands at the fire. "You've been maturing nicely." He rubbed his hands together.

"Hello in the shelter!" the two men heard from outside.

"Come on in, Benteen," Benson said. "Take a load off." He gestured to the wood round next to his before resuming his hand-warming.

"How's your time allocation?" Benteen sat.

"What time frame are you referring to?"

"I know you're busy, as we all are these days, but someone needs to report back to the other leaders at the landing. Can you spare a few days to report back?"

"I don't know, can we, Chris?"

"Who's all going?" Gunderson placed some fish close to the fire to cook.

"Just you two," Benteen answered. "We need to report that we've located and started to settle an acceptable area, but there's more. I'd have thought someone would have followed us, but so far none have made it this far. I'm concerned that they may be prevented from coming this far downriver, by Lantz's group, much like we were."

"So you want us to report back and see if any others want to come downriver?" Benson said. Benteen nodded. "And what are you authorizing us to do about Lantz if we find out they are interfering?" He rotated the fish in the fire.

"Authorizing?" Benteen laughed heartily. "Dirk, you've been quite an asset for us so far, and I want that to continue. But I can't *authorize* you to do anything. Any authority I have ends at the boundaries of our area, so you'll have to rely on your own skills. Nothing from me would carry any weight with the others, either with Lantz's group or our fellow new arrivals."

Benson said nothing. And Gunderson, taking his cue from Benson, remained silent.

"How important is it?" Benson said.

"This mission is very important to me. But to others outside our encampment, probably not important at all. Why?"

"Speaking plainly, what will happen to our shelter and our accumulated resources. during our absence?"

"It'll be untouched for at least ninety days. After that, I'll assume you've moved on."

"That seems fair, to me." Benson removed some fish from the fire.

"Good! When are you planning to leave?"

"I'd say, early tomorrow. It'll take us a bit to get organized."

"Sounds good." Benteen stood.

Benson got to his feet and the two men shook hands.

"A little later today, come to the encampment," Benteen said. "I have a few questions."

"I will." Benson sat again and resumed eating.

After Benteen left, Gunderson placed more fish near the fire to cook, and took a seat and selected his own bit of fish.

"So what's on your mind, Chris?" Benson said, when the silence became awkward.

"What makes ya think there's somethin' on my mind?"

"You had little to say when Benteen was here, and your silence continues after he's gone. So out with it."

"Are we workin' for Benteen now?" Gunderson said.

"Working *for* him? What would make you think that?"

"He wants ya to report to the others, and so we're goin'. It looks like we're workin' *for* him to me."

Benson looked at Gunderson. "Are you happy here? I mean, this encampment? These people?"

"They're okay, I guess." Gunderson shrugged.

"We helped to get them here. We continue to help them with some of the questions they have, but from my perspective, we don't work *for* anyone, but ourselves."

"But we're goin', at his request, so it looks that way ta me."

"Ever hear the saying, *looks can be deceiving*?"

"Yeah. So?"

"As you said, these people are okay. We could be around worse people, but that isn't my point. You and I are not owned by them. It suits my purposes, for now, to be close to them. It's difficult to survive without someone else around. The loneliness wears on you after a while. Sometimes, another voice, anyone else's voice, is welcome." Benson leaned in close to Gunderson. "This is something I'd prefer to discuss while we're on the road. But *this*," he motioned around the shelter, "is not what I have in mind for something permanent."

Gunderson nodded.

"Come on." Benson stood and clapped Gunderson's shoulder. "Finish up, and we'll go see what problems are plaguing Benteen."

The past twenty-one days had been interesting for Raymond Tutt. He had spent time getting to know Reyes and the surviving members of her small group, as well as is possible for such a short time. Now he was leading Timothy "Tiny" Daniels, Blandean Marchand, Elizabeth Reyes, and several of her group toward the mine, by way of the foothills, away from the river that everyone used for water and food.

"Do you know where you're going?" Reyes said.

"I know where I want to end up, but I haven't been this way before, if that's what you're asking," Tutt replied.

Reyes rolled her eyes. "Wouldn't it have been easier to follow the river? I mean, we'll end up in the same place, won't we?"

"Easier? Probably. But not necessarily better. Since we agreed to work together and combine resources, I'm looking for a more secure way to travel between the mine and your camp. A way that would allow us to move without Murdock's prying eyes. Or anyone else's, for that matter."

"You're not worried about getting lost?" Reyes asked. "What will we eat? Where will we get water? Personally, I think you're on a fool's errand."

"Who's more foolish, the fool or the fool who follows him?"

"What's that s'posed ta mean?

"If you think this is a fool's errand, then why did you come? You could've stayed home."

"I could have, but then I wouldn't be out here in the middle of nowhere, with a bunch of idiots who are lost. If you succeed, I'll know of a different route. If you fail, I can say I told you so, which would be very satisfying. There are wolves out here, you know."

"I know. Predators go where the prey is. It's a necessary risk. My people have been surviving on some tasteless fish. It's been a while since I've had venison, and my people could use the hides."

"But why are my people leading? Is that so your people can be eaten last?"

Tutt laughed. "Hardly! I've given your people bows that we made. With their skills, they should be able to make the best use of them."

"And your people can't do the same?"

"They could try, but they're not the experienced ones in this troop. We make the bows, but not everyone can use them effectively, and we've had trouble harvesting deer when we needed to."

"Should I take that as a failure of leadership?" Reyes asked slyly.

"Take it any way you want. I'm just stating facts."

After walking for three days, Reyes' and Tutt's small troop had entered the foothills of the mountains and were heading, roughly, downriver, picking their way around large boulders and narrow paths through the craggy landscape. Once in a while, they would see some tortured pines and would stop to rest. Elizabeth Reyes took every opportunity to rest under them.

"Are you *rested* yet?" Tutt said. *Every time we see a tree, she*

needs to rest. She's slowing us all down, and her incessant jabbering is
scaring away any game.

"I rest when I need to," Reyes snapped. "Until you came, I
didn't do much, physically, and definitely not in this desolate
hinterland. Climbing around this godforsaken place is tiring.
Besides, I'm finding I need a bath and something to eat. How
much further is it?"

"Our destination could be weeks away or just over the next
rise. How would I know? We've not been this way before."

"Lucky for you, I find you easy on the eyes. Otherwise, I'd be
at home where it's comfortable."

"Well, we're about out of water and food. If you'd have been
in better shape, maybe we could've gained some extra mileage
from the food and water we did bring!" Tutt snapped.

"If your men were better hunters, we'd have plenty of food
and water!"

"And if my men were better hunters, we wouldn't need
you!" Tutt clapped his hand over his mouth.

He had been thinking that for the past several days, but this
was the first time he had let it slip.

"Sorry," he said contritely. "That wasn't called for." He
walked away and refused to answer her inquiries as to what he
meant.

When they stopped for the night, they found an alcove just
off the trail they'd been following. It had started to rain, so
everyone had squeezed in to get out of the weather. It was
cramped, and the ones close to the trail were only half out of the
rain.

"Another fine mess you've gotten us into," Reyes griped,
from the back of the alcove.

The group resumed its trek after sunup, but hadn't gone far
before they ran out of trail. Ahead of them was a huge chasm
between them and the apparent continuation of their trek.

"Doesn't appear to be a way down." Tutt looked over the
edge.

"Not without more climbing equipment than probably exists on this planet," Marchand said.

Tutt took a deep breath and turned, making a circular motion with his hand. "Turn it around. We need to go back."

"Go back?" Reyes said. "Go back to where?"

A few men pushed her back against the wall that held the alcove. She stood watching the rest as they squeezed past. When no one answered, she shrugged and followed.

After a few hours of retracing their steps, they were once again in the scrub vegetation area.

"Tiny, you and Marchand go that way and see if you can find the edge of the terrace." Tutt indicated what he thought was downriver. "Be ready for anything. But if you see something we can eat, take it."

"I don't know what you're thinking," one of Reyes' men whispered to Tutt. "We should head back to our camp immediately. If you want to find a passage, you should do so by following the ridge downriver from our camp. None of us knows what is out this far, so we should retreat and try to figure out where we need to go. Besides, we only have enough food for a snack, and our waterskins are almost empty."

"I'm fairly certain my men will find the way and find something to eat," Tutt said, with more confidence than he felt.

"It isn't a weakness for a leader to admit mistakes," the stranger said. "If it were me, I'd go home and try to get up to this ridge from below. At least you'd know where up here you come out and what's required to navigate the ridge. You already know where our camp is, so finding it again shouldn't be a major issue."

Tutt looked at the man as he yelled for Marchand and Daniels to return. *Am I afraid of appearing weak? Should I be concerned with what others think of my leadership? Only as far as my people are concerned. Outsiders are... outsiders. So by definition, their thoughts don't matter.*

"I've decided that we need to return to Reyes' camp to

replenish, and then home, by way of the river," Tutt said, when Marchand and Daniels came up to him.

He looked around and saw Reyes and her men leaving them behind.

"What did Reyes mean by her statement?" Marchand said.

He and his compatriots were at the river, relishing the fish they'd caught after their wasted trip into the hinterlands on Reyes' part of the plateau. The three men were sitting close to the riverbank, with the river between them and Reyes' men, if they were around.

"I took it literally," Tutt said. "Bring me Murdock's head to gain my favor seems pretty clear to me. Her hatred for Murdock is so overwhelming that she literally wants his head. Don't know what she'll do with it once she gets it."

"I'm wondering what he did to warrant such a response?" Marchand said, between bites.

"Who knows." Tutt shrugged. "But the reason is irrelevant. What *is* relevant is that we now have to traverse hostile territory just to get home. I know there has to be a way to traverse the plateau ridge between our area and Reyes'."

"What were your reasons for seeking another route?" Marchand said.

"We need resources," Tutt replied. "We need lumber, venison, fish, this salmon-type, not the tasteless stuff we've been eating, and we need people. I'm certain we can trade our metal products for food. We can harvest our own lumber from this plateau once we establish a route of some kind, but it's the manpower. We need a number of the new arrivals. Or anyone else, for that matter. The aftermath of Wagner's rogue attack on the medical facility has left us undermanned. And our location has worked against our interests."

"Bein' behind the wall ain't helped neither," Tiny said, in the middle of chewing a bite of fish, some of the cooked flesh escaping his mouth as he talked.

Marchand and Tutt just looked at him.

"I wonder who *that* is," Marchand said.

Tutt and Daniels looked at Marchand, and then followed his gaze. Daniels started to rise, but Tutt put out a hand to stop him.

"Let them come to us," he whispered.

After a few minutes, the couple approached them.

"Excuse me," the man said. "May we share your fire?"

"That depends." Tutt rose to greet them with a smile. "Are you here to cause trouble?"

"No, we don't want to cause trouble. Just trying to get back to our group. I'm Curtis, and this is my sister, Angelica."

"Then come, Curtis. Share our fire." Tutt sat back down as the couple approached, and resumed eating. *Newcomers, by the looks of them. What are they doing out here?* As he chewed, he appraised them. *Neither have weapons or waterskins. That's reckless of them.* "What brings you out this far? The newcomers, I'm told, are on the next plateau down and a fair piece that way." Tutt pointed with his nose toward the stream.

"We're just trying to get back. We got separated," Curtis warmed his hands. "This is kind of embarrassing, but could you spare some water? We haven't had any for several days."

"You have an entire river of it over there. Help yourselves. I'm Raymond Tutt, by the way, and this is Blandean Marchand and Tim Daniels."

Marchand and Daniels nodded. Curtis nodded to each of the men. Angelica looked at the flames, refusing to look at the three men.

"Don't we need to boil it or something?" Curtis said.

"I don't know." Tutt shrugged. "Do you have something to boil it in? If you do, then by all means, knock yourselves out. We've not had any issues with drinking the water directly from the river. Not in the last five years, anyway. Now that you mention it, I don't think I've ever heard of anyone getting sick from it, unlike drinking from the river water back home."

Angelica rose and headed toward the river.

"Do you have any food you can spare?" Curtis said, after his sister was out of earshot.

Tutt chuckled. "There, again, is the river. It has fish in it. Delicious fish, if you ask me." Tutt popped another bit of fish into his mouth.

"Um...we're not accustomed to fishing." Curtis said chagrinned as he looked over the three men.

"Tiny, fetch another fish for our guests." Tutt smiled.

"But I just got dry," Daniels said.

"Go on, we don't want to seem inhospitable. Oh, and see to it the lady finds her way back unharmed."

Daniels got to his feet, took an arrow from his quiver, and walked to the river.

"Please excuse my companion. We get so few guests that he has forgotten his manners. How did you become separated from your group?"

"We were escorted upriver by Murdock's wife."

"Really? I haven't been upriver, myself. What's it like?"

"It's pretty much the same as here. Murdock has his house, and my brother and his family has theirs. Otherwise, it's about the same."

"Your brother? Is he a newcomer as well? And what is his name?"

"No, he's been here a while. Declan is his name."

Marchand darted his gaze to Tutt.

"Hmm… I *think* I might know him," Tutt said.

Angelica and Daniels returned to the fire, and Tutt watched them. Angelica sat next to Curtis while Daniels started the fish cooking. Neither said anything to the rest.

"Here. I've had enough, for now." Tutt handed his remaining fish to Angelica and licked his fingers. "I won't starve waiting for more fish to cook, and you two look like you could use it."

"Thanks." Angelica accepted the cooked fish.

She and Curtis pinched off some of the flesh and began eating.

"You're most welcome." Tutt smiled. "Now tell me, why are you two out here so... unprepared?"

"Unprepared?" Curtis said.

"Neither of you have any weapons of any kind. No water-skins. Can't fish, and doubtful you can hunt. So why are you out here?"

"We are out here to try to get back to our group," Curtis said.

"So you said, so you said. I ask because, from what you've said about Murdock's camp, it sounds like a good place to gain skills. Skills you'd need to survive. Not to mention that Murdock seems to be quite capable. He's been here the longest of any of us."

"There's more to it than just learning skills," Curtis said.

Angelica scowled at her brother.

"At this point, I'm just looking to make it downriver to our group, and that's all I have to say about my reasons."

"I can live with that, for now. You're both welcome to travel with us. We're heading home and will be going past the medical facility. From there, I'm certain you can find a way to get to wherever it is you're going. I had heard some of the newcomers had gone further downriver. To where, I have no idea." Tutt looked at the sky. "We'll be leaving soon, so if you're rested enough, you can follow along. Or you can stay here. Whatever suits you."

"We're ready now." Curtis got to his feet.

Angelica did the same. "Where is it you call home, Mister Tutt?"

"We have a growing mining concern. Ironwork, some copper. Nothing major, but we like it." Tutt also stood. "You might want to wrap up that fish and bring it along. Mustn't waste resources like food. We're sure to need it before we reach the medical facility."

"How do we do that?" Angelica said.

"Tiny, show Angelica how to wrap the fish for travel, and see to it the fire is out. You two can catch up with us. We won't be traveling too fast for a while yet."

Curtis kept looking back toward the place where he and Angelica came upon Tutt and his men. They had been strolling along for what seemed to be an hour.

"Worried about your sister?" Tutt said. "That's the fourth time you've looked back. I can assure you she's quite safe with Tiny."

"Of course I'm worried. To put it bluntly, we don't know you, and frankly I don't trust you."

"That seems fair to me. Trust is something you earn, and shouldn't be given lightly. I know all about that. What are your plans?"

"Like I said, our only plan at this point is to rejoin our group. After that, who knows? Why do you continue to ask?"

"Honestly, our group is looking for an infusion of new people. That's why we were up here. I wanted to meet with Reyes to see if there's a way we can benefit both of our groups."

Curtis gave Tutt a sideways glance. "You're hoping to convince my sister and me to join your group."

"Let's say, I'm hoping for you, your sister, or anyone else to have an interest in joining. Wanting to join is not enough. You have to be an asset to us, and it has to be a good fit for all concerned."

Curtis chuckled. "Well, that leaves me out."

"How so?"

"I've never really fit in anywhere."

"That may be to your benefit when it comes to our group. Everyone has been an outsider, before coming here and after. I

131

STEPHEN DRAKE

guess you could call us a group of outsiders." Tutt chuckled. "By the way, is your sister available?"

"Available? What does that even mean in this place?"

"I mean, no one has spoken for her? You'd be surprised to find what is acceptable in a frontier social environment."

"As far as I know, Angelica isn't spoken for. That's something she is quite capable of deciding for herself."

Tutt smiled broadly. "Speaking of which, here she comes with Tiny."

"Why do you call him Tiny? The last thing I'd call him is tiny."

"It's a rhetorical device, an antiphrasis." Tutt noticed the blank look on Curtis' face. "It's a way of speaking that actually means the opposite. Did you catch his first name?"

"Not really."

"His first name is Timothy," Tutt turned to meet the big man following Angelica.

Murdock wasn't more than a couple miles from the plateau edge, the one above the medical facility, when he saw five people coming toward him. He recognized Tutt, Marchand, and Daniels. His jaws tensed when he saw Curtis and Angelica.

What is she doing with them? It'll be a few more minutes before they get close enough to converse. I need to find out what's going on. Then after a long pause, a question ran through his mind. *Why am I so concerned about Angelica? I know she's not Rose. That momentary emotional trauma is gone and dealt with. I'm not overly concerned with Curtis, not after the report I received from Mei Lee. So why am I so concerned about Angelica?*

As he watched the others approach, Murdock prepared himself. He was standing in the middle of the trail with his spear. He drank water and shook out the tension in his shoulders

132

and arms. *I have no idea how this is going to go, but I need to be ready for anything.*

The five people stopped thirty yards from him and circled to talk. He rested a hand on the hilt of his twelve-incher.

Less than a minute later, Tutt continued to walk toward him.

"How's Reyes these days?" Murdock said.

Tutt's eyes grew wide. "What makes you think I saw this person... Reyes?"

Murdock chuckled. "If you didn't, then what are you doing up here? Of course you saw her. I know it and so do you."

"Where I go and what I do is *my* business, not yours. We're not looking for trouble, so let us pass."

"Sure, you're all free to pass. After I talk to Angelica. Privately."

"She doesn't want to talk to you, and neither do any of us. I'm the one who's stuck."

"She's an adult and capable of telling me that herself. Either let me talk to her, or you'll all be unconscious and I'll talk to her then."

Tutt frowned and looked back at his companions. "I'll have to ask her what she wants to do."

"Why? Either you're the leader or you're not. As a leader, you make the choices. So what's it going to be?"

"What about Curtis? Don't you want to talk to him as well?"

"Curtis has caused enmity between us. I have no *words* to speak to him, so he'd be well-advised to keep his distance from me."

Tutt walked backward a few steps before turning and moving back to the five members of his troop.

"Murdock wants to talk to Angelica," Tutt whispered.

"No way in hell," Curtis whispered back. "I have nothing to say to him!"

"Listen up, you! He said Angelica, not you. We'll wait here while Angelica goes to talk to him."

"Doesn't she have anything to say about it?" Curtis said.

133

"Not really, no. It seems to me to be a reasonable request. The alternative is not acceptable, and we have no way of preventing it. So Angelica, if you please, go talk to him."

"I refuse to let her!" Curtis said.

"Tiny, if he says one more word, shut him up." Tutt glared at Curtis.

"Angeli—"

Daniels put his huge mitt over Curtis' mouth and lifted him off his feet. Everyone else got out of the way of Curtis' flailing arms and legs.

9

In my opinion, the so-called sophisticated humans that come here have no idea what a real to-the-death survival fight is. Their first questions are always, "What are the rules?" and "Who's the referee."

— KEVIN MURDOCK, FAMILY CONVERSATIONS

Murdock watched the rest as Angelica slowly approached.

"It seems your brother isn't too happy."

"What is it you wanted?"

Murdock felt his emotions triggered at the sound of her voice.

"All I wanted was to hear from you that you prefer to be... elsewhere. Me and Declan were hoping you'd stay. For a while, anyway."

Angelica tilted her head to the right and narrowed her eyes. "*You* hoped? Why would you? You don't know me."

"Let's say, I know the effect your leaving would have on your *eldest* brother. You do know the people you're traveling with are dangerous?"

Angelica pursed her lips. "I'm of the opinion that *everyone* here is dangerous. *Some*, though, seem to be more dangerous than others. Besides, they're only escorting us to the medical facility. Not that it's any of your business, but we're planning to return to our pod group at the first opportunity."

Murdock nodded. "You *could* stay with your eldest brother."

"I could, but if I did, who would help Curtis? Declan needs nothing from me. I saw that immediately. But Curtis? Curtis is another story altogether. He's given his all to make sure he and I survived. I should repay that with... isolation, exile? What kind of a person would I be if I did that?"

"Some of the newcomers are located further downriver, if you choose to go that way. But I wouldn't go across the river on the same plateau as the medical facility. That is a long path with violence and pain at the end."

"Why should you care?"

"Call it... a debt." Murdock looked down as he felt his throat tightening.

"A debt? To who?"

"Your sister." He looked her in the eyes.

"That's the last of it." Zeke set the box of medical supplies in the corner of the room.

He, Annie, Irene, and Roy had worked for the past few days to get all the medical supplies out of the library pod and into the residence.

"Good," Irene said, without looking up from the microscope she was using.

"What are you doing?" Zeke came up behind her.

"I'm trying to determine if harmful bacteria exists in the river water. Bacteria that could be hazardous to humans." Irene rubbed her nose, then glanced in Zeke's direction, frowning. "A little whiff, aren't you?"

"I've been working hard." He backed away from her. "A hot bath would be nice, but I've failed to locate those facilities."

"Those facilities aren't readily available to everyone." She smirked. "Access to them is limited to me and Annie. Roy has access, but it's with his chosen group and their own bathing area."

Zeke cleared his throat. "I meant to ask you about the water. I've heard you should filter and boil all water, but I noticed Murdock doesn't."

Irene turned back to her microscope. "On Earth, that's true. But since we weren't born here, the bacterial and viral elements don't affect us? So far, Chun Hua is the only human born here that has no inherited genetic enhancements. We do have a filtering mechanism, here, but generally others don't. So far, no one has gotten sick from the water, as far as we know."

Zeke nodded. "So you're trying to determine if our immunity is from our being alien to this planet, or whether the pathogens here aren't strong enough to get through our natural resistance. Have you developed any theories?"

"Not yet. This is the first time we've had any kind of equipment to be able to detect the pathogens in the water. I haven't yet been able to determine if the filtered water still has pathogens in it. I do think boiling the water will kill most of the pathogens, but do we also need to boil the filtered water?" She shook her head slowly at the questions.

"What do I have to do to access the bathing facilities?"

"First, you have to decide if you'd rather bathe with me or Annie. Bathing alone is not an option at this point. Then you'd have to determine which of us want to bathe with you, if either of us does," she said, without looking up from her work. "And then there is our availability." She smirked, with her back to him.

"Is there anything I can do to help with your assessment?"

Irene pushed away from the table. "You already are. I've been sitting here for some time and find I need a distraction. So if you'll follow me, I'll see to it you get a bath, providing of course, that you would prefer my company over Annie's." She smirked at seeing his cheeks turn red. "There is always the river, you know."

"Annie is a sweetheart, but I'd prefer your company."

"Then follow me."

A few minutes later, Irene and Zeke were standing on the wall, as far as they could go away from the river.

"Put this on." She handed him a leather bag.

Zeke looked at the bag and then at Irene. "Put it on? Why do I need to put this on?"

"Because I want you to," she whispered. "Besides, there are things you shouldn't see."

"You don't trust me?"

"Trust is earned, so quit arguing and stick your head in the bag."

Zeke breathed in and blew it out slowly, trying to calm himself as he put the bag over his head.

"Okay, but I still don't understand."

"Leave it on no matter what happens."

"What's going to happen?" Zeke asked nervously.

"Well, it has been a while, so I may be a little out of practice."

"Practice? Practice what?" Zeke felt like he was floating, and gulped air in a panic.

After several minutes, he felt his feet on a solid surface again.

"Can I take this off yet?" He tried to keep the panic from his voice.

He heard something heavy rolling.

"Sure, you can remove it now."

Zeke snatched the bag off, but he was somewhere dark. So dark he couldn't see his hand in front of his face.

"Did that help with your panic?"

"No. Where are you? Where are we?" Zeke could hear the echo of their voices.

"Relax and let me lead you." Irene took his hand.

He steeled his nerves and allowed her to lead him. He had

noticed that the floor had turned to sand. After a few minutes, he heard water running and could smell steam.

"Stand there," Irene said.

He heard her strike a flint with her knife, and saw the sparks ignite kindling. Irene nursed the small flame into a bigger one. She was building a small campfire. As the flames grew, they lit the small cave.

"This is cozy," he whispered, as he looked around.

"The bathing area is over there." Irene indicated the direction with her nose since she was busy with the fire-building. "The water is hot, but watch out for slippery and sharp rocks."

In the growing light, Zeke could see the pools of water. "I don't see anywhere to disrobe—"

"There isn't one," she snapped. "I am a doctor, you know, so there's no need to be embarrassed. I've seen it all before."

"*Ahem*," Zeke cleared his throat. "I'm not embarrassed. It's just that I know I'm not a hard-bodied twenty-year-old anymore."

"So? Neither am I! Take off your clothes and wash them in the water first. They'll take a while to dry, so get to it."

It took Zeke no time to disrobe, and only a short time to get the heavy coverall washed. However, it did require both Zeke and Irene to wring them.

With his clothes washed and drying by the fire, Zeke settled back in the hot water. He had his arms on the flat rocks that formed the edge, his head back and eyes closed.

"What's this I hear about you wanting to know if I'm spoken for?" Irene entered the pool. "Why don't you try asking me?"

Zeke jerked up and looked at her. "Um, I meant no disrespect. It was more of a discrete inquiry. Or, I thought it was discrete."

Her face went from stern to laughing. "Christ, I was just pulling your leg, Zeke. Lighten up, would ya?"

He splashed water at her.

"Let's get a few things straight." Irene sat in front of the fire to dry. "I have no delusions about romance. I don't need any more friends. So what have you to offer that I don't already have?" She tossed a few more pieces of wood on the fire.

"I don't know if I have anything of value to offer." Zeke shrugged. "I am grieved to hear your views on romance. However, everyone needs more friends—"

"I have plenty."

"I can be that friend that will listen to anything you care to share, without the fear of being judged. Someone who'll listen when you need to vent."

"Have that already, in spades."

Zeke looked frustrated. "In the short time I've been here, I've seen you become uncomfortable when around others who are a couple. Call it a third-wheel feeling. I'm here to help you to not feel that way, or help with anything else you need. I'm not a doctor or a scientist, but I'll listen and give you my thoughts on theories you want to discuss."

Irene fidgeted. "So you'll be there to flatter me and not disagree?"

Zeke laughed. "Sometimes I don't know when or how to be tactful. I tend toward brutal honesty, I'd guess you'd say, but I'm no yes man. I won't flatter you, but I will give an honest opinion, and we'll undoubtedly have lots of disagreements."

Irene smirked and looked at him with a sideways glance. "Good answer! And what are some of your current observations about me?"

Zeke thought for a moment. "I think you are a handsome woman and you don't realize it, and I think you've spent too much time being married to your profession."

Harris looked at Zeke, mouth agape for a few heartbeats. "Medicine is a harsh partner." She averted her gaze. "It requires everything from its practitioners and returns too few moments of gratification." She paused for a long time. "I'm broken and have a lot of baggage. A *handsome woman?* I'm not sure, but I think I've been insulted."

"No, you haven't been insulted. The term, though archaic in our time, means a woman with the kind of refined beauty and attractiveness that requires poise, dignity, and strength of mind and character. Things that often come with age, not merely sex appeal. So you see, it's a compliment. As far as being broken, everyone who attains adulthood could be classified as broken. Adulthood seems to guarantee it, and everyone has baggage attributable to that attainment of adulthood. We are the sum of our experiences, both good and bad. That's the way I see it, anyway."

"So you're saying I have no sex appeal?" Irene whispered.

"I didn't say that. Being sexually attractive is a subjective matter. Beauty *is* in the eye of the beholder, you know?"

Irene moved to sit closer to Zeke, and leaned a shoulder into him. He draped his arm around her.

"You need to get rid of the beard," she whispered.

"How does Murdock keep his down?"

"He uses his six-incher, but he keeps it razor sharp at all times. Is yours?"

"I doubt it. I don't know how to sharpen it. There are a lot of things I don't know how to do... yet."

"I'm sure you can learn or manage to figure out most things." Irene chuckled. "I have faith in you. Now get dressed. We have work to do."

"There's something going on out there," flashed to Irene's mind, and she knew it was from Annie.

"What do you see?" Irene replied.

"Curtis and Angie talking to three slimeballs, the ones from the group that attacked us."

"So project yourself so you can listen in."

"I don't like doing that. It makes me think I'm invading someone's privacy."

Irene chuckled. *"Well, you are, but it can be forgiven if you learn something important."*

Tutt had made a point of leaning to one side as Angelica walked further downriver. It was obvious to Curtis that he was admiring Angelica's gluteus maximus.

"So what exactly are you saying?" Curtis said.

Tutt looked around nervously. "I'm saying that anyone who joins our group has to bring something to the table. TANSTAAFL, you know." Again Tutt looked around.

"Is there something bothering you?" Blandean also looked around nervously.

"I feel like someone is watching us," Tutt whispered. "You know, that feeling you get when you're sure you're being stalked." He shook himself all over.

"But I have nothing to offer except a strong back," Curtis said. "And what is TANSTAAFL?"

Tutt grinned. "TANSTAAFL is an ancient acronym for *there ain't no such thing as a free lunch*. The part about a strong back, that may be true at this point, but I'm sure things will change." He leaned once more to look at Angelica, "If you catch my drift."

Curtis followed Tutt's gaze. "Are you suggesting that I use my sister to gain access to your group?"

"I would *never* suggest such a thing." Tutt flashed a look of shocked insult. "I'd never condone such an action."

"But if I could *convince* my sister…" Curtis looked at Tutt.

"If your sister, of her own free will, came to us looking for sanctuary, being men of conscience, we'd have to, at the least, take such a request under advisement and give it the proper consideration it would deserve." Tutt once more leaned to glance in Angelica's direction.

The other three men followed his gaze.

"Uh-huh," Curtis said, dubiety apparent. "I think I understand."

"Say, you *are* a smart guy! I was *certain* you'd understand, eventually. If, or when, you decide to join us, cross the river and head that way." Tutt pointed toward his group. "I'll tell the guards to look for you," he said to Curtis' back.

Chun Hua's eyelids popped open and her hand went to her chest. Her heart pounded, breathing heavy and shallow. She looked around the darkened cabin while trying to remain motionless, and saw nothing. She strained her ears, but heard nothing out of the ordinary.

She knew her father—. Well, not *really* her father. Her mother had explained the living arrangements multiple times over the years. She knew Thomas Collier was her father, whom she'd never met. But the one who was always there for her when she was little was Murdock, the only person she thought of when she thought of the word *Dad*. She knew he was home, and everyone in the cabin was as safe as he could make it. But the nightmare had shaken her.

It was the same nightmare she'd had over the past two years. She knew it was a memory of events that had scared her when they'd happened, and they still caused her to wake in the middle of the night in a panic. The night two women burst through the door of the cabin, catching all inside unawares, threatening the life of Andy and Rosa, and taking the life of little Huo Jin. Additionally, they had injured her mother and caused the miscarriage of the baby.

At the time of the incident, Chun Hua had been terrified and Andy whispered to her to hide. The two crazed women hadn't known she was there. Her father, however, had been startled when she touched his hand, and it made her feel safer to know he was there and that things would work out. Just as now, she felt safer than when she'd first awakened from the nightmare, but she still couldn't get the images out of her mind when she closed her eyes. As she lay in her hammock, she could hear Rosa's soft breathing to one side, and Andy's louder breathing on the other.

Her heart still beating wildly, from the nightmare, Chun Hua got to her feet and tiptoed into Andy's sleeping area. She reached out to touch him.

"Another nightmare, Chunnie?" Andrew whispered, groggily.

"Same one," she whispered back.

She felt his hand take hers as he helped her into his hammock. She snuggled into his back, with her back to the log wall of the cabin.

He's a good big brother. She smiled. *I know we're the same age, but he was born first.*

After breakfast, Murdock was supervising Andy and Chun Hua sparring each other. Mei Lee was teaching Rosa a new kata, and supervised her practicing the ones she already knew.

"Stop!" Murdock got to his feet and approached the two older children. "What are you doing, Andy?"

Andrew looked at Murdock, contritely. "What do you mean, sir?"

"When you spar your sister, it's as much for your benefit as hers. Why are you holding back?"

"I wasn't aware that I was, sir,"

"Uh-huh. There were plenty of opportunities to tag her, and you either missed them or refused to press your advantage. I saw it plainly. So tell me what is going on with you?"

144

Andrew gulped as his face turned red, but he remained silent.

"Chunnie, are you trying to hit Andrew?"

"Yes, sir."

"I want you to lay him out. If he misses anything, I want you to take advantage. Fight as if your life depended on it. Understand?"

"Yes, sir."

"Begin!"

Murdock saw Chun Hua throw flurries of kicks and strikes, any one of which would be devastating to Andrew, but he deftly countered them all. Murdock did notice that Andrew hesitated to retaliate. The few times he did retaliate, his techniques were slow. Chun Hua blocked and dodged them all, but with difficulty.

"Stop." Murdock drew a hand down his face in frustration. "You two are not helping each other by holding back." He paced around them. "This is supposed to be training for the two of you. If you get the chance to hit each other, you should take it. Andrew, when you hit Chunnie, it helps her to know what it feels like to get hit. It teaches her to think about mitigating the impacts of those hits. If you have to fight someone and you don't know what it feels like to hit or get hit, the shock of the contact can paralyze you when you need them the most. Chunnie, hit Andrew. Hit him as hard as you can. He needs to be toughened up. Actually, you both do. You're not helping yourself by going easy on him, and it's not helping him either."

"I'm sorry, Dad, but I can't hit him," Chun Hua said. "I was trying and I couldn't get it done. He's just too fast."

Murdock furrowed his brow. Then he moved toward Andrew.

"Show me." He prepared himself to spar Andrew.

Chun Hua stood aside to watch. When it started, she could barely see them spar. Both were so quick with every technique they threw at each other.

"What's going on?" Mei Lee said, from behind her daughter.

"Father says I'm not trying to hit Andrew. I was really trying and I couldn't. He's too fast."

Mei Lee shook her head as she watched. "He is fast. I'll give him that. But I can see he isn't as fast as his father. I doubt anyone could be that fast." She looked at her daughter. "Are you taking it easy on Andy?"

"No, Mother, I'm not."

"I can understand it if you are, and there's no shame in admitting it." She watched Chun Hua for indications of deception. "You two have been raised together, and it would be natural for you to not want to injure someone close to you."

Chun Hua faced her mother. "True, we have been raised together, but we have both been trained together. During training, I know better than to take it easy on him."

Murdock and Andrew stopped.

"Not bad," he said to his son. "I can see why she can't hit you. Now explain to me why you can't hit her. You had no trouble hitting me when I left you an opening, but I could've tagged you several times." Murdock watched Andrew's ears turn red.

"I guess I'm hesitant because of the control required. I don't want to hurt her."

Without looking away, Murdock said, "Mei Lee, come spar with Andy. He needs someone to tag him."

Several minutes later, Mei Lee stopped and Andrew relaxed.

"Are you okay, Andy?" Murdock said. "Mei Lee did tag you a few times. A couple of them were a little on the hard side."

"I'm fine. A little sore in places, but that's to be expected."

"And you, Mei?"

"I'm fine. He tagged me a few times, but not too hard."

"In your opinion, is Andy taking it easy on Chunnie?"

"A little, yes. He could go harder with her."

"So what's going on with the two of them?" Murdock flashed to his wife.

146

"I don't know, but I think there may be something. It just hasn't presented itself yet."

In the silence, Chun Hua looked at Andrew and he looked back. They both saw a sad face.

"I have a question for you," Irene Harris said, without looking up from her work. She was about to finish for the day, and the pair was sitting in her lab area.

Zeke looked around. "You mean me?"

"No, I was talking to the mouse in your pocket! Of course, you. Why is it most of the people I've met since coming here have been rather... mean and nasty?"

"Back on Earth, did you spend any time in the real world?"

"I worked at a hospital or was in school."

"Not what I meant. Did you ever go out shopping or to a show? Go out for a drink or go on a date?"

Irene thought about it. "Not often. Why?"

"I'm not trying to be condescending. I'm trying to give you as good an answer as I can.

"In my opinion, the society we left was over-protective, self-absorbed, and delusional in that it tried to lay the blame for everything at someone else's feet. The if-he-wouldn't-have-done-this-I-wouldn't-have-done-what-I-did type. Add to that, the prevailing attitude was *I got mine, and it sucks to be you.* So impulse-driven and self-centered to the point that no one worried about anyone else, except maybe their wives and kids, and that's not something you could count on either. You take those people and transport them somewhere that, apparently, laws don't exist, without the required time to learn to be cooperative and to work as a team. During the westward expansion of the United States, the preferred mode of travel was wagon trains. The trips were dangerous and arduous, but through it all, the people surviving the journey learned to work together and understood survival meant teamwork."

"Hmm," Irene said. "Our pod was ruled by bullies, one female and one male. He was accustomed to getting his way by physical intimidation. She intimidated emotionally, by threatening being ostracized."

"Just out of curiosity, how many were in Murdock's pod, and how many survived."

"Murdock's pod? Twenty. Only he and his wife, Mei Lee, survived five years."

"Mmmm, I expected that. The survival rate is about ten percent on initial incursion."

"That low? I'd attributed their survival to Murdock's skills."

"Oh, his skills made a big difference, to be sure, but usually if you put a bunch of know-nothings in this environment, I'd say one-in-forty wouldn't make it five years. The ten percent survival rate assumes most know at least a little something about survival. Just out of curiosity, how many were in your pod?"

"We had two hundred."

"And how many survived the first five years?"

"I have no clue. No one reports on a regular basis those lost through animal attacks, accidents, starvation, internal aggression, and exposure in the previous year."

"Is it more than twenty?"

"There are more than twenty survivors from my pod, on this plateau. If I had to guess, our pod has close to fifty percent survival rate."

"I'd expect that. Those in Murdock's pod were to determine what it would take to survive and begin to establish an infrastructure. When your pod landed, survivors assisted some in your pod to help ensure survival. With more survivors in your group, I'm expecting more than fifty percent survival. How much more? I doubt we'll hit the sixty percent mark. But even then, fifty percent is a thousand people."

"But why are they so belligerent?"

Zeke looked at the floor and appeared to be ordering his thoughts. Irene had noticed that his lips would pucker and then be drawn into a line when he was thinking.

"When people first started out, they were tribal," he said. "They understood that to survive, there had to be cooperation between all the individuals. As their tribes grew, humans became more agrarian. Each individual knew how to do all the tasks necessary to survive. They all had a connection to the rest. There were some, though, that led the rest and felt they needed to be compensated for being in the leadership position. As they prospered, they formed into towns and cities, and as they did, they started to be more isolated from those who produced the food everyone required. In the late 20th century, things had gotten to the point where some would ask questions like, *Why hunt when you can just purchase the meat you want?* Which, if you think about it, is rather silly. In the first quarter of the 21st century, people would say, *Animals have a right to live, and that right supersedes the rights of humans,* while eating a hamburger. To me, that shows how isolated people had become. They wanted to eat, but had no idea where the meat they ate came from. And it didn't only apply to food. I'm pretty good at using a computer, but can I design and implement the programs I use? I know I can't, but there are some that can. Otherwise, we wouldn't have those things. Now can the person who created the software create every element that goes into the manufacture of computers? In my mind, that's doubtful. The belligerence you're asking about comes from fear. They are the most sophisticated humans to come along, but to get there, they have lost so much. The environment we now find ourselves in showcases their ignorance in the simplest of things. That lost knowledge and fear of failure, because failure means death, creates the belligerence."

"So you're saying they aren't responsible?" Irene said.

"I'm not saying that at all. They are responsible for their own actions, or lack thereof. But that doesn't mean I can't understand it. Do you know of any one of your pod mates that started out as an ass, and then changed for the better?"

Irene thought of Declan. "I can think of at least one."

"Okay, so what changed about that person?"

"I'd say the person I have in mind calmed down and quit worrying about food and shelter."

"Is there still a fear of failure in this person?"

"Yes, but it isn't the all-consuming issue it used to be. They aren't worried about dying at any second, all the time. That, and they matured."

"I know my explanation is simplistic and there are other drivers involved. Look at yourself. On Earth, you were a good doctor and you used all the tools at your disposal. When you first arrived here, were you worried about the finite resources you now had to deal with? Since you have finite resources now, would you be able to make some of the simpler things? Can you make a thermometer if you had to? How about a pencil? Paper?"

Irene pursed her lips. "I admit, I couldn't make any of those." she said chagrined.

Beware the ides of March.

— WILLIAM SHAKESPEARE, *JULIUS CAESAR*

S anittie Laust—no, that wasn't the name on her original birth certificate—was sitting on the ground close to the creek, watching those still at the landing site work.

When we first arrived here, I had no problem telling the guy taking our names what my name is. She smirked. *What parent in their right mind names their kid Hortense Winifred Lausvinchenco? Thank God I changed it as soon as I was old enough.*

Her parents hadn't argued much while she was growing up, but what a row it had caused when she brought up the reason for her name.

"You were named after my sister!" her mother had said, tears streaming. "She died at an early age."

Probably from the prospect of living her life with a name like Hortense.

"Are you happy now?" her father had said. "You made your mother cry!"

At her first grade school, she'd used her given name and was harassed and teased daily. Her teachers had tried to help, but *Tensy* was just as bad. Later, when she matriculated, she tried using Winifred, thinking *Winnie* wasn't as bad as Hortense, but invariably her classmates settled on *Fred*...at least, they did until someone found out what her given name was.

Being called *Horse Winnie*, with the accompanying sounds whenever she entered a room, for many years had driven her into the argument with her parents and had resulted in her name change at the ripe old age of fourteen. After much consideration, she had settled on Sanittie, a stylized spelling of *sanity*, went well with a truncated version of her last name. Lausvinchenco became *Laus*, and then *Laust*. Primarily because by the time she changed it, she had lost a good portion of her sanity. Her parents, of course, had been shocked and outraged at her decision, which pleased her no end.

Her reverie was broken when she noticed Erycca Valdez and Georgia Nyree heading her way. She stood and brushed off any dirt or grass that had stuck to the seat of her navy-colored coveralls—which is what everyone from this load of newcomers wore.

"What's up?" she said, as the two women came within voice range.

"Dirk Benson is here," Erycca said.

"So? How does that concern me?"

"He says he's here to inform the remaining leaders that Benteen has established a settlement, of sorts," Georgia said, "and he has the two that had gone with Murdock."

"So why tell me? I'm not the only leader here."

"You *are* the last one to be informed, though," Erycca said.

"Did you tell him that another group has already departed?" Sanittie paced.

"We did," Georgia said. "He said he had encountered them on his way here, and directed them as to where the others were located. What concerns me, and others, are the two... returnees."

"Why?"

"Well, they're related to Murdock, somehow," Erycca said. "I heard him making some sort of speech before he left." She paused, brow furrowed. "Are they spying on us? They certainly weren't gone long, but for what purpose? Personally, I don't trust them."

"I don't trust them either," Georgia said. "I'd just as soon they go somewhere else. Anywhere else."

Sanittie had been watching the others of her group continue to enclose the underside of the closest pod with sections of sod.

"Maybe we can send them on an exploration of the stream," she said. "We need resources, wood primarily, for doors and door jams, furniture, and other things. I've gotten the impression that no one has explored downstream on the plateau below, or further."

"How would that help us?" Erycca said.

"If we send fifty people downstream, mixtures from the remaining pod residents, there are bound to be some that won't make it back. With any luck, those two will be on the list of casualties."

"That'll work," Georgia said, "but I'd wait until we find out what their plans are. Who knows, they may have other ideas of where they want to go."

Murdock and Declan were standing on the edge of what Murdock called *the dread area*. Now, though, he felt no feelings of ill-will.

"What's the plan?" Declan fidgeted.

"I'm going to astrally project myself over this area and down into the depression—"

"What depression?" Declan said. "I don't see a depression here. All I see is tall grass and trees."

"The grass and trees are hiding the edge of a depression. When I first arrived, I came here and saw deer disappear over the edge. I found out later that there is a depression here hiding the Destroyers, like the wild pig I killed when I gathered poles. The depression acts to confine them. I plan to get close to the floor of the depression and scope it all out."

"For what purpose?" Declan asked nervously.

"Are you okay? You seem to be anxious about something."

Declan chuckled nervously. "You called this the dread area, and it certainly is that! I have this odd feeling of impending doom."

"The plan is to levitate a couple youngsters, or a mature sow and boar. I have a confinement already set up, but it will entail levitating them all the way home. Are you up for that?"

"I'll do what I can. How are you going to get out of the depression, and with the squealers?"

Murdock shot a look at his friend. "I'm not *physically* going down there. I'm going to project myself down, *astrally*. If I find some candidates, I'll levitate the squealers out. How else would you do it?"

"Astral Projection? What the hell is that?"

"Basically, astral projection is a willful out-of-body experience. When I do it, I can see and hear, but can't interact, so I'll be perfectly safe."

"You can do that? How are you going to levitate multiple objects?"

Murdock thought about the question a tick or two. "How have you been traversing the plateaus? I know you've been riding a mount from one plateau to another, so I'm wondering."

Declan flushed. "I've been walking them up and down the path."

"Why haven't you asked how to levitate yourself *and* your mount simultaneously? Why am I just hearing about this now?"

"Well, you've been busy… and I didn't think it was all that important. I had no idea something like that could be done."

Murdock looked sideways at Declan. "Maybe we need to pause so you can get some levitation training."

Declan was levitating himself a few feet off the ground while suspending two rocks. It had taken him a while to get the hang of accomplishing this task.

"Now keep in mind that levitating a rock is different than suspending a wriggling, squalling porker." Murdock tossed another rock into the air.

Declan didn't catch it. He did, however, manage to slow its descent. When it hit the ground, so did the other rocks, and Declan, who crumpled into a heap.

"How... was... that?" He panted.

"Not too bad." Murdock reached down to help Declan to his feet. "When it comes to levitating you and your mount, you should be able to do it by levitating just the mount, with you on its back, of course. I would get the mount used to it first, though."

After turning away, Murdock sat on the ground just off the path.

As his astral-self descended through the trees, Murdock could hear the Destroyers grunting and rooting around the bare ground. He hadn't gone far when he saw a boar, and not far away, a sow with several piglets.

Murdock deftly plucked the boar and sow, complete with piglets, off the ground. They started to squeal and try to wriggle free.

Declan heard a cacophony of squeals from the depression.

"They're on their way up," Murdock whispered to Declan.

"Try to grab the boar as soon as you see it. They're wriggling a lot, so hold him firmly, but don't crush him."

Soon, the boar cleared the grass covering the edge of the depression, and Declan, using his levitation skills, grasped the boar as Murdock released him.

"Maintain your concentration," Murdock whispered. "We now have a long walk. If you get tired, let me know and I'll do what I can to hold him."

Declan nodded as he started off toward home, the boar suspended in front of him.

Murdock was close behind, with his burden in tow.

It was close to sunset when Murdock and Declan arrived at the confinement Murdock had built, located a couple miles down-river from his cabin. When he approached the area, he noticed the high rocks, like sentinels, at the entrance. On closer inspection, he found that they were part of the mountainside. The entry looked more like a gate opening than a breach in the rock wall. The only way in, without climbing gear, was through the opening.

The opening was thirty-feet wide and a hundred-feet deep at the base, with smooth walls over forty-feet high. When first found, while in the entryway, Murdock had bent and probed the ground with his twelve-inch machete. He half-expected to hit loose rock, instead of hitting solid granite. As he stood examining it, it looked as if a twenty-two hundred gigajoule laser had sliced down the rock on the sides and across the bottom of the opening, and then lifted out the section of rock.

As he emerged from the opening, he saw what appeared to be an enormous flat oval with the opening behind him in a narrow end of the oval. Inside the oval, which appeared to be a mile wide and two miles long, was all grass. Murdock could see that this was a corral, of sorts—sheer mountain walls thick with

156

trees of all sorts formed the outside of the oval. From the entrance, he could see no water source, and the grass was over four-feet high. In some places, even higher.

When he had initially explored it, he found the center to be slough-like, with lush grass all around. To the upriver side, he'd built the enclosure for the pigs using slabs of granite ten-feet wide, forty-feet long and twelve-inches thick. He had also cut triangular pieces for the corners to hold the sides together, with the help of wooden poles inserted into holes in the blocks for stability and to give the pigs shelter. The finished enclosure was 120 feet by 280 feet.

"Do you think this is big enough?" Declan deposited the boar inside.

He had been embarrassed at having to ask Murdock several times for help on their way here.

"Better to have it bigger than we need, than too small." Murdock deposited the sow and piglets. "Besides, if our herd grows, there'll be room."

Declan scanned around the oval-shaped area. "What's up there?"

He had levitated himself to the top of the enclosure when Murdock had.

"I have no idea. I took a deer close to the entrance some time back, and haven't given it a full once-over. I know there's a small waterfall at the opposite end of this area, but other than that…" He shrugged and shook his head.

"Have you given any thought to moving our homes inside here?" Declan gestured toward the enclosure. "That entrance could be closed with a gate, or another feature that would keep out everyone. It's far more sheltered than where we are now. I can't help think if we'd been in something like this, then the tragedy…" He glanced at Murdock.

"Yeah?" Murdock snapped, and turned away from Declan. "Go on!"

Declan shook his head and remained silent.

"You're thinking that if we'd been established here, then I would have two more kids still alive? My wife wouldn't have been injured? Is that what you were thinking?"

"I didn't say that," Declan mumbled, head hung. "I didn't mean to imply anything. My brain went there, and it was out of my mouth before I could stop it. Sorry."

Murdock jumped off the enclosure wall and floated to the ground. He stormed off toward the entrance.

When Raymond Tutt, Tiny Daniels, and Blandean Marchand arrived at the wall that enclosed the mine area, the one erected by Murdock, he noticed that someone had dug a passage under the wall. What was a small hole which was difficult to crawl through to get under the wall, was now a wide, deep sloped tunnel under it.

"How long have we been gone?" Tutt said.

"Not that long," Marchand replied. "This is a pleasant surprise. It sure does make getting under the wall easier, and it appears large enough to haul in harvested deer."

Tutt grunted. *I wonder what other surprises await inside.*

As he moved into the mine, he glanced around at the weapons that were being carried by others. Some carried spears. Others carried bows, with quivers on their backs. Only one or two had what looked to be crossbows, with pouches of bolts at their waist.

When did we get crossbows? Who designed them? Granted, I've always had a passion for ancient weapons, but I always had trouble with the trigger mechanism when it came to crossbows.

As he entered the mine, in the first chamber were racks of weapons. More spears, bows, arrows, a few maces with spiked balls on the end, and crossbow bolts, but no crossbows.

As Tutt meandered to his office and living quarters, located one level down from the entrance, he saw Wagner sitting behind his work table, with a crossbow on the table.

"What are you doing in here?" Tutt scowled at him.

Wagner picked up the crossbow and studied it. "I'm working," he said, without looking up at Tutt. "Nice to see you *finally* decided to come back."

"I haven't been gone *that* long. You still haven't answered my question."

Wagner cradled the weapon across his lap. "You've been gone long enough that the others figured they needed a new leader."

Tutt looked shocked. "And I suppose that's you?"

"Say, you are a bright boy, aren't you! Yes, they figured I could do more for them than you could, with all your gallivanting around God's creation and back." He pointed the crossbow at Tutt.

"And are you now going to kill me? Is that how we ascend the opportunity ladder here?"

"Not if I don't have to. Raymond, you gave me a chance when I had no other choices. So to repay you, I'll give you a chance. You can stay here and be subservient to me and my instructions, or I'll eliminate you, here and now. The choice is yours." He grinned at Tutt mirthlessly.

"Can I leave?"

"I probably should grant that request, but I won't. You know too much to be allowed to leave. If I let you leave, you'd just go somewhere else, join another group, and then I'd have to contend with you working against me by working for my enemies. I've given you your choices. So what'll it be?"

"Can I at least think about it?"

Tutt saw Wagner's finger twitch and felt the bolt slam against his chest a moment later.

"Time's up."

Tutt slumped to the rock floor.

"Huh. I guess I need to see about modifying the hair-trigger on this thing," he said to a room devoid of other living beings.

He cocked and reloaded the weapon.

"Wagner! What the hell?" Marchand yelled, as he and Daniels entered.

"There has been a transfer of power here. Daniels, remove the body. And Marchand, you sit!"

Daniels looked at Marchand, confusion on his face.

"It's okay, Tiny. Take Tutt's body outside while I talk to Wagner," Marchand said, not taking his eye off Wagner and the loaded crossbow now cradled across Wagner's middle.

Tiny Daniels still hadn't moved. Marchand saw Wagner shift the aim of the crossbow toward Daniels.

"Daniels, you better start moving, or my finger may twitch again."

Daniels and Marchand both reached for their twelve-inch machetes, but before either could clear their scabbards, Daniels was hit with the crossbow bolt just under his ribs. Wagner dropped the crossbow, pulled his own twelve-incher and hit Marchand just under his ribs with the blade.

Once he stood free of the bodies, he replaced his machete and picked up the crossbow. As he left his quarters, another man was walking past. Wagner stopped him.

"Take out the trash." He hooked his thumb toward the room he'd just exited. "I'll be outside."

Johann Spitzer, Erycca Valdez, Dean Zelmiss, Bart Oldkampo, Parker Sheetzen, Camden Shultz, Sanittie Laust, and Georgia Nyree were sitting around a fire, located close to the center of the circle formed by the landing pods, waiting for the fish harvested from the river to cook.

"So I take it Xavier Alderman and his group, are well on their way downriver?" Oldkampo said.

"That's what Benson said," Spitzer replied. "By the way, shouldn't he be a part of this?"

"Benson isn't part of this gathering of leaders," Sanittie said. "He's not part of any group, from my estimation. Neither he, nor that kid... what's his name? They seem to be free agents, so to speak. Besides, there are things we need to discuss that don't involve them."

"Like what?" Sheetzen said.

"We have a couple of problems, as I see it," Sanittie said. "First, we have a pair of returnees. Does anyone else think it's a little strange that they would return so quickly?"

The others each nodded and grunted.

"What happened? Why did they leave us and where did they go?"

"I think I overheard Murdock claiming them as family before he left," Valdez said.

Again, everyone nodded.

"Has anyone questioned them?" Sanittie looked around the group. No one said anything. "Don't you think someone should? Or are we open to anyone just walking into our settlement? Another issue that concerns me is the weird-lings."

"To which weird-lings are you referring?" Sheetzen said.

"That group of fifteen that seems to hang around together," Sanittie replied. "They do what you ask them to do, but if you watch, they seem to migrate toward one another. They even sleep close to each other. I mean, I've seen friends do some of that, but come on! Even friends don't hang together like they do. Maybe I'm imaging things, but they give me the creeps!" She shuddered.

"So what are you suggesting?" Spitzer said.

"I don't know," Sanittie shrugged. "Maybe we can send them all, as part of a small group, to investigate further downstream, all fifteen and the pair of returnees." She leaned back and started eating.

"I suppose we could do that," Spitzer said, between bites. "Would that make you feel better, Sanittie?"

"It's not a matter of making *me* feel better. Just watch them for a while and see if they don't creep you out, too."

"That seems fair." Spitzer looked around to the nodding heads. "If we're bothered by their presence too much, then we send them downstream."

"I don't know if anyone's followed the stream," Nyree said, "but I think it's something that needs to be done at some point."

"And what if some, or all, don't return?" Shultz whispered.

Sanittie shrugged. "Then I guess they don't return. Problems solved."

"You seem to be disturbed by something," Emily whispered to her husband. "Care to discuss it?"

"I think I set Kevin off." Declan cuddled his wife.

It was night and the pair lay in their hammock. All the children were asleep.

"What makes you say that?"

"After putting the porkers into their confinement, I mentioned that maybe the tragedy wouldn't have happened if we were inside the oval basin. It looked like it could be easily walled off and others would have difficulty getting over it."

"Seems reasonable. So what set him off?"

"I don't know. He accused me of implying that he failed in some fashion. I don't know what's going on with those two. Murdock is short-tempered, and Mei Lee is becoming a wild woman."

"I agree. Before the tragedy, she never would have gone off on Curtis as she did on the way here."

"I think the changes in their behavior are caused by the loss of the two kids. Has either of them shared since?"

"Not that I'm aware of. Whatever is eating at them, I hope they get it settled soon."

"I have noticed that Murdock spends a lot of time away from Mei Lee. It's as if he can't be around her."

"As many of you are aware," Wagner addressed the group at the mine, "Raymond Tutt, Timothy Daniels, and Blandean Marchand are dead."

A number of people began to grumble.

"We know!" someone yelled from the center of the crowd. "We want to know why *you* killed them."

"We've been here for several years and still have an issue getting enough to eat. We gave Tutt plenty of time to do something about it, and he did nothing. On top of that, he gave away the weapons he retrieved from Murdock." Wagner rubbed his newly healed right hand. "He decided to just take off exploring… for a month. What did we do in that month? With everyone's help, we managed to make a number of these fine crossbows." He lifted one overhead. "And because of it, we managed to harvest a couple deer. Isn't it nice to have red meat for a change? Was Tutt here? These crossbows shoot a bolt faster, with a flatter trajectory, and further, making it easier to defend and feed ourselves. With the taking of more game, we will be able to clothe ourselves as well. We've spent a long time being incarcerated, unjustly, and since Tutt disappeared, we've managed to get a good start on a defensible entry that allows us to walk through as men, instead of crawling like animals. We've turned our *prison* into our *fortress*. We've managed more in the month of Tutt's absence then he could in *years*."

A man stood toward the back of the crowd. "I happened to like Tiny Daniels. I saw no reason for him to die. Explain yourself!" The man sat back down.

A number of those around him clapped him on the shoulder.

"Marchand was, as many of you already know, a weasel. The only loyalty he ever showed was to himself and his own needs. Timothy was honest and loyal, but he wasn't the sharpest crayon in the box. His mistake was in trusting Marchand and being loyal to him instead of remaining loyal to Tutt."

"That's bullshit! You're lying," someone shouted from the middle of the crowd, without standing.

"Being one of Tutt's most trusted advisors, I overheard Marchand trying to sway Tutt, behind the scenes," Wagner said with a straight face. "I'd also heard Marchand, using his weaseling ways, trying to turn Daniels against Tutt and gaining Daniels' trust and loyalty. It was Marchand that shot Daniels. I took matters into my own hands by killing Marchand immediately. That is all I have to announce. Everyone can go back to doing whatever you were doing. Stoddard, I want you to come to my quarters." Wagner left the disgruntled survivors, with Harvey Stoddard on his heels.

Wagner entered his quarters, formally Tutt's. Stoddard stopped to look around the passageway outside the room before finally entering.

"So what are you planning?" he whispered.

Wagner sat and reloaded his crossbow. "This section of this plateau needs to be unified."

"You mean, we're going back to Rogers'?"

"Not in the way you mean," Wagner looked sideways at Stoddard, with a smirk.

"War? We're going to war with them?"

"I prefer the term *unification* over *war*. If you think about it, there aren't many left from our pod. A dozen here, who knows how many of Rogers' group are left, the farmers, which have been exposed to the elements all this time. All are in need of unification." Wagner grinned, as he usually did when he thought about going to war with the rest.

"I've heard Tutt mention a group on our side of the river and one plateau up. It was something he wanted to do—contact them and see if there was a possible trade opportunity."

Wagner appeared shocked. "Okay, then they're susceptible to unification as well."

Stoddard looked at Wagner with a blank expression.

"What?" Wagner said.

"I'm trying to decide if you're out of your mind or just dumb. Maybe you're both. We can only field a dozen troops, at most. You don't think you're biting off more than you can chew?"

"Over the years, I've been studying those that hunt for Rogers' group. It's always the same few. Only recently have they been given bows and arrows, thanks to Murdock. I doubt they have the expertise necessary to repel a concerted attack. Besides, my plan is to injure everyone who comes out to fish or hunt. Without food, they'll have to exit the cave and will be out in the open, where they're the most vulnerable."

"What about those in the open?"

"The farmers are not fighters. They'll knuckle under faster than you'd think. Besides, I may have an ally in that camp."

"And the one's upriver from us?"

"They, like the farmers, are most likely fewer in number. Maybe they can be incentivized to join us."

"What's your endgame?"

"Ultimately, I want my property back!" Wagner said, through clenched teeth.

Stoddard looked confused. "Property? What property?"

Wagner glared at him. "I had a cart, several hides, assorted tools, and two women. I mean to have them back!"

Stoddard stared for several seconds. "As I recall, those were items that belonged to Murdock—"

"And he couldn't defend his claim on them. They are mine!"

"Why go to war with those not involved? Why not go after Murdock personally?"

"The plague known as Murdock is everyone's concern. They didn't stop him when they had the chance. So now they are complicit in his crimes. Now, then, we need more of the maces and crossbow bolts. I don't want anyone to run out of either."

He has lost his mind. Stoddard exited Wagner's quarters. *My memory of those events differs significantly from his. True, he stole everything Murdock had with him, including the women, but Murdock took them back. By whatever rules Wagner is functioning under, the stuff he says was his now belongs to Murdock. Unless he's changing the rules to benefit himself. I just hope he doesn't get us all killed.*

Gundersen and Benson had established a camp not far from the circle of pods.

"What are they doing?" Gundersen looked over the pods in different stages of enclosing.

"They're trying to enclose the undersides of the pods," Benson said. "Pretty smart, actually."

"But why? I don't get it."

"They're on this plain, which is lacking trees for building. They're using sod to enclose and insulate the underside of the pods. Apparently, they're planning to spend the winter here. If it gets as cold as I expect, the sod will insulate them from the cold, wind, and snow. It increases the available living area and should help hold the heat in and keep the predators out. All this without an external structure."

"But aren't there heat-shield tiles on the underside? They're designed to radiate heat away from the pods, aren't they?"

"True. If they don't remove them, sleeping inside on the decks will get cold. Removing the tiles would allow them to build a fire inside the confined space and warm everything. Otherwise, they'll only have heat in the underside area."

"Do they know?"

"They should. If they don't, they'll find it out in the middle of winter." Benson settled in. "I assume you're taking the first watch?"

"Yes, of course. Shouldn't we tell them?"

"About the heat-shield? Nah. If you can figure it out, so should they. Sometimes you don't help anyone by doing their thinking for them."

Benson snuggled down and turned his backside to the fire.

People say I don't fight fair. I never understood that. There is nothing fair about a fight. If it's a fight worth having, it's worth winning. Why would you not use all you know and all you have to win? Like I said, fighting fair is a strange concept.

— KEVIN MURDOCK, FAMILY CONVERSATIONS

Alvin Jones was preparing mounts for a deer hunt.

"Have you ever hunted before?" Alvin asked Zeke, as he finished his outfitting of the mounts.

"Never, but I'm willing to try! Irene... um... Doctor Harris says I need to know how it's done and what's all involved. She says it's so I don't take it for granted."

"Do you? Take it for granted, I mean."

"I understand that this is a frontier. At this point, we have no means of a wide distribution of food and everyone has to do their part to sustain themselves. I'd like to think I don't take anything for granted."

"Another point—do you know how to use that?" Jones glanced at the bow Zeke was carrying. "Can you shoot it somewhat accurately and responsibly? Or do I need to worry about getting shot?"

"I will make a concerted effort not to shoot you," Zeke said, unsure if Jones was joking or not.

"I would 'preciate that." Jones chuckled.

"If I do shoot you, you can be assured it will not be intentional, and you have my sincerest apologies in advance."

"A fat lot of good an apology does me. The plan is to use the mounts to get close to the herd of wild deer. You'll have to shoot from a mounted position. Can you do that?"

"After hours of practice, I can now hit what I intend out to about twenty yards. It remains to be seen if I can accomplish it while mounted. Is this the only way to hunt deer?"

"It's not the only way, but unless you feel up to endless hours of tracking and stalking, at the end of which you may not get close enough to take a shot, it is more efficient. We'll be hunting on the plain, so the techniques differ. The mounts, being deer themselves, will afford us a means to get closer to more targets than you could hope for otherwise. Out here, in this Great Wide Open, it's hard to sneak up on the deer. They can see you coming for miles, and they'll smell you long before they'll see you."

"How do others hunt?" Zeke said.

"Murdock, being more of a mountain dweller and used to using trees to hide, either stalks or hunts from a stand, or some other feature that gives him the advantage. Wolves hunt in packs. They can chase the deer for hours and hope to cut the weak from the herd. We don't want to startle the herd. We want to blend in. Do you understand all that, Professor?"

Jones, of late, had taken to calling Zeke *Professor*, as a means of showing that even though Zeke may be well-educated, he was still ignorant of certain life skills. A fact that Zeke was already painfully aware.

"From this point forward, don't talk," Jones said, as both men settled themselves astride the mounts. "Don't nock an arrow until we're in the midst of our targets. You can control your mount with your knees once we are in the thick, freeing your hands to shoot. Your mount knows what to do, so trust her."

Zeke nodded, and both men rode off toward the stream.

———

Ted Wagner, with four of the miners, crouched behind trees close to the walled stockade that protected Reyes and the rest of her group. They had spent a number of days traveling. Climbing the ridge had been hard, but they'd managed. Once on this plateau, they followed a path that led to this stockade. Everyone was on high alert when two men exited the stockade and started off toward the river by way of a well-worn path.

"Everyone stays hidden," Wagner hissed to his followers. "We have to surprise them, so we have to use the trees for cover. If you see something, say something. No kill shots, either. Shoot to wound, not kill. Chico and George, you two go back a hundred yards or so, cross this clearing and position yourselves to ambush those two on their way back. Stay hidden from them and the stockade. I want them injured so they can call out to their fellows. When they come out to help, we'll take them."

Everyone nodded.

"It's a good plan," Fred whispered, after the two men had gone. "It beats attacking them when they're all locked inside and have plenty of cover to defend themselves."

Wagner glared at Fred. "So nice to know my plan meets with your approval. I want the rest of us to secret ourselves as close to the stockade as possible. Be ready to shoot to wound without getting shot ourselves. We may be few in number, but with surprise on our side, we should be able to gain a victory."

———

Chico Hernandez and George Robinson had hid themselves behind trees and not far off the path, by lying down. Each wore leather boots, breechclouts, and Gora-style cloaks, all made from deer hide. Since they had left the fur on, they blended into the shadows cast by the surrounding trees. Their positions allowed them good visibility of the stockade gate as well as the path.

Shortly after they were in position, they heard the two men from the stockade talking as they approached. When the men reached the agreed upon trigger point of the ambush, Chico and George fired their crossbows, aiming for their targets' legs. Both men hit the ground, as did the fish they'd been carrying, and they started screaming for help.

Chico and George, hurried to reload their crossbows and were ready when four more men came out of the stockade. Once in range, they fired again, taking down two more men. Per Wagner's instructions, they maintained their positions and remained motionless. The two uninjured men picked up the dropped fish and proceeded to help the injured into the stockade. Before they could gain the safety of the stockade, they were also hit in the legs. All the injured were wailing and screaming for help.

"I don't know who you are, but you just pissed off the wrong people!" said a female voice, from inside the stockade. "You just wait until Murdock hears about this. He'll have your hides stretched on his barn walls."

Upon hearing Murdock's name, Wagner and his men began to wonder if this was Murdock's home.

"Bring him out!" Wagner yelled back. "I welcome him to stick his nose into matters that don't concern him. I put him down once and I'll do it again."

One of his men touched his arm. Wagner glared down at him and the man shook his head.

"Murdock isn't here right now," said the female voice. "But

I'm expecting him momentarily. You better clear out while you can."

"Surrender your holdings!" Wagner said. "We're prepared to wait until you all starve. We mean to take your stockade. If you wish to survive, then exit now while you can."

"What's to prevent us from shutting and barring the gates?"

"Then your injured men will die. None of us will lift a finger to help them. Come out now and save your men and yourselves."

"What are you going to do?" Bass Heartly said. "We can't outlast them. We sent the pair to get fish because we're in dire need of food. The other four were sent to help the pair into the safety of the stockade, and, now they lay outside bleeding and wounded. You and I are all that's left, so what are you going to do?"

Elizabeth Reyes looked around the inside of the stockade that had been her home for so many years. To her, it was a squalid place. Too hot in summer, too cold in winter, and too much pain and suffering associated with it.

"My first instinct is to leave and let them have this place," Reyes said. "If it weren't for their attack, we probably would have left before winter. I don't like the idea of being forced out."

"Well, we *are* being forced out," Bass said, "and our comrades are dying as we dither. Make up your mind."

"Go out and speak to them," Reyes finally said. "I need some assurances for our safety."

"And if they don't deign to give you assurances, then what? You've already misled them into thinking we have some special relationship with Murdock. They obviously didn't buy it."

"Speak to them anyway. Work the best deal you can get. I'm tired, Bass. Tired of the weight of leadership."

"Can we parley?" Bass called over the stockade wall.

Wagner's eyebrows shot up when he heard the word *parley*.

"We have them now," he whispered to those around him. "We've already won." Wagner inhaled deeply and shouted toward the stockade, "One person, unarmed. Any tricks, and they'll be killed immediately."

Wagner didn't have to wait long for the gate to open enough to allow one person to come out.

"Walk straight away from the gate and stay within the clearing," Wagner said. "Keep him covered. Anything untoward, and you are free to shoot to wound," he said to those close to him.

"Who's going out to talk with him?" said one of his compatriots.

Wagner straightened and readjusted his cloak and weapons. "I am."

He stepped from the protection of the trees and strutted toward the man, who looked bedraggled and defeated. His clothes were threadbare and hung off his body. Wagner could tell he had been through a lot, including starvation.

"What is it you wish to parley about?"

"Our leader requires some… assurances," Heartly said.

"You are defeated. In spirit, if not in fact. What assurances does your leader require and why should I grant any of them?"

"Magnanimity would be a good reason. You are victorious, and so can afford to be magnanimous, I'd think. All we're asking for is you to spare our lives, including those injured."

"I'll grant it when your leader and any who remain inside come out and bow down to me. There is a certain pleasure I can get from Murdock bowing before me."

"Um… about that. That may be a problem."

"Why is that a problem?"

"Our leader, against all advice, tried to use Murdock's name in an attempt to scare you off."

Wagner's face heated. "That was foolish! And if I'd said

either Murdock surrenders or I kill every one of you, then what?"

"You could, but Murdock wouldn't do anything about it. I guess you could say we burned that bridge a while ago." Heartly smirked and shrugged. "We have no way of contacting him."

Wagner started storming around the hapless Heartly. "I want this… this fool of a leader brought before me. Restrained, if you must, but do so immediately. Now get out of my sight before I kill you where you stand."

Heartly ran back to the stockade.

Wagner called his men to him. "Send someone over to help those injured men. I don't want them dying just yet. But tell everyone to be ready. We could still be attacked. If we are, kill them all."

As Wagner continued to storm around, yelling at the sky, Heartly and Reyes shuffled toward him. He stopped his ranting when he saw the pair approaching.

Heartly shoved Reyes to her knees at Wagner's feet. "This is our leader. Elizabeth Reyes. She is the one who lied to you."

"You lied to me!" Wagner roared.

"You attacked a peaceful compound," Reyes said. "What did you expect?"

Wagner backhanded the kneeling Reyes across the face, sending her sprawling. Blood started to leak from her lips as she tried to get to her feet. He kicked her in the stomach, raising her off the ground a few inches, and she fell onto her back, gasping for air and holding her ribs.

"Who else is inside the stockade?" Wagner roared at Heartly.

"N-no one else. We were all that was left."

Wagner motioned to his men to advance on the stockade, and his men ran to investigate.

"You better hope my men don't get so much as a stubbed toe, otherwise you're all dead," Wagner spewed through clenched teeth.

It was a couple hours later when Wagner called for his captives. He was sitting with his back to the cave that Reyes had been using as her own throne room. All his men had been fed the fish that Reyes' men had gathered.

Wagner stood, with a small fire between him and his captives. "Today you were defeated by a superior force. I claim the area from the river to the mountains, as my own. Additionally, you are all now my property, for me to do with as I please. Not wanting to be vengeful, I'm going to allow you the opportunity to join us, of your own volition. I need fighting men and hunters, and because of your survival, I'm assuming you know how to hunt and use the bows we found.

"I'm also assuming that Tutt was here and gave you the bows. He is now dead, as are his two companions. So any deal you had with him is null and void. You are at my mercy, and to be merciful, I'm allowing you the choice to join me, freely. What say you?"

"What about Reyes?" Heartly said.

"I have no use for a lying wench, especially one that would argue and plague me for the rest of my days, or until I tire of her. But I'll give her a choice. I have men here and elsewhere who haven't been with a woman for a long time. She may be of use in that capacity."

"I'm of more use to you as an advisor," Reyes whispered. "I've surrendered to you. This place and these men are now yours. But I, on the other hand, know things you don't. Information is always a commodity."

"That may be true, but how can I trust you to be truthful? Besides, anything you know, your men would know, and knowing they'd be rewarded for such information would be a big incentive."

"There are things that my men don't know. There are observations I've made and kept to myself. There are people that

175

Murdock has surrounded himself with. But these observations I intend to keep to myself for now. I need assurances that I'll be there when Murdock finally falls. I want to see that for myself."

"I'll make sure you see him fall," Wagner said, with venom. "So tell me what you know."

"Privately, I will... eventually," Reyes said, seductively. "Publicly, I'll keep things I know to myself."

Reyes saw Wagner's face take on an intense smirk. "You don't trust me?"

"About as much as you trust me," Reyes returned the intense smirk.

———

Zeke and Harris were bathing after his return from their successful hunt.

Zeke and Jones had taken a deer. Zeke, however, hadn't made the kill-shot which resulted in more fresh meat.

"Did you learn anything from your hunt with Jones?" Harris snuggled closer to Zeke in the hot water.

"Before coming here, I mistakenly viewed hunting as being more like shopping." Zeke smirked. "I had no idea how many things can go wrong to ruin your chances. Since Jones made the kill, I got to experience firsthand how much work is involved in the whole process."

"Did you get along with Jones?"

"Eventually. He does have a ...quirky sense of humor."

"As do you. What are your views on psychic abilities?"

Zeke sat up straighter and tried to peer around Harris' head, which had been resting on his chest.

"Are you serious?"

"Serious? Yes. I just want your opinion."

Zeke cleared his throat, as Irene had noticed, was his habit when discussing subjects that made him uncomfortable.

"Some of the listed ones are sheer hokum, like the ones prefaced with *clair*— clairaudience, clairsentience, all the ones listed under clairvoyance. Some, however, I suppose are possible, but I haven't witnessed them personally. Is that what you're asking, or did you have something more specific in mind?"

"What about telepathy?" Harris asked hesitantly.

"What about it? I know it's supposed to be the ability to transmit and receive thoughts from others. But like I said, I've not seen anything that convinced me it was actually possible."

"Telekinesis?"

"Isn't that supposed to be the same as levitation? I've heard of others supposedly having that ability, but I've not witnessed it. Why are you asking? Are you going to tell me that you, a learned woman of science, read tea leaves? Speaking of tea, I'd love some Earl Grey hot, if you please. Or do you prefer reading chicken entrails? Not that I've seen a chicken, or any other fowl around here."

Zeke thought he heard Irene snort, but in previous experience with her laughing, she shook, as most people do. He didn't feel her shaking at all, but he did feel her chest rise and fall as she breathed.

"Do you trust me?" Irene said, after a long pause.

"That's a silly question. Of course, I do."

"Can I trust you?"

"Of course! Why would you ask that?"

"Those of us in-the-know have agreed to keep a well-guarded secret. I'm trying to ascertain if you're trustworthy enough to be… enlightened. Are you?" Irene moved away so she could look at Zeke's face.

"I'd like to think I'm an enlightened person. So please, enlighten me."

"On this planet, there are life forms that are far superior to humans. Their intellect is as far above us as we are above mice."

"I read a book once, where the mice were hyper-intelligent, pan-dimensional beings. So you don't mean those kinds of mice?" Zeke interjected jovially.

Irene slapped his wet bicep. "I'm being serious! If you can't take me seriously, then I'm not so sure I should tell you." She turned her back to him and crossed her arms.

"Are you pouting? I thought you were beyond that kind of emotional manipulation."

"All women pout in one form or another, no matter our age. Sometimes it's the only way we can get a man to pay attention to us."

Zeke tried, unsuccessfully, to stifle a laugh. He made a motion as if to put on his serious mask.

"Okay, I'm seriously listening and paying attention to whatever you have to say. Please continue."

Irene turned and glared at him. "I'd also appreciate it if you'd keep your comments to yourself until I finish."

"I promise to be all ears."

"You better, you... you man, you, if you know what's good for you," Zeke heard inside his mind.

It was Irene's voice, but he had been watching her full pouting lips and they never moved.

Zeke's jaw dropped.

Annie Cooper was visiting Heather Stevens and Alvin Jones at their home, on the opposite side of the river from the medical facility. She was listening to the small talk in the main room of the cabin, with some of her consciousness, while a smaller part was paying attention to the enlightenment of Zeke Jakes by Irene Harris. Annie and Irene had previously discussed that enlightenment, and had received approval from Murdock and Beron for it to take place.

"Did I say something funny?" Heather said, after hearing a chuckle escape Annie.

"No, I was just thinking of something funny. Sorry."

Heather nodded to Alvin and he left the cabin.

"I have something important to discuss with you," Heather said. "I had a discussion with Murdock back when he, Harris, and Zeke went to get the pod that's now parked outside the medical facility."

"What did that discussion concern?" Annie had discussed it with Harris and Murdock, so she knew what was coming.

"Communication. Specifically, the type of communication you, Harris, and Murdock enjoy. As I told Murdock at the time, and I reiterate now, I want in."

Annie pursed her lips. "As Murdock told you, that was something you decided to forego when you chose not to join our tribe."

Heather looked crushed. "I know. That was then, and it was a mistake. I chose to not be lonely over something *I knew* was better."

Annie glanced down at her feet. "Why are you with Alvin? Do you love him?"

"Love? I wouldn't go *that* far." Heather looked sad. "At the time, I was lonely and wasn't thinking too clearly, or wasn't thinking with my brain. Later, we just sorta …needed each other to survive. Admittedly, there are times I wish I had somewhere else to go."

"And other times?" Annie said.

"I'll admit that I'd miss him. But there's a reason we have no kids." Her head was down, her back turned to Annie.

"Are you crying?" came to Heather's mind.

Heather's head snapped up and she spun to face Annie.

"What did you say?" Heather's expression showed fear.

"You heard me the first time."

Annie saw Heather's chin quiver and tears start down her cheeks.

"Stop that," Annie said. "It's time to put on your big girl panties. You have been given a gift, but it is limited."

"Limited? In what way is it limited?" Heather brushed the tears from her cheeks.

179

"You are not connected directly to everyone, just to me," Annie stared at her. "That's mostly because the rest don't trust you completely, and with good reason. At the time you were asked to join, I'd lobbied for your inclusion. That you declined the invitation hurt all who had vouched for you—me, Doc Harris, and Murdock.

"Murdock? You're teasing me!"

"He was impressed with your observational skills, that you spoke your mind, and your loyalty. I lobbied for you because of all the time we spent as prisoners, and during observations and conversations, it took me a while to trust you, but I did. And still do. Consequently, I'm the one tuning you in, so to speak. So don't abuse it. You can use it if you need help or just to chat, but the latter is best kept to a minimum. Also, you will have to watch what you think."

"Watch what I think? Who can do that?"

"You do it by disciplining your mind. Try meditation. It worked for me. If you don't, you'll wear out your welcome, and I'll have to tune you out."

"But how will I know it's working?"

"A fair question. Clear your mind."

Heather did some deep breathing in an attempt to clear her mind.

"Good enough for a test," Annie said. "Now think of something I wouldn't already know."

Heather did as requested.

"No, the size of Alvin's... um, ...member doesn't interest me in the least. And neither does your assessment of his oral skills. Annie closed her eyes and rubbed them. "That's what I meant by watching what you think. And you don't need to shout, either."

Heather's mouth fell open.

Just as Heather was getting her composure under control, Alvin entered the cabin.

"Sorry to interrupt, but one of your old friends is here, Heather."

180

It was then that Annie noticed the crossbow slung over his shoulder.

"Stay behind me, Heather." Annie turned and extended an open hand toward Alvin before he could train his crossbow on anyone.

Alvin slammed against the wall and crumpled to the floor. Annie headed for the door, with Heather on her heels. Upon opening the door, Annie saw several men, some injured, some not, and a lot of loaded crossbows aimed at her.

"Well, well, well!" said Ted Wagner. "I didn't expect this pleasant surprise." He grinned at the two women. "Part of my lifelong task was to return you two to my... um, care."

Heather looked one direction and Annie looked the other, trying to determine which way to run.

"Running will afford you nothing," Wagner snarled. "You two belong to me now, thanks to Alvin."

"Now what?" flashed to Annie's mind, from Heather. *"Not again! I can't go through that again."*

"Stay calm and follow me no matter what." Annie brought her extended arms and hands together in a clapping motion.

A concussive wave extended out from her to about fifty feet beyond the would-be attackers, and everyone was knocked off their feet. The few crossbows that fired had sent their bolts into the air and away from their intended targets.

"Now run!" Annie sprinted toward the medical facility.

She could hear Heather panting behind her.

"Irene, I need help. We'll be under attack soon. Inform the family."

"Heather, keep running and don't be shocked by what happens," Annie flashed.

When Annie reached the river, she levitated Heather and herself over the river and over the wall of the medical compound.

"What the—" Heather said, as her feet touched the grounds inside the walled enclosure.

"Come on," Annie said, and both ran to the portcullis.

Seeing it closed and secure, Annie levitated above the tunnel and ran to the stone gate. Seeing it closed, she breathed a little easier.

"Okay, Heather, what the hell happened!" Irene Harris strode into the courtyard.

Heather turned to see Harris accompanied by a much slimmer and shaven Zeke Jakes. It shocked her to see them together.

"Um… I'm still trying to figure it all out myself," Heather replied. "Annie and I were having such a nice… conversation, when Alvin came in saying something about an old friend."

"Alvin had a crossbow when he came in," Annie said.

"And I assume he didn't have one when he left you two alone?" Irene said.

"Hell, I've never seen a crossbow until a few minutes ago!" Heather replied.

"Where did they get crossbows?" Zeke said. "They would be the next logical improvement from the bows we have and the ones they used to attack us before. But where did they get them?"

Irene glared at him, and Zeke decided now wasn't the time.

"Who was it that attacked you?" Irene asked Annie and Heather.

Annie chuckled. "They didn't actually attack. I didn't give them that chance. I hit them with a concussion wave before they could do anything. It was Ted Wagner."

"Him again? Damn, that boy is persistent." Irene smirked. "Not too bright, though. I'm sure Murdock will have a few choice words for him."

Annie frowned. "You and I both know it won't be words."

———

It took more than a few minutes for Alvin to come to his senses and get to his feet. When he opened the door, all he saw were bodies all over the place.

He strode around, checking to see if any were still alive, and was surprised to find that everyone was still alive. They'd just been unconscious.

"What the hell hit us?" Wagner said, when he started to come around. His head ached and he didn't know from what. "And where the hell were you, Jones? I thought you were going to take care of restraining the women?"

"I was going to, but that bitch Annie hit me with something. I just woke up a few minutes before you did. What happened out here?"

"Annie...again!" Wagner managed. "We had her covered as soon as she opened the door. She clapped her hands together and wham-o. We were all tossed assholes over tea kettles. Where did she go?"

"I'm not sure." Alvin said. "But my guess is back to the medical facility. She would hide in there and wait for someone to rescue her."

"Someone? Or Murdock?" Wagner grinned.

"Are you spoilin' for a fight with him or sumpthin'?"

"Or something," Wagner spewed. "I have a score to settle with him."

"I hope it's important." Alvin shook his head. "If not, then you'll be dyin' for nuthin'."

"You let me worry about that. I want to know the best way into the medical facility."

"The best way is in through the door." Alvin chuckled. "But failing that, there isn't any. I guess you could throw yourself off the cliff, but that's a good forty-foot fall. You hit something before the ground, you could be dead. You hit the ground, you could be dead. So, there ain't no *good* way in, except the door."

Wagner thought about the situation for a while. "Would waiting them out work?"

"They are five. Six if White is there, which I have no inkling if he is or not. They have a fresh side of venison and plenty of water. I'd say they could stand you off for a month or more."

"Can't wait that long." Wagner shook his head. "How was it constructed? Can we pull down the walls or the door?"

Alvin Jones looked at Wagner. "First, no one knows how it was built. I'd heard something about Murdock doing it all himself, but that was probably just rumor and exaggeration. Second, I've seen the size of the blocks used. If you look, you can see the seams from here. Most of the slabs are twenty feet by thirty feet by two feet. You do the math of how much the granite would weigh and how many men it would take to pull down a free-standing block. Add any supports at all, and I'd say it'll come out to be more than you'll ever see. Third, if you were able to tunnel under the wall, you'll have to fight your way up and inside the main living quarters on the third floor. You'd lose more men than you got just to get inside the wall. The most inexperienced person inside is an old guy, a newcomer. For no more than I've seen him practice, he ain't no slouch. The rest are dead-shots. Meaning, you give them a shot, you dead."

"It can't be as impossible as you think, Jones. I'm sure there's a flaw somewhere that can be exploited."

"Here's a kicker for ya. Murdock is on his way here right now. So just sayin', the clock's tickin'."

Cry havoc and let slip the dogs of war!

— WILLIAM SHAKESPEARE, *JULIUS CAESAR*

The area around Murdock's and Declan's homes was a flurry of activity.

"Who's going?" Declan asked the adults sitting around the table.

"I have to," Murdock said. "We all know who is attacking. I've stated many times that I protect the medical facility—how can I now abandon them?"

"I'm going," Mei Lee said. "Annie and Irene are friends, family. I can't stay behind."

"I'm going," Emily said, just as Murdock was about to object. "For the same reason as Mei Lee."

"I'm going," Declan said, as Murdock was raising his arms to object. "I'm going for my friend, my brother. To watch his back, because he needs it."

Murdock raised his arms. "As much as I appreciate it, I think our resources are best served by Declan and Emily staying behind. You have kids to raise. No one will watch my back like

185

Mei Lee. I would rather go alone, but you all wouldn't have that."

"Do you have a plan?" Declan said.

"Sure. Defend the medical facility." Murdock shrugged. "I'd think that would be obvious."

"Not what I meant. Do you care to share any details of your plan?"

"How can I do that before I see the situation? All I have right now is the most general of goals."

"Okay. Well, if you need anything, just ask. We'll keep the home fires burning."

"Just not so hot that you burn down the house," Murdock teased.

"*Is everyone okay?*" Murdock flashed.

"*We're fine, so far,*" Irene replied. "*Where are you?*"

"*Mei Lee and I are sitting on the edge of the plateau just across the river from you. Anything new in the situation?*"

"*Nothing. They do shoot over the wall periodically, but we still have no idea what they want or the why behind it. Alvin is on the outside, you know.*"

"*How's Heather taking it?*" Mei Lee flashed.

"*Surprisingly better than I would have thought.*"

"So how do you want to handle this?" Murdock said.

Ted Wagner was doing his best to get his men placed at regular intervals around the three assailable sides of the medical facility. He had sent a runner to the men who were poised outside Rogers' cave complex. Their instructions were to prevent any aid coming from anyone inside.

When Wagner looked around, his gaze seemed to gravitate to the plateau.

He grabbed a man and pointed toward the plateau edge. "What is that?"

"Looks like somebody sitting on the edge, to me." The man returned to his assigned task.

Wagner looked around for Alvin Jones and sauntered in his direction, when he spotted him. As he moved, he kept glancing up to the edge.

"What do you make of that?" Wagner asked Jones, indicating the plateau.

"Looks like someone's curious about our doin's," Jones said, after staring at those on the plateau.

"I'm wondering who they are. It can't be Murdock already. Are we missing anyone?"

"I'm not in charge of keepin' track of your people."

"Do you think you could hit them with your bow?"

"'Tis a bit far, but I can try."

Jones raised his bow and drew the arrow back. As he did, he elevated his target point. When he was happy with conditions, he released the arrow.

He and Wagner tried to watch the arrow's flight to see where it would land, but it passed from their view.

Wagner gave up on seeing the arrow land, and turned. "It's too far for me to—"

"Duck!" Jones pulled Wagner down just as an arrow whizzed past their heads.

Wagner jumped to his feet and glared up at those sitting on the edge of the plateau. He heard Jones moving around behind him.

"Look." Jones was holding two arrows, one metal, the other wooden.

"So?"

"The metal one is what I shot. The wooden one is what just missed us."

"Are you having fun?" Mei Lee said.

"As a matter of fact… yes." Murdock chuckled as he re-slung his bow over his shoulder. "It's been a long time since I've been this… entertained."

"Well, stop antagonizing them. You aren't helping the situation."

"Was I supposed to help the situation, or help Irene and company?"

"Ideally, I would hope you'd do both."

"So what are we going to do about Heather?" Murdock asked. "I was a little put out when I heard Alvin had changed sides."

"Isn't that Irene's call?" Mei Lee asked. "She's the one in charge of the medical facility, and by default, all those inside its walls."

"It is…and it isn't," Murdock said. "Irene may be in charge of the medical facility, but I'm in charge of keeping the Oomah safe. If I thought Irene was making a mistake, should I say something or let her make her own mistakes? I normally lean toward letting her make her own mistakes. That being said, I'm the one who talked Heather and Alvin into moving their operation up here. So it falls to me to fix it."

Mei Lee looked at Murdock compassionately. "There's nothing for you to fix. You helped them get established on this plateau—more help than I would have provided—and they've made their own choices. It's not something you need to fix. Now we have family members under attack. To me, that seems the more immediate problem. What are your intentions?"

"My intentions? My intention is to do nothing—"

"What!" Mei Lee shrieked. "You intend to do nothing?"

"Calm down, Mei. You didn't let me finish. I intend to do nothing I don't have to. I built the medical facility with an attack of this nature in mind. Each block making up the wall is over a hundred tons. To pull down a single block would require more men than exist on this planet. The residence area has its bulk under the edge of the plateau above and is three-stories tall. Add to that it was designed with limited access to those who can't levitate. Since none of the attackers can, it's my opinion that they are unlikely to enter the living quarters, even if they gain access to the inside of the compound. If someone does manage to gain entry, then I'll do something. However, everyone carrying on down there," Murdock pointed to the commotion at the medical facility, "needs to learn something. Our friends need to learn to trust their own skills, and they need to trust my skills."

"And what do the attackers need to learn?"

"They need to learn that just because I built something, it doesn't mean that taking it will be easy or beneficial."

"So our friends and family aren't in any danger?"

"The danger is real, but it isn't the same as they believe it is. Short of explosives, the attackers won't gain entry. The pressing danger is from a stray arrow or two and complacency. If anyone inside the wall would take up their bows, they'd drive off the attack. The simple act of shooting back would give the attackers pause."

"What makes you think that?"

"Before coming here to this planet, most of those below us were limited. They had no idea what it takes to win a fight for survival. They're used to things being fair. They're used to disputes being refereed by someone—police, courts, someone to keep things from going too far. If you're in a fight for survival, there is no such thing as fair. In fact, if you're not doing absolutely everything you can to win, then you aren't trying hard enough."

"*Have any of you tried to fire back at your attackers?*" Murdock flashed to Irene. "*Just the act of fighting back should drive off some, if not all.*"

"*Annie and I can't. We are precluded from harming anyone because of our Oath.*"

"*So you're saying you two are martyrs to be crucified on your caduceus?*" Murdock flashed to Annie and Irene.

"*Actually, it is called the rod of Asclepius,*" Harris replied. "*A caduceus is something else.*" Harris flashed back, with some contriteness.

"*I stand corrected.*" Murdock smiled.

"That was an interesting point," Annie said to Irene.

They had all been crouching in a corner, far from the arrows flying over the walls.

"What was?" Heather looked from Annie to Irene, and back.

"What do you think?" Irene asked Zeke.

"About what?"

"Does my Hippocratic Oath prohibit me from defending myself?" Irene looked down.

"I don't know, does it?" Zeke shrugged. "It's not for me to tell you what the oath you took means to you. Only you can answer that."

Zeke got to his feet and pulled his bowstring a few times. "Your oath doesn't preclude me from defending myself." He moved closer to the outside area.

Annie nodded at him and donned her quiver and tested her own bowstring.

"Annie, sit down!" Irene said. "Your Oath!"

Annie looked at Irene. "The oath you took means something to you, as mine means something to me. I have the right to defend myself and I will. I'll worry about the implications of the Oath after the crisis has passed." She turned to follow Zeke outside the living quarters.

Zeke and Annie hurried to the crenelated section of the outside wall, stopping several times to avoid incoming arrows.

"Aim as best you can," Annie said to Zeke. "They won't quit if you don't try to hit them."

"I've never killed anything with a bow." He panted.

"Me neither," Annie smirked. "First time for everything, though."

The pair split to opposite ends of the protected wall and started to return fire.

"What the hell is going on!" Wagner said. "Why are the fighters backing away from the wall?"

"Maybe they don't like gettin' shot at." Alvin pointed toward the facility wall.

Wagner could barely see arrows being fired down at his men from the top of the wall. As he marched toward a few of the men retreating, one caught an arrow in the shoulder. The man whirled and yelled in pain, dropping his bow.

"Take him back out of range," Wagner told a couple of men who were advancing to the rear.

"All those in the open, rush to the wall!" Wagner said.

Just as he finished giving the command, his shoulder was yanked down from behind. An arrow narrowly missed him.

"What the hell are they supposed to do once they get to the wall?" Jones said. "Once they're in a position next to the wall, they're trapped, or at best, ineffective. So what's the point?"

"Maybe we can tunnel under the wall."

"You have no idea what you're doin', do ya?" Jones castigated. "I've been inside those walls. If any make it under the wall, they'll be picked off from inside. You won't get anyone to go first through the tunnel, even if you succeed in diggin' one. Those castley-lookin' structures will allow those inside a way ta shoot down at the men at the wall, and they'll be protected while they do it. Your best bet is ta retreat. For now, anyways."

After thinking about it for a second, Wagner nodded.

"All you guys in the open, grab the wounded and fall back to

191

my cabin," Jones yelled. "The rest can stay behind cover for now."

Just before dark, Annie and Zeke heard someone yelling, "Medic!"

Annie peeked over the wall. "What do you want!"

"We need medical attention."

"You should've thought of that before you attacked us."

"Annie! We are medicos! We need to tend the injured," Harris flashed to Annie.

"Why? We didn't ask them to attack us. Why should we put ourselves at risk?" Annie responded.

"We have to do something."

"Leave your injured next to the wall and move away," Annie yelled.

"How far?"

"We can see some distance. We won't open the gate as long as we can see you."

"You have to help the injured," someone pleaded.

"That might have been true once, but now we reserve the right to deny service to anyone for any reason."

Zeke started laughing while he peeked over the wall.

"You're the only medical professionals on the planet. You have to help."

"By not following my directions," Annie said, "you're reducing the potential survivability of your fellows. Move the wounded to the wall and leave."

She peeked over the wall and could see several of the wounded being helped to the base of the wall.

"Zeke," Annie whispered, and motioned for him to come to her position. "Keep an eye on the uninjured. I want them out of sight."

"Any ideas on how we can determine if the uninjured have moved

off?" Annie flashed.

"I'll make sure they are far away from the wall while you transfer the injured inside," Murdock replied. *"I would, however, be very careful that there aren't any false injuries. They could fake injuries just to get inside."*

"I'll gather all the arrows I can find outside the walls," Annie said to Zeke. "Irene will be out to assess the injuries, and with Heather's help, get the injured inside. We need you to provide over watch. If you see someone that could present a danger, raise the alarm and fire at them."

Zeke nodded.

After the attackers had moved out of sight, Irene levitated the door of the medical facility. Annie placed precut logs near the corners to hold the stone open. Zeke, who was walking the platform above the formed tunnel, watched Irene hurry around the injured. She was, with Heather's help, disarming the injured before they were moved inside the door. They were lined up under Zeke's feet, against a wall, weapons piled just inside the door.

Zeke had noticed that the door was raised and lowered inside a track cut into the stone walls on either side of it. The door faced upriver. *How did Murdock managed a door like that. One would think the door would be more of a drawbridge style. The top of the wall I'm walking already looks like a castle. Why not go all out? How do they open that door? A solid stone that size would be heavy.*

"About fifty tons," Murdock said, from behind Zeke.

Zeke jumped and jerked around. "What?" he said, voice quavering.

"That door weighs close to fifty tons. That is what you were thinking, isn't it? That's what everyone asks about the door."

"How did you get up here, and where did you come from?" Zeke frowned.

Murdock gave him a whimsical look. "There are things you need to know, and there are things you don't need to know. What you just asked belongs in the second group. You weren't paying attention to everything, just to the immediate threats." He smirked. "Which is a good thing. It's what you're up here to do."

Zeke turned his attention outward, with a scowl. "I don't like being surprised like that. It makes me uneasy."

"Lots of things make *me* uneasy." Murdock sat on the edge of one of the crenels. "Did you manage to hit any of the attackers?"

"I don't know," Zeke snapped. "Did any of them say I did?"

"I don't know." Murdock exhaled. "I haven't asked any of them yet. I'm asking because I know how you'd feel about it if you did."

"And exactly how would you know?"

"I know you aren't angry with me right now. You're upset with those that forced you to do something you don't like doing. You're resenting them because they forced you to defend your-self, something you clearly have resigned yourself to doing, and that you, nonetheless, find distasteful. You need to let it go."

"And how do I do that?"

"You're a smart man. You know we're not in a situation that could be considered civilized. This is the wild frontier. People will take advantage of those they perceive as weaker. It takes more intestinal fortitude than most think to live out here."

"They attack us and then they want our help?" Zeke growled. "That's delusional!"

"It shows how little they understand about surviving. They didn't necessarily want to kill you. They want you to surrender to them and their policies. However, if you refuse to surrender completely to them, they will kill you."

Zeke nodded. "Too bad they can't leave the peaceful alone."

"The way I had envisioned things working is people go out and do what they can to survive. Groups would support each other and care for each member of the group. Everyone would work together for the benefit of their group. Those that are able to hunt, hunt. Those who can't hunt, gather whatever edibles they can find. Everyone helps with the building."

"Too bad things seldom work out that way," Zeke added. "Human nature says those who can get others to produce for them, will do all they can to do it. Those with no morals won't develop any morals out here."

"They may… if someone teaches them the benefits of having morals."

Both men chuckled.

Chris Gundersen and Dirk Benson were setting up a pair of ropes to rappel down the cliff face close to the stream and the pods. Curtis and Angelica Griffen were trying to grasp the concepts involved in rappelling as it was being explained to them by Benson. Fifteen others stood around taking in the information, but strangely remained to themselves and asked no questions.

Benson had just stepped off the cliff, as did Curtis Griffen, when a tall, slight female with long, wavy, brown hair, blue eyes came bouncing over to Gundersen and the rest of those waiting their turn to rappel off the cliff, to the plateau below.

"Wait up!" She ran up.

"We ain't goin' anywheres fast," Chris said, without taking his eyes off those rappelling. "No need to run."

"Nice!" she said with a high level of sprightliness. "I didn't want to be late for any instructions. I have this thing about being left behind."

Chris glanced at her and noticed an apologetic look.

"I'm Melanie …Burton." She thrust out an open hand.

Chris looked at her hand and made no motion to take it. "Sorry, but I'm a little busy to be shakin' hands right this second." He felt a flush run across his face.

Melanie's face turned red and she shrugged. "Sorry. I didn't think... which is something else I usually do... don't do... whatever."

"Apologies not necessary, Mel." Chris shrugged. "Just watch when I set up the next pair. You'll get it."

Melanie's face clouded. "Do I look like a Mel to you? My name is Melanie. M-e-l-a-n-i-e. Not Mel, Lanie, or Mimi, or any other name you care to call me. If we're going to be traveling together, everyone had better see to it they use my name correctly. Just making sure you all understand that before we get off on the wrong foot."

Chris looked at her, shocked into silence. He glanced at the rest of the group, then turned his gaze back to the task at hand.

Angelica chuckled and turned her back on Melanie.

"You got something to say?" Melanie said to Angelica.

"Oh, Mel, get over yourself."

Chris tried to keep his face hidden as he grinned. After a few seconds, he chanced a glance at Melanie. He saw her glaring at Angelica, her face turning deep red.

Just as the sun was setting, the group of twenty that had rappelled down from the pod landing had reached the next plateau by following the stream.

"Everyone, get camp set," Benson said. "We'll spend the night here and rappel down to the next plateau in the morning."

"How far downstream are we goin'?" Chris Gundersen said, as he built a campfire.

"What I'd like to do is head downstream for a few days," Benson placed a couple fish he'd caught and cleaned, to cook. "However, I seriously doubt this group will hang together that

196

long." He sat close to the fire to tend the fish. "If you need a way to light your campfire, come get an ember."

Gundersen got up to fill their waterskins.

"Could I trouble someone to help me?" Melanie said.

"And you are?" Benson replied.

He was enjoying looking at the tall, leggie girl standing across the fire from him.

"Hey, Melanie." Chris entered the firelight.

"Aren't you going to introduce me?" Benson asked Gundersen. "Who is this luscious tidbit?"

Chris looked at Melanie, and even in the firelight, could see her blush.

"This is Melanie—"

"Melanie Burton," she said.

Chris turned. "Melanie, this is Dirk—"

"Dirk Benson." He rose to his feet and leered. "What is it you need?"

"I'm having a bit of trouble getting a fire going. Do you think Chris could help me with it?"

"He could." Benson smiled back at her. "Or I could."

"I just need a little help." Melanie shrugged.

Benson smiled as Chris dropped the waterskins. "Chris, give the lady a hand, won't you?"

Gundersen shrugged and followed Melanie to her campfire, carrying a burning stick.

"You got a fire ring?" he said, when they had traveled the short distance.

"Yes," Melanie said, softly. "And I have some wood in it. Just couldn't get the kindling to start."

"That's easy enough to rectify."

"I'm glad. I'm not really comfortable being out here in the dark. Those fifteen over there are about a fifteen on the creep-a-zoid meter. The brother and sister are about a ten or eleven, and Benson is about a nine."

"Benson is a nine?"

"Didn't you notice that little interchange? It struck me as being creepy." Melanie hugged herself and chafed her arms.

"Next thing, you'll be sayin' I'm creepy." Gundersen smirked and blew on the coals to get the small fire going.

"You will be soon enough," Melanie mumbled. "When you get older, that is. You are *male*, after all."

"You got a lot of brass sayin' things like that and askin' for help." Chris stood. "Your fire is goin', so enjoy. But you better figure out what you gonna do next time."

"What's that supposed to mean? Are you refusing to help me in the future?"

"Depends." Chris shrugged. "On what you have ta offer the rest of us *creeps*? That is what you called us?"

"Did you get her *fire* started?" Benson said, as Chris entered their campsite.

"Her *campfire* is going." Chris hunkered down to get his fish, which was now overcooked. "She's got some strange notions." He popped a piece of fish into his mouth.

"How so?" Benson said, as he ate.

"She thinks all men are *creeps*, as she put it."

"Feminist!" Benson chuckled. "You're right. She has some strange ideas, and they'll get changed soon enough. What did you say to her?"

"Basically, I said she better come up with some way of returning favors."

Benson laughed louder. "How'd she take that?"

"Don't know. Don't care." Chris shrugged. "She gotta learn that, out here, people will help, but it ain't all one-way. Sometimes all that's required is a kind word or a smile. Being called *creep* or *future creep* ain't the way ta influence people and make friends."

"Sounds like you could be getting sweet on her. Next thing

you know, you'll be wantin' to move in with her," Benson whined, "and leave your poor old mentor out in the cold to fend for his-self."

Chris laughed heartily. "Not frickin' likely!"

"Hello inside!" Ted Wagner yelled at the gate of the medical facility, accompanied by Alvin Jones. "Let me in!"

"Not by the hair of my chinny chin-chin," Murdock said, from his perch high above the gate. "Look, Zeke, it's Teddy Wagner. What is it you want, you little cucaracha?"

Jones started laughing and Wagner looked at him.

"What? What does that mean?" he whispered.

"He called you a cockroach."

"Why did you call me a cockroach!"

"Because you're a plague, just like cockroaches. A plague with a tiny brain—a constant source of irritation. And if you're not careful, you'll get squashed, just like a cockroach."

"I *demand* entrance to reclaim my warriors!"

"And if I refuse to admit you?"

"Then I'll attack to free my men from your torturers."

"I'd pay money to see that. I imagine it will be rather difficult, though. We have collected quite a number of arrows, both inside and out. I guess we'll see you again once you re-arm. Oh, and by the way, we've had no injuries. All the injuries are on your side. True to form, you require others to pay for your mistakes and ambitions."

Jones was watching Wagner and noticed that Murdock's baiting was working, as evidenced by Wagner's reddened face.

"Let me catch you out in the open!" Wagner said.

An arrow hit Wagner in the thigh, most of it poking out from the back of his thigh.

"*Ahhhh!*"

Jones started to grab Wagner to help.

199

"I'd leave him if I was you," Murdock said.

Wagner was writhing on the ground as he tried to pull the arrow out. Jones raised his hands and stepped away from him.

It took several minutes for Wagner to calm down and quit screaming.

"Piss-poor shot, Murdock!" he said. "I thought you were good at shooting."

"I hit exactly where I intended."

"Then you're dishonorable! You can't even face me. You have to shoot me from cover. While I was under a flag of truce, no less."

What the hell is Wagner talking about, Jones thought. *We have nothing to use as a flag for anything. I warned him that making demands at the gate could get him killed.*

Murdock chuckled. "I saw no flag, and I didn't grant you access to the gate of this facility. You are trespassing, and as such, will suffer the consequences of your actions."

Jones heard Wagner's screaming again. The wooden arrow pulled itself the rest of the way through his thigh. Once it cleared his leg, the arrow flew off toward Murdock's position. Wagner passed out. Jones took a step toward him.

"Leave, Alvin, while you're able," Murdock said.

"But he's injured. If you let me, I'll remove him." No response.

Shortly, Jones heard the gate rise, and Murdock walked out, the gate closing behind him.

"Take him." Murdock said. "But be advised—if I see him anywhere, I'll end him. You think this an idle threat?"

Jones shook his head rapidly.

"You're not as dumb as you look, Alvin. You want him? Take him. If I *ever* see him, it will be *the very last time.* He has outlived any tolerance I may have had. He won't see or hear me. I won't be reasonable. There won't be any bargaining. I won't feel pity or remorse. He'll just be dead."

Murdock turned and re-entered the medical facility.

It's been my experience that a word to the wise is seldom sufficient.
People just can't believe you're serious, until you show them. Then it's,
"Why is he so mean?"

— KEVIN MURDOCK, FAMILY CONVERSATIONS

Alvin Jones was checking Wagner's injury when he
came to.

"Where am I," Wagner said, groggily.

"You're in my house, which we'll have to leave," Jones said.
"You've really done it this time, Ted." He shook his head.

"Done what?"

"Murdock has had it with you. He said that if he sees you…
anywheres…you're dead." He offered Wagner some water.

He took a drink. "I've been threatened before."

"You were out of it, so what was said was as much for me as
it was for you. T'weren't no threat. Felt more like a promise."
Jones finished packing. "So I've decided that we need to vacate
the premises. I gave orders to the others to fall back to the mine
area."

"We aren't retreating! I refuse to retreat, when we've taken so much. I refuse to give it all up."

"Okay." Jones nodded. "Let me rephrase. I'm leavin'. Everyone who had been followin' you has already left. Don't know where—you were out of it for some time. Right now, we're in the house that Murdock built, and I'm leavin' before he comes around to evict me. After what I saw at the gate of the medical facility, I want no part of anything you got cookin' when it comes to Murdock or anyone he's protectin'. Nope, not interested. Everyone who was following said the same thing as they left."

"What did you see? What was it that made you turn on me?"

"I saw the arrow stuck through your thigh, pull itself out and take off back to Murdock. No one touched it, but off it flew just the same."

"Anything Murdock said wasn't serious."

Jones shook his head and stared down at the floor. "I've known Murdock for a while, just like you. Has he ever struck you as a jokester? To me, he has always struck me as being a most serious individual. A man of singular focus, an enduring commitment, and a dynamic force of will. Someone you really shouldn't mess with. And yet you keep on doin' it. Does *don't poke the bear* have any meaning for you at all?"

The half-smile on Wagner's face disappeared.

It had been several days since the small group had first rappelled down the cliff face by the pod landing. At first, they tried to cross one plateau a day, spending the mornings rappelling and the rest of the day walking. After the third day, that all changed. Until then, the trees seemed to be getting denser with each plateau. The beginning of the third day began by rappelling into a dense forest.

The order of the rappelling remained the same each day, so

Benson and Curtis were the first two over the edge, and Gundersen and Burton were last. When Gundersen and Burton reached the bottom of the plateau edge, they saw how much undergrowth was present. It appeared to be an ivy-type vine, lavender on the sunward side of the leaves, and deep blue-green on the underside.

"So now what, Benson?" Curtis Griffen said, with his balled fists on his hips. "This undergrowth is going to slow us down, you know, probably to the point that we won't be able to get to the plateau edge for weeks or months, if ever."

"Are you in a hurry, Griffen?" Benson said. "You have an appointment somewhere that I don't know about? So it takes us a while to get off this plateau. Have you noticed the size of the stream on this plateau? It's significantly larger. Not as big as the river, but bigger than it was on the plateau the pods landed on. This appears to be able to support our group more easily."

"But this undergrowth will stifle our movement."

"The undergrowth seems to be vines. That's exactly what we'll need to build a more permanent shelter. You're just looking for problems, rather than seeing possibilities. We've started on an open plain, and now we have a dense forest of large trees. Possibilities, Curtis, possibilities."

Gundersen, being one of the last ones down, coiled the ropes the way Benson had instructed him to make them ready for use on the next edge. He carried them to Benson and Griffen for them to carry to the next edge.

"And what happens if me and my sister decide to call it quits here?" Curtis said, as Gundersen came up to give them the ropes.

"Then I'll bid you farewell and move along." Benson took his rope from Gundersen. "Just let me know so I can give your rope to someone else for the next ridge. So decide. You have until we're ready to move, else we'll move on without you two."

Gundersen, Benson, and Griffen had all been standing close to the trees. Gundersen saw that the vines didn't get close to the stream. As he took off his waterskin to drink, he noticed it was empty. So he set off for the stream, but his feet refused to work and he ended up face down on the vines.

"What the—" Griffen noticed his own feet were anchored.

Benson bent to try to help Gundersen to his feet. He tried to shift his feet for leverage, but found they wouldn't move. When he looked down, he noticed the vines starting up his legs. He pulled out his eighteen-inch machete and started to cut the vines holding him. With the first cut, there was an ear-piercing sound that caused pain inside his skull. He glanced around and noticed that everyone was trapped by the vines.

Angelica Griffen was in the process of taking a drink from her waterskin when she saw the panic growing as everyone realized they were trapped. She dropped her waterskin without replacing the stopper and some of the water spilled on and around her feet. The vines released her feet and shrunk away from the dribbled water.

"Water! Use your water skins to splash water on the vines!" She dribbled liquid from her waterskin on the others' feet.

When they were released from the vines, they gathered at the edge of the stream and filled their waterskins to try and release the others. By the time they got to Gundersen, he was almost covered in the vines.

"Ow!" he screamed, as the vines retreated from the water being splashed.

It felt like they were ripping his skin.

When everyone was free of the vines and congregated at the stream's edge, they all did a self-evaluation. Gundersen, however, was being stared at by Benson.

Since Chris was the only one who'd lost his footing and fell into the vines, he seemed to be the only one injured. His injuries were limited to places the vines managed to touch the bare skin of his arms, which were exposed most of the time during the march.

"Remember me saying to keep your arms covered?" Benson

said to him. "It appears that these vines will work themselves into the pores of exposed skin. Once under the skin, their retreat in the presence of water causes them to rip away, opening up wounds."

"Who knew these vines were alive?" Griffen said.

"Are you joking?" Benson replied. "Of course they're alive. All vegetation is alive when it's green and growing. But this is something else. These vines seem to be able to trap the unwary. I'm wondering if it's just us, or is it anything that wanders onto them."

"Probably anything that wanders in." Chris tried to get his arms to quit bleeding by submerging them in the stream. "Apparently, this place is more dangerous than we believed."

"Did anyone else hear that ear-piercing noise?" Benson said. "I tried to cut myself free, but the noise was terrible."

"Yeah, I heard it, too," Griffen said. "Couldn't tell where it was coming from, but it felt like someone was pushing a hot needle into my brain."

"Have a lot of people poking your brain with hot needles?" Benson asked Griffen, who was standing, looking downstream. "It looks like it's clear of the vines if we stay within the boundary edges presented by the stream."

"What would've happened if Angelica hadn't found that water was the weapon to use?" Melanie said.

"We would all have been trapped and eaten by the vines," Chris got to his feet and rolled down his sleeves. "Thanks, Angelica," he said, as she was filling her waterskin.

Angelica just flashed him a quick, mirthless smile.

"How are all your patients?" Murdock asked Irene, as she joined him at the fire he'd built in the courtyard.

She exhaled. "They'll live. Most of their injuries were self-inflicted. Most from stumbling with an arrow exposed. One was shot from behind, in the shoulder. I think it was a case of friendly fire."

"Were any of the injuries caused by Annie or Zeke?" Murdock put another log on the fire.

"Not that I could see. Why?"

"Are they going to be able to defend you, or themselves, if the need arises? I mean, I know they can shoot at someone attacking them, but can they do actual damage? Can they kill if they need to?"

"I'm sure Annie and Zeke were doing their best."

"What's your plan for Heather or any of the patients who want to stay?"

Irene shrugged. "I don't know. I haven't thought that far ahead yet. Heather can stay if she wishes, and Zeke, of course. The rest... I haven't decided."

"Well, you probably have a few more days. Or are they all ready to be released?"

"They can go any time. If they develop any complications, they can come back."

"I wouldn't let them leave with the crossbows or the long-bows. Or you could confiscate all their arrows."

"I can't do that. Their weapons belong to them and I have no use for them."

Murdock paused a long time. "They attacked you, without provocation. Their weapons, as far as I'm concerned, are confiscated as a price for their aggression. Not wanting them to be totally defenseless, I'd let them keep the personal weapons—machetes, hatchets, that sort of thing. But the rest, they lose."

"Whatever you think best, Kevin."

"You seem tired, Irene. More tired than I've seen you in a long time."

"I am, Kevin. I guess I need more help than I have."

"What sort of help?"

"The kind of help you already have and I don't. The kind you can't help me obtain." Irene gave a weak smile.

Irene, Annie, Mei Lee, Heather, and Zeke had gathered, at Murdock's insistence, in the notch in the cliff that led up to the next plateau. It was a large area. Annie, Irene, and Mei Lee recognized it as the immediate area outside the cave that Irene and Annie had been using for bathing.

"As you may have noticed," Murdock said, "I enclosed this entire area so if Heather manages to obtain a deer for taming, she has someplace to house it. Also, enclosing it keeps out those who don't have our best interests at heart."

"Why did you call us here?" Heather said.

"Two of you have shown interest in some… personal disclosures. Before that can happen, we need to know we can trust you. We are, or have, put a lot into developing relationships with you. Do any here find Zeke or Heather unworthy?"

No one spoke.

"Since those here find you worthy, we will initiate you into our tribe."

Murdock remained quiet while a form began to appear. Little by little, an enormous bear materialized in front of everyone.

"This," Murdock gestured, "is Beron, leader of the Oomah. Those of us who know him, trust him implicitly. Before our trust was given, he had to trust us. This was achieved by opening our minds, our thoughts, to him. Ezekiel Jakes, will you open your mind to him?"

"I will," Zeke said.

Murdock nodded at him. "Heather Stevens, will you open your mind to him?"

"I will."

"The rest of us will stand guard over our friends while Beron determines their acceptability."

207

Alvin Jones had shown himself at the pods a day after Wagner regained consciousness. He volunteered to lead the next group downriver.

He had spent the last seven days leading his group downriver, without incident. When they reached the farmers, Jones had the opportunity to talk privately with Nels Osterlund and informed him of all the things that had evolved in the past few years.

When they had reached the newcomers' encampment, the one downriver from the farmers, a number of Jones' charges decided to join them, the rest choosing to proceed further downriver.

Over the years, Jones had heard of Jeffery Carter. How, during the first migration of the two hundred, five years prior, he had chosen to walk off and leave his charges to their own devices.

Now, sitting atop his mount at the top of the ridge, seeing the next plateau some three hundred feet below, he felt much the same as he imagined Carter felt. *I'm getting closer to doing the same as Carter. For two cents, I'd leave these idiots and explore. Carter left, I think, to explore... and escape. Escape the bullshit that comes from all the politics. I wonder what happened to Carter. No one has seen hide-nor-hair of him since he left.*

"We're all ready to continue, Mister Jones," the newcomer said.

Mister Jones. He laughed to himself.

He motioned onward and slowly descended the ridge, letting his mount pick its own way down. The rest of his group followed close.

Ted Wagner, being injured, knew he wouldn't be able to keep up with Jones. Besides, Jones had acted like he didn't want to be anywhere around him.

Must be what Murdock had told him. It couldn't be my sunny disposition. He laughed.

Wagner had figured that the best place for him to go was to the mine area. But to get there, he'd have to make a beeline to the ridge leading down to the farmers, and then cross the river. That would keep him far enough downriver from Murdock and those in the medical facility.

It's going to be a long walk. It won't be the victory parade I had planned, but I can get my people working on making things better for the next time. I don't know why Murdock spared me, but that's his mistake. I'll be back at him again, and next time, things will be in my favor.

Zeke and Heather heard the others as they began to recover from their sharing with Beron. To them, it all seemed like they were sleeping in a room with a conversation going on and hearing everything, though you appear to be asleep.

"Irene and Annie will be in charge of the training required for both," Murdock had said. "First should be levitation and telepathy. Those being the skills most needed."

"That would be a big help," Irene said. "As soon as Zeke can levitate, he can take care of his own bathing."

Everyone laughed.

"You didn't seem to mind too much last time," Annie said. "You looked quite… um…relaxed when you returned."

Annie, Mei Lee, Murdock, and Irene all laughed.

"Welcome back." Murdock grinned as Zeke and Heather opened their eyes.

"So what's the verdict?" Zeke got to his feet.

"You, like others before you, have special access for learning," Murdock said.

"That doesn't sound too good to me," Heather replied.

"It means you two have, what I call, a special dispensation. The same one that everyone else has."

"Special dispensation means..." Zeke shook his head.

"Basically, you will not be held to the code of conduct the Oomah have instituted. You are all under me. I am responsible for your conduct during your training and indoctrination."

"So you'll be held liable if we do something we shouldn't?" Heather said.

"That's what it means," Mei Lee said. "Speaking for myself and the kids, we would appreciate it if you didn't get Murdock killed."

Everyone chuckled, except Heather and Zeke.

"What would have happened had we been found... lacking?" Zeke asked Murdock, as everyone sat around the campfire eating and talking.

"Don't know, but why worry about it now?"

"It's something I shouldn't be worried about, but I am. I can't help but feel like I wouldn't live long if I were found lacking. What is it about *you* that makes you so special to the Oomah?"

Murdock shrugged. "I was the first human they contacted, and I have been protective when it comes to humans interacting with them. Other than that, maybe that I've been around them for so many years. I have no other ideas."

Zeke chuckled. "Well, the reasons you gave may have gotten a few people in, but certainly not all. There has to be more to it."

"Why? Why does there need to be more to it, I mean? The Oomah know I'll take care of things should someone I vouched for do something ...untoward. I doubt anyone I've vouched for doubts I will do what I have to."

Zeke looked around. When his gaze caught Irene's, she nodded almost imperceptible. As his stare met each member, including Heather, they gave a little nod.

"So Zeke, tell us," Mei Lee said. "What are your thoughts on your experience with Beron?"

"Hmmm… I'd have to say it was enlightening, for both him and me, and it was different from anything I've ever experienced before. In some ways, it was indescribable. In other ways, it was warm, familiar, and comfortable. I'd say both of those, simultaneously."

"How about you, Heather?" Irene said.

"Since I've been here a while, I had sorta gotten used to some of the things that always went unexplained. Now, I know. And honestly, it frightens me a little."

"What frightens you?" Mei Lee said.

"I don't know, and that's what frightens me. I know a little more now, but it's the stuff I don't know. It's like, I'm not sure if I wanna know, and I'm almost sorry for knowing what little I do." Heather hung her head.

Murdock nodded. "For now, we'll all be training our newest members in what they need to know. Once they're comfortable with the telepathy, they'll be free to travel unaccompanied. Until then, they need to be accompanied when getting too far outside the immediate area of the medical facility."

Zeke and Irene were sitting in the cave that was used for bathing.

"There are some things we need to get straight." Irene soaked in the hot water. "Since I'll probably be the one teaching you telepathy, which is strange to me, you need to stay out of my head."

"Why does it seem strange?" Zeke was soaking next to Irene.

"Before I was otherwise indoctrinated, I was certain that telepathy didn't exist and was just so much hokum." She chuckled. "As I recall, I was adamant about it. Just goes to show how much can change if you maintain an open mind."

"Will there be an issue with you teaching me?" Zeke asked.

"Not unless you make it an issue."

They both lay back in the water and were quiet for some time.

"I don't know," Zeke said. "I don't think I knew enough to have an opinion about telepathy."

"Are you aware that I didn't voice that question?" Irene smirked and looked at Zeke.

He looked confused. "You didn't? I clearly heard you ask what my opinion was on telepathy."

"That's something you need to get clear. What's telepathic and what's verbal. We all answer in the same fashion as the conversation came across. Since I asked a question telepathically, you should, to maintain protocol, answer telepathically. Otherwise, you may offend or confuse someone."

Irene turned and slapped Zeke's face. "You need to guard your thoughts as well. Just so you know, I'm not that type of woman!"

Zeke rubbed his face. "I wasn't aware I was thinking anything offensive. Sorry!"

"That's one of the hazards of telepathy. A person has so many thoughts every second of every day. We have become used to not having them heard. Since you're just starting out with telepathy, you'll have stray thoughts, unless you button them down. I happened to find that stray thought you had offensive. You, of course, must suffer the repercussions of that…leakage."

"You're not going to cut me any slack, are you?" Zeke was still rubbing the side of his face.

"Not a bit!" Irene grinned. "There are too many here that can pick up on that sort of mental leakage. So until you get your thoughts under control, I don't want you leaking anything that should remain private."

"But did you need to slap me so hard?" Zeke whined.

Irene wore an evil grin. "Yes! Maybe the pain will help you to not think about those things."

"You're not saying a lot." Annie looked out over the wall.

She and Heather were sitting close to the parapet.

"Don't have a lot to say," Heather replied.

"This is what you wanted, you know, when you asked about the communication we use. I'd think you'd be happier about it. Why so sad?"

"Just lonely, I guess. This is the first time since I got together with Alvin that I've been without him. Granted, dealing with him was trying, most of the time, but you get used to someone being there."

"I've wondered about something, if you wouldn't mind answering?"

Heather took a deep breath and let it out slowly. "If you're looking for information about Alvin or my life with him, then not now. Let me get used to his absence, and then I might answer you. How do you start with telepathy?"

"Mainly, you just clear your mind. If someone is sending a thought to you, you'll know." Annie chuckled. "Before I was indoctrinated, when I was tending Phylicia, I was needing Irene's help and found my thoughts screaming to her that I needed her."

"What happened?"

"Irene heard me and came to my call, which I consciously made but doubted anyone could hear. She was at Murdock's, and you, me, Phylicia, and Kimberly were outside Reyes' camp."

Heather grinned with her eyes closed. "I remember. Fun times!" She chuckled sarcastically.

"*You will have to learn the difference between telepathic and verbal,*" Annie flashed.

"Is there a difference?" Heather kept her eyes closed.

"*There is. if you think about it, you'll know if you actually heard something. There were times when I wasn't sure, until I really thought about it. The other thing to learn is how to keep your thoughts private.*"

"Huh. Hadn't really thought of that." Heather scowled. "But I guess you'd have to. You could go nuts, otherwise."

"You need your own thoughts. Some of us have a running commentary going on in our head most of the time. You must have something private. We've grown up with thoughts being private. Now that there's a possibility of them being transmitted, privacy becomes even more important."

Heather nodded. Both women were quiet for some time.

"Can I ask you something?" Annie said.

"You can ask..." Heather smirked.

"Were you even aware that part of our conversation was telepathic?" Annie wore a sly grin.

Heather sat up and looked at Annie, eyes wide.

It had taken longer than expected to reach the end of the current plateau. Even though the stream was straight and clear on both sides for several feet of the gripping vines, there were the thickened trees to deal with. In some areas, the trees were so thick they presented a barrier that forced them to go around.

"Another fine mess you've gotten me into, Benson," Curtis said, during one of the many stops they had to make.

"How'd ya figure?" Benson replied. "You could stay behind any time you like. You're not tied to the rest of us, so you're following because you choose to."

"And just where am I supposed to go?"

"You can go anywhere you choose to. You can go crazy, or you can go to hell."

Griffen glared at Benson.

"Just giving you suggestions." He shrugged.

When they had finally reached the end of the plateau, they realized it was blocked by trees, to the point that they couldn't penetrate them to rappel.

"So Dirk, now what?" Gundersen said.

"What would you suggest, Chris?"

"We could head toward the river."

"That would force us to cross the vines."

"True. But it should be possible if we fill our waterskins and soak our feet."

"How? We'd run out of water before we got very far."

"Not if we sprinkle it before us and travel quickly. We'd have to push fast, but I think we could make it to the river. Who knows? We may not have to go far to get out of the vines. We won't know unless we try."

"Hmm, we may be able to just run across," Melanie said. "After all, no one has tried jogging across the vines. We know if we stand still long enough, they'll tangle us up, but how long does that really take? It could be that a brisk stroll will be fast enough not to fall prey to them." She looked at Gundersen. "Feel up for a challenge? You go in, walking close to the edge, and see how quick they grow to trip you up."

Gundersen scowled. "I'm up for it. Are you?"

Melanie looked back at him. "I'm ready for anything *you* are."

They both took off, each with their own waterskins filled. They started walking, slowly at first, to find out the slowest speed without being tripped up.

After a short time, they found that any walking pace was sufficient to avoid being trapped. Stopping was the problem, as no one could walk for hours without stopping.

When everyone was rested and waterskins topped off, Benson called for everyone to follow him and not to stop. Just as he was about to give the order to proceed, one of the fifteen called for Benson's attention. After a short discussion, Benson was back, giving the order to proceed to the remaining five.

The remaining five walked for many hours. When it was dark, they stopped, partially to see if the vines were active at night. When they found that they're movements, or lack thereof, went unhindered in the dark, it took no time for them to build a small fire and rotate guarding.

Before sunup, they had broken camp and were on the move again. A few hours later, they broke out of the dense forest and the vines.

"It looks like we can go back to our normal routine now that we're literally out of the woods." Benson chuckled. "Question is, do we rappel off this edge here, or do we travel to the river before finding our way down?"

"We need food," Bronson said. "And since we don't have any, I'd say go to the river."

"I agree with Melanie," Curtis said.

"We could use some food and water," Gundersen said. "We could also use downtime. Time to get ourselves together before we decide where to go."

Benson nodded. "I concur. We need to de-stress before going on, if that's what we choose."

Once everyone had their say, some water, and a little rest, they pressed on to the river, though none knew how far that was or how long it would take. As they traveled, Benson led, watching for an attack by man or beast, or surprising a feeding animal, while Gundersen brought up the rear, on the lookout for anything that would attack from behind.

I hope we can just get to the river without anything else going wrong. He kept Melanie in view.

People waste all kinds of time by not planning properly. Some say they can't afford the time to properly prepare, but they can afford to start over when they realize they're not prepared? You never know what you're going to need until you need it.

— KEVIN MURDOCK, FAMILY CONVERSATIONS

Once the remaining five had left them, the fifteen and the entity that controlled them, circled and stood motionless.

It is good to find a protected area, the entity thought. *There is the thickness of the trees to prevent penetration, the vines, and the isolation. Living in the branches of the trees would be best. There is the need to remain unnoticed. Should anyone happen upon us, we can absorb them. But first, we need to grow and exert more control.*

During the long trek, the individual parts of the entity had been exerting more control over their hosts. By the time they had reached this heavy-forested area, control of the hosts was complete, though fragile at times.

The enemy is here. Their position, when vulnerable, remains unknown. But that will change eventually. We are nothing if not patient.

Mei Lee and Murdock were hunting in the area close to the battlefield. Both had their bows at the ready.

"*Heather has asked us not to shoot her tamed deer, should we encounter one,*" Mei Lee flashed to her husband.

"*I'm not hunting deer. I'm hunting those that attacked the medical facility.*"

"*You seem to be upset that the battle didn't last longer*" Mei Lee flashed.

"*That isn't what I'm upset about. I'm upset that more of these ... idiots don't pay for their ignorance in a more expeditious way. I'd just as soon live in peace and quiet, but they won't have it. They insist on conflict. They seek the death that comes from their instigated battles. Can you imagine if they treated others with civility as readily?*"

Mei Lee chuckled. "*That won't ever happen, so you don't need to worry about it. From their point-of-view, they're being civil and see no reason for the resistance from you and others. They feel they're entitled to everything.*"

"*They're wrong. No one is entitled to anything. You work hard to improve things for yourself and your family. That doesn't entitle someone else to come along and take away everything you've worked for.*"

"*Well, they believe, because there are so many of them,*" Mei Lee continued, "*that they can force the issue and you should see the folly of your beliefs and allow them to have whatever they want.*"

Murdock chuckled. "*Yeah, like that's going to happen.*"

Mei Lee laughed. "*I'm on your side. What we do to make our family's lives better, that's ours, and no one else has a right to it. If we take a deer, it belongs to us and no one else has a right to it—*"

"*Wagner and his ilk would argue that because they are stronger than you, they can take it from you.*"

Mei Lee frowned. "*And I have the right to place an arrow in their solar plexus to defend my property.*"

"*That you do, Mei. That you do.*" Murdock stalked off toward the ridge leading up and toward the stream.

Mei Lee followed. When she saw the deer, she nocked an arrow and drew back her bow.

"*Let it down, Mei. Don't fire. That's one of Heather's tame beasties.*"

Mei Lee slowly let down her bow and held it loose in case another target presented itself.

"How do you know it's one of hers?"

"Look at the antlers. Heather and Alvin kept their tame ones' antlers cut back. If you look, you can see the royal and bay antler parts are square-cut."

Murdock crept to the deer, whispering to it, as he'd seen Alvin do. It took him a while to place his hands on the animal. Mei Lee had removed the length of rope she kept wrapped crosswise on her body, and handed it to Murdock.

"Do we ride?" Murdock finished tying a halter and attaching his length of rope to be used as reins. "Or do you prefer to walk?"

"Why would I walk if I don't have to?"

"I don't know." Murdock swung up onto the mount. "Maybe you feel you need the exercise." He grinned as he reached down to swing Mei Lee up onto the mount.

"Are you saying I'm fat?" she settled in behind Murdock, bow ready and arrow in hand.

"Fat you're not." He took up the reins. "You could stand to gain a couple pounds, though."

Mei Lee chuckled.

"Does Irene need a deer?" Murdock said, before they'd gone far. "If she doesn't, I figure she soon will, with Heather and Zeke residing with her and Annie."

He turned the mount to amble toward the stream.

Curtis and Angelica Griffen, Chris Gundersen, Dirk Benson, and Melanie Burton had been at the river a couple hours. It was time enough to get a small fire started, catch a couple fish and get them cooking.

"What do you want to do?" Benson cut a portion of fish and began to recline to eat it.

Gundersen said nothing as he ate, his knees pulled up and feet flat on the ground.

"We haven't decided …yet." Curtis took enough for himself and his sister.

"How 'bout you, Mel?" Benson said, around another bite of fish.

Gundersen laughed.

"Why ask me?" she said. "Are you going to leave me out here in the middle of nowhere. Alone? Would you really be that heartless?"

"Hmm… you call it bein' heartless," Benson said. "I don't. You're free to do as you please. But if you ain't ready to fend for yourself, then that's on you. But that ain't what I was askin'. Do we relax here for a couple days, or move on? Personally, I could use a good sleep before movin' on, but I don't see needin' much more'n that."

"Where the hell are we?" Melanie said.

"Two terraces down from the one Benteen's group is on," Gundersen replied, without looking up.

"That doesn't tell me much," Melanie said.

"That would be… three down from the pod landing," Benson said.

"Still doesn't tell me much."

"Well, hell, darlin'! Let me get out our map so's I can show you." Benson said sarcastically, as he went through the motions of checking in his pockets.

"Ha, ha! Very funny. You're a real comedian. So we're lost?"

"Nope, not lost at all. I know which way to go to get to others. That ain't what I call lost. Hell, Gundersen knows more about where we are than you do. That tells me he's paying attention." Benson shot Melanie an accusatory glare, then looked at the siblings. "If we're going on, rather than going back upriver, are we going to cross at the next plateau down, to the stream and continue downstream? Are we going to just follow the river? Or is it going to be both....or neither, or some other combination I haven't thought of yet? Our original mission was to follow the stream, to explore the regions that border on the stream. Yes, we met with an impassable barrier— impassable to us with what we have for tools and the time and effort we want to expend—so we were forced to go to the river. Now that we're at the river, I haven't seen any sign that people have come this way. Doesn't mean they haven't, it just means I haven't seen any sign of it. My plan is to rappel down from this ledge to the next one down, and follow the ridge to the stream and continue downstream. If the rest of you don't want to do that, just let me know. We can discuss it and make our choices from there. You all have until tomorrow morning, by the time we reach the ground of the cliff edge on our way down, to let me know. If you don't want to rappel off this plateau, then we can discuss that. But that would require the discussion to happen before we rappel. Those are your choices."

The sun had gone down and everyone was bedded down close to the fire. Gundersen had already made up his mind to follow Benson, wherever he decided to lead.

Murdock and Mei Lee were leading the mount when they'd returned to the medical facility. The animal was burdened with a wild deer that Mei Lee had taken shortly after the couple had found the tamed one. Murdock levitated the one that was in pieces and wrapped in its own hide, onto the level where Irene and Annie stored their meat. While Annie, Irene, and Heather were getting the meat stored, Murdock led the pack animal to the enclosure he had recently made.

Zeke had followed Murdock and the pack animal.

"I was thinking," he said "how much trouble would it be to move the library inside the enclosure?"

"For me, not too much trouble." Murdock looked askance at Zeke. "For you, it would be quite difficult. Why?"

"Our attack has demonstrated, to me at least, that care should be taken to ensure the library's safety. Especially with all the barbarians that seem to need it most, and understand that need the least."

"Why, Zeke, whatever do you mean? Are you saying that our fellow inhabitants are savages? Say it isn't so!"

Zeke laughed heartily, as did Murdock.

"How do you process the hide?" Heather asked Mei Lee, as the rest of the animal was stored.

"I could tell you, or Murdock could tell you, or you could look it up in the library. I'm busy right this minute, and I'm certain Murdock is also otherwise occupied, so…"

"Without having an alternate means of obtaining information for so long, the library isn't the first thing I think of, and it probably should be. Sorry. I guess I'll be looking it up, with Zeke's help."

"*Speaking of Zeke…*" Mei Lee flashed to Irene.

Irene snapped around to glare at her. "*Don't even start with me on that subject.*"

"*Sorry, didn't mean to upset you. I didn't know it was such a sore subject.*"

"*It isn't really. It's just something I'm not used to dealing with.*"

"*Is he pressuring you?*"

"*Oh, heavens no. He's been great, actually. I think it's me pressuring myself. I've never had a beau. Never had the time, nor the incli-*"

nation. Now, though, it seems to have reared its ugly head, leaving me at a loss." Irene laughed loud enough that the other women heard her.

"Are Mei Lee and Irene having a conversation?" Heather whispered to Annie.

"If they are and you aren't hearing it, then it's private. Keep your nose out of other people's business," Annie flashed, without turning around. "Did you get that?"

Heather turned to Annie and smiled. "I got it."

"Well, damn!" Benson looked over the edge of the cliff and out to the horizon.

The siblings, Curtis and Angelica Griffen, himself, Gundersen, and Burton had walked downstream.

I have no idea how long we've been gone. Benson looked out. *I've lost all track of time.*

What he saw, standing on the edge of the current plateau, was water. He couldn't tell if it was an ocean, a sea, or a lake. Around the C-shaped shore was something that looked like sand for a fair distance from the water. He looked down at a drop that appeared to be five hundred-foot. Since the *strange fifteen's* plateau, he noticed the height of the plateau edges had increased significantly.

"How far down do *you* think it is?" Benson asked Gundersen.

"Nary a clue." Gundersen was holding onto the end of one of the climbing ropes they had been using to rappel from one plateau to another. "The end seems ta be a ways off the bottom. I'm thinkin' we need ta tie on the second and see if they reach."

"Are you strong enough to hold them?" Benson said. "Can't have you dropping them, and they will get heavy. Would be hard to explain, and even harder to get off this plateau."

"I can handle the weight. Just tie it around my waist. That way, I can't drop it."

"But it could pull you off the edge."

"Least I won't drop it." Gundersen shrugged.

Benson nodded and took off the second rope. He and Gundersen had become the designated rope carriers. Gundersen handed Benson the end he had been holding, straightened the rope and started tying the end around his waist. Benson knew the ropes being tied together would make them heavy. He had been carrying half of it since they left the landing pods. He pulled up a length of the rope and stood on it. Then he joined the two ropes with a zeppelin bend. With the ends secure and Gundersen thirty yards from the edge, he tossed the rope over the cliff. He watched as it became taut and the weight of it pulled Gundersen a few steps closer to the plateau's edge.

"You got it?" he asked Gundersen, and received a thumbs-up.

As he looked over the edge again, Benson could see the end blowing in the wind. He motioned for Gundersen to come closer as he fed the rope over the edge.

"Damn, damn, double-damn." Benson saw the end of the rope still blowing in the wind, and Gundersen was standing next to him. "It's further down than the amount of rope we have."

"How much further?" Gundersen said. "I mean, if it's just a bit further, someone could drop down."

"But how would you get down there? You're too big for me. You're too big for all of us, probably."

"It's his weight, plus the weight of the rope," Curtis said.

"Curious?" Benson glared at Curtis.

He looked around. "The closest tree is too far from the edge to be useful. I'd say go to the river and see if there's a way down there or somewhere along the route that may afford a path down."

"He has a point," Gundersen said, after Curtis went to stand with his sister.

"All this time and he finally comes up with something

useful." Benson let out a deep sigh. "Okay, let's pack up and move toward the river."

"I say we stay here," Curtis said to Angelica.

They were whispering while they ate, away from the other three. They had spent the day crossing the plateau looking for a way off.

"I think we need to stay with the rest," Angelica said. "At least until they get closer to the shore. Like you, I'm tired of the constant crossing of the plateaus with little diversity in the scenery. This group obviously doesn't seem to know anything about planning."

Curtis cocked his head. "You want to continue to the shoreline? Why? Seems like a huge risk with little return, to me."

"I've always wanted a beachfront home." Angelica closed her eyes. "I've always found the sound of waves crashing on the shore to be most relaxing. I can almost hear it from here."

"Really? I can't hear anything over the din of the river. Wish I could turn down the volume on that. I happen to like absolute quiet. That's what I'd call heaven."

"But there is no place that's totally soundless."

"Thus, my disappointment." Curtis noticed Benson coming toward them.

"What say you two?" Benson said.

"I say try to find a way down to the shoreline," Angelica replied.

Benson gave Curtis a questioning look.

"Personally, I couldn't possibly care less," Curtis said. "I find this entire place a constant crashing of noise and constant irritation. I just hope for a peaceful nights rest."

"What's irritating you now?" Benson said. *It's always something with this guy.*

"Why should we risk our lives on finding a way down? I say

225

wait until someone else comes up with a way down that doesn't involve a risk to us. I'm in no big hurry to go anywhere."

"So why are you still with us? You could've stopped anywhere along the way. I don't think anyone would've complained."

"What do you do when others don't want you around?" Curtis shrugged. "Our return to the pods was met with suspicion. We—" he used two fingers with a hand gesture to indicate himself and his sister— "had little to say about where we went and with whom. We were taken advantage of by Murdock and the rest of his followers. Since we had no choice then, we have no choice now. If I had my way, we wouldn't be out here at the ass-end of nowhere."

"Like I said, you could've stopped anytime."

"And do what? We have no idea how to survive out here. Sorry, but I'm not the great white hunter Murdock is. I'm told we're related to his first wife, not to him."

"And you don't put yourselves out to learn, either. You've had plenty of time to learn something… anything. But you're apparently *refusing* to. Both of you."

"Hmmpf!" Angelica turned away from everyone.

Curtis grumbled, crossed his arms and turned his back on everyone else.

"They aren't no help at all!" Benson grumbled, as he returned to the fire and Gundersen and Burton. "I still don't understand why those two need their own fire," Benson indicated the siblings, with his nose.

"What did they say?" Gundersen asked.

"*She* wants to look for a way down, and *he* doesn't care either way. Every day, I wake up and hope those two will decide to leave. But they don't." Benson took a deep breath and let it out slowly. "Oh, well. I guess we can't have everything. What do you two think?"

"About finding a way down?" Gundersen said. "I'd say it cain't hurt to look."

"I agree with you two," Melanie said. "I am a little more adventurous than those two," She indicated the siblings, "and I'm enjoying this little jaunt through the hinterland."

Benson and Gundersen looked at her, disbelief evident in their expressions.

"What?" Burton said. "I *am*. Enjoying myself, I mean."

"Do you understand what we're doin' out here?" Benson asked her. "We're here to explore the area for possibilities on settlements. We ain't here to have fun."

"But who's to say we can't have fun anyway? Is it against corporate policy or something?"

"Okay, keep your head and your feet," Benson tied the end of a rope around Melanie's waist and thighs. "We'll anchor you, should you need it. I'll be watching from up here while Curtis, Angelica, and Gundersen pay out the rope."

"Okay. I'll watch for a pathway that may be cut into the cliff face." Melanie tried to dispel the nerves in her stomach. "What if I need something?"

"Like what?" Benson said.

"Like a shovel or other tools?"

"That's easy. We don't have anything useful. No pitons or a climbing hammer to drive them. No extra rope, and no grapples. So that makes things easy." Benson chuckled. "Just be careful of your feet and hand placement. Stay as close to the face as you can. If you get into some kind of trouble, we'll pull you up."

Melanie was blowing out through her mouth, trying to calm herself, while shaking her cramping hands.

"Why was I selected again?" She started off the cliff, backward.

"Because you're the smallest and lightest." Benson smiled. "You're strong and fit, more so than Angelica, and it will be easier to pull you back up or prevent you from falling the rest of the way, should you slip. Just stay relaxed and aware, and you'll do fine."

Melanie started off the cliff, keeping her body close to the rock face. *I've got to be out of my ever-lovin' mind.* Her waist passed the edge.

Gundersen, being at the end of the second section of rope, was the anchor for Melanie. He had the rope tied around his waist to prevent accidentally dropping it, should Melanie fall. Curtis and Angelica were holding onto the rope close to the joined ends. Benson was lying on the edge, looking over, watching Melanie climb off the cliff.

They had all agreed that they should at least check to see if it was possible to climb off this plateau. They'd already checked, and they knew they didn't have enough rope to lower someone, and they had also checked to see if there was a path down, as there had been on a few of the other plateaus. From what Gundersen had seen, it looked like the face tended to cut toward being convex, rather than a parabolic bank.

Melanie was chosen because she was the thinnest of the remaining five, as well as being the shortest. She had balked at being volunteered, but she was as curious as the rest. She'd been assured that the rest of their group could hold her.

I hope she doesn't slip. Chris inched forward at Benson's motioning the rest for slack in the rope. *I don't agree with her. Hell, I don't even like her much, but I don't want her to fall or get hurt.*

What the hell am I doing? Melanie slipped over the edge of the plateau. *I must be out of my mind.* The edge rose to her chest and she gripped the edge.

She hadn't ever been climbing. She had done some rock climbing at her gym, but not the real, life-threatening kind. She knew it was a long fall should she slip on loose gravel or from a hand-hold break or a loss of balance. Melanie was stressed to the point that her muscles were cramping and she had barely started her decent.

It isn't the fall that'll kill you. It's the sudden stop at the bottom. She chuckled inside. *Why would my mind make light of a situation like this?*

"Probably to break the tension," she answered aloud.

The sound of her own voice seemed to calm her as she crept along a narrow ledge her feet had found before her arms were too short to reach the top of the ridge. The ledge ran downward, away from the river, which was rushing over the edge less than fifty feet away.

"You found a ledge?" Benson said, from above.

"Yes, a small one," she replied, without looking up, irritated with him for talking to her when she needed her concentration. "Now I just hope it doesn't just end...or break off," she muttered.

When she had moved down far enough that it required her to let go of the edge above her, to drop further, her hands didn't want to.

"Carefully let go and find something else to hold on to further down." She willed her hands to obey.

She probed around the rock face, down from the top, seeking a new hand-hold. Finding one finally, she breathed a sigh of relief and slid her other hand down to the same level.

"You may want to speed it up a little," Benson said, from the safety of the ledge above. "It'll be dark before you reach the halfway point, at this rate."

"If you don't like it, we can always switch places, you know.

I'd be more than happy to" she said aloud and added, "asshole," she murmured.

Melanie chanced a look at her feet and couldn't see the ledge her feet had found. She blinked a few times, trying to clear whatever was obviously obscuring her vision. Then she noticed the colors and shades in the stone.

"Great! The shadings make features invisible. That's all I need. To climb this cliff blindly."

She jumped when her foot stepped off into nothing, and a hand was in the air. She managed to recover, and with her heart in her throat, held her position to calm her banging heart. She tried to crouch once she regained her grip to see if she could find another purchase for her foot. . Melanie held her breath while searching for something to hold her weight, and let it out when she did.

This is crazy… this is crazy… this is crazy. She sought purchase on the same level, with her other foot.

When she was finally on another ledge, she paused long enough to look around. That was when she saw a shallow niche below her present position and away from the river. She worked toward it.

"Where are you heading?" Benson yelled down to her.

"There's a niche down from me, away from the falls," she called back.

She was afraid that if she should go much further toward the falls, her voice would be drowned out by the roaring water.

"Where's the other rope?" Melanie said. "Do you have enough on this rope to hold me? If so, I can direct the placement of it so we can come down there instead of trying this treacherous climb."

It took some time to direct those above to get the rope in the proper place, and for her to climb over to the niche in the cliff face. As she was about to climb into the niche, she saw why it had gone unseen. The plateau edge overhung the niche about forty feet above it, thus hiding it from anyone above.

Shortly after Melanie had climbed into the niche, Benson climbed down the second rope and was hanging some distance away from the cliff face.

"Swing out," Melanie told him. "Swing out and time your drop to land in here. Whatever you do, hang onto the rope as best you can."

Benson nodded and started swinging. It took him several tries to accomplish the dismount without taking the longer drop of several hundred feet.

"This is small." Benson looked around and took some water. "It does, however, allow someone to be lowered further down from here. We can take a turn around some of these spires." He touched the rock formations on either side of the entrance. "There appears to be space around it, and it's big enough to hold the heaviest of us."

"So what do we do now?" Melanie said. "Do you take a turn around a spire while I climb down further? This niche won't hold everyone, but it is big enough to allow us to rest on the trip down."

"I'd say this resting place is only big enough for two of us at a time," Benson said. "So before someone else can come down, we have to find the pathway down since we're already here."

"There's a problem you need to know about," Melanie said. "The coloring and shading of the rock face. Its wear and erosion makes it difficult to see footholds and handholds. Looking down, I could not see the differences. It seemed as if they disappeared, like I was looking at a smooth rock face. I had to find them by feel."

"Luckily, you had the skills to get us this far," Benson said, "and you're the only one with the proper shoes for climbing."

"These aren't the proper shoes for climbing." Melanie put

one foot out on its heel. "These are just a basic hiking shoe. It's what I used to wear all the time."

"Well, they're better for climbing than anything we're wearing." Benson chuckled.

"Another problem is, this may be a one-way trip," Melanie said.

"How do you mean?" Benson replied.

"Assuming we can get down from this rock face, how are we ever going to get back up there? We've had to use two ropes and five people, all with no climbing equipment or experience. I doubt we have the tools necessary to survive here, so how do you propose to get them here? Climbing out the way we came will be problematic."

"Good point." Benson frowned. "Normally, I'd say things will just work themselves out. But since few know where we are, it could be some time before someone comes looking for us. I doubt they'd be bringin' the tools we'd need as well."

"Well, right this second," Melanie said, "we have the means to easily go back the way we came. If we release one rope, which we would have to do to preserve it for any amount of time, we're not getting out again."

"You've raised some good points," Benson frowned again. "What would you suggest?"

"Honestly? I'd climb out of here and put it to a vote. I certainly don't want to get stuck here."

Never mistake quietness for ignorance, reflection for acceptance, or forbearance as a weakness. With every decision, I try to be sure I'm making the correct one. I don't want to eliminate someone, and then find out it was an error. I can't fix that. If I'm quiet, I'm watching. I reflect on the situation to make sure I know what's happening. Some mistakenly think that because my wrath isn't heaped on someone immediately, I'm afraid to do what is necessary.

— KEVIN MURDOCK, FAMILY CONVERSATIONS

Chris Gundersen was hunkered down, cooking fish for himself and Melanie Burton just under the cover of the lean-to he'd built, while it rained. Periodically, a hiss could be heard when a raindrop fell onto hot coals or the hot rocks surrounding the fire.

It had been raining the majority of the time that Benson had been gone, three days now. They had all voted that someone would go back to the pods for tools and extra rope, and maybe bring more people. Benson was selected for his expertise in solitary travel and his persuasiveness. He left the remaining four to fend for themselves until his return, and no one knew when that would be.

The land, like most of the plateaus they had experienced, seemed to be rolling hills devoid of trees, from what they could see from the river. The trees were across the river and seemed to be thicker here than where Benteen and the rest of their group had chosen to build.

The river seemed to drop in level the closer they got to the plateau edge. It wasn't a large drop, just fifty feet or so before the water went over the plateau edge.

On his own, Gundersen had found a suitable crossing of the river, and after crossing, had dropped and limbed trees large enough, about six-inch diameter logs at the base, to work as a small footbridge across the river. He'd chosen a point about two-thirds of the way from one plateau to the next. Upriver, from this point, the water was close to the river's edge and made fishing more accessible. It also made water retrieval easier.

"Wish there was a drier place to sit." Melanie was sitting in the back of the small lean-to, shivering.

"You could move closer to the fire," Chris said. "It's plenty warm over here."

"Have you seen Curtis and Angelica today?"

"Only for a second or two. I gave them another fish when they failed to harvest their own." Chris came over and handed Melanie her portion of the fish and found his own place inside the hovel to enjoy his meal.

"How long do you think it'll take for Dirk to get back?" Melanie said, as she ate.

"It'll take as long as it takes." Chris shrugged. "I have no idea how many miles we are from the pods or even Benteen's group. For all I know, he ain't even there yet."

The pair ate in silence for some time.

"What are you going to do today?" Melanie said.

"I need to enclose the lean-to more and strengthen the walls for protection from animals." Chris looked around at the interior.

"That'll be a lot of work. It ain't easy to drop the trees with an eighteen-incher."

"Anything I can do to help?"

"You can gather more debris and more limbs."

Melanie scrunched her nose.

"So what's Gundersen doing?" Curtis said.

"He's eating," Angelica snapped, as she tried to cook the fish Gundersen had given her.

"I'm getting kind of tired of eating fish all the time."

"Then get something else! I'm getting tired of your ingratitude for the things I do for you." She continued to tend the fish cooking, her back to Curtis.

She heard him scuffling around inside their lean-to, and then she was pushed out of it and into the rain.

"Get out! Get out and stay out!" He turned and faced her as he tended his fish.

Angelica got to her feet slowly and stood to look at Curtis, hair becoming scraggly and dripping in the rain, mud on the knees of her coverall and some smeared on her face.

"That was supposed to be for both of us." She pointed at the fish.

"*Pfft*... I don't think so. I'm tired of you getting your way all the time. We're here because of what you want."

"Really? You want to go there? It's all because of you we're out here at all! I was happy to stay with Declan and his family. But because of your racism and misogyny, we have been driven out into this... wilderness. You did that all on your own!"

Curtis glared at her and fingered the hilt of his twelve-incher. "I'd leave if I was you. While you still can!"

Angelica stomped, and stormed off toward Gundersen's lean-to.

Chris and Melanie watched Angelica storm toward them. They had only heard the final bit of yelling, which is why Chris had set their lean-to some distance from Curtis' and Angelica's.

"Mind if I join you?" she said, from a short distance.

"Sure," Melanie replied, before Chris could say anything. "Are you okay?"

Angelica entered the hovel to sit beside Melanie on the ground.

"Did he hit you?" she asked.

"He just shoved me, is all." Angelica looked at the ground. "Not like it would be the first time if he had."

"Why do you put up with him abusing you?" Gundersen said.

"He *is* my brother. One of them, anyway."

"You have another brother?" Melanie said. "Is he here, or back on Earth?"

"He's here," Angelica mumbled.

"There's a little fish left. Would you like it?" Melanie said.

"Thanks. I would. I didn't get a chance to eat today." Angelica accepted the offered food.

"So what set him off this time?" Melanie said.

"He said he was getting tired of fish." A tear started down Angelica's cheek. "I guess I am, too. My temper went off a little, and I told him to find something else." She shrugged. "Then I got pushed out."

"That is going to be an issue," Gundersen said.

"What is?" Melanie said.

"Eating fish all the time. We're gonna need lots of stuff—clothes, boots, weapons. Things we ain't gonna find just lyin' around. A deer or two would go a long ways toward us bein' independent."

"Have you seen any deer sign lately?" Melanie said.

"Nary a one!" Gundersen replied. "Don't think they're down

here. If they're only on higher up plateaus, then we in trouble." He got to his feet. "You stay here. I'm gonna look around a bit and do some thinkin'."

"So do you think your brother would help you out? Have I met him? Is he cute?"

After his injury healed, Wagner found his way back to the mine. On the way, he accumulated as many of his fighters as he could find. Several of them had been injured and treated by the medicos, and had then disappeared.

"How long, Ted?" Elizabeth Reyes said.

"How long for what?" Wagner replied.

"How long are you going to hide here? To look at you, one would think you're afraid."

"I am! Murdock has, in no uncertain terms, told me that if he sees me, I'm dead. Doesn't that warrant a little trepidation?"

Reyes looked at him. He still wore the makeshift bandage on his thigh.

"It would, if it were anyone but Murdock. You know as well as I that he doesn't mean what he says. *All hat and no cattle*, I think is the idiom."

Wagner looked at her in disbelief. "What makes you say that? From my dealings with Murdock, he has always backed up his statements. So I'm curious. Where's your proof?"

"He said to us that he'd see we had plenty to eat and that he'd take care of us."

"Really? That doesn't sound like the Murdock I know. The man I know would let you starve, if he had his way."

"Well, modesty prevents me from giving a reason," Reyes said, flirtatiously.

"*Ha-ha-ha*," Wagner laughed. "With you, it's false modesty. There's nothing *modest* about you, Liz!"

"*Hmph.*" She scowled at Wagner, crossing her arms across her chest, and turned her back. "There's no need to be insulting. I can say that Murdock has *a thing* for me—"

Wagner was holding his sides and laughing to the point of breathlessness.

Dirk Benson was tired and cold. He had left the others to run back to the pods to get more tools, rope, and maybe more people. He was three plateaus up from where he left Gundersen and the others, when he could go no further.

Benson had been traveling as rapidly as he could. Climbing the plateaus had been difficult and nerve racking for him alone. If he were to fall, no one would know where the others were and wouldn't likely find out what happened to them.

I have an idea we were sent to get us out of the way. He cooked fresh fish under a tree with low-hanging bows. *I know the fifteen oddballs were sent out here to get rid of them. Were Curtis and Angelica sent to get rid of them, too? Why was me and Gundersen sent? We didn't do anything to them to want us out of the way.* Benson thought about Curtis and Angelica while he ate. *They would give the others pause. Why did they go and why were they returned? They did say they returned of their own volition, but why go at all? Obviously it has something to do with Murdock, but what? I'll have to remember to ask them when I get back... if I get back.*

"Mind if I join you?" came from behind the tree Dirk was leaning against.

He snatched up his twelve-incher as he turned around. About twenty feet away was a large, unkempt man. He looked to be in his fifties, but some of the apparent age could be from the stress of survival. His auburn hair was straight and scraggly-looking. His hazel eyes flashed when he noticed the drawn twelve-incher.

"If you wanna be alone, say so." The man slowly moved his

hand to his own twelve-incher. "I ain't in the mood for trouble, but if that's your intention, I'll oblige you."

Benson heard no boast in the man's statement. He did hear a confidence that told him to be wary. This was no newcomer.

Benson stood straighter and slowly put away his machete. "Sorry, but you gave me a start." He smiled a little. "Wasn't looking for company, and wasn't expectin' anyone."

The stranger moved his hand away from his machete. "Sorry 'bout that. I'd almost decided you were a mirage." He chuckled. "Been awhile since I been around people."

"You gotta name, stranger?" Benson resumed his position.

"Name's Carter. Jeff Carter," Carter made no motion to shake hands, and just hunkered down opposite Benson. "Whatcha doin' out here all by your lonesome?" He opened his hands toward the flames.

"On a mission, of sorts. Dirk Benson's my name, by the way."

"What sorta mission, Benson?"

"You want some fish? I got plenty. I'm one of a small party investigating the stream."

Carter chuckled. "You're a bit off track, then. The stream is that-a-way." He indicated the direction of the stream, with his nose, then picked out a good-sized piece of fish and raised it to Benson as a way of saying thanks.

Benson chuckled. "Yeah, I know. We managed to find a way a fair piece downstream."

"So where's the rest?" Carter said, between bites.

"They're waitin' for me to get back with tools and people." As Benson ate, he tried to remain vigilant and relaxed at the same time.

"Hmm..." Carter started as he looked around. "Since ya don' got much, you must be goin' rather than comin'. Mind if I ask where you comin' from?"

Benson squinted at Carter. "It's a bit soon to be pokin' noses into each other's business."

Carter chuckled. "Yeah, it is. Not bein' nosy. Jus' curious. Makin' polite conversatin'."

"Understood. You live around here? Just askin' so I don't step on any toes, if you take my meaning."

"I do, matter of fact. You must be from the new arrivals that landed a while back."

"Is it so obvious?" Benson wore a slight grin.

"Mostly your dress. It gives you away. Get you into some skins, and you won't stand out so much."

"How long you been out here?"

"Some would say too long." Carter chuckled. "Not long enough, others would say. Five years? Maybe? Don't really know. Heard the noise of the new ones landin', but only one. So must be five years."

"Anyone out here with you? You been alone all this time?"

"Yup." Carter shrugged. "Just me. Ain't seen hide nor hair of anyone since. Til now, anyways." He stood when he'd finished his fish.

Benson watched him closely, especially when he moved. *He moves quick, deliberate. Do I have something to be concerned about with this hermit? Five years out here alone will do some damage to your sanity.*

"Which way you goin'?" Carter said.

"The plan was to follow the river up. That won't cause you trouble, will it?"

"Which side of the river?"

"The other side. Why?" Benson had crossed the river to take cover, as the trees on the other side were few and far between.

"Easier way up on this side. You can do as you please, but this side is easier for the next couple plateaus."

"Thanks for the information. Are you leaving?" He didn't know why, but he didn't want the man to leave. Not just yet, anyway. *Am I missing Gundersen's company that much?*

"I seem to be makin' ya uncomfortable." Carter shrugged. "Guess it's been too long 'tween conversations." He chuckled.

"No need to leave. I could use the company."

"For how far? I ain't goin' up from this plateau."

"I need to, but it's always better travelin' with others, even if it is just a little while."

"How long you plannin' on bein' on this plateau?"

"Now? Not long. Quick as I can get to where I'm goin', quicker I get back. Sayin' that, would like to spend time on this plateau, if you're willin'."

Carter frowned. "I ain't much for havin' friends. Had no use for them before."

Benson nodded. "Understood. Just didn't want to intrude by passin' by this way again."

"You ain't intrudin'. Just don't come lookin' for me. If I want comp'ny, I'll find ya."

Benson stood and offered his hand to Carter.

Carter looked at it as if it were something he wanted to take, but was leery of the gesture.

Chris Gundersen had finished breakfast and was outside the lean-to. The rain had slowed to a drizzle, one that would soak you before you realized it. He was trimming limbs around the base of a huge tree, under which, the bare ground was drier than inside the leaking lean-to.

"You better watch yourself, *boy*," Gundersen heard from behind him.

He remained calm and didn't flinch, even though his heart had come up into his throat.

"And why is that?" he said, without turning to look at Curtis Griffen. "I fail to see the need of *me* watching myself, when you seem to have taken it on yourself to do it."

He dropped the limbs and turned toward Griffen, who punched toward Gundersen.

Gundersen turned his head with the punch and it only

landed a glancing blow, but was still a stunning one.

"I'll give ya that one." Gundersen glared.

The other man was preparing to throw another punch.

"Do it and you'll be fending for yourself!" Gunderson rotated his jaw to work out the soreness.

"Think so?" Griffen scowled. "You're gonna do what I tell ya to do!"

"Bite me!"

The punch from Griffen came from the pods and traveled at roughly the rate of a strolling cow. Gundersen simply leaned back while pulling his twelve-incher. Griffen, now off-balance from the missed haymaker, leaned forward more, and Gundersen stopped his fall with one hand while placing the tip of his machete at the base Griffen's neck, the handle close to his ear.

"So do I make your sister mourn your passing?" Gundersen whispered.

"You don't have the guts!" Griffen spat, and immediately felt the tip of the machete bite into his skin. He felt the warmth of his blood starting to flow. "Okay! Okay!"

He felt the machete ease up.

"You're going to go back to your lean-to and stay there," Gunderson whispered. "You come 'round me again and I'll finish this."

"Okay." Griffen nodded.

Gundersen removed the machete and pushed Griffen, who stumbled and then slipped and did the splits. He grabbed his inner thighs and yowled.

Gundersen went back to doing what he was doing.

"What the hell?" Angelica came to Curtis' bellows.

"He attacked me!" Curtis said.

"What the hell is the meaning of this?" Angelica yelled at Gundersen, indicating the bleeding cut on Curtis' neck.

"What's going on here?" Melanie had heard the commotion and followed Angelica.

"That beast stabbed my brother!"

Melanie pursed her lips and looked toward Gundersen, who hadn't bothered to aid Curtis.

"We don't know what went on, so don't jump to conclusions, Angelica."

"What's to know? My brother is cut and bleeding, and is lying on the ground in pain. These facts speak for themselves."

Melanie continued to watch Gundersen. "I'm not so sure," she mumbled.

The rain had started again. Chris entered the lean-to and placed a cleaned fish on the hot rocks to cook.

"Nothing to say?" Melanie said, as Chris sat close to the fire.

"About what?" He tended the fish.

"Don't play innocent with me," Melanie whispered. "You know I'm asking about your little altercation with Curtis. I want to know what went on."

Chris looked at her. "And who exactly are you to demand anything from me?"

Melanie stared at him, slack-jawed for a few seconds. "I thought we were friends enough that you'd feel comfortable enough to talk."

"I'll talk to you any time." Chris returned his attention to the cooking fish.

"So talk to me! What happened out there?"

"Does it matter?" Chris frowned.

"Curtis is saying you attacked him."

"What do you think happened?"

"Honestly, I don't know." Melanie blew out a breath. "It's why I was asking *you*."

"I know what happened. Curtis knows what happened." Chris shrugged. "The rest is just noise and nonsense." He looked around the lean-to. "What happened with our house guest?"

STEPHEN DRAKE

"She now has to take care of her brother after he was brutal-ized by you." Melanie looked at Chris, trying to get some sort of reaction from him, "But you're trying to change the subject. I want an answer."

"*Want* in one hand and sh—"

"Language, if you please!" Melanie scolded.

"I was speaking English. It *is* the only *language* I know. What *language* did you want me to use?"

"I don't think you need to swear."

"And I should see to your needs, why?"

"*Argh!* You are so frustrating!"

"Why, thank you!" Chris flashed a toothy grin.

"That brute!" Angelica helped her brother into their lean-to. "Who does he think he is?"

"Are you gonna make us something to eat?" Curtis sat grinning.

"What did you do with the fish I left this morning?"

Curtis shrugged. "I ate it."

"All of it? How can you still be hungry? What am I going to eat now?" She looked at her brother and he shrugged. "It's all right. I'm not hungry at the moment. I'm just too livid to eat! A part of me wants to go over there and give him a piece of my mind!" She started to break sticks and put them on the fire.

Curtis was sitting back with a smirk on his face.

A hot coal and an errant breeze caused the fire to blaze to life. At that moment, Angelica had turned toward Curtis, and in the light of the blaze, saw a fleeting, smug grin on his face.

Did I just get played? Did he fake being injured just to get me to come back? Was I wrong to think Gundersen started the altercation? Maybe he finished it and Curtis, after having his ass handed to him, decided to play on my and Melanie's sympathies. It wouldn't be the first time he'd done such a thing.

Her anger rose. She threw more wood on the fire, then left the lean-to and stormed over to Melanie's.

"Melanie, we need to talk! Gundersen, take a hike."

"I think you're confused." Gundersen frowning at her. "This is *my* shelter! You want privacy, take it into the woods."

"Come on, Angelica." Melanie got to her feet and exited the lean-to.

"Take it easy on Gundersen," Angelica said, when they'd gone far enough.

"Why?"

"I'm suspecting my brother instigated the altercation between them, and Gundersen finished it." Angelica chewed on the inside of her cheek. "I think my brother's screams were for my benefit. I think he's faking."

Melanie's eyes grew wide. "Why would he do that? Would he really fake it?"

"Who knows why Curtis does anything? You'd asked me about my brother. My brother, his wife, and their kids are where we were before we came back. Curtis started his racist comments to someone he shouldn't have, and had his ass handed to him by our older brother. I think Curtis would lie, cheat, steal, maybe even kill if it meant he'd get what he wanted."

"But that would mean—"

"Yup." Angelica nodded. "He's an asshole! I just thought you needed to know before you got into it with Gundersen. What has he said about it, if I may ask?"

Melanie shook her head. "Nothing. He's said nothing about what happened. No pleas of innocence. No pleas of being mischaracterized."

"Well, that's all I wanted to tell you. I would have told you earlier, but I caught him smirking at my ranting."

"So now what?"

"I honestly don't know. It's quickly getting to the point that I can't stand to be around him anymore."

"Your own brother?"

Angelica nodded. "My own brother."

"Hello in the camp!" echoed a voice familiar to Gundersen.

According to Gundersen's count, it had ten days since Benson had left.

Gundersen exited his lean-to and ran to his friend. The pair hugged and shook hands.

Melanie and Angelica had built their own lean-to and were sleeping together.

Curtis Griffen trudged out of his lean-to. He was curious if Benson had managed to get the tools or the people they needed. Other than that, he couldn't have cared less if Benson made it back.

Melanie and Angelica lined up in front of Benson and greeted him with grins and hugs.

"It's nice to see y'all again!" Benson said. "Come on in!" he yelled toward the river, waving. "We got some tools, thanks to Benteen. But they do need to be returned before winter. We got another fifteen people from the pods, and we got two more lengths of rope."

"You think it'll be enough rope?" Curtis smirked at Gundersen and Benson.

"It should be enough to get some of us down to check it out."

Benson caught Gundersen glaring at Griffen. *I'm sensing bad blood between these two. What went on while I was gone. I don't think I was gone all that long, but I have lost track of time.*

"Let me get the newbies settled, and then we can talk," Benson whispered to Gundersen. "Where's your shelter?"

"Over there." Gundersen pointed to his lean-to.

"I'll get with you soon and I want to hear how things went here." He patted Gundersen on the shoulder as he turned him toward his lean-to. "I don't know what went on while I was gone," he said to Griffen, as Gundersen was walking away, "but if you caused any unnecessary trouble for my friend there, you and I are going to have a *conversation*. You get my meaning?"

"Blow it out your ass! I don't answer to you or your butt-bud—"

Gundersen turned at the sound of someone getting hit and everyone else saying, "Ow! That'll leave a mark!"

He saw Griffen on the ground and Benson shaking his hand and flexing his fingers.

Angelica stalked over to her brother and kick him in the ribs. "Serves you right!" she said, to the unconscious form, and stormed off.

Gundersen was tending his lean-to, repairing and building up the insulating bows.

"What's with garbage mouth?" Benson watched Gundersen.

Gundersen shrugged. "He's just a horse's ass," he said, without turning.

"That, I think, is an insult to horses everywhere." Benson chuckled. "I take it there's a bit of bad blood between you two?"

Gundersen shrugged. "Only about twelve pints worth." He gave Benson a rundown of the altercation six or seven days prior, and the consequent fallout from it.

"Sorry you had to go through that." Benson chuckled. "I'd a thought you and Mel would'a got together a little more."

Gundersen's ears turned cherry red.

"What happened there?"

"Nuttin'."

"She is older than you, but not a lot. Patience is a virtue. Don't be in a rush."

"What did Curtis say that caused you to punch him?" Gundersen asked.

"He was just being himself—an ass. More importantly, what happened that caused his sister to kick him?"

Chris became fidgety. "That was from him playin' Angie when we had our... um, issue. He tried to play Melanie and his sister. Almost got away with it, too."

"I hear you handled it... uniquely." Benson chuckled. "I found someone *unique* myself on my little trip."

Gundersen perked up. "Who was that?"

Benson laughed. "It's funny. The guy startled me. But I think he was quite unique. He was someone I'm interested in learning from."

"Learning from? I thought you knew all you needed to know?"

Benson looked to Gundersen with a shocked look. "If there's nothing else you learn from me, learn this. Never stop learning. I don't care how much you think you know, you can never know everything. Learn all you can, for your entire life. You'll be happier for it, and with any luck at all, you'll learn one very important thing."

"And what's that?"

"If you're lucky, you'll live long enough to learn just how much you don't know."

"I'll keep that in mind."

"As soon as you think you know something, try teaching someone else. You'll see for yourself how much you missed or forgot. If I could, I'd hang with Murdock."

"I know, for the learning."

"Exactly! I'm sure there are things he knows that I'll never get anywhere else."

"You sound like you're leavin' tomorrow. You ain't, are ya?"

"I am. When we wake up, we're goin' off this ridge and see what we can see." Benson smiled.

"Can we throw Curtis off the ridge and see how long it takes for him to hit the bottom?"

"Ya know... that sounds like a good idea. I don't think he'll like it, but his sis might."

16

It is the height of human arrogance to think mankind is the epitome of everything. In actuality, they're hairless apes, cowering inside themselves, in the dark. There is so much more that humans don't understand.

— KEVIN MURDOCK, FAMILY CONVERSATIONS

E veryone had gathered at the edge of the plateau. They were off by a day, as everyone who had traveled here needed a day to recover. Nonetheless, they were now well-rested and ready to explore.

They had tied all the ropes for climbing together, and tied one end around Melanie since she was the most experienced climber, as well as the lightest.

"We're gonna do this a little different," Benson said to Melanie. "All you need to do is climb down a little ways and we'll lower you the rest of the way."

"You want me to trust that you've tied the rope ends together in a way that'll hold me? Yeah right! Not gonna happen. Get someone else."

"Lucky, we have just the candidate." Benson winked at

Melanie. "We all took a vote and have selected Curtis Griffen to be the first one over the edge."

Curtis marched over to Benson. "This is an outrage!" he roared. "I refuse! None of you have any authority over me."

"For my money, the rope would be optional," Benson said. "I should mention that Gundersen had the perfect means to find out how high this edge is. It called for you to take a deep breath, and then we push you off the edge as you yell the whole way down."

"That's outrageous!"

"Relax. I decided it wouldn't work because you couldn't possibly yell loud enough to be heard all the way down. Besides, no one knows the math needed to figure it all out from our crude measurements."

Curtis' face was bright red and he was silent. He turned a pleading face to Angelica. It took several seconds before Benson broke down and guffawed.

"Quit teasing Curtis," Melanie said. "I'll go. Just make it quick, before I change my mind... again."

As Melanie was walking around, trying to keep from hyper-ventilating, she noticed that someone had managed to find and prepare six-inch diameter logs to ease the rope over the edge without the danger of sharp rocks cutting the running end. Someone had formed a U-shape with the logs, and the one that went over the edge was smooth and free of bark. When she turned around, she could see ten people on the rope at various points, and the rest were ready to relieve them, should the need arise.

Melanie turned her back on the edge and started down close to the U-shape construction. The rope was paid out per Benson's directions, and she remained panicked as she was lowered over the edge.

It took Melanie a while to reach the bottom of the ridge. The trip down had been uneventful. Her fears about the rope joins were, thankfully, unfounded.

Once she was on the ground, she noticed that she was at least twenty feet away from the rock face. She untied herself, drew her twelve-incher, and started to explore the area as the rope was being retracted for Benson's trip down the ridge.

While she waited for Benson, Melanie noticed the ground had a high sand content and was covered by something similar to the creeping plants they had already encountered. She managed to keep her feet moving, even though she couldn't detect any movement by the vines. She breathed easier when Benson was down.

"Good thing we got more lengths of climbing rope." Benson untied himself. "It took nearly all of it to reach the bottom."

"Who else is coming down?" Melanie watched the rope retract.

"I told them to send down Gundersen and Angelica, and then send down some of the tools. I figure we can do the initial exploration of the immediate area. No need to endanger everyone."

"How are you going to get everyone down here?" Melanie watched the next person being lowered.

"Not everyone will come down here. We need to find another way up to allow more than ten people down here. Until that happens, it will be a long tedious job to go up and down the ridge."

When Angelica landed, Benson was there to untie her.

"Stay close," he said. "At least until me and Gundersen can check out the area. While we do, I would like you and Melanie to untie the tools that will be coming down after Gundersen. I'd stand close to the rock face while they are coming down, though, just in case."

"In case of what?" Angelica said.

"In case something comes loose or isn't tied securely. If something falls, you're gonna want rock over your head."

As they waited for Gundersen, Angelica and Melanie strolled toward the rock face. They wandered around and finally found good-sized stones to sit on that were close enough to the face to allow them safety while those above lowered the tools.

Once Gundersen was down, he and Benson drifted away from the area before the tools could be lowered.

"See that?" Benson whispered.

"See what?" Gundersen said.

"See how the rock face is cut in?" Benson motioned the curved shape. "The overhang is large. It's going to make getting back up there difficult by climbing."

"Looks impossible to me." Gundersen shaded his eyes as he looked up.

"Nothing's *impossible*. Just extremely difficult for us with the equipment we have."

"Like I said—impossible."

Both men laughed.

A few days after their arrival at the shore, Benson had discovered many traits about the land below the plateau edge. It was a peninsula. The water was brackish to saline, depending on how far from the shore you were. The only fresh water was that which flowed off the plateau. When the river flowed over the edge, it gathered in a pool. The overflow created a rapid flowing water area that snaked around as it emptied into the C-shaped bay. The water away from the shore appeared to be lavender. The reason for the colorization was undetermined.

The beach was several hundreds of yards wide of dark brown sand, devoid of plants. The few trees and grasses were confined to an area around the river that flowed off the upper plateau.

Standing with his back toward the plateau edge, to his right, was the immense C-shaped bay.

Over the coming years, we'll explore this shoreline. Benson stood looking at the surrounding water, with his hands on his hips. *There is some land, but not much, and the soil has a high amount of sand. That would make it easier to dig until we hit rock.*

"What do you think?" Gundersen walked up to Benson.

"About what?"

"About what we found down here?"

"I think we'd be better off on the plateau. Up there, we have more arable land. There is more game the further we go away from this... *sea,* for lack of a better term."

"I'm sure there are edible fish in this *sea,*" Gundersen said.

"I'm sure if there is, then there's something there to eat it and maybe us, too. How are your boat-building skills?"

"I know more about survivin' up there," Gundersen pointed to the plateau edge, "than I do about buildin' boats and such."

"Can you swim? It would be ill-advised to put anyone on a boat when they can't swim."

"Don't swim well. My swim skills are more like rocks than those of fish."

"As I stand here looking at the ridge, what I notice is the lack of the stream waters flowing over the edge. Maybe we should see if it goes over the edge. And if so, is it a drop or is there an easier way up or down?" Benson took in a deep breath and let it out slowly and loudly. "It's worth investigating. To me, anyway."

"What's your suggestion for the two women?"

"I want to check out the ridge around the stream. I can take Mel with me and leave you here with Angie." Benson watched for a reaction from Gundersen. "You two could see if there is a way across the river to see how far the ridge goes that direction," he said, when no reaction was discerned.

"And we meet up back here?"

"Yeah, in about two days. Three at the most."

"If you say so." *Three days stuck with Angelica and her uppity attitude. Joy of joys!*

Melanie and Benson had been trekking toward where the stream should have been flowing off the ridge above. At sundown, they found a place to camp close to the ridge wall they'd been following.

Benson had found dry driftwood lying on the sand, and got a small fire started.

"What's the plan for winter?" Melanie warmed her hands.

"My plan is to find a place more permanent in the coming weeks, and lay in for winter." He was putting the finishing touches on a pole he was fashioning.

"Laying in? Laying in what? And what is that?" She pointed at his project.

"You lay in provisions. Accumulate enough food to get us through the winter. This?" He stood and pulled out his eighteen-incher, then placed the machete in the groove he'd been working on.

Melanie heard a distinct click as the machete was locked to the pole. "What's that supposed to be?"

"My version of a pudao. Or it will be when I'm finished with it. I need to find cordage to secure the blade, though."

"What good is it?"

"It's an effective weapon. Light enough to slash around, or to poke from a distance greater than a man's arm length. It's more close-in than a spear or pike, and can, if properly applied, disembowel someone or something."

"And…what are you planning to use it on?"

"If someone attacks me, I should be able to defend myself easier than to be in *their* weapons range the whole time. Besides, I may be able to use it to harvest a beastie for food and other things."

"I think you're wasting your time. What's the plan for tonight?"

"You can sleep and I'll watch. When I get tired, I'll wake you."

"That sounds good to me, just as long as I get some sleep." Melanie slid down.

They had built their fire inside a ring of boulders. Melanie had been sitting on the sand and leaning back on one. Now she was lying with the boulder at her head. Her eyelids kept popping open as they lowered. It took some time for them to stay closed.

"Where are we going?" Angelica snapped. "Do you know? Or are we just wandering around?"

"I have an idea where we're going," Chris mumbled. "Why don't you announce our presence a little more? I think there may be a few animals a few miles away that don't know we're here."

"No need to mince words. What exactly are you saying?"

Again with the snooty attitude. "Don't mince words? All right, shut the hell up! You need to be quiet. You know, the opposite of your normal volume." Gundersen scowled.

"Are you trying to *silence* me?" Angelica ranted.

"Let me put it another way. I'd give most anything right now for a gag and a set of earplugs."

"Well! I never—"

"Yeah, I can believe that. Look, we don't know what's out here, so we need to disturb as little as possible. So shut it!"

Angelica glared at Gundersen, mouth agape, but said nothing further.

Gundersen turned away from her and resumed leading away from the river, following the shoreline. He'd found that walking on the ground close to the sand was easier going than the sand itself, even though the sand silenced their footfalls. Periodically, he would stop and focus on the ledge. He thought there might be an easier way up to the plateau, but there might not be.

After an hour, he stopped to drink. "What's that?" he whispered.

Angelica looked at him with a frown, and then looked around.

"Ah, it's only silence. Something I thought was gone forever." Chris chuckled.

Angelica narrowed her eyes and gave the universal single-finger salute to his back.

As sundown became imminent, Chris found a small clearing not far off the course he was charting. When he entered it, he found dry deadfall for firewood and got a fire started.

"You can talk now if you want. As long as you keep it down." He worked on the fire, then turned to look at her when there was no response.

Angelica was glowering at him, with her arms crossed.

"I wanted you to bite your tongue, but didn't mean for you to bite it off." He smirked.

"I fail to see anything funny." Angelica said, in a low tone. "First you say to be quiet. Now you want me to talk. Make up your mind."

"When we're walking, yes, be as quiet. Melt into the background. Here, it's okay to talk if you have something to say, and if you're with someone who wants to listen to you. I was just giving you the option to talk."

"Why should I do anything you say?"

"You know, the more I listen to you, the more it confirms that your cornbread ain't quite done in the middle."

Melanie had no idea how long she'd been asleep. She had no idea she *was* asleep. She seemed to be following herself along the beach, at the edge of the purple sea. Her image turned to her.

The eyes were gone and the sockets looked burned out, scorched and blackened skin surrounded them. Scars ran down the pallid face, deep crevices down both cheeks and across the forehead.

"You don't belong here," a deep guttural voice rasped, apparently a few yards away. "Leave! Now!"

"But how?" her real voice said. "We're looking for a way up the ridge."

"You don't belong here," the guttural voice repeated, much closer. "Leave! Now!"

"Now-*now*, or later-*now*?"

"You will die if you remain."

Melanie could feel the fetid breath on her face.

"Leave! *Now*!"

"We're trying!" She sat up.

"Mel? You okay?" she heard Benson say, while someone, likely Benson, was shaking her shoulder.

"What?" She cast her gaze around, disoriented. "Where was I?"

"You were right here," Benson whispered. "You were asleep. You didn't *go* anywhere. Musta been one helluva dream."

Melanie dropped her head into her hands and tried to slow her breathing. "Nightmare, more accurately."

"Care to discuss it? Might help. Couldn't hurt."

"It was just a nightmare?"

"Had to be. I've been right here, and you didn't go anywhere."

"Then why do I feel sand between my toes?"

Angelica knew she was asleep and relaxed. She knew she was dreaming, even as her apparent trip to the shore of the purple sea seemed real. While she stood in the sand and watched the waves lapping on the shore, she felt something on her legs. She looked down and saw wide leaves of what looked to her like seaweed, coming out of the sand and wrapping around her legs.

Her heart rate sped up as she struggled to relax and kept mentally repeating that it wasn't real.

When she looked up, in an attempt to ignore the seaweed, she saw someone coming from the sea. It was a female, naked except for some stray leaves of seaweed draping off her shoulders and hair. As the stranger got closer, Angelica could see it was... herself.

"This place is forbidden to you. Be gone!" said the gray-skinned apparition. The voice was guttural and sounded like someone talking with a throat full of water—that bubbly quality.

"We are searching for a way off the beach," said the dreaming Angelica.

"Do not tarry. Be gone! Or be destroyed!" the apparition's deathly pale face blocked out all other images from her vision.

Angelica squeezed her eyes shut and tried to force herself awake.

"Get away!" Angelica's eyes popped open.

"Wake up, Angel," Gundersen whispered, from his position opposite her, the fire between them.

"I'm awake."

"Bad dream?"

"No, I think I had a vision."

"A vision? What's that s'posed ta mean?"

"For years, I've been a lucid dreamer. That's when you know you're dreaming and take control of it. What I just experienced was much more than that."

Chris remained silent for a while. "So how do you know your vision was more than a dream?"

Angelica chuckled, and then turned away from his direct gaze. "You're a skeptic."

"'Course." He shrugged. "Actually, I don't believe in visions or in, what you call, lucid dreams. Dreams are just random thoughts. It's your brain trying to figure out unresolved problems. No more. No less."

"If you would've seen what I saw, you'd agree with me," Angelica said.

"But I didn't *see* anything, and no one could. I just think you're crazy, and hallucinatin', on top of ever'thing else."

"Nevertheless, we have to get off this beach. Vision or not, we *have* to get back up the ridge."

Melanie got to her feet for the third time in as many minutes, and was pacing.

"Why don't you lie back down and relax?" Benson said. "If you'd relax, I'm sure you'd go back to sleep."

"That's exactly what I don't want. I don't want to go back there again!" Melanie had her back to Benson, but he could see her hug herself. "We need to get off this... this sandy area. If we don't, something bad is going to happen. I can feel it."

Benson shook his head. "You can't know that—"

"And you don't know it won't."

"If it does, it don't mean nothin'. I believe in what I can see and touch and hear. Don't believe in visions or the like."

"No one is asking you to. I'm just saying we need to get off this area."

"Okay, okay. First thing in the mornin', we'll see if we can find a way up."

"I'd feel better if it was now."

At daybreak, Angelica refused to continue.

"We need to go back. We need to get off this sand immediately, if not sooner."

"So we should just turn around?" Gundersen said.

"Yes! We need to get back and get hauled up the ridge."

"But we were supposed to explore this area for a way up, other than being hauled up by a rope."

Angelica grinned at him. "Okay, you do that. I'm going back, right now." She turned and started her trek back to the rope.

Gundersen put out the fire and followed her. He didn't know what else to do, but he knew exploring is safer with more explorers.

Before first light, Melanie, who hadn't returned to sleep, and Benson, who hadn't slept at all, were already heading back to the rope. They didn't argue or even discuss it. Melanie left and Benson had no choice but to follow.

It took them several hours, hurrying, to get back to the rope. Benson arrived shortly after Melanie. She was already tied and was just getting her feet lifted.

"I'll send down the rope for the rest of the equipment as soon as I get up there," she called down to him.

Benson stood staring at her feet, then began pacing. *Sure didn't take her long to beat feet back here. Her nightmare must have really shaken her. Did it shake me, too? I seem to be a little antsy about getting back up the ridge. I wonder how Gundersen and Angelica fared. Are they already up to the top of the ridge?*

When he looked up again, Melanie was close to the top. *Better get the equipment ready to be lifted.*

He headed over to the pile of tools, and was collecting them when the rope hit the ground and moved some of the pieces. It took some time for him to get the tools tied onto the rope. They had come down in several lifts, and have to go back up the same way.

After tying on the first load, Benson moved back toward the ridge, waving a hand. He didn't know if anyone could see him, but he noticed the tools started to be hauled away. While he was tying the second load of tools, Gundersen and Angelica came running to the river. Benson waved and finished tying the load. He moved away, waving, and the tools started up.

"How long you been here?" Gundersen said, breathless.

"Long enough to get Mel and most of the tools lifted."

"Glad we caught you when we did."

"Enough small talk. Get me off here," Angelica said.

"You can go the next trip, Angel." Benson turned his attention back to Gundersen. "What happened? Find anything?"

"Only thing we found was a reason for Angelica to panic. She woke up insisting she'd had a vision of some kind, and we needed to get the hell outta Dodge."

"Same with Mel. Very odd. She didn't say anything about a vision, but she beat me back here and was starting to be hauled up by the time I got here."

"Nice of her to wait." Gundersen chuckled. "Angelica fled the camp and I had to catch up after putting out the fire. It must be us. Maybe we smell or somethin'."

"It's you. I always smell like a patch of posies."

As Gundersen was guffawing, the rope came down and Angelica tied herself before the two men could react. Benson waved when he saw she was secured, and watched as she was hauled away.

While they waited for the rope to return, they had been staring out to sea. There appeared to be a disturbance under the water off the crescent-shaped beach, and it seemed to be moving toward them.

"I think we need to get off the beach," Gundersen said.

"Worried?" Benson asked rhetorically. I don't know what's

causing the water to be so disturbed, but I agree with you. We need to get outta here."

The rope slammed onto the ground.

"Get the rest of the tools tied on and hoisted out." Benson pulled out his eighteen-incher and his hatchet, and stood between the disturbance and the rope.

Once the tools were tied on, Gundersen pulled his own weapons and stood with his mentor.

"What the hell are you doing?" Benson said. "Get the hell outta here. I'll do the best I can to hold off whatever's coming."

"I ain't goin' nowheres," Gundersen said stoically.

"Look, kid, I'm old. You're not. Get outta here."

As the two men watched, the roiling water moved closer to the beach. The rope hit the ground behind them.

"Look, Gunny, you need to leave! Get outta here while the gettin' is good. Either you go, or I'll knock your dumbass out and tie you on. Now move!"

Both men backed up to the rope. Gundersen got himself tied on and then swung his leg up and hooked his foot higher on the rope as the ground was falling away. He grabbed Benson's wrist, and both men were hauled into the air. Just as their feet left the ground, a beast emerged that looked to be a giant version of a Komodo dragon. It pulled its bulk onto the sand.

"You're gonna have ta climb up here," Gundersen yelled. "I cain't haul y'all the way up the cliff. Climb up here and grab the rope."

As the pair where being hauled up into the air, the dragon had gotten fully onto the sand and was heading in their direction.

"I ain't no worm on a hook, you ugly sumbitch!" Benson yelled.

"Climb up here! Forget the beast and climb up here."

Benson looked down and saw the ground was twenty feet away. He peered at the dragon again, and its bulk obscured his view of the beach. *I doubt I'm high enough yet. That ugly thing could probably still latch onto my leg and pull me down, and Gundersen with me.*

"Let me go, Gunny."

"Get your old ass up here. I don't know how much longer I can hang onto you. You wanna be lunch for that beastie?"

Just as Benson pulled himself up a little, a younger, smaller dragon used the back of the older one and tried to grab Benson.

With the people hauling on the rope, pulling the pair up, the dragon missed by inches, but Benson's foot hit the top of the beastie's head.

"*Ahhh!*"

"Pull yourself up, dammit," Gundersen said. "Quit screwin' around and get up here."

"I think my ankle's broke."

"If you don't get up here, you're gonna be lunch. Climb, dammit!"

After straining every muscle he had, Benson managed to climb up Gundersen's body to grab the rope tied around Gundersen's waist. About halfway to Benson's goal, Gundersen released his foot and allowed his body to resume a more natural posture.

Benson grimaced while sitting on Gundersen's lap and holding the rope.

"My ankle is killing me!" he said.

"It almost caused you to die, that much is true."

"Why?"

"Why, what?"

"Why did you risk your life for mine?"

"Why not?" Gundersen shrugged.

***

"Get Benson up here," Melanie ordered the men of the extraction team.

"Careful," Gundersen said, from his position just off the edge of the plateau. "He may have a broken ankle."

"How'd he break his ankle?" Melanie said.

"One of those beasties jumped up and tried to grab him. Because of you up here hauling us up, the beastie missed and its head hit his foot or ankle. I didn't see it, but that's what he said happened."

"Since you had a hold of him, why didn't you see it?"

"I was hangin' upside down with him spinnin' us both around. I can have them lower you down so you can try to copy it and figure it all out, if you feel the need."

"I was just asking. I don't want to know *that* bad, so I'll pass on your offer."

Benson was helped up onto the plateau and was away from the edge, when Gundersen managed to climb the rest of the way to the top of the ridge.

"Speakin' for myself, I'm tired of feeling like bait on the end of a line." Gundersen untied the rope, then shook out his legs and arms.

"See!" Angelica said. "I told you I had a vision. I told you we would die if we didn't get off the sand."

"Rather pleased with yourself ain'tcha?" Gundersen said. "I'll admit that you gave the warnin'. And I'm glad I decided to follow your suggestion. Is that what you wanna hear?"

"Close enough."

"We've had time to compare notes," Melanie said to Gundersen. "All I can figure is some… entity warned us away before those monsters arrived. I, for one, can't figure it out."

"I'm just glad we all made it back in one piece," Gundersen said.

"What were those things?" Melanie asked.

"Benson said something about Komodo dragons, but I don't know what he meant. You'd have to ask him."

"I plan to," Melanie said. "I plan to."

17

It's all about the journey, not the destination. Uh-huh. Sure it is.

— KEVIN MURDOCK, FAMILY CONVERSATIONS

M elanie was watching the monsters on the beach they had just vacated. From the distance, they looked much smaller and less terrifying. Even though they were down on that beach a day ago, all four explorers were ready to put some distance between the monsters and themselves. Gundersen had checked the plateau for any sign of game animals. Finding none, they decided to head back upriver until they found sign of the deer.

Everyone left and headed back. Melanie stayed behind several minutes to get a final look at the beach and the monsters occupying it, before turning away to follow the rest.

Benson's ankle was examined by someone who had followed him to the plateau. The examiner didn't think Benson had broken his ankle, just severely bruised. Benson was carried off the plateau, which grated on him.

Gundersen stepped into Benson's shoes and was making the

decisions, and the rest had decided to follow, for now. They all had made it plain that it wasn't anything permanent.

Gundersen was a day ahead of everyone else. His job was to search for deer sign, and hopefully, find a herd. If he couldn't find anything, then he would move on after half of the followers had gained the plateau so they could help the rest.

———

"Why are we going back?" Curtis whispered to his sister, as they were following a few people back from the lead.

He could see Benson being carried out on a makeshift stretcher.

"We're leaving the beach because of the visions and because of the monsters that claimed it," Angelica whispered back. "I don't like it, either, but we have no weapons to battle those beasts. At least, not yet."

"Do I need to question you about Gundersen? I know you spent time alone with him."

Angelica glared at her brother. "What did or didn't happen is none of your concern. He's just a boy, and I'm attracted to men."

"I know that about you. You're my sister, and I'll see to it you are well taken care of."

Angelica laughed. "Since when has that ever been any concern to you? You've always made sure you would come out on top of any deal, no matter the cost to anyone else. And I'm supposed to believe that *now* you care about me, your sister?"

"Then why didn't you stay with Declan?" Curtis frowned. "You had your chance. Why didn't you take it?"

"You really don't want an answer." She looked at her brother in disbelief.

"Yes, I do. I really want to know."

Angelica nodded. "Okay, just remember, you asked for it! You hit me! You've dared to raise your hand to me too many times through the years. The last time was done in the presence of Declan's wife, and because of her witness, our older brother, her husband, kicked your ass. I watched it and rather enjoyed it, if truth be told. I enjoyed it enough that I'm planning on finding someone to kick your ass on a regular basis. I'm going to make sure you suffer!"

Curtis stared at his sister, eyes wide, mouth agape. He said nothing.

———

Murdock, Mei Lee, Declan, and Emily were gathered outside Declan's cabin. All the children were inside sleeping while their parents were enjoying quiet time before bed.

"So who won the war?" Declan said, as the adults sat around a fire in the yard.

"I wouldn't say it was a war, exactly," Murdock picked up a stick and was poking at the coals. "It was, however, a learning process for Doc, Annie, Zeke, and Heather."

Mei Lee nodded. "And it was an opportunity for Kevin to antagonize someone."

"That, too." Murdock laughed.

"So why did you say it was a learning process?" Emily said.

"Doc, Annie, Heather, and Zeke had to learn that freedom isn't free. You have to stand up for yourself and defend yourself."

"I would've thought Annie and Heather would've known that," Declan said, "after all the time they'd spent with us."

Murdock looked at Declan with a strange expression.

"Why you lookin' at me that way?" Declan said. "I know you have to be prepared to defend what's yours."

"You may know it, but until you actually have to, you have no idea what you'll do or how you'll act. I was lookin' at you that way because I don't remember you having to defend yourself against an attack of that magnitude."

Murdock turned to Mei Lee. "And I wasn't antagonizing

them. They started it. They fired at us first. I returned fire only to let them know they better be the best they can be before coming after me and mine!"

It was then that the adults all felt a familiar presence.

"*Beron, my friend,*" Murdock flashed. "*Have you been well?*"

"*Have been well,*" Beron responded to all present as he became visible.

"*Did Bridget come with you?*" Mei Lee asked.

"*Not this time,*" Beron replied.

"*What brings you to visit?*" Declan flashed.

"*You sibles safe.*"

"*Sibles?*" they all asked.

"*Excuse! Wrong words?*"

"*Sibles... siblings?*" Emily flashed. "*Those with same parentage?*"

"*Ah, yes, siblings. They safe.*" Beron flashed.

"*Don't understand,*" Murdock replied. "*Were in danger?*"

"*Share?*" Beron flashed.

Murdock entered the sharing state and was standing next to Beron in the sharing state realm. Each of the others joined and materialized with Murdock.

"What's this about?" Murdock said.

A sleeve of the black robe raised, and the sky changed to show the view of the beach with the Komodo dragons on it.

"Siblings were here, but now safe," Beron said.

"I don't recognize that area," Murdock said. "Where is it?"

"Far down water."

This caused them all to puzzle on the meaning.

"Down... river?" Declan said.

"Yes, downriver. Far away."

"So you warned Angelica and Curtis to leave that area before those... those things could harm them?" Murdock said. "How did you warn them?"

"Same as Murdock," Beron answered.

Murdock chuckled.

"What's that supposed to mean?" Declan said, irritated.

"Back before Beron and I met," Murdock said, "he tried to warn me off an area. He did it in a dream. Didn't work on me, but I bet it shook up Angelica and Curtis."

"No Curtis," Beron said. "Only females."

The view of the sky changed to a view of Angelica and a stranger.

"I know her," Declan said. "Melanie... Burton, I think was her name."

"So you warned them and everyone is safe?" Murdock said.

"No. One injured."

The sky changed again and showed a man.

"Dirk Benson," Murdock said. "I know him. He's talented, but needs to learn more. How bad was the injury?"

"Unknown," Beron said.

"*Annie, are you up for a trip?*" Murdock flashed.

"*Not now. Maybe in the morning. What's up?*"

Murdock communicated everything he knew about the situation and Dirk's injury.

"*Tomorrow. I'll take Heather with me,*" Annie flashed to Murdock.

"*Travel as quickly as you can without showing off too much,*" Murdock replied.

"*Understood. Tomorrow.*"

It took the group five days to find a plateau with an acceptable amount of deer, in Gundersen's opinion. As he stood at the top of the plateau, listening to the river and waiting for the first arrivals of the rest of his group to gain it, he tried to figure out which plateau this was and how many plateaus it was to the landing spot.

According to Murdock's information, the pods landed on the third plateau, presumably from some major land event or structure. I'm currently standing on the third plateau from the beach. Now, then, how many plateaus are between the two?

"Damned if I can remember," Gundersen said, just as Mackenzie Braddock cleared the top of the ridge behind him.

It didn't startle him since he had marked their passage of the last mile or so to the base.

"Talking to yourself, again?" Mackenzie said.

"I'm the only one who'll listen to me these days." Gundersen laughed.

He had noticed that Braddock always seemed to be close by, especially since Dirk's injury. He didn't mind, but when he stopped to think about it, it was a bit on the creepy side, in a stalker kind of way. He tried to not think of it in those terms. He figured she was in her late teens or early twenty's—he couldn't always tell how old a woman was just by looking—and Dirk had told him to quit thinking like that.

"Never tell a woman how old you think she is," he'd said, one night. "Always shade it to closer to sixteen, if at all possible. Women like to know they look younger than they actually are."

They'd had a chuckle over that one.

"And if she's too rude or not to my likin'?" Gundersen had said, between guffaws.

"I ain't gonna tell ya what to say in that case. Just be advised, you could get murdered in your sleep."

"So is this the place?" Mackenzie came up beside him.

Whenever he looked at her, he always seemed to be looking down at the top of her head. He was becoming attracted to her long brown, baby-fine hair she kept in a ponytail. He noticed that her part was always straight and her scalp was always clean.

"Not here. Upriver apiece," he replied. *Why is my tongue getting in the way of itself.* "It's not too much further."

Mackenzie nodded and drifted back to those clearing the edge. Gundersen knew, from having gone through this before, one of the last ones up would be Benson and Melanie. The last ones were always Angelica and Curtis.

They're last so everyone else could walk away and leave the trouble-twins behind. Nobody likes them much, and they don't do anything to ingratiate themselves to the rest of the group.

He knew they weren't twins, but they were double-barreled trouble.

It was early morning when Heather saddled up her mount. She and Annie were making a trip of unknown duration, for medical purposes. Annie had brought a bag of medical supplies and other sundries, which Heather secured. When they were ready, Heather took the lead position on the mount, with Annie behind her. Both women carried bows as well as their usual component weapons—two machetes, a hatchet, a rope, a skinning knife, a whetstone, and a flint. Annie had been trained by Murdock in the use of the tools, including as weapons. Heather, though she had left Murdock's protection for some time, was starting to get back into it.

As the mount plodded along, following the river's flow, Annie had trouble staying awake.

"How do you do it?" she said.

"Do what?" Heather replied.

"Stay awake. Between the plodding and the swaying of this animal, I'm having trouble staying alert."

"Sometimes I don't." Heather laughed. "I have to trust this animal to take me where I want to go. Sometimes the trip has a lack of... mental stimulation. When that happens, I do sometimes fall asleep. Usually, though, I hum to myself or sing. Usually, I'm walking and have to be alert enough to put one foot in front of another. Up here, I feel like my head is in the clouds and the swaying motion is having its effect."

"Okay, so you keep an eye out to the right. I'll take the left, and if we need to, talk or sing."

"You don't want me singing." Annie chuckled. "I've been told that I sound like a cat being strangled."

"Yeah, I ain't no velvet voice myself, but if you can stand it, I'll give it a go."

"Oh-h-h, I'd love to be an Oscar Mayer wiener..." Heather started, with vigor. "That is what I truly like to be-e-e."

"Wait...what is a wiener? And what's so special about an Oscar Mayer wiener?" Annie asked.

"I have no idea. It's just a song. I think my Dad used to sing it to me, but I have no idea what the lyrics mean, or all of them, for that matter. You know any songs?"

"The only song I know is the chorus of 'Oh, Susanna'."

"Is that all you know? I'd think it wouldn't be a proper song with just a chorus. Needs a bit more than that. Maybe we shoulda had Zeke lookup some travelin' songs."

"Maybe." Annie chuckled.

"Do we know where we're going?"

"Downriver is all I know. There's someone with an ankle injury. Now you know as much as I do."

"Seems rather thin on the information."

"It's something you get used to. I was told the information came from Beron. So though it lacks details, it is accurate. I think it may be a group with Angelica and Curtis in it."

"Those two? Aren't they related to Declan?"

"Yes, his siblings."

"What're they doin' out here? You'd think they would be staying with Declan, or somewhere close to him."

"You'd think so. From what I know, Curtis raised a hand to his sister and Em interrupted them."

"Bastard! That explains what *he's* doin' out here, but not her. Personally, I woulda shot his ass."

"I've not been made privy to the details. So I can't say."

"Maybe we should ask her," Heather said.

"Maybe." A long pause. "And maybe we should keep our noses out of it."

"Are you comfortable with this pace?"

"Sure. You could go faster, if you think we can."

Heather kicked the beast into a trot, setting both women bouncing.

"You okay with this?" she said.

"For a little while. Too much of this is going to make my breasts hurt."

"Oh-h-h, I'd love to be an Oscar Mayer wiener…"

"Heather, please stop," Annie said, after the fifteenth time. "I now have that stuck inside my head. Thanks!"

"No problem, Annie. Just tryin' ta help!"

When they had arrived at the point that Gundersen had chosen for a more permanent site, it was midday. As everyone was preparing a meal, Gundersen decided to check on Benson.

"How ya doin', Dirk?"

"I need to get to my feet, somehow. I'm tired of not being able to do what needs to be done."

"Just take it easy, Dirk. I'll help ya get to your feet, but don't go doin' nuthin' to reinjure yourself."

"I'd appreciate it if you could find me somethin' to shape into a crutch." Benson smiled as Gundersen got him upright, with an arm over the younger man's shoulder.

"I'll see what I can find."

"Is this where you're thinkin' of buildin' a shelter?" Benson hobbled around. It'd be better to build it on the other side of the river."

"I know."

"What type of shelter?"

"Lean-to, to start with. Don't know any other kind."

"You could make Celtic roundhouses. They aren't too complex. They just require a lot of work."

"Let's get everyone together and you can explain it."

It was getting close to nightfall, and Gundersen was across the river looking for a good spot to build his and Benson's roundhouse.

Mackenzie came over. "Whatcha doin'?"

"Tryin' to find a good place to build a house," Gundersen said.

"Does it matter so much? I mean, with all the houses that'll be built here, this whole place is going to change."

"Maybe so." Gundersen walked around the area.

"Am I bothering you?"

"No. Sorry, but I have a lot on my mind. It's a lot of responsibility, and I ain't used to it."

"What is?"

"Bein' in charge."

Mackenzie started to laugh.

"What's so funny?"

"You think you're actually in charge of something? I hate to break it to ya, but you ain't in charge of shit. You do what you're told and that's all."

"Is that right? And how would *you* know?"

"I know 'cause I listen. Most people pay me no mind. Most times, I'm ignored, invisible. You can hear lots of things when people don't see ya and forget you're around."

Gundersen plopped down on a rock. He looked at her and noticed, possibly for the first time, that she had a good face. She wasn't what others would call pretty, but he found comfort in her features. Her hazel eyes were bright and lively.

"Why you tellin' me this?" he said.

"'Cause I kinda feel sorry for ya. You been stressin' over nothin'."

"I don't need, nor want your pity," he said, rougher than he'd intended.

"Good! Wasn't givin' ya any. Look, I like you. You're tryin' to do what you think others are expectin' of you. Most of us listen to Benson 'cuz he's older. It's obvious that he knows stuff."

"I know stuff, too."

"Maybe, but ya don' know enough for people to trust ya. Ya gotta prove yourself, or that's what I hear."

"You seem to hear a lot… maybe too much."

"Mind if I ask you somethin'?"

"What?"

"How old are ya?"

"Why?"

"Just askin'. Tell me or no. Don't really care either way."

"Fifteen."

"Thought so. I ain't trying to put down whatcha been doin'. For a fifteen-year-old, you been doin' better than most. You seem to have a good head on your shoulders. Few more years and you'll do just fine!"

"Do? Do for what?"

"You ain't quite marryin'-high yet." She chuckled. "When you are, I may be interested. Hell, I ain't husband-high myself yet."

"I got no idea what you're talkin' about."

"Yeah, probably not. Cogitate on it all, and you'll get it… eventually." She chuckled as she rejoined the rest, leaving him to his thoughts.

Heather was busy tending her mount as Annie was getting a fire started and catching them some fish. They had managed to get off the fourth plateau.

"Two plateaus in a day? We seem to be makin' pretty good time," Annie said, while preparing the fish for cooking.

"Don't count on traveling that slow all the time," Heather said. "We could speed up some before we get to where we're going. Without the possibility of someone watching, we might navigate the terrace-edges faster."

"I was meaning to ask you about that. Have you done any work with your mount and levitation?"

"She does pretty well, if I do the levitatin'. She may panic if you do it, even though you're probably better at it than I am."

"We'll have to see. How are *your* skills coming along?"

"Fair, I guess. You'd have to run me through some paces for an assessment."

"Well, I'm sure we can do some of that on this trip."

"Sounds good to me," Heather finished her fish. "Didn't we bring some venison?"

"We brought some, just not enough. If they have some at our destination, then great. If not, it may fall to us to hunt one down. So how are your bow skills? Tracking skills?"

"Tracking isn't what it should be yet. I'm not bad with the bow."

Annie saw an expression cross Heather's face.

"What is it?" she said.

"I'm still a little queasy about taking a life, human or deer."

"Why is that?"

"I know we need to hunt deer, but I've spent a lot of time taming a few. It's just difficult." Heather looked at the fire.

"And shooting at people?"

Heather's face contorted into several expressions. "I don't like it. I know I have to be ready to do it, but I don't like it."

Annie smiled. "Good! I'd be worried about you if you did like it. If pressed to it, could you shoot Alvin?"

"Alvin was okay, I guess. He was a good companion to me, but that was about it. I could wound him, but I don't think I could kill him. His betrayal wasn't surprising. So when do you think we'll get there?"

It had been three days since their arrival here, and Gundersen was, with Mackenzie's help, getting close to having the walls done. He was having trouble with mixing the clay and straw to get something that would stick to the waddle walls. So far, the mixtures he'd tried had fallen off when they dried.

"Why are you having such a hard time?" Benson hobbled over to Gundersen's mixing area.

"I don't know," he said, frustrated.

Benson watched Gundersen work the straw and clay together.

"Ah, your mix is too dry," Benson said. "Don't be afraid to use more water. You want it wet enough to stick, and you'll be smoothing it with your wet hands, so don't make it so dry."

"Hello in the camp!" a woman's voice sounded, from across the river.

Benson hobbled around to see. Two women sat atop a large deer. The one in control of the beast was dressed in a buckskin dress and looked familiar to him. They both jumped down and started to untie a bag.

"I'm Annie Cooper, and I take it you're the one with an ankle injury?"

Benson nodded, dumbfounded.

"This is my associate, Heather Stevens. Have we caught you at a bad time?"

"No, come on over." Benson waved to the pair.

Then he remembered who Annie was. She was the one who had given all the new arrivals their first once-over on arrival.

"Tie your beast over that away a little," Benson said. "We're trying to build a house here."

Annie nodded to Heather, who complied.

"And you are…" Annie extended her hand.

"Dirk… Benson. This here is my friend, Chris Gundersen. Clean off the mud first, Chris. Lady don't want your muddy paw to shake."

Gundersen used water to clean off his right hand before offering it to Annie.

"Nice to see you both again," she said. "I don't know if you remember, but—"

"You gave us the once-over when we all first arrived," Benson said. "I remember."

Annie smiled. "It's always nice to be remembered. Now, about your foot. Is there somewhere I can look at it?"

"As you can see, this here rock is about all we got at present."

"That'll be fine. How long ago was it injured?"

"About seven days. Maybe a little more."

"Have you had your shoe off since the injury?"

"No, we've been travelin' up here since it happened. This ain't the place to be barefoot."

"Mind if I take off your shoe? I have to get a good look at it." After receiving a nod from Benson, she started to untie the binding. "Tell me if this becomes too uncomfortable for you."

She slipped the loosened shoe off in a smooth motion. Benson gasped.

"Your sock needs to come off as well. I can try, or your friend can…"

"No, you did fine with the shoe. I trust you."

"It may hurt some." She tried to roll down the sock and off the foot. "You okay?"

"Just fine, ma'am."

She smiled. "Just Annie is fine."

She saw deep purple all around the ankle and across the top of his foot, and it was extremely swollen.

"Can you move it at all?"

She placed Benson's calf on her thigh, allowing his foot to be suspended. It twitched as Benson attempted to rotate it.

"Well, since you can move it, it's unlikely that you broke anything. You have, however, bruised it significantly. You should have had your shoe and sock off and the foot in cold water as soon as possible. That would've helped with the swelling."

"It was an emergency situation." Benson chuckled.

"Well, we'll be staying around here for the next couple days. I want it soaking as much as possible to get the swelling down."

"Um… okay. I guess that'd be okay. Soak it how?"

"The river works. The water is cold. I still don't know if it's broke or not, which is why we're staying for a few days. If I find it is broken, we'll be transporting you to the medical facility to have Doc Harris look at it."

"Um… okay…" Benson said unenthusiastically.

"So for the time being, get your foot into the river."

Gundersen, who'd overheard Annie, had picked up a round of wood and was carrying it down to the river's edge.

"Come on, old man, let's get you down to the river." He got Benson to his feet.

"I'll give you *old man*, you whippersnapper." Benson leaned on the younger man as he hopped to the river.

"Glad they're friends," Heather said.

Both women noticed they were the object of curiosity by the others in the group.

"Well, Doc, is he gonna live?" Melanie watched the two at the river.

"First of all, I'm not a doctor. I'm a nurse under the direction of a doctor. Secondly, yes, he'll live. If he bites the big one, it won't be because of his ankle. Not directly, anyway."

"Melanie Burton." She extended her roughened hand.

"Annie…Cooper." She took the offered hand, "And this is Heather Stevens."

"Is she a nurse, too? I remember you from our arrival." Melanie nodded to Annie.

"Nah, I'm just the LPN's go-fer," Heather said. "Nothin' special about me."

"Funny, you don't look like a burrowing rodent. Everyone is rather curious about you two. They weren't expecting any medical treatment this far out. Staying long?"

"Um… not an animal. A go-fer…as in *go fer this* or *go fer that*." Heather smiled.

"*Uh-oh,*" Annie flashed to Heather. "*I think we're being sized up as competition.*"

Heather flashed her version of a cat hiss and growl to Annie.

"Not staying long," Annie said. "Just a couple days to make certain Benson's ankle isn't broken. Then we'll be off."

"Okay. I'll let the others know," Melanie said.

"*Did you hear the 'good' in her tone?*" Annie flashed to Heather.

"*Sure did. You ready for the question of how we knew Benson needed medical help?*"

"*Sure. I'll tell them the truth.*"

Heather was in the middle of drinking when Annie sent her message, causing Heather to spew water.

"*Very funny!*" Heather replied.

"*So your control over your responses from telepathic communication needs work. It's imperative that others don't know we can communicate that way, so you can't react.*"

Annie walked down to the river to check on Benson.

"How's the ankle?" she said, from some distance.

"I'll live, maybe." He chuckled. "The cold water sure feels good on it. Probably should've been doin' this all along."

"Probably." Annie smirked. "Can I ask you something?"

"Sure." Benson shrugged.

"Our being here isn't going to cause any… um… issues, is it?"

"Not as far as I'm concerned. Do you need something from me or from us?"

"Nope. Don't need anything from you or your people." Annie paused for a couple seconds. "Would a deer help?"

"You mean as in venison?"

Annie nodded.

"It would help me and Gundersen. We have to make range weapons, and I'd need to take a deer to start. But with my bum ankle…"

"Tomorrow, Heather and I will see what we can find for game. I mean, we could use some venison while we're here."

"Well, I for one, would like it if you spent your nights inside our house. Yeah, it's still under construction, but it's safer than sleeping out in the wild. You're more than welcome to it, for your help with my ankle."

"Is our mount going to be okay?"

"Should be. Is it yours?"

"No, it's more Heather's pet than anything else. She was teaching me how to control it when we arrived. I would be upset if something happened to it. Heather would be inconsolable."

Benson nodded. "I'll see to it that Gundersen explains it to everyone else before nightfall. I'd say nothing should happen, but these people do as they please, even if it is contrary to my wishes."

"I'd appreciate that. And I'm certain that Heather would appreciate it as well."

"I have a question, if you don't mind?"

Annie nodded.

"How did you know I needed medical attention? There was no way one of these people could get a message to you. I just can't figure out how you knew."

"Honestly," Annie exhaled, "you wouldn't believe me if I told you. Suffice it to say, a friend of mine knew of your injury and told me."

"Seriously? You expect me to believe that?"

"Well, the only other answer I can give is it's magic. You choose which is more palatable to you and your sensibilities."

18

My Sensei told me once that your biggest hindrance to most everything you do sits on top of your shoulders. It's between your ears. Your own mind can talk you into most everything, and can also work against you.

— KEVIN MURDOCK, FAMILY CONVERSATIONS

Easy, *Annie. Breathe. Make sure the breeze is in your face. If the deer looks at you, don't move. You can do this.*

Annie had left Heather and her mount a short distance behind her while she'd crept up on the herd of deer.

Pick one target and stay focused on it. Don't focus on the entire herd.

Her target turned away and dipped its head to eat.

Quietly nock an arrow. Annie took a metal arrow and nocked it onto her metal bow.

She had practiced enough to be proficient. The noise the arrow shaft tended to make against the metal riser made her cringe as she drew it back. She inhaled during the draw, exhaled during the hold, and released the arrow at the end of the exhale. The deer stumble before running off. She pulled an arrow and stuck it into the ground where she was standing, then moved away and emptied the contents of her stomach.

"*Did you hit it?*" Heather flashed to her.

"*I think so,*" Annie replied, once she got her nerves under control. "*It ran off like it was hit. I'll look for a blood trail in a few minutes.*"

"*Correct, Annie,*" Murdock flashed. "*Don't be in a rush.*"

"*Where are you?*" Heather flashed to Annie.

"*Right now,*" she sighted back to the arrow stuck in the ground, "*I'm about two hundred yards toward the stream from you, and a little downstream.*"

"*Find a blood trail?*"

Annie's gaze locked onto some large splotches of bright red on the blue-green blades of grass.

"*Just now. You can start heading my direction. Just take your time.*" Looks to be a lung hit, judging by the color.

Annie started creeping along the blood trail and remaining on alert for any other beasts looking to steal her prey. It took her some time to find her prey. When she did, it laid still, eyes glazed. Her stomach churned and threatened to empty itself again.

My first kill. I may have been excited about my first deer, but now I'm sad. I know I had to do it to eat, but it doesn't mean I can't regret it.

It didn't take Heather long to lead her mount, with Dirk Benson and Chris Gundersen on its back, to Annie and her prey.

"There you go, gentlemen," Annie said. "Your turn."

Gundersen dismounted and helped Benson down. Benson was having trouble hobbling along, and would periodically bump his foot on a tuft of grass or a small rock, causing him to cringe. Once the men arrived at the deer, Benson began giving Gundersen instructions on how to gut the animal. Annie watched silently for a bit.

"Be careful with the hide," she said. "You'll need it. Actually, you'll need a lot of hides."

"Good point, Annie." Benson then resumed telling Gundersen what to do. "Look at this, Annie," he said, after a short while.

"What is it?" She got closer to look at the carcass.

Benson brushed a bloody finger across her forehead.

"What the hell?"

"You did say this was your first. You're now blooded."

Annie glared at him and thought about wiping off the blood.

"Leave it, Annie," Murdock flashed. *"If I'd been there, I'd do the same thing. Wear it proudly."*

"Fine!"

When the men were finished quartering the deer and wrapping it in the hide, Gundersen got Benson remounted and they all headed toward the river. After crossing the river, Benson was sat on the log round and told to soak his foot while Gundersen washed the quarters and dispersed them amongst the rest of the group. He had kept one hind quarter—which he hung inside their roundhouse—and the hide, with the head attached. The hide was draped over a thick tree-limb.

"Chris, you get to see how to brain tan a hide," Benson said, when Gundersen had returned. "Hopefully, Miss Annie will instruct us on that task. That was somethin' I never learned to do."

"I'll tell you what I know. Annie chuckled as she kneeled to look at Benson's ankle. "Does that hurt?" She rotated the foot.

"Not bad," Benson said, through clenched teeth.

"Uh-huh. You need to be more truthful with me. I need to know. An honest response would make my job easier."

"Okay, yeah, it hurt quite a bit, actually."

"That's better." Annie smirked. "I didn't feel anything that would indicate a break. Was there any sharp and intense pain when I rotated it?"

"No. You just made it throb more."

"Well, then, I'd say we can leave tomorrow. You'll eventually recover full use, depending on how much you overwork it instead of taking it easy until it heals."

"Um… okay. So soon?"

"Yes, we've intruded enough. Tomorrow, we leave."

"Well, then, I'm insisting on you joining us for dinner tonight."

Annie smirked. "Okay, Dirk. We accept."

"We have a dinner date tonight," Annie flashed to Heather.

"I don't have a thing to wear," Heather joked.

"Dirk would like that, but Chris would have a heart attack."

"I don't know. I've seen how Chris has been eye-balling that girl. Mackenzie, I think is her name. By the way, what's the occasion for tonight?"

"Because tomorrow morning we leave."

"Well, I, for one, will be glad to get home to a nice hot bath."

"Me, too!"

Annie spent the rest of the day explaining, mostly to Benson, how to tan the hide. Gundersen was finishing up the roof on their house while listening to Annie.

Heather helped Gundersen by gathering tall grass from across the river and binding them into shocks. On one of the trips, she was approached by Mackenzie.

"How's Benson comin' along?" she said.

Heather continued gathering the tall grass. "He's doing better, I guess."

"Good! Glad to hear it. So when are you two leavin'?"

"I was just told that we'll be leavin' tomorrow mornin', not that it's any of your business."

"There are some of us that feel you two need to be movin' on."

"Who are these people that feel that way?" Heather grinned as she glared at the much younger girl. "Are they here with you to explain to me why I should leave?"

"No, I was selected to pass on the information." Mackenzie glared back.

"First off, little one, you don't tell me or Annie what to do. Second, show us a little more respect. There'll come a time when you'll need us. How are you or the others going to feel when we decline due to your lack of ...hospitality?"

"Like when? When are we ever gonna need you?"

"Like when you're pregnant and ready to deliver. When you're all big and hurtin' and scared. How would you like it if we just declined?"

Mackenzie tried to rush toward Heather, but stumbled and fell. She scrambled up and took a step, and fell again.

"You really don't wanna fight me, little girl," Heather said, without turning to look at her.

When Mackenzie gained her feet, she took a step and fell again. She looked at Heather, puzzled.

"Clumsy, ain't you." Heather took her load of grass and headed toward the river and Benson's house.

"How much more you gonna need?" Heather asked Gundersen, once she was at the house.

"Don't know yet. Should be getting' close, though."

"*We got a problem,*" Heather flashed to Annie.

"*What problem?*"

"*That girl Mackenzie was going to assault me while I was across the river.*"

"*And what did you do?*"

"I made it so she couldn't keep her feet. It allowed me to finish what I was doin' and leave without touchin' her."

"Did she tell you why?"

"Not in so many words. I think she was tryin' to intimidate me into leavin' early."

"I've been expecting that since we first arrived. Stay alert and let me know if anything else happens."

At sundown, Annie and Heather were sitting on a log round in front of the central fire inside Benson's roundhouse. Annie looked around at the waddle walls covered with clay. When she looked up, she noticed the smoke gathered at the peak of the roof.

"Aren't you afraid of a spark catching the roof on fire?" she said.

"No," Benson said. "The smoke should filter through the thatched roof, but up there, a carbon dioxide layer builds, so sparks won't start anything on fire."

"That's the theory, anyways," Gundersen added with a chuckle.

"Yeah, that's the theory." Benson laughed. "Ask me in a year. If I'm still around, you can always come back to check my theory for validity."

Annie and Heather selected their portions of venison. Benson and Gundersen selected theirs.

"A special thank you goes to Annie for this meal and for the company." Benson wore a broad smile.

"And for prettying up our humble house." Gundersen smiled, too.

"And to Heather for all her help and support!" Annie said.

"To Heather *and* Annie," the two men said.

About halfway through the meal, a female cleared her throat at the doorway to Benson's house.

"Excuse me, Dirk, can we have a word or two with *your* visitors?" Melanie said.

Several women were gathered at the door, all of which had a scowl on their face.

"That's up to them," Benson said. "I'll not presume on our guests to talk to you if they're unwillin'."

Annie got to her feet and approached the women. "What is it?"

"You need to discipline your *girl*," Melanie said.

"And why's that?" Annie said. "She's not *my girl*. She's her own woman."

"Whatever she is, she assaulted one of the younger women here." Melanie crossed her arms and glared at Heather.

"What do you mean by *assault*?" Annie said. "Did Heather touch this... girl... in any way?"

"Well... no."

"Then it wasn't assault, now was it?" Annie grinned and glared at the women and crossed her own arms. "Any other complaints... *ladies*?"

"We feel that this arrangement is... improper," Melanie said.

"Improper? In what way?" Annie said. "Are you the arbiter of what is proper and what isn't in your society? Perhaps if you'd specify what the impropriety is, then we could address it."

Melanie's face turned red. "As the women of this group, we reserve the right to determine what is proper and what isn't." She continued glaring.

"And you also have the right to live alone. I'm certain most of these men could find... other women... should they desire it." Annie returned her glare. "Besides, *ladies*, my companion and I will be leaving first thing in the morning, so, you have nothing to fear from us. We came here unescorted, and we intend to leave the same way. Your claims are safe from us." Annie went back to the fire.

"What the hell was all that about?" Heather flashed to Annie.

"Jealousy, pure and simple. You didn't touch Mackenzie, but they used it as an excuse to confront us about the untenable situation."

"What was all that about?" Benson said. "And what was all that about claims?"

Gundersen's curiosity was evident on his face and he listened intently.

"Either some, or all, of those women feel they have a claim of some sort on you two," Annie said.

"What? Why, that's just craziness!" Benson said emphatically. "I know for a fact I've never given any of them a reason to think that way. Have you, Chris? Have you been dallyin' with any of them?"

"I have no idea," Gundersen said. "I have no idea what you mean."

"You know, in an intimate liaison with one, or more, of them?" Gundersen gave him a blank look.

"Are you havin' sex with any of them? Sorry, for the bluntness," he said to Annie.

"I'm not offended," she said. "I'm a nurse. I've heard it all, and probably said it all, before. And I'm sure Heather isn't offended with plain speaking."

Heather shook her head. "Not offended at all."

Gundersen turned a bright red. "I have no idea what you mean," he said, with downcast eyes.

"Are you still a virgin?" Annie asked Gundersen.

"Um... ah... um... I... *think* so," Gundersen said finally.

"So Annie, as you can see, I got no idea what they're talkin' about."

Annie looked at the two men and could see the confusion on their faces. "Oh, I have no doubt that you two know nothing about it. I'm certain it's something they have fixated on in their own minds. To them, it's okay to compete amongst each other. But it isn't okay for us, being outsiders, to come in and jump their claims, so to speak."

It had been hours since everyone had turned in for the night. Annie hadn't been able to sleep. Her mind was in turmoil over the women confronting her and Heather.

If it would have been up to Heather, we'd have battled it out.

"Trouble sleeping?" Heather flashed. *"Them uppity women get your nose outta joint?"*

"Maybe."

"Shoulda knocked a few heads together. Woulda been more satisfyin'."

"Probably." Annie got to her feet.

"Annie, what the hell are you doin'?"

"Hush now! Go to sleep. I know what I'm doing,"

As Heather stalked upon Benson, she could hear Gundersen's deep, even breathing. She looked down at Benson in the dark and saw he was about to speak.

She gently put a hand over his mouth and whispered, "Hush," into his ear.

A few minutes later, she lowered herself, with her buckskin skirt hiked up around her hips.

Thirty minutes later, she got off Benson and went back to her own sleeping area.

Just before first light, Annie and Heather were awake and packing the rest of their equipment onto their mount or about their person.

"Tryin' to sneak away?" Benson hobbled up to them.

"Not at all. We were going to wake you before we left," Annie lied.

Benson looked around as if checking for ears that could be listening.

"About last night," he whispered.

"What about last night?" Annie whispered back. "Did something happen that I should be aware of, because if so, I'm sorry I missed it." She smirked.

"But—"

"No buts. Nothing happened and I want to keep it that way."

"Okay, then, if that's the way you want it," Benson whispered.

"Glad I could help you out with your ankle. You need to keep off it as much as you can for a while yet. Soak it whenever you can."

"Thank you for the deer meat. Take care on your way home. Oh, before I forget, we had fifteen odd-balls with us when we left the landing area. Near as I can figure it, they should be on the next plateau up and over by the stream. If you go that way, be extra careful. There're vines that'll creep up your legs and trap ya, or your feet. Takes water to get them to let loose."

"Thanks for the information. We're always looking for more info on this place." Annie swung up onto their mount's back and slid back to let Heather swing up and take charge of the beast.

Benson raised his hand and had a quizzical little smile as he watched Annie and Heather ride away. Gundersen came out of the house, stretching. He walked over to Benson and looked in the same direction as his mentor.

"They leave?" He tried to stifle a yawn.

"Yup. They gone," Benson mumbled.

"You okay? You ain't usually this quiet this time of the mornin'."

"In some respects, I'll never be the same."

"What's that 'sposed to mean?"

"Never mind, Chris. Get breakfast going. We got stuff to do. We're burnin' daylight!"

———

"What was that?" Heather said.

They had been riding at a walk for more than an hour.

"What was what?" Annie replied.

"Oh, come on! Don't tell me you're gonna play it *that* way."

"What are you talking about, Heather?"

"I wanna know about last night."

"What about it?"

Heather turned to look at Annie. "Nope! I ain't gonna let you pull that. I wanna know what last night was all about."

"Honestly, I don't know yet. It's been so long, and those harpies thinking we were there to upset their applecart, I was just thinking I should take what I want. So I did. And I'd appreciate it if you'd keep it to yourself."

"What about Beron and Murdock and everyone who can read our thoughts?"

"They can't read our thoughts… exactly. We have to share them. Have you seen anything from Murdock or Mei Lee about anything intimate with them?"

"Can't say that I have," Heather said, after thinking about it a while.

"Did you think they don't have any thoughts of an intimate nature? When we share, we share what we want. So keep it to yourself. I'd appreciate it."

"What about Murdock and Mei Lee?"

"They won't ask, out of respect. They'll wait until I'm ready to tell them, if ever. Doc Harris won't ask either. Same reason."

Heather shrugged. "Okay, if that's the way you want it."

"*Murdock,*" Annie flashed, "*we're heading back. All is well with me and Heather. Just before we left, we were told about fifteen …others. Did you want us to check it out?*"

"*Where are these …others, and who are they?*"

"*We don't know who they are. They're just referred to as oddballs. Fifteen of them and they're up one step and over by the stream. That's all I know.*"

"*Go to the stream. There should be a ridge above it in the direction you travel to get there. Go up on that ridge and proceed homeward. You should pass where the fifteen are. I would like you to observe them for a while and report back. Don't contact them in any way until after you report to me."*

Annie confirmed the message.

"Have you thought of what happens if you got knocked up last night?" Heather said.

"We need to head to the stream. If I'm pregnant, then I'm pregnant. No big deal."

"No big deal?" Heather said, after changing course. "To you, it may be no big deal, but how would Benson feel about it? Don't you think he deserves to know?"

"Not particularly. He's just the sperm donor. He doesn't have a right to know anything. He doesn't know me and isn't likely to, either."

Heather chewed on the corner of her lip. "If, as you say, it had been a while, then he knows you like no one here does. I think you're wrong about Benson. I think he needs to know, should you be pregnant. But I won't tell him. I promised to keep it to myself and I will."

Annie breathed a sigh of relief and touched Heather's shoulder. "I appreciate that."

"Oh, you're not off the hook with me! I won't tell him, but I will harp at you until you do. It's the price you pay for me keeping your secret."

It was close to the end of the day when Heather and Annie arrived at the stream. They decided to move downstream far enough to be out of sight of the suspect ledge where the fifteen should be located.

Both women emptied their waterskins and refilled them with fresh water. They found wood for a small fire to cook a portion of the venison Dirk had insisted they take. Heather hobbled her mount and staked it out so it could drink and browse as it wanted. By the time it was dark, they had a nice little camp set and were sitting around the fire, waiting for the venison to cook.

"Do you think Murdock would make us bows like his?" Heather said. "The metal ones are better than nothing, but his bow seems more natural and easier to keep quiet."

"I don't know. You'd have to ask him."

Annie did agree with her assessment, though. She had managed to sneak up on that deer, but the bow and arrow made a lot of noise.

"What does Murdock want us to do?" Heather said.

"Observe. We're to observe these fifteen, and nothing else at this point. We are to stay away from them and stay safe."

"Have you ever been up there," Heather turned to look up on the ridge towering above them.

"I have once, I think. But that was back when we first arrived. I don't think I've been up there since. The part I was on was way upstream, toward home, from here."

"I'm just wondering what's up there, is all." Heather turned back to the fire.

"What did you do to that girl who was going to attack you?" Annie checked the venison.

"I used my powers, which is how I think of them, to force her feet to get in the way of each other and trip on rocks or tufts of grass, the swing of the leg or not step high enough, that sorta thing. Worked pretty good, too. She stumbled enough that I could get back without rushing."

"Yes, it did." Annie chuckled. "The meat should be cooked now." She selected the one she'd set aside."

"Did Benson ever explain what happened to his ankle in the first place?" Heather picked up her portion of cooked meat.

"Yes, he told me." Annie took a bite. "But I'm not too sure he knew what he was talking about. When you're being attacked, the animal attacking is usually larger in the re-telling."

"Except for Murdock," Heather added as she ate.

"Ha-ha-ha. Yes. I'd have to agree. Murdock doesn't exaggerate at all."

"I don't think he knows what that is." Heather chuckled. "Oh, sure, he'll pull a leg or two, but not exaggerate the facts."

Both women got quiet and quit laughing. Both looked sad.

"I miss home," Annie mumbled.

"I know. Same here." Heather snuggled into her.

They stared at the fire.

By daybreak, both women were awake, fed, and packed to continue on their trip.

By the second day of this long trip, the mount had gotten used to Annie levitating it while Heather held the reins. Usually, Heather controlled the pace and direction, and Annie did the levitation when required.

Annie, Heather, and their mount were levitated up to the ridge that followed the stream. Heather was leery of this portion of their trip since the ridge they were on was off-limits.

"Sure hope we don't get unconscious for bein' up here," Heather said, as soon as the mount's feet hit the ground. "I heard about the punishment that some have received for bein' up here, and I don't want no part of that."

"From what I know, Beron caused nightmares for those who broke the taboo. We're now part of Murdock's household, so we're allowed."

"You *know* that? Or are you just *hoping*, like me."

"I know I'm part of Murdock's household. He has said so. Beron has said so, and I feel it. Don't you?"

"'Course I do!" Heather said. "But I'm the new kid on the block and still don't know all the rules and all the expectations."

"Sure you do." Annie chuckled. "It doesn't change. All you have to do is settle in, you know?"

"So you're just happily skipping through life? Everything is good and gettin' better all the time?"

"Well, not so much. I've asked Roy about any births that have taken place in the group he lives with."

"What did he give as a count?"

"He's said no more than five babies born over the last five years. Those weren't all born to one household, if that's what you want to call what they have. With the other groups, the birth rate is zero, or close to it, from what I've seen. That troubles me. The only ones with some births are Murdock and Declan."

"You have any theories as to why?"

"Mei Lee miscarried due to an injury, as you remember. Emily seems to be fertile as a turtle. Those in Reyes' camp could have been zeroed because of being close to starvation for most of the five years. The farmers could be hiding their kids. Those in Raymond Tutt's…" Annie shook her head, "nobody knows. You and I were there once, but I didn't hear or see any kids. Did you? And then there's you. Some of us, like me and Harris, haven't had males around that were of interest to us. You did, for some time."

"As far as the farmers go, they weren't hidin' any kids," Heather said. "They were all too busy to get around to havin' any, or were starvin'. Those with husbands, and well-fed, were …avoiding getting pregnant."

"Avoiding? How can you avoid it for five years?"

"There are ways. In my case, yes, I was with Alvin for the past two years, but neither of us wanted to be married. We didn't want the added responsibility of kids. It was all we could do to feed ourselves."

"But how did you avoid it?" Annie asked innocently.

"Think about your biology and what's required to become pregnant. Can you think of anything, any technique that would work to avoid pregnancy? I can think of several, off the top of my head."

"Is this subject matter embarrassing you?" Annie asked.

"Yes. It's personal and private!"

It took Annie and Heather the better part of the day to reach the area of the fifteen. Heather was holding their mount two hundred yards away, while Annie was creeping closer to the edge.

Here is Annie Cooper, hunter, nurse, and ninja extraordinaire, sneaking up on her prey. Annie chuckled. *If this wasn't such a serious matter, it would be comical. I have no idea what I'm doing crawling around, spying on people who may be different from others.*

Shortly after crawling over a small rise, she found the edge. All around was enough high grass to cover her if she stayed low. As she peered through the stalks of grass, she could see a few people below her. She was trying to ascertain what they were doing, but it looked like they were just milling about.

"Murdock, I'm here," Annie flashed. *"I'm at the ridge edge."*

"Good! Send me all you're seeing."

As she did so, she felt like she was lying on the grass, watching, and Murdock was there with her, watching. *I wonder if I opened my eyes wider, if I'd see him lying here next to me.* She chuckled. *Annie Cooper that is the most ridiculous thing I've ever heard.*

She opened her eyes and her mind to allow Murdock to see everything she saw. As she scanned along the stream below, she knew there was a purpose, but it was so subtle that she didn't see it right away.

Heather was holding the reins of her mount two hundred yards from where Annie was supposed to be. She had paced around a bit, drank water, and finally sat on the ground.

I wonder how long this is gonna take. How am I to know Annie didn't fall off the ridge? What do I do if she does? Do I call Murdock or

297

someone else? If I did, how long will it take them to get here? Heather laughed. *You big baby. Are you intentionally trying to scare yourself? Maybe you like having something to worry about? Is that it? Just relax and enjoy the downtime.* Heather took a deep breath and let it out slowly. She had been carrying her bow, mostly to get used to its weight. *Maybe carrying this will strengthen my arm. Not real confident with its use, though. Maybe Murdock gave us these because it takes time to make a bow. Maybe he is seeing if we can get good with these. Can I shoot wooden arrows from the metal bow? How about visa versa? Stop it, Heather. Slow your mind. You're talking yourself into issues you know nothing about. There is something to the saying, don't borrow trouble from tomorrow, as today has plenty of trouble in it.*

"Heather," Murdock flashed. "*Stay where you are. Do not get closer to the edge.*"

"Okay." *Has something happened, and how would I know?* "*I was told to stay here by Annie, so why are you telling me the same thing?*"

There was a long silence.

"*Annie has been taken.*"

19

What is YOUR truth? How is it different from MY truth? Truth is objective, not subjective. I'm unconcerned with YOUR truth. My only concern is THE truth.

— KEVIN MURDOCK, FAMILY CONVERSATIONS

Annie regained consciousness and found that she was bound, but not by ropes. She looked at her wrist and saw that there was a vine of some kind wrapped around it. She focused on the vine and lifted it slightly. The pain was tremendous, which told her it was penetrating her skin.

"Do not struggle," came a male voice, from somewhere behind her head. "The vines are primitive but effective. They have had many years to evolve."

"Why am I being held?" Annie asked with some ire.

"Why were you spying on us?" the male asked.

Annie tried to communicate with Murdock. She remembered having that mental connection at the time she was grabbed.

Grabbed? I was grabbed... shit.

"There is no need for you to communicate with those agents

of our enemy," the man said. "We have severed your communication link."

Well, that explains that. "You haven't told me what you're doing with me." Annie tried to struggle against her bonds. *The vines aren't weakening. That's not good. Worse, I have no levitation abilities or telepathic abilities. I hope Murdock comes and is ready for these jokers.*

"We are ...curious about you," the man said.

"We? Who are you talking about? Who is this *we*?"

"We. We are Teknarah. We are a collective mind. A hive-mind, if you will. Have you not heard of us? Strange, that."

Teknarah...Teknarah... something about that sounds strangely familiar. Something about Teknarah and Oomah. These bindings make remembering difficult.

"We are much older than you or your kind."

Annie started to cry, silently. *How long will it take Murdock to get here? Will he come alone, or will Beron accompany him? I don't think I can hold on very long. I'd thought I was stronger than this.*

"Annie, where the hell are you?" Heather flashed. *Still no answer, and that was the fifth time.* "Dammit girl, if you ever get home again, you ain't leavin' my sight. And I don't care who says otherwise!"

"Where are you, Heather?" flashed to her mind, from Murdock.

"I ain't moved since you said I shouldn't. Are you close?" I know it's like asking are we there yet, but dammit I want—no, need to know. God, I hate this being out here in the middle of nowhere and alone bullshit.

"We're on our way, so be patient and stay strong. Can you tell me what happened?"

"No, I can't. I was left two hundred yards behind to take care of the mount and build a camp. I don't know what happened because I couldn't see her at all."

"Busy yourself with those tasks, please. We'll need them when we

arrive. But don't go near where Annie was. I need a trail to follow and I don't want it disturbed."

Heather sat on the ground and cried. When she was all cried out, she gathered rocks for a fire-ring and plenty of deadfall branches for firewood. As she was cutting up the wood, she started crying again.

Dammit, Heather, quit your blubberin'. Murdock is on his way. He'll do what he can for Annie. He's gotta. She's family! She inhaled deeply and let out a trembling exhale. *Just calm yourself, girl.*

———

Murdock was at home, mentally connected to Annie, seeing through her eyes, when it went dark.

"Mei Lee, I need to go to Annie. Something is drastically wrong and I can't make contact."

"Who is going with you?"

"I'm thinking Declan and Beron, if they're available."

"Was she alone?" Mei Lee asked.

"No, Heather was with her. There were two hundred yards between the two of them."

"Have you contacted Heather? If not, do so before you bother Beron or Declan."

Murdock cleared his mind and contacted Heather.

"Where are you, Heather?"

———

Murdock was pulling his cart, which had been packed with everything he felt he would need, including extra waterskins, and Declan was riding on it. Declan's job was to keep everything on the cart. Murdock had packed it in a rush and some things didn't get secured as they should have. Besides, Declan riding one of the mounts wouldn't be able to keep up with Murdock.

"Is Beron joining us?" flashed to Murdock's mind from Declan.

"He'll join us en route. I'm going to travel as fast as I can for as long as I can. I owe it to Annie and Heather."

Declan felt the same way. Currently, though, he was occupied with trying to keep everything on the cart, including himself.

The cart quit bouncing and Declan looked around and saw the ridge pass by under the cart.

"Which way are you going? Are we at the ridge already? We just left a few minutes ago." Declan flashed.

"We just left the ledge that separates our ridge from the next one down, close by the stream. Be sure to hold on!"

While being in the air disconcerted Declan, it didn't frighten him. He had done a fair bit of levitating in his time here. But it still caused him concern when it was without warning while traveling at high speed. He likened it to the flutter he used to get back on Earth when a car went over a hill and his stomach dropped.

It wasn't long until the wheels of the cart were again on solid ground and the bouncing resumed.

At least I'll see Beron in action. Declan returned to wrangling things on the cart. *I've never seen Beron—or Murdock—for that matter, in action against another entity. This ought to be something to see.*

It was getting close to sundown when Heather saw Murdock approaching, pulling his cart. *Hopefully, he brought some things to make the camp safer and more comfortable.*

The closer he got, she could see that Declan was riding in the cart.

That makes sense. No mount available could keep up with Murdock when he's on a mission. They might be faster, but they don't have his stamina.

Heather knew the tamed deer, the ones used as mounts, were fast and could go far, compared to most humans. But not in Murdock's case.

"Are you okay?" He stopped close to her.

"I'm fine. Better now."

"Declan, please help Heather get the camp up to snuff with the gear we brought. Beron will be here soon. He's coming in from a different direction."

"Come on, Heather. We have lots of things to make us comfier." Declan put his arm around her shoulder to guide her away.

At his touch, Heather buried her face into his chest and wailed. He did his best to comfort her.

"Heather," Murdock said softly, when she seemed to be slowing down. "Do you know if Annie knew not to make contact?"

"Sh-she knew," Heather said, while sniffling. "She said she wasn't going any further than she needed to, but she did need to see."

Murdock nodded to Declan, who lead her away.

"What is your availability?" Murdock flashed to Doctor Harris.

"You already know the answer to that. What do you need?"

"We've just arrived, and Heather seems close to a breakdown."

"She'll be fine. She's stronger than even she knows. She's probably just glad to hand over any responsibility for Annie. I do have things set for any emergency, so just get Annie here as soon as possible."

"I agree with your assessment of you staying home. The fewer of our people here, the fewer targets they'll have. I was just looking for advice on Heather."

"Just give Heather a little time to calm herself and she'll be fine."

"Okay, we'll keep you apprised." Murdock terminated the connection. *"Annie, can you hear me? We're close by. Let us know you're okay."* He waited for a reply. *What could possibly block telepathic communications.*

"Talking can be blocked," flashed to Murdock's mind, from Beron. *"Takes practice, power, and knowledge."*

"Are you close?" Murdock replied. *"What did you find out?"*

Beron became visible and was a hundred feet from Murdock.

"Have tried seeing into camp?" Beron said.

"Not yet. I was waiting for you. If they're strong enough to block Annie from contacting us, I wanted someone more powerful than me, just in case."

"Declan, get me a deerskin," Murdock called to Declan, who then came running over with the skin. "Thanks."

Murdock spread the deerskin on the ground and lay on it. He closed his eyes and projected his astral self to the stream below.

While Murdock's astral self floated a few inches off the surface of the stream, he took time to look around. As he drifted toward the bank, he was slowed. *That's something new. It's more difficult than it should be.*

Before his astral self could reach the vined border, someone stepped from behind a tree and stared straight at the astral projection.

"You cannot come here." The man slapped Murdock's projection, causing it to snap back into Murdock.

Murdock bolted upright, his eyes wide. *"That was different!"*

"Happened?" Beron said.

"Someone slapped my astral projection and sent it flying back into me. He saw my astral self and talked to it. I haven't seen that before."

From Beron's silence, Murdock inferred Beron hadn't seen it either.

"There was also some kind of vine border...or ivy, close to the stream."

"I think Annie knew something about the vines," Heather

said. "She was told by Benson that the vines released their prey if water was dropped on them."

Murdock and Beron looked at her with a puzzled expression.

"That's what I heard. I didn't make it up, you know!"

"No one said you did," Murdock said. *Vines that release with water. Never heard of anything like that.*

"*Can you hold water?*" Murdock flashed to Beron.

"*Unknown.*"

"If Annie is being held, it can't be by conventional means," Murdock said. "She'd escape in no time. Being tied up will teach you that. She has to be held where the living plants can hold her. If water was dumped on them, maybe she'd be able to get free."

"How much water are you thinkin'?" Declan said.

"Hmmm... good question. But a moot one if no one can levitate water."

Murdock looked toward Beron and saw what looked like a ball of water forming and growing. Murdock walked upstream a short distance and saw that the stream water was flowing into the ball. As the ball got bigger, the stream bed, downstream, began to show.

"What's Beron doin'?" Declan said. "Where's all that water comin' from?"

"He's taking the water flowing downstream and making it flow into a ball of water," Murdock said with a chuckle. "Smart...and impressive!"

"But how much will it take to be enough?" Declan said.

"I have no idea. I don't know if this is a test to see if it can be done, or an attempt to weaponize the stream."

"How much water will it take?"

"Depends. If it were me, I'd make it big enough to drown out the rats who kidnapped Annie."

"But wouldn't that drown out Annie, too?"

"Possibly. The water is primarily to make whatever is holding Annie release her. Maybe then she can levitate out of danger. As with all weapons of this size, the more accurate the weapon, the smaller it needs to be for effectiveness."

"Meanin' that if we knew where Annie was, the smaller the water ball would need to be?"

"Basically."

Murdock turned his attention to the trail Annie left. As he followed it, the closer to the ground he got to see if he could ascertain how they had managed to capture Annie. By the time he was at the edge of the ridge overlooking the stream, he was flat on his belly, peering over the ridge.

He could see that the stream's water level had dropped significantly. A few people were rushing around the trees. He reached out his hands to pull himself further, to look over the edge close to the base of the ridge on this side of the stream. It was then that something grabbed his wrists.

Murdock felt himself being dragged further toward the edge.

"Declan, need water fast! The vines have me!" Murdock flashed.

By the time Declan pulled off his waterskin and got it opened, Murdock was already over the edge.

Murdock was being pulled over the ridge. He didn't fall, though. He'd managed to levitate away from the ridge, and the vines trailed down from his wrists, to the ground. And they were reeling him in. He changed his focus and he managed to free his right wrist, but the vine had reattached itself to his left. With his free hand, he brought out his eighteen-incher and severed the vines with a single swing. By the time he accomplished this, he was only two feet off the ground at the ridge base.

"Nice of you to join us," a male voice said.

"You have one of my people," Murdock said, as his feet touched down.

"Yes, we do. We caught her spying on us."

"She was, at my instruction." Murdock looked the man over and wasn't impressed.

He'd seen him before, a most unremarkable person.

"Why?"

"I wanted to know what you're doing here by yourselves and away from the rest. Some would say you were acting strange." Murdock smirked. "To me, that warrants investigation."

The man narrowed his eyes. "We do not know your name. We do, however, know you as an agent of our ancient enemy."

Murdock glanced around. *We?* "The person you have is an agent of mine. I'd like her released… unharmed."

"There is time to discuss her …situation," the man said. "We want to know how you managed to escape from the vines." He looked at Murdock, expectantly.

"I prefer to keep that to myself," Murdock answered guardedly.

"Perhaps something a little easier, then. Why is the level of the stream dropping?"

"Without the release of my agent, I can't see my way clear to give you the information you want."

"What is there to stop us from taking you? You made a grievous tactical error in coming here, you know. We are conversing with you out of courtesy. We insist on answers."

The man moved quicker than Murdock had ever seen a man move, but not as fast as Murdock. Consequently, Murdock wasn't where the man expected him to be.

"Impressive," he said, without turning to face Murdock.

"I don't react well to threats… or violence," Murdock said quietly.

"I can see that," the man wore a puzzled expression. "How is it you can function?"

"What do you mean?"

"We are blocking all communications you and your agents utilize. How is it you can still move so quickly?"

"I'm special," Murdock quipped.

"Indeed! We see that now."

"My agent, unharmed, if you please?" Murdock asked. "Or would you be more comfortable if I looked for her myself?"

"You will not find her." The man scowled. "Not unassisted."

"I wouldn't be so sure if I were you." Murdock flashed a sly grin. "I'm pretty good at finding hidden things."

Declan was shocked to see Murdock's feet disappear over the edge. His first instinct was to grab for Murdock's feet, and dropped his waterskin in the process.

"*Kevin just went over the edge,*" Declan flashed to Beron.

A moment later, he could see Murdock cutting the vines and lowering himself. *I sure do hope he'll be okay. I don't wanna explain to Mei Lee that I let somethin' happen to her man.*

"*And what, exactly, would you have to explain?*" Mei Lee flashed to Declan.

"*Sorry, but I must be flustered or somethin'. I guess I'm broadcasting thoughts. Never mind.*" *Whew, keep your thoughts to yourself, Declan.*

"*Murdock unharmed,*" Beron flashed to Declan. "*I maintain contact.*"

"*How? Ain't they jammin' us, or interferrin' with us or somethin'?*"

"*I blocking sensing me, and maintain contact with Murdock. As curious as Murdock and need answers.*"

"*All that and buildin' the water ball, too?*"

Declan got no response.

What's gonna happen when all that water hits. Sure hope Annie can hold her breath. I'm thinkin' total inundation.

Annie felt the vines move across her throat and begin to tighten. Then they went across her forehead.

The longer I lay here, the more they'll disable my ability to escape.

"No need to distress yourself," the man said. "Once the vines have you, you will not escape. We could aid you, but why?"

"Why was I brought here?"

"Lots of reasons, but mainly because we can."

She could hear the smile in his voice.

"Killing me does you no good, you know." *He's having way too good a time at my expense.*

"Who said anything about killing you? Quite the contrary. We intend to see how well you fare against the vines. We suspect they will eventually crush your skull, finishing you in a slow, relentless pressure. Some of us think it will snap your neck first. It remains to be seen."

"So I'm just a science experiment?"

"Aren't we all?"

The man looked at Murdock. "We can see that more effort needed to have been made during the selection process. It may have been a mistake to send you here."

Murdock narrowed his eyes. "What does that mean? From what I discerned, the selection process was rather random."

The man chuckled. "Was it? Initially, the criterion was clear. If a human had a brain, one not in use by them, then we kept them. All others were to be sent here. Now we think that could have been an error."

"An error? I think the error was on your part. You shouldn't have come here. That was the error you made."

The man chuckled again. "The error was not taking advantage of human drive. Clearly, there are some of you with the drive to move your species forward. We look at you and see the evidence. Acquiring you would have been to our benefit. More intense scrutiny would have turned out your secrets, as simple as turning out your pockets. Haste does indeed cause waste of materials."

Murdock levitated and drifted over the vines, out of their reach. The man looked shocked at the display of power. He rushed toward Murdock a few steps, and then slammed into something.

"I want my compatriot!" Murdock held the man by the neck.

The man's feet kicked.

"I'm done with you! Release her now, or suffer the consequences!" Murdock threw the man down onto the vines.

"You will pay for that!" The man's voice raspy, as he got to his feet.

"Will I?" Murdock smirked. *"Now, Beron!"*

The man turned as the light seemed to diffuse and cast rainbows all around. Then he saw a gigantic ball of water descending to the trees a hundred feet from the stream. Everything seemed to be moving in slow motion for the man. Trees were bending to accept the weight of the water ball, and began to snap when the weight became too much, which caused *booms!* to echo.

To Murdock, the water ball popped like a bubble breaking when seen from a high-speed camera. The edge, broken by the trees, broke all around the ball, and the water leveled trees in the impact area. Murdock rushed around looking for Annie.

Annie was gasping for air. The vines had crept over her chest and hips and tried to pull her into the ground.

Then they released her, and she flew into the air. She had been trying to levitate herself against the pull of the vines for the last several seconds. At first, her flight through the water was refreshing. But the longer it went on, she wondered if she'd ever get through it. The water-logged air was making her soaked leather dress extremely heavy.

"*Annie! This way, Annie,*" flashed to her mind, from Declan.

When she looked around to get her bearings, she saw Beron and Murdock gathering the other humans as the land below was flooded. When she peered at the edge of the ridge, she saw Declan and Heather waving her over to them. She allowed the beckoning to guide her exhausted body. When she landed, she collapsed.

When Annie regained consciousness, she panicked, not knowing where she was. She could still feel the vines holding her. But when she sat up, nothing hindered her but a hand.

"Easy, Annie, it's just us," Declan said.

Annie opened her eyes and looked around to see that she was in a tipi. She was naked, covered with a large hide. Heather had Annie's buckskin dress hung close to a fire in the center.

"Hey, Heather," Annie said, "why are you trying to burn my dress? Are you that jealous?"

Heather turned toward her, and then away.

What's got her panties in a twist.

"*You've given us all quite a scare,*" flashed to her mind, from Irene. "*We're glad you're okay... or will be soon.*"

"*Are you nearby?*" Annie replied.

"*No. Murdock felt that it would be better not to expose everyone*"

"*Where is Murdock?*" Annie flashed to Declan.

"*He and Beron are questioning those they pulled from the flood waters.*"

"*Are they somewhere close?*"

"*Depends on what you call close. They're further downriver than you and Heather went.*"

Declan left the tipi.

"Heather, what's wrong?" Annie said.

Heather glared at her. "You really piss me off, sometimes."

Annie was taken aback at her bluntness. "How so?"

"You went off doing shit that Murdock sent you to do, and you did so without giving me a second thought. You left me all alone out here in the ass-end of the planet. I had no idea what to do or how to do it." Heather stopped to try to catch her breath.

"Wow! I thought you knew there would be times I'd have things to do that may require you to be alone. Sorry if that wasn't made clear to you."

Heather looked down. "It was… sorta. I just don't like it much. I've gotten used to havin' you around. When you were lost, so was I."

"But you did fine. You did what you knew to do. You did so quickly and efficiently. And you were never alone."

"That's somethin' we can talk about later." Heather winked.

"So am I forgiven?"

"Silly question." Heather grinned. "I was just upset. I don't much like being out here all on my lonesome. And I was worried about you." She shrugged.

Murdock and Beron had fifteen people on the ridge just above the Purple Sea. They were on the ridge that marked the forbidden area to all not affiliated with Murdock.

"Now, then," Murdock said, with the man that had detained him earlier. "I want answers, in detail."

"And what about what we want?" The man smirked. "A negotiation is all about *we get something, you get something*."

Murdock glared. "I require information …from you. I'm not here to *give* you anything. Except possibly, release."

The man looked at him, questioningly. "We do not understand."

Murdock smiled, coldly. "You will. You are Teknarah, true?"

The man cocked his head. "Yes. You know of us?"

"Quite assuredly. My friend has told me all about your kind."

The man looked at Beron, who towered over the humans. "He does not speak! That is but an animal."

"An animal? He is the one responsible for the flood that dislodged you. He has trained me, and because of that training, I have learned all I want to know about your kind. My questions will refer to the interaction of your kind and mine on Earth."

"And we want guarantees," the man said.

He had recognized his ancient enemy as the Fifteen were fished from the flood waters.

Murdock smiled. "I can only guarantee your next breath as long as you answer me honestly. Currently, I am staying my friend from exacting what he wants to do to you and the rest. We can do this here or down there." Murdock pointed over the ridge, leading down to the dark beach.

"Do you know what's down there? On Earth, there was an animal known as the Komodo dragon. Not a dragon in the classical sense of the word, but still quite formidable. Their saliva carried enough bacteria to kill the healthiest in days. Being a monitor lizard, they swallowed their smaller prey whole. A bite was all that was required to capture. If something escaped the teeth, then they had sickness and death to look forward to.

"Those down there make the ones from Earth look like babies. They are gigantic, and they bury their eggs in the sand down there in the summer. Or so I've been told. They are waiting for their eggs to hatch. Anything that goes down there now, they will eat, usually with multiples aiding in the rending, if they can."

The man ventured a furtive look over the edge and saw some of the beasts roving far below on the sand.

"We think talks should proceed up here, in safety," the man said.

"Just so you know. I don't care to know what your human name is, or any of their names."

The man nodded. "Understood."

"You gave me an answer about the selection process. I want it explained better than what you've told me."

The man looked puzzled. "We do not know exactly what you require. So we will try to make it more… plain. Have you known humans that have no idea what they think unless someone else tells them what they should think? They are told where to go and what to do. They are not much above the apes they descended from. Those are ones at the top of our lists.

"Humans, who aren't that intelligent anyway, as a species have few members that ask why. There are some that will ask why at everything. They take great joy in getting others to explain it. Some do it for fun to see how far someone else is willing to go. Others, however, question from a place they will never be happy until they know and understand why. Why the sky is the color it is. Not to be foolish, but from a genuine desire to know all that is knowable. They are the ones that are dangerous. They are the ones that, when given an order, ask why. Why should they? Why is this person superior to me, when clearly they aren't? Why should I obey? You could say, it is the *why* and the reason for asking that is dangerous."

Murdock frowned. "So we were selected because we asked why?"

"There are ways to ask that question without saying or thinking the word. I'm sure you have seen those that will just look at you when told to do something. They do not do as ordered, and you know they will never bow to the whims of others. Teknarah rule by ruling those that will cooperate. All others are useless to us, except for advancing our sphere of influence."

"But you're ruining societies. As you say, there are few that ask why, but they are the drivers and the risk takers of their societies. Without them, society becomes… bland."

"That is what we require."

Murdock shook his head. "So you sent us here so we could tame the place for you?"

"That, and the Oomah."

"What about the Oomah?" Murdock growled.

"They are our ancient enemies."

"So?"

"We have no difficulty with saddling them with a bunch of questioning apes with little to no intellect."

"You called me an agent of the Oomah. How did you know that?"

"Partially a guess. The rest, we surmised. Enemies know each other. Even if it has been eons since they've seen one another. They… sense it. Ask your master if it had sensed us. I am certain it will be affirmed. Besides, to us you smell, like they have infected you."

Some say nature is cruel. And it can appear that way to us, but is it really? Why do those who say nature is cruel, crave being in it? Is it the testing? As humans, we crave the testing, even though we fear it.

— KEVIN MURDOCK, FAMILY CONVERSATIONS

"**D**eclan, go ahead and take Heather and Annie home," Murdock flashed.

"What about you?"

"I'll either catch up to you, or will be at the medical facility shortly after. I'll keep you posted. The important thing is to get Annie and Heather home."

"Has the Teknarah threat been neutralized?"

"It hasn't been eliminated, but it has been rendered ineffectual, for now." Murdock broke contact.

What does that mean? No matter. I'll get him to clarify it when he gets back, whenever that is.

Declan found Heather as she was returning with fresh drinking water. "How's Annie doin'?"

"She'll be right as rain soon." Heather said. "Why?"

"Just got the word to get you two home. I was wonderin' if she's okay to travel."

"She can travel, but she ain't walkin' too far yet."

"Well, she can ride, then. We'll be breakin' camp soon, so get her ready."

An hour later, Declan was having problems with getting Heather's mount harnessed to the cart.

"Heather, your mount is being ornery."

Heather chuckled as she finished packing up the tipi. *"She's not a draft animal. She's only known riders, and doesn't understand what you want from her."*

When Heather reached the cart, she saw Declan trying to get her mount to back up so he could attach the cart to the harness he'd finally gotten on her. Heather dropped the bundles next to the cart and sprang up onto the mount's back.

"It's okay, girl," she cooed, while patting the mount's neck. "He's okay, mostly."

"Gee, thanks. You've named our animals, but you haven't given your own a name?"

"Oh, she has a name." Heather grinned.

"So is it a secret? What is it?"

"Batibat. Battie, for short."

"What kind of a name is that?"

"Look it up if you wanna know." Heather grinned at him.

An hour later, the cart was packed and Annie, riding in the cart, Heather, riding Battie while she pulled the cart, and Declan, who was driving the cart—or so he told himself, after the trouble of getting the beast harnessed to it—were on their way to the medical facility.

While he was waiting for Beron to return, Murdock slowly turned, eyes closed, focusing, feeling, for humans. When he located them, small lights in his mind indicated where they were. His *locater*, as he called it, for he lacked the words to describe it any other way, was similar to a small black screen. The *screen* didn't show topographical features or elevation, only the rough direction. He knew the information would become closer to reality once the distance was reduced. He had used it before to locate Annie and the others that comprised the Fifteen. He had used it when he confronted Tutt, Tiny Daniels, and Marchand. His misinterpretation of it had led him to be grabbed by surprise. All-in-all, though, he thought of it as useful.

Murdock knew it wasn't a radar- or sonar-type of a locator. He felt, rather than knew, it must be tied into his astral projection abilities. Same basic concept, just different levels of use and experience requirements.

Because of this latest excursion, Murdock had finally seen what was at the end of the river and the stream. He hadn't seen or followed the river that ran from the meadow atop Mount Oomah, the one for the spring gatherings, over the falls and through the area of the destroyers, but he assumed it either emptied into the Purple Sea or merged with the stream.

I'll have to follow it to be certain. It would make a good canoe trip. One I can take with Andy, as soon as I make a canoe. He chuckled. *It could curve away from the stream and end up somewhere else entirely. But then, what's in the area on the other side of that river?*

"Ready?" flashed to Murdock, from Beron.

"Are you back?"

Just as he'd sent it, he saw Beron making himself visible. *"Guess so."* Murdock chuckled. *"Where did you deposit them?"*

"Away."

From the years of being associated with the Oomah, Murdock knew a single word could be taken as a word or as an entire paragraph. From Beron's tone, Murdock knew the Fifteen were somewhere never to be seen again on this part of the planet.

"Scans for future!" Beron sent.

"I agree. All future pod landings need to be scanned for the Teknarah infestation. Is that something I'll be able to perform?"

"Locate Teknarah hard. Needs most exposure to find."

"More exposure?"

"Need scan those here now."

"You mean now-now, or later-now?" Murdock received an affirmative in the immediate. *"That will take a while."*

"Can do on way home."

Dirk Benson was sitting at the river, on his round, soaking his ankle. It had been ten days since Annie and Heather had left and the rest of their company had gotten back to something resembling normal.

"How's the ankle?" Murdock appeared behind Dirk.

"Holy sh—" Benson rose, grabbing for a weapon. "Murdock, you scared the bejesus outta me!"

"Sorry."

"No, you're not. What can I do ya for?" Benson sat back down.

"I have some news that might be of value to you and your people here."

"What kinda news? We don't get around much. The rest 'cause that's the way they want it, and me 'cause of this ankle."

"Get your people together, and I'll tell everyone at the same time. Just bring them across the river. That's where I'll be." Murdock strode off and crossed the river.

"What did *he* want?" Angelica followed Murdock with her gaze. "I was on my way here and saw you two talking." She turned to face Benson.

"Says he's got news for us." He cringed while taking his ankle out of the water.

"What kind of news? If *he's* got news, it can't be good."

"I dunno." Benson covered his foot and put his shoe back on. "I guess we'll see, later. He wants us all to gather on t'other side o' the river."

"You know, Benson, you should pay more attention to the way you talk." Angelica prepared to leave. "T'other? Dunno? Please!"

Benson straightened and cleared his throat. "Angelica, are you the grammar police? Speaking for myself, I'll talk any damn way I want to. And if you don't like it, you can stick it right up your arrogant, pompous, self-aggrandizing ass!"

"Well! I never—"

"Yeah, probably not. Now, then, go around and get everyone wrangled across the river."

It took some time, but finally everyone was across the river and milling around.

The news I have isn't all that important. Murdock watched them gather. *But it affords a way for Beron to scan everyone here to see if the Teknarah had infected any of them.*

"Everyone!" Benson said. "Hey! Shut yer pie-holes! Murdock has news."

Murdock stood and everyone quieted down.

"I don't know if any of you were aware of the small group that wasn't far away. There were only fifteen of them. Well, don't go looking for them, because they are no longer there. It has been determined that they were... um... infected by those that sent us here. That threat is no more. They have been dealt with."

"What did you do? Kill 'em off?" said a guy from the crowd.

"No. They've been relocated. I suppose, if you wanted to go find them, you might be able to, but I wouldn't count on it."

"Oh... *those* fifteen," said someone close to Murdock. "Fuck 'em. Just a buncha weirdos, anyways. They kept to themselves, the antisocial asses."

"Good riddance!" someone else said.

"Anyway," Murdock continued, "the area they were in was infested with a vine that would creep, strangle, and kill. We had to render the vines harmless for a time, so be advised that the area will be… damp… for some time."

"Was Annie all right?" Benson said.

"You knew she was there?"

"No, but I did warn her about the vines and what stops them. I figured if you're comin' here to tell us about those fifteen, then she went there and got into a pickle."

Murdock's eyebrow rose. "I'm glad you mentioned what you found out about neutralizing the vines. It allowed me to get her out of her… *pickle* barrel, so to speak."

"How damp are you talkin'?" Benson whispered. "*Downpour*-damp?"

"Closer to *Noah*-damp," Murdock whispered back.

Benson sucked his teeth. "Yup, that would be pretty damp… for a good long time. Just so Annie is okay."

"She's a little worse for wear, but she'll recover."

Benson's face loosened.

"*Nothing*," flashed to Murdock's mind, from Beron, who was invisible a few paces behind him.

"Well, that's all I have," Murdock announced, as he prepared to leave.

"Stay with me and Gundersen tonight?" Benson said. "It'll be sundown soon."

"Love to. Can't, really. Next time, maybe," Murdock said.

"Are you in that big of a rush?"

"I have lots of people to inform. You know how it goes." Murdock smiled. "By the way, are you planning to go to Benteen's or to the landing site?"

"Not 'til my ankle is up to snuff. Why?"

"I'll pass that on. I'll get to Benteen's and the landing area sometime in the next few days. I brought it up because I think Annie would like to see you, if you're in that area. Just go upriver until you see a structure resembling a castle."

"A castle?"

"You'll see, if you want to. Got to get going. Lots to do. Be well."

Murdock and Beron were camped at the base of the ridge up to step number six when the sun set. Murdock found it interesting that there were ten steps, as he called them, to Mount Oomah.

"*Location?*" Murdock flashed to Declan.

"*The top of the ridge above where we found Heather,*" Declan replied. "*What's your location?*"

"*A couple steps down from you. If I were you, I'd go upstream until you get to the second step, then cross-country to be above the medical facility.*"

"*The second step...is...*"

"*One step up from the landing pods.*" Murdock shook his head. "*I thought you knew that.*"

"*Oh, I did. It gets confusing when you lose track of where you are because you're bouncing around in the back of your cart. You know, like I was when we left on this rescue.*"

"*Yeah.*" Murdock chuckled, "*I was rushed, then. Beron is checking everyone else to see if others have been infected by the Teknarah.*"

"*Understand. It'll delay you a little as you make your way upriver. Be sure to let Mei Lee know.*"

"*She already knows.*" Murdock lay down and relaxed.

Once he broke the connection, he consulted his locater and saw a single light a fair distance away, but closer than the next bunch of lights.

Tomorrow, I'll see who that is.

It was close to midday. Murdock and Beron were hidden by a hillock a few hundred yards from the river.

"*Remain quiet*," flashed to Murdock, from Beron.

"*He won't know we're here*," Murdock replied, after checking wind direction.

As soon as they had levitated to this step, Murdock shook himself to see if anything he wore or carried would make noise and silenced them.

"*Are you scanning him?*" he flashed.

He received an affirmative from Beron.

Who is this guy, and why is he out here alone? As he focused on the man's face, he flashed to all members of his tribe, "*Does anyone know who this is?*"

"*I do*," Emily replied. "*That's Jeffrey Carter.*"

"*And who's that?*"

"*Hmmm... not one of my favorite people. He was the initial leader of the 140 that we followed away from Phylicia and Palmer. He walked away after we were down on the third step, leaving me in charge. I'm surprised he's still alive.*"

"*Suggestions?*"

"*Leave him alone. Don't contact him. The only thing you can count on with him is that you can't count on him. Saying he's unreliable is an understatement.*"

"*Will do.*" As generous as Emily is, she does have limits.

It took Murdock and Beron the rest of the day to reach the bottom of the step up to the fifth plateau. He noticed that, not only did the distances between the steps become longer, the ridges became higher the closer to the Purple Sea he traveled. Going the direction he was, the ridges would get less high and the distance between would get shorter.

When he'd left on this rescue mission, he didn't pay close attention to the distances. He took notice, however, when he escorted the fifteen to the point Beron had taken them before he disappeared with them. And now it was becoming painfully obvious that he was much further from home than he wanted to be.

Before coming to this planet, Murdock had gone months without seeing another human being. He gave no thought to distances he needed to travel. But now, being out here with Beron, away from Mei Lee and the kids, he missed them. He missed the chaos and the noise the children created.

The more he thought about it, he found that he missed Declan, Emily, and all their kids as well. He smiled whenever he thought of them. He smiled even more when he thought of his entire tribe.

They're all a good bunch of people. Each one has their positive aspects that benefit the entire tribe, and few truly negative ones. I wonder if Annie will let the rest know of her midnight tryst.

It was close to sunset when Murdock pulled himself over the top of the ridge on the fourth plateau. Beron, invisible, had already levitated to that point. It wasn't long before Murdock saw a camp across the river and over a mile from the plateau edge he'd just navigated.

"Who are ya and whadaya want?" said a man holding a spear, of sorts.

It wasn't much more than a sharpened stick, actually. Murdock couldn't tell much as the gloom of evening was coming quickly, but he couldn't use his night vision yet. It was still too bright out.

"Murdock. Here to see Benteen."

"Was he expectin' ya?"

"I don't know, was he? Did he become clairvoyant recently?"

No reply.

"Well? Bid me entry or bid me farewell. I won't stand here all night while you try to decide."

The man moved over to Murdock to get a better view of him, holding the makeshift spear at Murdock's middle.

"We was told you was dead. Got any proof who ya be?"

"What would you need for identification?"

"I haven't decided yet." The man smirked.

Murdock brushed the makeshift spear to one side, punched the man in the solar plexus, causing him to gasp. Before the man knew it, Murdock was behind him with a twelve-inch machete at his throat.

"Now, then," he whispered into the man's ear. "Do you want to lead the way to Benteen? Or would you rather I find him myself?"

"I-I'll takes ya," the man said, between gasps.

Murdock followed him with his machete at the man's back. "Anyone jumps me, you die first. Get it?"

The man nodded.

"You're not as dumb as you look." Murdock chuckled.

Before long, the man and Murdock stopped in front of a makeshift lean-to.

"Mister Benteen," the man called out.

Murdock could hear someone moving around inside the lean-to. Finally, Benteen showed himself.

"Benteen, you really need to inform your security people on how to do their job." Murdock shoved the guard away from Benteen and himself.

Benteen gulped. "Murdock. I wasn't expecting you. Come in."

He offered the opening to Murdock, and he ducked into it.

"What can I do for you?" Benteen asked once he was inside.

"I need someplace to bed down tonight," Murdock said roughly. "Also, I have some news for you."

"News? What news?"

"Tomorrow. Right now, I'm beat. Where can I stay?"

"Only place we have available is Benson's place. It's about thirty feet past the last hovel upriver."

"That'll do. Benson did offer me a place to stay when I last saw him."

"And when was that? We haven't seen him in quite some time."

"Couple a days ago."

"How is he?"

"Injured his ankle and is recovering. Gundersen is a great help. But I'll clue you in before I leave."

"So you won't be with us long?" Benteen asked nervously.

"Not long. I'll be on my way before midday tomorrow. Unless I get disturbed… then it could be a while."

"Disturbed?" Benteen chuckled nervously. "Why would anyone disturb you? I'm sure everyone will be cooperative."

"Uh-huh."

It didn't take Murdock long to find Benson's campsite. Since it was for him and Gundersen, it was a significantly larger room than Benteen's. Murdock found kindling and firewood and got a fire going.

With the fire going, this temporary wickiup-style of branches and debris would keep him cozy. *I must remember to thank Benson for his building skills.* Murdock made himself comfortable away from the door.

The next morning, a little before sunup, Murdock was up and collecting a fish to eat. While it cooked, he gathered more wood and kindling to replenish what he'd used, plus a little extra. Benteen came over to him while he was stacking the wood.

"What's your plan for this place?" Murdock offered Benteen a place to sit.

Even though he couldn't see him, Murdock knew Beron was close by and had passed the night wandering around the other campsites, scanning the people.

"Benson is our designer, of sorts." Benteen sat. "He has said we need to build housing to withstand the winter winds and cold. We haven't decided where to build yet, but it will be in this general area."

"As far as security goes, you need to improve it. If I'd been someone else determined to kill off you or your people, I wouldn't have had any trouble. Who told you I was dead?"

Benteen's eyes grew wide. "Who said that?"

"The idiot you had for a guard last night. I asked for you specifically, so he should have called out to someone smarter than he was to decide who I was. If they couldn't, then someone should have escorted me to you, or you to me."

"Yes. He's new to guard duty. His ...training on procedures will be enhanced... immediately. Now, then, tell me of Benson and Gundersen?"

"He said he's planning on a trip up this way when his ankle is up to it. By the way he was hobbling around, I'd say another ten to fourteen days. Gundersen has been helping him out. Together, they've gotten twenty-some-odd people settled in further downriver."

"How far downriver?"

"Oh, couple hundred miles ...or thereabouts. Could be a little less. I'd suggest waiting for him to send word to you. You could send a runner to him, but it would take a while to get there. I'd send word to the landing area that anyone heading that general direction to stop here and use them to pass messages."

"Huh. That would work."

"It would have to be oral, unless and until someone figures out the whole writing thing again. Who would've thought paper and pencils would be something so difficult. A lost skill, I suppose."

"Any other suggestions?" Benteen asked.

"Yes, build a smokehouse. You'll need it to store meat through the winter, and you better get someone trained on tanning hides. Otherwise, you'll never make it through the winter. It gets frigid and you'll be limited in your exposure time."

Benteen nodded.

"Plenty of water, wood, and meat, and you'll get by. After

your first winter, you'll figure out what you need to do and you'll get it done."

"Otherwise?"

"Otherwise, I'll be burying your corpses...after the thaw, of course."

Benteen gave an uncomfortable chuckle. "Of course."

"I'll let you know when I leave." Murdock ate his fish.

Benteen left and drifted back to his campsite.

"Send everyone that can wield an ax to my camp," Benteen said, when he passed one of his charges.

———————

"I take it everyone was clear?" Murdock flashed to Beron, as he exited the camp.

"No infestings."

"Farmers are next. I'm not looking forward to seeing them."

Murdock received a questioning feeling from his friend.

"They're an arrogant bunch," he flashed. *"They didn't know what they had with Heather and Alvin, and now probably blame me for losing them. If we didn't need to go there, I wouldn't."*

———————

Clearing the farmers turned out to be easier than Murdock had expected. He and Beron observed them from the plateau edge above them. It didn't take long before they were on their way to the medical facility. It was sundown when Murdock and Beron arrived. They were met at the gate by Harris, Annie, Zeke, Heather, and Declan.

Everyone clapped Murdock on the shoulder, and they led him inside and secured the gate before celebrating.

"Oh, my God!" Declan brought over some meat for Murdock.

"What?" Murdock said.

"What's that on your face? Are you... smiling?"

Everyone turned toward Murdock and laughed.

"Shut up." Murdock chuckled.

"Funny, I don't recall ever seeing you smile... and definitely not like that!"

"I smile. Ask Mei Lee. She'll say I smile."

Declan smiled broadly. "I know, just teasing you a little. Besides, that smile looks good on you. You need to do it more oftener."

After hours of backslapping, storytelling, and joking, the impromptu party was quieting down. Murdock sought out Annie.

"Can we talk?" he whispered to her.

"About?"

"About what happened with Benson."

"What about it?" Annie turned away.

"I was thinking... of everyone human on this planet, I've known Mei Lee and you the longest."

"Yes, we've known each other a long time."

"What you do is your business. But you may want to clamp down on your... ah... transmissions before you do something. For the most part, everyone ignores any unexpected leakage...of thoughts, at times like those. Most of us realize it and try to ignore it; we are all adults here, after all. It's when you try to hide it ...that makes things like this ...difficult.

" Everyone knows, but no one will say anything to you, except that they are willing to rejoice with you, if there becomes something to rejoice over. Does any of that make any sense to you?"

Annie nodded. "If there is ever a reason to rejoice, then I'll be sure to let everyone know." She shrugged and grinned at him.

"Are you going to scan the rest of the humans?" Murdock flashed to Beron.

"Did."

"Result?"

"Clean." Beron replied.

"Then I'm going home in the morning, unless you need me for something."

"Young ones of age?"

"Why do you keep asking that? Every year you ask, and I'd like to know why."

"Remember snake?"

"Yes, I remember. Why?"

"Was test. Same test we give to our young ones."

Now it all makes sense. Why that was the only snake I've seen in ten years. Why the Oomah selected me to contact.

"So you want to put my young ones through the same test?"

"Yes. Required."

"It's a test of adulthood and accountability?"

"Yes."

"Humans aren't mature at nine years old. They won't have their adult musculature until they reach fifteen years, at the earliest. I must figure out how to tell Mei Lee about this, as it concerns Chun Hua. She won't take it well."

"Misunderstanding. Not female young one. Only males tested."

"She's still not going to like it."

———

"No! Absolutely not! I refuse to let Andy participate." Mei Lee stormed around the main room of their cabin.

"It's important, but it isn't for a few years yet," Murdock said. "It's going to be important that Andy is accepted by the Oomah, isn't it?"

Mei Lee glared at her husband. "Yes, it is important that the Oomah accept Andy, but can't they do it based on who he is and who his father is?"

"From what I understand, a male has to pass the trial to be

acceptable. Right now, everyone in our tribe is acceptable because I passed the trial within a couple days of arriving here. If something were to happen to me tomorrow, no male humans are currently acceptable from the Oomah point of view."

"Declan?"

Murdock shook his head.

"Zeke?"

Murdock shook his head again. "Only me. I'm the only adult male human acceptable to the Oomah, at this time. I don't like it either, but it is something that needs to be done. I'm thinking of taking this issue up with Beron, as far as Declan and Zeke taking the trial."

"Why does it always fall to you?" Tears started to fall down Mei Lee's cheeks. "He may not be of my body, but Andy is nevertheless my son, and he always will be."

"My first step to my status with the Oomah was based on the trial. Until I passed it, I would not be acceptable for further contact. Since you've been there all this time, you know how much we've relied on the Oomah. Without their help and friend-ship, humans wouldn't have survived here. This last episode with the Teknarah has really slammed that home for me. Without Beron, we never would've known who they were or what they wanted. Not to mention how to eliminate the threat they represent to us here."

"Speaking of eliminating the threat, what did Beron do with the Teknarah?"

"Since an infestation of Teknarah is possible here, Beron has decreed that he will scan any newcomers immediately upon arrival. They will then be transported to what I understand to be an island. The waters of which are surrounded by those huge lizards, but the island has no way for the lizards to get on it."

"So he created his own Molokai?" Mei Lee asked.

"You mean, the leper colony?"

"Yes."

"The leper colony wasn't the entire island, as some believe. Kalaupapa was the leper colony, not the entire island."

"That's a distinction without a difference to me."

"In the case of the Teknarah, I agree with you. The point is, Beron decided where to put them. He decides who goes, because after this bunch of newcomers and who they were, specifically Curtis and Angelica, I'm apparently unable to decide who should go. He knew what it would do to me and Declan if they were found to be infected when they first got here and removed."

"So he's being kind?" Mei Lee said, with sarcasm.

"He thinks he is. More importantly, I think he is trying to be."

"But it's Andy!"

"It isn't like the trial is tomorrow, Mei. We have time to prepare. More importantly, we have time to prepare and train Andy."

"We have been training him since he could stand. That's how we chose to raise our kids. What more can be done? We know what the trial is and we know how the trial should end."

"Do we? The trial is more than just killing a damned big snake. It's a test of survival, strength, both inner and muscle, and reflexes. What I gathered from Beron was what I did and *how* I did it, that's what mattered. From my memory of the event, I didn't seek out the snake that was hunting me, even though I could feel I was being stalked. It was the snake's choice to attack, not mine. The way I did it was with a single swing of an eighteen-incher, quick and clean, that and staying out of the way while it was in its deaththroes. Afterwards, I hauled its carcass into camp and started feeding everyone who wanted some. I didn't waste it or kill it for no reason. It was a gift from nature ,and I accepted it as such."

Mei Lee resumed her pacing, arms crossed. "Sugarcoat it all you want. Justify it to your heart's content. It'll still be Andy, our son, being tested."

21

Rose was my first wife, my first love. After her death and after I took Mei Lee to wife, I realized something. I realized that Rose was the first time I fell in love, and you never quite love another woman that way again.

— KEVIN MURDOCK, COLLECTED SAYINGS

"What are you going to do about the lack of a diverse diet?" said Elizabeth Reyes. "Summer is gone and winter is well on its way. I'm done with starving in winter."

"What do you mean, what am _I_ going to do about it?" Wagner matched her attitude. "I'm not! You want a more diverse diet, so go get it yourself. We have what we have. If that ain't good enough, then blow it out your—"

"Watch your mouth, ass-hat!" Reyes said. "There's a lady present!"

"There is?" Wagner looked around for someone else, with a shocked expression.

Reyes glared at him. "If you wouldn't have screwed the pooch on taking the medical facility, then we'd be in a better position to demand game from the others. At least we'd be out of this damn cave."

"You've been outside since coming here?"

Reyes nodded. "You know I have."

"Then you can leave anytime. Don't let the doorknob hit cha where the good Lord split cha."

Reyes crossed her arms and started tapping her foot.

"Starting a new job as a metronome?" He chuckled.

Reyes uncrossed her arms and moved over to him to whisper into his ear. "At least I've been outside since that last battle, rather than hiding down here."

Wagner jumped to his feet and backhanded her. "You know damn well why! You know I have a death mark hanging over me."

"And so do I," Reyes spat, while rubbing the side of her reddened face. "What are you going to do about it?"

"I'm open to suggestions."

"We could always take a group and go up to the next plateau. While setting an ambush for Murdock, the rest could be harvesting deer."

"How are we going to get up there?"

———

Wagner and Reyes were staring up at the cliff face. A group of their men had climbed up and were waiting for the rope to be thrown down. When the rope was sent down, Wagner tied himself on and was lifted up to the next plateau. Once he was up, the rope was sent back down.

"You know," Wagner said to one of the men, "we need to rig up some kind of boom. Something counterweighted. We'll need it to lower deer or people."

Reyes shivered as her foot touched the ground on this plateau. The one she used to live on. The one where she'd buried so many.

"Leave me a couple men while you take the rest to the river," she said. "I'll get something to use as a lift for carcasses. You worry about the ambush."

Murdock and Mei Lee had traveled to the medical facility. Murdock was there to help Zeke with modifying the water generator to a wind-driven one. Mei Lee came to get a checkup from Irene before winter. Since her surgery for the stabbing, Harris had insisted on her having a checkup at least every year, just before winter.

"How long did it take you to carve the blades assembly?" Zeke said, as he and Murdock erected a small tripod tower to hold the blades and shaft.

"It took me a while. The hard part was finding something to use as glue," Murdock said. "Each of these blades has two shafts attached to it. Those shafts are bigger than arrows, and had to be attached to the curving blades. I managed to find sap oozing from firewood, which is extremely hard once it cooled. The bond to the blade is stronger than the wood itself. The blades aren't really carved. They're just thinner planks I steamed and twisted. The carved parts are the collars for the shafts to pass through. The bottom collar is glued to the two-inch diameter main shaft. The major carving was done on the shaft to get it to mate up to the shaft of the generator. You did say you didn't want the generator up in the air."

"I didn't want to work up high in the winter winds," Zeke replied.

"Do you think this will work in here?" Murdock looked around.

At Zeke's insistence, he'd moved the library pod inside the notched area that held the small cave everyone at the medical facility used as winter living quarters and year-round bathing.

He had closed off the opening to allow Heather's mount a corralled area to run free.

Murdock placed the library pod in the middle of the opening to get the most out of the sunlight on the solar panels. Most days, the winter sunlight would be diffused, thus the need for the generator. But there are those days of clear sky, no winds, and cold temperatures.

The top of the wind conversion tower was only slightly taller than Murdock's six-foot stature as he stood on top of the pod.

"It should," Zeke said. "Granted, I haven't been here during the winter, but I asked Irene and Annie, and they confirmed that the winds tend to howl through this gap. The wall you erected, to keep Battie corralled, may interfere with the prevailing winds. If nothing else, I can monitor the speed and direction of the wind during the winter."

Mei Lee, riding Donder, was on the second plateau. She'd come up to this plateau to harvest a deer for Harris and everyone else in the medical facility, and to escape the incessant chatter of the women. Everyone had noticed Annie's slight bulge in her tummy, but still, she didn't say anything to the rest. Mei Lee figured she'd get to it soon. It was becoming hard to ignore.

Mei Lee and Murdock had noticed that the deer avoided the area of the recent battle, forcing deer harvesting one step up. She was leisurely riding, with her back to the river and her eyes closed. *This is so relaxing. The wind smells so good. There is the promise of cold in the scent of it and it's as noticeable as the winter wind toward the end of its season, which will carry the promise of warmer temperatures.*

She opened her eyes and scanned the horizon for anything moving. She readjusted her grip on her bow, with an arrow nocked and ready. She used her knees to steer Donder in a curved direction that would eventually lead them downriver and close to the bank, but that was hours away. For now, she could see for miles.

It almost looks like I can see into tomorrow.

Wagner, Heartly, and several other men were hiding in the trees along the river. They could see the start of the open plain on the other side.

"How visible are we here?" Wagner said.

"I have no idea," Heartly responded.

"Send someone over to the other side of the river to let us know who and what is visible from the other side."

Heartly nodded and gave silent orders to someone, while Wagner looked across the river.

"Are you sure they'll come this way?" Wagner said.

"Yes. I've observed them going and coming on the other side, for years. The problem is, where are they now? Are they at home? Are they at the medical facility? Are they traveling over by the stream? We have no way of knowing."

"I'll not be very pleased if this *hunt* is …unfruitful," Wagner said.

"We are here for deer, right?" Heartly asked.

"Of course! If we see a deer, I want the men to open fire on it, *after* I fire. I don't want to chance a miss. There should be absolute silence among the ranks."

"And your concerns for Murdock?" Heartly asked.

"How concerned would you be if there was a hit out on you? I'll not be taken unawares."

The man Heartly had sent across the river returned, and a few men resettled themselves.

It had taken hours, but finally Murdock and Zeke were standing on the ground, looking at the spinning generator cap.

"You have it plugged in?" Murdock said. "Some juice should be generating now."

Zeke ran inside the pod. "*Yes! It works.*"

"Have you used the smokehouse?" Murdock said, when Zeke returned to stand next to him.

"Annie has been training me and Heather on everything related to it." Zeke fidgeted.

"You have something to ask?"

"What do you think of me and Irene?"

"What do you mean, what do I think? You two are adults. Does it matter what *I* think?"

"I may have been around when you were made, but here, you're the Big Kahuna. Besides, Irene needs your blessing, as head of our tribe." Zeke chuckled. "*Our* tribe. Who'd a thunk it!"

"What's that supposed to mean?"

"I meant nothing derogatory. I just find it strange to refer to myself as part of a tribe. When I think in those terms, it makes me laugh."

"She doesn't need anything from me. She's a big girl now and can make up her own mind. I mean, she is older than me, and a doctor."

"What's that supposed to mean?"

"I have no idea, but it sounded good, didn't it?" Murdock laughed.

"Well, would you tell her that? I told her that already and she didn't listen to me."

"If she doesn't know it by now, then she never will. *Mei Lee, where are you?*" Murdock flashed.

"*I'm hunting on the second step.*"

"*Any luck?*"

"*Not really. I'm just enjoying a gentle roam with Donder. Most of the time, my eyes are closed.*"

"*So, you're not hunting, you're communing,*" Murdock flashed.

"That would be a good way to put it. Between you and me, the cackling women were making me crazy. I find myself looking forward to the silence of winter."

"Are you coming back to the medical facility? Or do I meet you on the way home?"

"Why don't you meet me on the way home. I'm not in the mood to go back. Just look for me along the river."

"Well, you do need to be aware of your surroundings, you know."

"Stop! Just stop, Kevin. You've reminded me thousands of times over the years. Don't you think I'm aware? There is no one up here anymore. With the assault on the medical facility, everyone that was up here has left. You've scared them all off. Now leave me alone. I'll be fine until you get here, and there's no reason to hurry. I'll be riding toward you along the river, so you should have no trouble spotting me."

Wagner knew it was past midday, but he had no idea how much past midday.

"Anything exciting?" Reyes came up behind him.

"Nothing here. You see anything back there?"

"No. We did rig a boom lift. It's crude, but it should function." Reyes looked toward the open plain across the river. What's that?"

Wagner perked up when he saw what Reyes did. Across the river was a deer, strolling, with… *a rider.*

Wagner quietly alerted the rest of the men.

"You can't," Heartly whispered. "That deer has a rider. A small rider. You can't fire on them."

Wagner's nostrils flared in anger. "Your men will fire after I do, or I'll have them all executed. Get to your position!"

When the deer looked in his direction, Wagner froze. When it looked away a few seconds later, he raised his crossbow and took careful aim. With his gnarled hand, he squeezed the release.

Mei Lee, letting her mount take her wherever it wanted to go, sat with her eyes closed, though she held her bow and nocked arrow. Her eyes popped open when she felt an intense pain in her thigh, and her mount stumbled and fell, pitching her toward the river.

When mount and rider had finally come to rest, Mei Lee was trapped with the huge dead deer lying on her leg. She was only briefly aware as the pain in her thigh had intensified as she went unconscious.

Wagner, Reyes, Heartly, and the rest of the men, crossed the river and stood over their kill. They had fired half-a-dozen arrows, from longbows as well as bolts from crossbows, all at the same time. Every one of the arrows hit their mark on various parts of the deer. They would find out later that three arrows were kill shots—two into the heart and one that passed through the lungs.

As they crept up, Reyes and Wagner looked down with supe-riority on the unconscious form of Mei Lee. Heartly rushed to her to check for pulse and breathing.

"She's still alive." He turned toward Wagner and Reyes.

"More's the pity." Wagner cradled his readied crossbow and fired.

The bolt hit Mei Lee in the exposed part of her chest, just above the yoke of her dress.

Heartly's gaze became downcast as he rechecked Mei Lee's pulse.

"I want everything salvaged that can be," Wagner said. "I want the deer quartered, preserving the hide, the brain, and the back-strap tendon."

"What about Mei Lee's belongings?" Reyes said.

"I said everything. Her clothes, though, won't fit you. She

was a lot shorter and not so," Wagner indicated her breasts, "well endowed as you are. The bow and arrows should work for someone close to her size. The rest, anyone can use."

"What about her body?" Heartly whispered. "Shouldn't she be buried?"

"When the men gut the deer, they'll leave what we won't use. Toss her into the middle of it, like trash."

"She was always trash. And now she is again." Reyes cackled.

"Make sure they recover the arrows and bolts." Wagner strode toward the river.

Heartly crossed himself and mumbled a prayer over Mei Lee's body. *You're all going to get yours.* He glared at Wagner's back. *You're nothing more than a pack of hyenas. The lion will scatter you all, once he sees what you've done. And I'm in there, too. He won't differentiate between those that were there and those that gave the orders.*

Murdock had just levitated up to the second plateau from the far end of the cleft he'd been working in with Zeke.

"Where are you, Mei? I'm up on the second plateau and heading toward the river. Where are you?" He took several steps, and then remembered that his wife hadn't yet responded. *"Mei? Quit playing around and answer me. I know you didn't want to be disturbed, but this isn't funny."* He took a few more steps and noticed the quiet. *"Has anyone heard from Mei Lee?"* he broadcast to all who could hear his thoughts. *"I was supposed to meet her, and now she isn't answering. Anyone hear from her?"*

The silence was deafening.

By the time Murdock had reached the river, Irene and Zeke were there.

"Anything?" Zeke said.

"Nothing," Murdock replied. "What are you two doing up here?"

"I've never known Mei Lee not to answer when I call her," Irene said. "And I called to her telepathically as soon as you sent the wide-cast. No answer, so we're here to help."

Murdock used his locator to see if there were any humans around. It showed him a clump of lights heading away from the river, miles away. He struck out upriver, with Irene and Zeke in his wake, who had fallen behind since they weren't used to the pace.

It took some time for Murdock to come upon the pile of intestines and lots of blood.

"It looks like someone took a deer here." He looked at the surroundings. "That's odd," he said as he turned toward Zeke, "there's no—"

Zeke grabbed him and turned him away from Irene. "Don't do it, son!" he said, as Murdock struggled to get free.

He easily threw off Zeke. Irene levitated a small, naked body from the middle of the pile of intestines, covered in blood.

———

"*Declan!*" flashed to Declan's mind, from Irene Harris.

"*Hey, what's up, Doc?*"

"*Stuff a sock in it. This isn't a time for jokes. You have Murdock's kids?*"

"*Yes. Why?*"

"*Keep them there. Get ahold of Beron and have him find Murdock. Immediately!*"

"*What's the rush, Doc?*"

"*Mei Lee's dead.*"

Declan fell on his butt, inside his cabin, mouth agape.

"What's wrong with you?" Emily said after hearing her husband hit the floor, and then seeing his tears.

Declan glanced at Andy, Chun Hua, and Rosa, and shook his head at his wife.

"Hey, kids, I think it'll be a while before your parents get home. Is there anything you need from your place? Why don't we go check." Emily escorted them out of the cabin.

"Beron, Murdock needs you!" Declan flashed.

Beron's response was his normal questioning.

"Murdock's mate… is dead. He needs you immediately!"

It wasn't long before Emily came back with the kids. Declan left the cabin and went to his pottery shop. Emily followed.

"What's wrong," she whispered.

"Mei Lee… is dead," Declan barely managed. "Harris just told me…any questions, ask her."

———

Doctor Harris and Zeke were washing the blood from Mei Lee's body when Beron arrived.

"He's gone across the river. He said nothing when he left," Harris flashed to the enormous bear.

Beron disappeared.

"Do you think he understood?" Zeke brought back more water in the waterskins.

"More than either of us." Harris took the waterskins.

"What are we doing now?"

"We're getting her ready to transport to the medical facility. I need to know what the hell happened. Maybe that'll tell me who."

"You don't know? Murdock seems to know."

"Right now, he's hurt and angry. More so than I've ever seen him. He thinks he knows who did this, but I want to be sure." Harris poured the water over Mei Lee and handed the waterskins to Zeke when they were empty. "I do pity the poor, dumb bastards he runs across, though." She got to her feet.

STEPHEN DRAKE

"Murdock looked like he went a little crazy. And why Beron?"

"Beron and Murdock have been friends since Murdock first came here. You should've known that already. Anyway, Beron dispatched the idiot that killed his first wife. Beron has been a friend to Mei Lee as well. Now she's been killed, stripped, and thrown away. A little crazy? Naah. They're both a lot insane. I let Beron know because at least Murdock won't be alone if he gets in over his head. Sometimes when you go over the edge like that, you can become overwhelmed. But at least he won't be alone."

Heartly was following everyone else in their party as they made their way to the lift.

"You know," he said, to Wagner when they'd stopped for a rest and water, "you've really fucked yourself. What makes it worse is you fucked each of us as well."

"What the hell are you talking about, Heartly?" Reyes said. "You need to be more respectful."

"What do you think Murdock will do to every damn one of us?" Heartly said to Wagner.

"What can he do?" Wagner replied. "He has no proof of anything."

"Proof? You think he's going to need proof?" Heartly laughed. "If you think that, you're a bigger fool than I originally thought you were. When he catches up to us, no one will survive. And that's if we're lucky."

"Lucky? What's that supposed to mean?"

"Have you ever heard the expression, *skinned alive*? That would be a cakewalk compared to what he'll do."

Murdock was consulting his locator while following the blood trail he'd picked up on the opposite bank of the river. It was leading in the same direction of the lights in his locator.

Whenever he thought of Mei Lee, he'd stop long enough to sob. Then after getting a grip on his emotions, he would turn off his emotion as best he could, and continued the pursuit.

While he traveled, others tried to contact him telepathically, but he ignored them. He could feel his rage swelling inside and driving him onward. Someone would pay for what they did to his wife, and he was okay with it. His rage was justified. All that mattered now was the quenching of that rage.

When Beron caught up to him, nothing was said between the friends. Beron levitated Murdock onto the back of his neck to travel faster, but Murdock kept a close eye on the trail.

This is a trail I will not lose.

It had taken Irene Harris and Zeke a few hours to levitate Mei Lee's body toward the medical facility. Even though Zeke didn't know Mei Lee as well as the others did, it still broke his heart to see the impact the loss of this one life had on everyone else.

"Would you like me to levitate her for a while?" he whispered.

He'd seen Irene crying while attempting to keep the body lifted.

It was then that a large bear became visible in the middle of the trail. Irene walked up to the bear and hugged around the neck.

"Who's that?" Zeke asked Irene.

"This is Bridget. She's Beron's mate, and a dear friend to Mei Lee."

"What does she want?" Zeke asked.

"Only to honor her dead friend and help her live friends in the worst of all hours. She's going to levitate Mei Lee for me."

"But I can help."

"I know, I know, dear man. Let us see to our friend in our own way? Please?"

Zeke moved to Irene and put his arm around her. She buried her face into his chest and wailed.

Annie and Heather were pacing around sobbing and weeping and holding each other.

"We need to get this out of our system now," Annie said, during one of the quieter spells. "Irene is going to need us to help her. She's performing an autopsy on her friend, our friend. I owe it to Irene and Mei Lee to be professional for as long as I can after she gets here."

"What am I supposed to do?" Heather said.

"Do your best to console Zeke while Irene works. If he doesn't need consolation, then just be there with him. He didn't know Mei Lee as we did, but the little things we remember will help him to know her. Be a strong friend, if nothing else."

"Has anyone told Murdock's kids?" Heather said, after a long silence.

"The kids are with Declan and Emily. They'll see to the kids and explain things to them, tell them what's happened, until their father gets home to answer any questions they may have."

"This is something we're not going to get over quickly," Heather said, as the tears started again.

"What do you think?" Wagner asked Reyes.

"About what?"

"About Murdock."

"What are you asking? Are you asking if we're in deep doo-doo? Yes! But she had it coming."

"What makes you think that?"

Reyes looked at him. "Are you having regrets? I'm asking because you seem to be showing remorse."

"What if I am? I'm entitled to be remorseful."

Reyes laughed heartily. "It won't matter to Murdock if you're remorseful or not when he catches up to us. You know that, don't you? Heartly was right, you know. Murdock will not care about anything except revenge when he gets here."

"I know," Wagner mumbled, hanging his head.

"And you? You'll be set aside for *special attention* when he gets a hold of you!"

"I know! Now kindly shut your damn mouth, or I'll rob Murdock of slaking his rage toward you."

"Give me the chance, and I'll be sure to tell Murdock who finished his wife off. She was alive until you shot her in the chest, you mealy-mouthed, pencil-di—"

Wagner wiped his blade on Reyes' shirt after dipping his twelve-incher into her throat, just above the meeting of the clavicles. He made sure to go deep enough to cut her spinal cord.

Damn, I thought she'd never shut up. He replaced his twelve-incher in its sheath.

When Irene and Zeke finally arrived at the medical facility, they took Mei Lee's body into a room that Irene had set up for exams.

The last time I saw you was in this room. Irene took more water and gently washed off the rest of the gore from the body, then began her examination. *Only two injuries penetrated her skin? She has one thigh injury and one chest injury. The thigh injury has something in the wound.* She took out a clamp and fished out the object —*a piece of buckskin. Knowing Mei, this is part of her leggings. How did they go this high on her thigh?*

"Did anyone see Mei Lee leave here?" Irene flashed to those in the medical facility.

"*Yes, she rode out with Donder. Why?*" Heather replied.

"*Just asking.*"

Irene put the fabric sample into a test tube and stoppered it for further tests. She then then rotated Mei Lee's leg, the one with a hole in it.

Lower leg has multiple fractures and patella dislocation. Looks like her mount fell on her leg, breaking it several times. She examined the chest wound. *Just above the heart, several broken ribs.*

"*Can someone bring me an arrow without the broadhead?*"

"Here." Annie entered shortly after the request and handed the arrow shaft to Irene.

She inserted the shaft into the chest wound. "See that, Annie? The arrow shaft entered at a steep angle." She propped up the body to check the exit wound, and found dirt in it. "I thought so." She nodded.

"What, Doc?"

"Well, it's my considered opinion, at this point, that Mei was shot through the thigh while astride her mount. I found bits of animal hair and rawhide in the wound. The arrow you brought me is one we took off the attackers a while back. But if you look, I bet I could get two shafts side-by-side in either wound. That tells me that the shaft of the weapon was close to twice the diameter of this one."

"Crossbow bolt."

Irene nodded. "After laying her on her side, the angle of entry on the chest wound is rather steep and angled toward her pelvis. From the size, it's a crossbow bolt and was fired at close range. The chest shot was the one that killed her. She was in a lot of pain, probably unconscious, from the leg wound and fractures. From what we know of the possibilities, I'd say she was killed by Wagner, or his group of cutthroats, or both. Also, considering where she was found and the condition of everything, they stole everything she had on her and threw her away. If the bastards would've gotten the mount off her leg and let me know, she'd still be alive. Hurtin' pretty bad, but still alive. "The

348

chest wound, from what I can see, nicked the top right side of her heart and hit her spine. Thankfully, it ended her without more pain. I don't think she was conscious anyway, from the trauma I found in her leg."

Both women stood there looking at their friend.

"You gonna tell Murdock?" Annie said, as the tears started again.

"Tell him what? That his wife was killed by murdering thieves who ended her life without any remorse or contrition? He knew that when he took off after them."

"Then why the exam?"

"I needed to know, for me, and maybe the kids. I needed to know if I could make a case to end them. I have, and I'm now satisfied that Murdock is on a righteous crusade. There is one thing, though."

"What's that?"

"I'm glad I won't be in earshot when he finds them. The screams are going to be loud, long, and justified."

Murdock and Beron caught up to what was left of the group, at the ramshackle boom lift. There were only a couple men and they were trying to get off the ridge.

"Say hello to my little friend." Murdock slid up to the pair.

They could see a huge bear's head over Murdock's shoulder.

"He's not so little, but he'd like to have a conversation with you concerning my wife."

22

Vendettas are something I engage in only after careful consideration. Too often, they go on too long and cause more pain than the original act. However, there are times when they are justified... and needed.

— KEVIN MURDOCK, FAMILY CONVERSATIONS

Murdock paused his vengeance campaign long enough to see Mei Lee laid to rest next to Rose. Those in attendance were members of Murdock's tribe or the Oomah. Murdock and Beron were there covered in the blood of the murderers they had managed to catch, so far, before being called away.

Andrew, Chun Hua, and Rosa Lea where there, standing on one side of the sarcophagus, while Declan, Emily, and their kids stood on the other. Because of Murdock's quick response, he'd managed to retrieve Mei Lee's clothing. She was entombed in the dress and leggings she wore most often.

Murdock, looking like a wild savage, dripping blood mixed with tears and sweat, looked down at her.

"This is the blood of those that took you from us." He touched her face, smearing it with blood. "They will pay! They will all pay! I'll see to it personally!" he said with sadness and anger.

Jeez, Louise, Declan thought. *I hope he knows when to quit. Granted, he did just arrive, but he coulda cleaned up a little.*

Behind Andy, Chun Hua, and Rosa were Zeke, Irene, Annie, and Heather. They had all escorted Mei Lee's body to this spot with the help of Bridget. All were silent and reverent. Each marked the passage of their friend in their own way.

When the cover was placed on the sarcophagus, Beron beckoned all the humans to join him. He led the way to the chamber with the pools inside Mount Oomah.

As each one entered, they remembered that Murdock and Rose had lived here, and Murdock, Mei Lee, and the kids had stayed here when gathered for various reasons over the years. Harris had once doctored Murdock here when he was attacked and left for dead by Wagner.

"Each you invited enter sharing state for last wishes," Beron flashed to everyone.

No one declined.

As Murdock entered the sharing state, he could see Beron and Bridget, though he couldn't tell one from the other, as all the Oomah looked the same—all cloaked, shadowy figures. Everyone else appeared as they did outside the sharing state, except for Murdock, who was now free of blood and gore. Everyone gathered in a circle.

An image began to form in the center. The image solidified into a three-dimensional one.

This must be what a hologram looks like. Murdock stared at it.

"In an effort to carry on something Rose started, Bridget has agreed

to hold my final message. In the event that I should pass on, it is to be shown to those who meant the most to me. So if you're seeing this, you know where you stood in my estimation. First, to my husband, Kevin." The image looked at the ground. "*You may have been a hero to some, once in a while, but you were my hero, always. You rescued me and were there whenever I needed you. You always treated me as an equal, always, which is more than most wives can say. To Andy, you've always been and will always be my son. I helped deliver you, and even though you weren't of my body, that never mattered to me and doesn't change anything. To Chun Hua, my Chunnie,*" the image grinned, "*you were always the light of my life. I know your father feels the same way. To Rosa Lea, you were named after the greatest woman I've ever known. Grow strong, and you will do great things as well. Everyone here is dear to me. I tried to make how I felt plain to everyone I met. Those I didn't care for knew it without a doubt. Everyone else is here, especially Beron and Bridget. They are both dear to me, relied upon by me, and held in the highest esteem by me. I've never been one for public speaking, so I guess that's about it. Just want to say thanks to everyone for everything you did for me. It was appreciated more than I usually let on.*"

The image of Mei Lee faded.

"*This was shown at this time to allow heal during long sleep,*" Beron said.

One by one, everyone exited the sharing state.

When Declan and Emily recovered, Murdock was waiting.

"Take the kids home," he said. "I'll be there when I'm done."

Murdock's appearance was shocking to Declan after seeing him in the sharing state, all cleaned up.

"Anything you need, you know I'll do it for you," Declan said.

"I know, and I greatly appreciate it."

"What's the status?" Declan asked.

"Reyes is dead, by someone else's hand. I found her dead. A few of those following orders had a chat with Beron and me. They didn't last long. Wagner escaped to the mine, his stronghold. He sacrificed several men to me and Beron to manage it."

"How much longer will it take?" Emily said.

"It'll take as long as it takes." Murdock shrugged.

"You do have kids to care for, you know," Declan said.

"Are you judging me?" Murdock replied. "Before you do, ask yourself what you'd do if something happened to Emily," he hissed. "I have to finish this, you know that. And I will."

"But at what cost?" Declan said.

Murdock turned to look at his three kids. He frowned at Declan and left, saying nothing to the children.

"What's wrong with Father?" Andy asked Declan, as they walked home.

"He's angry, Andy. Angry and hurt." Declan looked to the boy with compassion. "From what I understand, when your mom, my sister, died, your dad was torn up. Now Mei Lee has been killed, and he's gone a bit …crazy."

"Chunnie and I saw a little of that when Huo Jin was killed. Will he be coming home?"

"What he's doing, he feels he has to do. He probably thinks he's doing it to keep everyone safe. But everyone dies, sooner or later. Sometimes it's by someone else's hand. Sometimes it's just bad luck. Violence and vengeance always take a toll."

Andy gave Declan a strange look and he dropped back to walk next to Chun Hua and Rosa.

"What were you talking about with Uncle Declan?" Chun Hua whispered.

"Just asking about Father," Andy whispered.

"Find out anything interesting?" Chun Hua asked.

"I think Uncle Declan is a pacifist. I don't think he understands Father."

"Why do you say that? He's been around him a long time."

"He thinks Father's anger is unnecessary and that he should be here, taking care of us."

"But he *is* taking care of us." Chun Hua looked sideways at her step-brother. "He's making sure that when we leave the safety of this plateau, we'll be safer, less likely to die at the hands of others, as Mother did. Besides, we're not babies. We can take care of ourselves, for the most part."

"I know. I think Aunt Emily and Uncle Declan were asked to take care of us to give them something to do, to feel useful."

"Why doesn't she like us to call her Auntie Em?"

"I have no idea. Maybe someday we'll find out."

———

Wagner was standing inside the entrance of the mine, watching the snow fall.

Look at it comin' down. Can't see shit outside ten feet. It's like everything just drops off. At least I won't have anything to worry about, as far as Murdock is concerned. He'll be holed up somewhere. This may be the first snow this year, but it won't be the last.

As he turned away from the entrance, he gave orders to admit no one, and strolled to his quarters far below the surface, where it was warm.

We've suffered a lot of losses. Wagner strolled through the empty tunnels. *Time to recruit newbies. Murdock's vendetta has been taking its toll. Maybe we need to pack it up and find somewhere else to live. Someplace not so ...out of the way. Maybe in the spring. Definitely not now. Soon, it'll be too damned cold to go outside at all.* As he moved, he could hear his footsteps echoing in the tunnels. *I think I was too quick to execute Reyes. She did make a good bed warmer. I just couldn't take the tonal quality of her voice any longer. It really grated on my nerves.*

When he reached his quarters, Wagner marveled at his trophies. He had Mei Lee's bow and arrows hanging on a rock edge sticking out from the wall opposite his bed. As he removed his shirt, he turned to get into his bed and was startled by Murdock standing there.

Before he could react, Murdock hit him at the pressure point stomach 5 and Wagner's lights went out.

It was some time before Wagner regained consciousness. He had no idea how long he was out. When he woke up, he was suspended somewhere in the mine by his wrists, gently swaying. He extended his feet, in an attempt to touch the rock floor and failed.

"Welcome back," Murdock said, with a cheerful tone. "And how do you feel today?"

Wagner waited until Murdock was directly in front of him, and closed his mouth and inhaled through his nose to hock a loogie. Murdock gave Wagner a quick punch to his solar plexus causing his breathing to be interrupted in a spasm.

"Is that all you got?" Murdock said. "Somehow, I expected more from you. You can keep that vile crap to yourself. Now, then. You're alive right now because I want answers. You can, of course, refuse to answer my questions, but that will result in me…" Murdock smiled and cocked his head, "releasing some of my aggression onto you. Now that'll be fine, because I have a lot of aggression stored up. A mountain of it, you could say. Regardless, you will not survive this …encounter. You already know where we are, so why don't you scream or something? Take my word for it, there is only one life here other than yours and mine. There is no escape, no bargaining, nothing you can do to stay my hand. But I *will* have my answers, one way or the other."

"You do whatever you want. I ain't tellin you shit!" Wagner spat.

"Really? Well, we'll just have to see about that. But before we do, let's finish out the introductions. I have with me a friend, a dear friend, who you haven't met yet. He was also a dear friend to my wife. He would like to have a brief conversation with you. Beron, if you please?"

Wagner heard something moving behind him as Murdock backed up. Whatever it was, it was ambling into his field of vision. What he saw caused him to jerk and tug on the ropes holding him. Standing directly in front of him was a colossal brown bear, standing on all fours.

It had to drop his head significantly just so Wagner could feel the exhalations coming from its nose, on his forehead. It was easily the biggest bear he'd ever seen.

The bear inhaled and roared at his face. It was deafening and seemed to go on forever. When the roaring stopped, Wagner could feel spittle running down the side of his face, and the pounding of his heart.

"Wow!" Murdock said. "That was sure one big, loud roar. If there was anyone else here, you'd think they'd come arunnin', wouldn't you? Even if for no other reason than to see what caused a roar like that?"

"M-maybe," Wagner said.

"Maybe? Huh. I was impressed, and you should've been, too. Careful. If you offend Beron, he could take it personally and eat your gizzard… while you're alive. You do know that's how Ben Palmer died, don't you? He was eaten alive by a family of mountain lions, or what passes for them here. He'd fallen through a tree and broke a bunch of bones. Mama lion found him and brought him home to her kits to eat. They'd done a pretty good job of it, too, before I found what was left of him and saw to it he got planted. I mean, he was already dead and mostly eaten by the time I found him. Does that sound like something you'd enjoy, Teddy Ruxpin?

"Don't call me that," Wagner spat.

"And why not? Are you going to beat my ass, or some such

other nonsensical threat? Let me tell you, ass-wipe." Murdock poked him in the chest. "I could have one foot in the grave and still be able to clean your clock. You pose absolutely no challenge to me. No challenge at all. Never have, never will."

"Fuck you!" Wagner said, through clenched teeth.

"Language." Murdock came over and gave Wagner another punch in the solar plexus. "That filthy tongue of yours is offending me. Maybe I should remove it." He grinned at Wagner. "You remember when I got Preston Freeman to watch his tongue, don't you?"

Wagner remembered Nels telling him about it, but he gave no outward sign.

"Oh, come on. I know Nels Osterlund told you about it. Anyway, if you don't watch your language, I could do the same to you."

"You do that, I won't be able to talk." Wagner smirked.

"True, true. But you know what? I *can* take off a toe every time I have to remind you about your language. That'll hurt like hell and won't prevent you from talking."

Wagner paled.

"Recently, I found Liz Reyes' body. Tell me what you know about that."

"I just got tired of that stupid bi—um, woman's mouth. She was bat-shit crazy, you know."

"She had some deep psychological issues." Murdock nodded. "Stemming mainly from exposure and starvation. Those around her were starving and freezing, and she could do nothing about it. As a result, she internalized it and started to blame others. So you, being morally superior, decided to end her life."

Wagner gulped.

"You had no more compassion than that? What about Raymond Tutt, Timothy Daniels, and Blandean Marchand? I was actually starting to warm up to Daniels. What happened with them? Did they just get in the way of your agenda?"

"Something like that," Wagner said, in a low tone.

STEPHEN DRAKE

"Was it something *like* that, or it was *that*? There is a difference, you know. And what about my wife?"

"What about her?" Wagner sneered.

"Why did she have to die?" Murdock said, his voice tight and his hands clenching convulsively.

"I don't answer to you, asshole."

"You're right," Murdock said, in a jovial tone. "I must say, when you're right, you *are* right."

He stepped out of Wagner's view for a few seconds, then came back carrying a round of wood and placed it close to Wagner's right foot. He grabbed Wagner's leg and punched the pressure point just above the knee on the outside of his thigh. He put Wagner's tingling right foot on the round and pulled his six-inch knife from his boot sheath. Then he placed the edge on Wagner's pinky toe, just at the end of his foot, and in a smooth rolling motion, sliced off his toe. Blood leaked everywhere and Wagner screamed.

Murdock again disappeared and came back with a red-hot piece of steel rod, the kind Wagner's men used for arrow shafts, and touched it to the stub of the toe. Again, Wagner howled, the smell of burning flesh stinging his nose.

When Declan, Emily, their kids, Andy, Chun Hua, and Rosa had returned home, Andy, Chun, and Rosa turned and went to their father's cabin. Declan, shocked that they would do that, followed them, leaving Emily to corral her brood inside their own cabin.

Declan tried to open the door, and knocked when it failed to open.

"Yes?" Andy opened the door.

"What are you doing, Andy? I thought it was clear that you were going to be staying with Emily and me until your father gets home."

"Respectfully, Uncle, that was your understanding, not ours. We're perfectly capable of taking care of ourselves. We have, after all, been doing so for a long time."

"But your father—"

"Our *father* expects us to fend for ourselves in his absence. It's the way we were raised. He expects self-reliance, always. You know that. Our father didn't ask you to look after us. That was done by others, probably Auntie Irene. She still thinks of us as *little*."

"I disagree! You are going to be staying with me and Em." Declan glared at the significantly smaller boy.

"Respectfully, *Uncle*, we're staying *here*. Be assured, if we need anything we'll let you know."

"Look here you little... you little..." Declan fumed.

"You little... brat?" Andy inhaled and exhaled loudly. "Do I need to fight you on this? I don't want to. Really I don't, but I will if you insist."

"Emily! What do I do?"

"You're the adult. Start adult-ing!"

"But he is challenging my authority. He says he'll fight me if I insist."

"Oh, well, that would be embarrassing," Emily chided.

"Yeah, it will be... for me. He's his father's son. He's been trained his entire life. I've never won a fight with him, and he's only nine!"

"Well, then, you figure it out."

"Look, Andy. I don't want to fight you. I know you're upset and want to come home. We'll do it your way for now. You should have plenty of everything you need, but if you need anything, anything at all..."

"I know." Andy smiled. "We'll ask."

He closed the door, leaving Declan standing with his hands in his pockets.

"Now, then, you want to tell me what your major malfunction is with me?" Murdock said.

To Wagner, it seemed he'd been hanging by his wrists for a long enough time to stretch him to the ground.

"You stole from me!" Wagner spat.

"*I* stole from *you*. What, exactly do you think I stole from you?"

"You stole two women, a cart, bow and arrows, deer hides, and other weapons and tools."

Murdock started laughing. "Those items that can be owned weren't yours. You took advantage and knocked me in the head with a rock. Anyone else would have died. You stole from me. I took it back. Besides, you can't own a person. Not here, anyway."

"You asked, I told you. I refuse to argue the finer points as to what can be owned and what can't." Wagner ground his teeth.

"And because of that, you decided to kill my wife?"

"Nobody steals from me," Wagner said, through clenched teeth.

"You stole from me, tried to kill me, and it's my fault you killed my wife? Do I have that about right?"

Wagner nodded.

"So how did all that turn out for you? Wouldn't it have been better to try to get along? As I see it, we're almost done here."

Murdock grabbed some rope and tied Wagner's foot to a round of wood that was bigger in diameter than the length of Wagner's feet. He tied it tight enough that Wagner could have walked with the rounds, like shoes. This freed Murdock's hands.

"Are you ready, Teddy?" Murdock said.

"I'm ready to be done with the likes of you. You're a coward. Torture is the tool of cowards. Do your worst."

Murdock pulled his six-incher and placed the edge on a toe and rolled it, severing the toe. This was followed by the hot iron. Blood, screaming, and the smell of burning flesh permeated Wagner's awareness. He waited for shock and pain to render him unconscious. But the release unconsciousness would offer wasn't happening.

Hours passed this way, until Wagner had no more toes. It was then that Murdock went behind Wagner. He started to feel slices to his back. They hurt, but not too bad. He was confused.

"What are you doing?" Wagner said, tired of the pain and the smells.

"I decided that you have become immune to the pain from amputation. I wish to explore your resistance to nerve stimulation."

Wagner felt a pull on his skin and his skin ripping and pulling away from his muscles.

"How does that feel? I plan on doing this slowly, all over your body. Doesn't that sound like fun?"

Murdock sat crossed-legged on...nothing...but air. His buckskins looked dark in the flickering firelight, stained with blood. His face was ghoulishly streaked with blood. In front of him lay Wagner, panting at times, tossing his head from side to side at other times. Every so often, a whimper would escape his sleeping lips. Beron was nowhere to be seen, as he was miles away in a warm cave.

"How long?" Beron flashed to Murdock.

"How long before he realizes that what he's seeing isn't real?"

"You kind imagine great. Long time yet."

"How long can you maintain it?"

He felt Beron grin, if such a thing was possible during telepathic communications with a bear creature.

"I would like it to be so ingrained in his brain that he'll experience it every time he sleeps."

"Will make certain." Beron flashed.

Murdock left Wagner's quarters, carrying everything that belonged to Mei Lee. He first went deeper into the mine. As he proceeded, the men he surprised tried to defend their territory by attacking first. They were quickly dispatched. With each person dispatched, their weapons would float around Murdock, as if the ghosts of those killed were battling their living cohorts for Murdock.

The deeper into the mine he went, the more weapons were accumulated. When he'd reached the end of all the tunnels, Murdock turned and exited the mine, with a shield of weapons preceding him. When he came to Wagner's quarters, he stopped long enough to glance inside. Wagner was still deep in the throes of his personal nightmare.

At the mine entrance, Murdock picked up his parka and donned it before stepping out into the snowstorm.

It was six days since the funeral of Mei Lee Murdock when Kevin Murdock opened the door to his cabin. Seeing his children there wasn't a surprise. His indicator had told him three were inside, and he'd figured it was his kids.

"Andrew," Murdock said in his stern voice.

"Father."

"Chun Hua." Murdock looked at his eldest daughter.

"Father."

"Rosa Lea," Murdock looked at his youngest.

"Daddy."

It then struck Murdock that none of his children were smiling.

He exhaled loudly. "It's done."

"Good," Andrew said.

"All of them, Father?" Chun Hua asked.

"They've all been punished," Murdock said, the fatigue evident in his carriage and expression.

"How many are still alive, Father," Chun Hua said.

"One."

"Why?"

"He will forever be trapped in a living nightmare of never-ending pain. He'll live that way until he chooses to not live that way any longer."

"The point was to terminate everyone who had a hand in our mother's death," Andrew said.

Murdock looked at his children, saddened. "All of you are young. When you get older, you'll realize that there are worse things than dying."

The children all seemed to accept what Murdock told them.

"Get out of your clothes and take a bath, Father," Chun Hua said. "We'll eat when you've removed the gore."

"Bossy, aren't you?" Murdock smiled at her.

"Someone has to be. Now that Mother is gone, that chore has fallen to me."

"What happened to you staying with Declan and Emily?" Murdock asked Andrew.

"After the funeral, we decided that we belonged *here*. We aren't babies, and they tend to treat us that way."

"They may not understand," Murdock said, "not completely, but they're good people and their heart is in the right place."

"Get your bloody clothes off and bathe!" Chun Hua said.

"Yes, ma'am." Murdock smiled as he made his way to the spa.

"*I'm home,*" Murdock flashed to everyone in his tribe.

He had finished bathing and was sitting in the cabin, in his winter pants, eating, while Andrew was busy cleaning his buckskins.

"*About time!*" Emily flashed.

Murdock could tell she was upset.

"*Good!*" Declan flashed. "*I'll be there shortly.*"

That sounds ominous. Five will get you ten it'll be something about the kids going their own way. By the way the messages were being sent, he knew they were personally connected to him and not general messages to everyone.

"*I know the timing isn't the best,*" Irene flashed, "*but you need to know, Zeke is off the market and so am I.*"

Murdock chuckled. "*About time.*"

"*I'm pregnant,*" Annie flashed.

"*Is that something you wanted?*"

"*Yes, it is.*"

"*Thoughts on letting the father know?*"

In the pause, and due to Murdock knowing Annie's manner of speaking, he knew she did the *exasperated exhale* thing before answering.

"*Not at present, but I suppose I must... someday.*"

"*Someday soon?*"

"*Don't push it!*" Annie flashed.

When there was a knock on the door, Murdock called, "Come in, Declan."

Declan opened the door and glanced around at all three children.

"Can I talk to you... alone?"

Murdock gave one of his faraway looks. "Define alone?"

"Outside the presence of the children."

"And where are they to go while we have this...conversation? This is their home, and they can hear whatever you have to say."

"Very well then. I was tasked with looking after your kids, and it wasn't a big deal, you know that. But then Andy disrespected me. Right after the funeral, too. I decided I'd wait and take it up with you."

"Okay. You've said what you wanted to say. Happy?"

Declan stared, mouth agape. "Far from it. He needs to be disciplined."

"Andrew," Murdock said, without taking his eyes off Declan. "Did you disrespect Declan?"

"No, sir," Andy said. "I prefaced my remarks with the word *respectfully*, and I meant it, too."

"Sounds like he didn't disrespect you, in my opinion."

"But we were supposed to look after them while you were away."

"Did I ask you to?"

"Irene did, and it was no imposition. We enjoy their company."

"I appreciate that, but Irene doesn't run my household."

"But they're just little kids."

"Yours are little kids. Mine are small adults."

"Your son threatened to fight me to stay here."

"He did, did he?" Murdock looked at his son. "Andrew, Is that true?"

"Yes, sir. All three of us decided that we were better off at our home. Uncle Declan didn't agree, so I volunteered to let him know we were serious. I was respectful about it, though."

"But he's an elder. What have I told you about your elders?"

"You've said to respect them," Andrew said, eyes downcast.

"Apologize to Declan."

Andrew took in a deep breath and let it out slowly. "Revered Uncle Declan, I apologize for my lack of vocabulary—"

"Wait, a minute," Declan said. "That wasn't it at all—"

"Declan, it isn't respectful to interrupt an apology," Murdock said. "You expect him to respect you, so give him the same courtesy when he is apologizing. Andrew, continue."

"I apologize for my lack of vocabulary. I didn't know the words or the proper way to tell you that, in this matter, I am more capable than you. My sisters and I have been surviving here longer than you have and were raised to be self-reliant, by our father. I'm sorry that I failed to impress that on you and convince you of your error."

"There you go." Murdock smiled. "He's apologized to you. Feel better, Declan?"

Declan looked confused and got what Rosa called a *scrunchie face*.

"Not really, no."

"You look confused. What is causing your confusion?"

"I'm not sure."

"Well, he did apologize for his shortcomings. That is what you expected, wasn't it?"

Declan looked like somebody had hit him and knocked him silly. "You know, I think I'll just be going home. You'd think I'd learn after all these years that coming here is just going to cause me more confusion. I'm not certain, but I think I was just insulted."

"Well, thanks for stopping by so we could get this matter behind us. Let me know if I can help you out in some way."

Declan left, closing the door behind him.

A few seconds later, Andrew and Chun Hua tried to stifle a laugh.

"I, however, do know if he was insulted," Murdock said ominously.

The children became quiet.

"He was...and we need to talk about your apologies, young man!"

23

Some would say dealing with my hellions is difficult. The difficulty results from looking at them like they're normal kids. What is normal? My kids are who I raised them to be, and I'm happy with that.

— KEVIN MURDOCK, COLLECTED SAYINGS

The winter, much like the winters that had passed before, was bitter cold, filled with days of high winds and snow. Murdock and his children spent their days repairing clothing they would need after winter, making arrows, and playing games.

Murdock presented Andrew with Mei Lee's bow and quiver of arrows, with the understanding that he would give them to his sisters when he'd outgrown it. Murdock presented Chun Hua her mother's winter wear. The remainders of Mei Lee's meager possessions were divided evenly between the three children. Mei Lee had taken to marking her machetes and hatchet with a stylized *MLM*.

Minimal time was spent with Declan and Emily and their kids. Murdock felt he needed the time with his kids to re-establish the connection between them. None of the children were resentful of the lost time while their father was on his vengeance campaign. What they resented was the loss of their mother at the hands of *outsiders*, those who didn't belong amongst the living. Many times, everyone in the cabin would stop what they were doing and weep for their loss.

Those at the medical facility passed the winter by trying to stay busy. Annie's pregnancy advanced as expected, and Doctor Harris predicted she'd deliver by the beginning of summer.

Heather spent most of her time in the library pod.

Zeke and Irene spent all the time they could together. Annie and Heather gave them as much privacy as they could manage.

Winter took a heavy toll on the newest arrivals since it was their first. Of the two thousand that had arrived, 1,980 entered winter and nearly half were gone by the time their first winter ended.

Casualties were mostly from exposure and starvation. There were a few deaths from cabin fever. Two people lost it and took out four others. And then those in charge of the two who'd lost it ended them for murdering others.

Mackenzie Braddock spent her first winter with Chris Gundersen at the downriver site, while Melanie Burton spent her first winter with Dirk Benson at his temporary shelter with Benteen, on the same plateau with the farmers. The men had made no promises and had no understanding with the women. They'd gone to great lengths to make it known that everything was platonic and for mutual survival. The women took the situation more personal, and by the end of winter, were showing signs of ownership of the men.

The farmers had taken in a few of the newcomers. Since the

farmers were well-versed in surviving the winters, none of those newcomers died.

Those who remained at the pod landing site had the heaviest casualty count. No one was used to winter weather, so no one had the clothing to withstand the extreme conditions, and no one knew how to insulate the pods against the cold.

A few individual leaders who'd figured out that doing anything was better than doing nothing, partially enclosed a few of the pods and managed to keep fires burning under the pod. However, they had missed the estimated fish count necessary to survive. At about the middle of winter, those still standing had consolidated into larger groups. Some cannibalism did occur.

No one had seen or heard anything from the Lotus Eaters since the attack on the medical facility. Roy White, the EMT from the previous landing, was the in-house medical person for them, and usually reported to Irene Harris after winter ended.

Murdock had shown up at the medical facility with his family in tow, just as Irene, Annie, Zeke, and Heather were moving back into the main part of the facility. There were several patches that were free of snow, and the river would be free-flowing soon. The Oomah had not yet emerged from hibernation.

"What are you all doing here?" Irene opened the gate. "Isn't it a bit early in the year for you to be out and about?"

"I have to do my rounds, and I thought I'd bring the kids so Zeke could assess their scholastic levels." Murdock laughed.

"Well, come on in. You're always welcome here." Irene tousled Rosa's and Andrew's hair as they walked past her. "Zeke is around here, somewhere. I swear he knows when to disappear when I need him the most."

Murdock said nothing.

"Zeke? Company!" Irene yelled. "He should be here directly."

"I have no idea how long it'll take for my rounds. I'm not particularly fond of the children seeing what I will possibly see, so is it all right if I leave them here while I'm gone?"

"That's a silly question. I'm always glad to spend time with them. But what's wrong with Declan and Emily?"

"We've had some words after."

"After what?"

"After, after." Murdock huffed. "They're here, primarily, so Zeke can get their education started. I didn't think it would be such a big deal."

"It's not. I was just curious is all."

Murdock was looking out over the wall. It was a crisp evening and his breath was visible.

"Tough day?" Heather came up from behind and leaned on a kneeler on the crenelated wall.

"They all seem to be tough lately," Murdock said, quietly.

"Don't they though?"

"When I announced I was home, you didn't answer. Can I ask why?"

"I figured you were in your own headspace and didn't need my input on anything. Besides, I had nothin' to offer. I knew you were hurtin'... and so were the kids. I figured you'd let me know if you wanted to talk."

"Not a big fan of talking," Murdock responded.

"Yeah, I noticed. Me neither."

Murdock chuckled.

"Are you leavin' soon?" Heather said, after an extended pause.

"Yeah."

"Mind if I tag along?"

Murdock shrugged. "Isn't Annie going to need you here soon?"

"She's not gonna need me. She has Irene, and no one here is all that busy anytime."

"So where are you goin'?" Murdock asked.

"Away."

Murdock was up early the next morning. He kissed his kids and exhorted them to behave, and then disappeared over the wall.

He had started for the pod landing area since it was the closest. It didn't take him long before he caught up to Heather riding Batibat.

"I thought you wanted to leave with me?" Murdock said.

Heather shrugged. "I figured you'd try to slip out."

"What made you think I was going this way?"

"You got it backwards. I had no idea which way you were going, or even if you were going. I just went. So from my perspective, you followed me."

Murdock chuckled. "You know, it's dangerous for you to be out here alone."

Heather shrugged. "I ain't worth the effort. Besides, I won't go gentle. I been survivin' for a long time before comin' here."

Murdock and Heather were stopped at a makeshift city gate when they arrived at the pod landing area. Murdock could see several of the pods somewhat enclosed.

"Where do you think you're going?" a man said, obviously a guard.

"Who's in charge here?" Murdock replied.

"Several people. It depends on your business here."

"Well, we're going over to the stream to get a camp set. You go tell whoever that I'll be over there and ready to talk whenever they get around to it." Murdock turned upstream and started off.

"I can't let you do that." The guard stepped into Murdock's way.

He glared at him. "I've not had a good winter, so don't."

"Don't what?" the man smirked derisively.

In a flash, Murdock had his twelve-incher at the guard's throat. The guard stood still and said nothing, his eyes were bugging out.

"Heather, make a note."

"I'm ready."

"Landing area unfriendly. Off-limits, and no assistance until further notice." Murdock released the guard and turned to go.

"What was all that about?" the guard said.

Murdock stopped. "Every spring, I go around and help those that survived the winter. If they're rude to me, like you were, I mark them as off-limits. That's off-limits to any of my tribe. That includes, of course, the medical facility and its personnel. So sure hope your inhospitality doesn't get your people wiped out."

Murdock turned to go, and Heather followed.

The pair headed off toward the river and the plateau edge, when a woman came running up to them from the pod landing area.

"Excuse me, Mister Murdock," said the breathless woman. "I'm Erycca Valdez. I'm one of the leaders. The guard had no idea who you were, so please come back. We'd like to talk to you, at least."

Murdock looked at Heather. She shrugged, and they both turned around. At the city gate, they were admitted without further incident.

"What was that about me making a note?" Heather said, as they made camp by the stream.

"It was something for their ears." Murdock chuckled. "The mere threat of cutting off access to medical treatments should be enough to compel anyone's cooperation. You were there. You saw and heard. I'm not unreasonable, but I won't be intimidated. I've been here too long for that. If it were up to me, I'd go peacefully through life. But others won't let that happen. I won't attack first, but I won't just stand there and be attacked either."

"I can understand that." Heather nodded. "I wouldn't just stand there either if given a choice. I wish I knew a little of what you know."

"You've had the basic training over the years."

"Yes, but we both know it's not enough most of the time."

"So," Murdock put fish on to cook, "what did you mean Annie doesn't need you?"

Heather shrugged and said nothing for a long time.

"You ever feel like you're in everyone else's way?" she asked breaking the silence. "Don't get me wrong, Annie, Irene, and Zeke have been great, but I can tell a make-work job when I see it. Since I've been at the medical facility, it's all been make-work."

Murdock had nothing to say. Both ate in silence.

"I need to take an animal for this group tomorrow." Murdock covered himself with a deer hide. "You up to helping?"

"Do you *need* my help?" Heather asked quietly. "Won't I be in the way?"

"I can always use the help, especially when it comes to skinning and such, but most people don't like the mess."

"Can I ask you something?" Heather asked after another long pause.

"You can ask. But I reserve the right to refuse to answer."

"What is it about your bow?"

Murdock chuckled. "You're referring to when I first rescued you, Phylicia, and Kimberly?"

"As a matter-of-fact, yes."

"Are you familiar with the Odyssey by Homer?"

STEPHEN DRAKE

Four days after leaving the medical facility, Murdock and Heather arrived at Benteen's camp.

"Murdock!" Benteen said, with a big grin as they came into camp.

"Benteen," Murdock said stoically.

"Nice to see you made it through the winter okay." Benteen led the pair to the large cabin.

"I always seem to make it through without too much trouble. Your shelter needs chinking." Murdock approached the door.

"I know. It was the last thing we built before the first snow." Benteen held the door for them.

Murdock and Heather strolled to the large fireplace, looking around, removing mittens as they approached.

"Was this big enough for all of you?" Murdock said.

"It was, but Benson decided that being in here day in and day out gave him claustrophobia, so he and Melanie would spend several days at his shelter."

"Is Benson around?" Murdock said.

"I'll send someone to find him. What brings you here?"

"I've made it a habit to check on newcomers after their first winter, to see how they fared and if they need anything." Murdock looked around with a more critical eye. "It appears your people did just fine."

"We had our moments, but we came through it okay."

"Murdock." Benson limped over to the fireplace.

"Benson," Murdock replied, after giving him a once-over. "Can we speak privately?" he asked Benteen.

"Of course," Benteen said, with a shaky voice, and then left the structure.

"*This him?*" Murdock flashed to Heather.

"*Yup.*"

"I hear," Murdock said, when he was sure they wouldn't be overheard, "that you're going to be a father."

Benson was silent. He stood straight and his mouth fell open.

374

"No judgments from me. I'd like to suggest you make a trip to the medical facility." Murdock warmed his hands.

"Um... how... what..." Benson stammered.

"Never mind that. You need to ask. Or offer. Just do something."

"What the hell is *she* doing here?" Melanie said, after the door slammed open.

"Oh, Christ," Heather mumbled.

"Trouble?" Murdock whispered to Heather.

"Nothin' I cain't handle," she purred.

Melanie had come over to Benson and was hanging on him. Benson looked uncomfortable with the situation.

"I thought this was a *private* conversation," Murdock said.

"Anything you can say to Dirk, you can say to me." Melanie smiled like a Cheshire cat at Heather.

"I'm sorry, Dirk, I had no idea—"

"Mel, back off," Benson said roughly. "Don't mind her, Murdock. She has some rather *strange* notions."

"So is this one of your *clientele*?" Melanie asked Heather.

Heather, who had been sitting quietly next to Murdock on a round of wood, got to her feet and looked at the men.

"Excuse me." She started to leave.

"Yeah, keep on walk—"

Heather turned and punched Melanie dead in the face. She then strolled to the door.

Murdock and Benson tried to stifle their laughter, with limited success.

———

"Heather, what are you doing out here?" Murdock said, as he got their camp set for the night.

She'd caught and cleaned fish for them.

"Ask me again sometime and I might tell you." She finished prepping it to be cooked.

"I'm serious. I really want to know."

"I'm looking for somewhere to go. Somewhere I feel comfortable. Somewhere I feel like I'm contributing."

"And if you don't find it?" Murdock asked.

"I really don't know. I hadn't thought that far ahead. What about you?"

"Me? You know why I'm out here."

Heather noticed he turned away from her when she asked difficult questions.

"I know what you tell me you're doing, but I think it's deeper than that." She watched his silhouette in the firelight. "I remember what you were like before…"

"Before what?"

"Just before." Heather turned away from him.

Both were silent while the fish cooked.

"Tell me about Declan and Em," Heather said, as they started to eat.

"It was kind of funny, actually." Murdock helped himself. "Declan and Andy got into a bit of a tiff after the funeral."

"About what?"

"About where my kids were going to stay while I was … busy. Andy told him he would fight Declan if that's what he wanted." Murdock laughed. "And once I got home, I made Andy apologize. And he did." Murdock gave a full-throated laugh. "But it wasn't the apology Declan thought he was getting."

Heather chuckled. "I bet that pissed him off."

"Actually, it confused the hell out of him. Andy had him to the point that he didn't know if he was coming or going."

They both laughed.

"Declan said they were just little kids," Murdock laughed.

Heather was laughing, too. "And what did you say?"

"I said his were little kids and mine were small adults."

They both roared.

"You shoulda seen it," Murdock said while laughing.

"Wish I woulda," Heather said, laughing.

Then they both stopped laughing and ate in silence.

"More fish?" Murdock said.

Murdock woke in the middle of the night. The cold woke him and he draped the deerskin over himself as he got more wood and put it on the fire, which had nearly gone out. As the fire blazed up, he glanced at Heather and noticed she looked strange. He went to her and felt her face, and it was ice cold. He turned her head toward the fire and saw that her lips were blue.

"Heather," He shook her.

No response.

"Come on, Heather! You can't do this to me." He started chafing her arms and shoulders to get the circulation started again. He lifted her and sat her close to the fire. Draped his deer hide over the one she still had on her shoulders. He took her ice cold hands, they, too, were ice cold, and patted them to try to stimulate her circulation a little.

"Goddammit! Wake up!"

"There's no need to yell," Heather said, groggily. "Shit, it's cold! Can you turn up the heat a little?"

Murdock stood and took off his parka and slipped it over her head. He gathered more wood and put it on the fire, hoping it would kick out more warmth.

At sunup, Heather opened her eyes and looked around, disoriented. She was sitting up, partially, closer to the fire than she'd remembered, and was she wearing Murdock's parka? Also, she wasn't alone under the deer hides. Murdock was there with his arms and legs wrapped around her.

"What the hell happened?" she whispered.

Murdock opened his eyes. "You okay?"

"Why wouldn't I be? Am I wearing your parka?"

"Yes, you needed it last night."

"Why?"

"I woke up because I was cold. I got more wood on the fire and noticed you were blue."

"Well, I was a little sad last night..."

"Not that kind of blue, ya goof. Your lips were blue, and your hands and face were ice cold."

"Musta got a bit nippy sometime in the night." She gave a sheepish smile.

Murdock looked at her face and could see the color was back into her face and lips.

"Do you feel okay now?"

"I'm still chilled a little. Feel like a popsicle, like I been sleepin' in a freezer."

"I think you were until I got the fire going again. We aren't in any big hurry. You just stay under the hides until you feel warm." Murdock got out from under the hides.

"Sonofabitch, it's cold! You done let all the heat out."

"Sorry. Couldn't be helped." He put the leftover fish close to the fire to warm it, and then he gathered more wood.

"I was warmer before you got out from under," Heather said, when he came back. "Get your ass back under these hides and get me warm." Her teeth were chattering.

Murdock removed the hides and quickly got close to her and restored the hides.

"Better?"

She grabbed his hands and wrapped them around her. "That might help."

"Sorry about this morning," Murdock said.

They'd spent the day under the hides, trying to get Heather warm.

"I wasn't expecting the weather to get so cold and I was a bit under-prepared for two of us on this trip."

"It's okay. Glad you woke when ya did."

"So am I. Didn't want something bad to happen on my watch." Murdock chuckled, nervously.

"I guess that would depend on your definition of bad. And don't worry, I ain't holdin' ya to nothin'. I understand you was just keepin' me warm."

"You know, sometime during the night, while I was trying to get you warmed and revived, I thought of my daughters."

Heather looked at him out of the corner of her eye. "Yeah?"

"Yes, and I was thinking, would you be interested in being a governess?"

"A what?"

"A governess. My kids are a handful, even for me. I'm going to need help with them. My daughter is ten now, so…"

"So you don't know how to explain things to her? Say, in a couple years?"

"There's that. Irene could explain it, but I don't think Irene and Zeke want my daughters parked on their doorstep all the time. I had planned on taking Andy with me when I go hunting, but I don't like leaving the girls alone. I sure could use the help."

"Is this one of those let's-find-Heather-something-to-do things?"

"To be clear, I have no designs on you, other than needing your help."

"Good. I have no interest in you either."

"If you like, I'll build me a room to sleep in outside the cabin."

Heather looked at him with a shocked expression.

"Or it can be for you… with a lock and its own fireplace."

"How much control will I have over the kids?"

"How much do you want?" Murdock asked. "I'll explain it to

them that you're not their mother and aren't trying to be. That you're there to help me keep tabs on them, especially when I'm gone."

"How much do they know about the Oomah?" Heather gathered the hides around her.

"They grew up with them. They don't know everything, but they will eventually. They have to finish growing up first. So what do you think?"

Heather looked at him, soberly. "I think you need to understand what you're getting yourself into.

"That tiff with Melanie wasn't the first, and I doubt it'll be the last. When Annie and me were tendin' to Benson's ankle, we basically got booted from their camp, too. The womenfolk were being rather protective. I don't understand why, but they insinuated that me and Annie were a couple of hookers trying to get at their menfolk."

"Surely, you're joshing me."

"Not a bit, and don't call me Shirley. Maybe it's me, I dunno. Maybe it's the blonde hair and blue eyes. Maybe it's my name, but everyone thinks I'm a bimbo. I'm not. I may not be the brightest crayon in the box, but even I know that what Annie did wasn't fair to anyone. Not to her, not to Benson, and not to her baby. But what do I know? I ain't no hooker neither. Just so you know, you have competition for the job offer. I was thinkin' of just bein' by myself before you made the offer. Now, then, if you take me to your place to be a nanny to your kids, you need to know you're gonna catch three different hells of shit from ever'one. And when I say ever'one, I mean *ever'one*. Declan and Emily ain't gonna like it 'cause it don't seem proper, you just widowered and all."

"Um, that would be widowed," Murdock said.

"Shut up when I'm talkin'. I gotta get this out while I can. Irene and Annie won't like it neither. Same reasons as Declan and Emily. But they won't *say* you have a whore livin' in your house with your little kids. They don't call me that, but they think it. Prob'ly 'cause I ain't smart like them. So you need to think about it long and hard. If you still want my help, you got it. But you gotta consider what I said."

Heather turned her back and sobbed.

It took five more days for Murdock and Heather to get back to the medical facility.

"Irene, would you mind if I used your spa?" Murdock said.

"You don't need to ask, you know that. What we have is yours."

"*Heather, meet me at the spa,*" Murdock flashed. "We had a bit of an emergency on our jaunt downriver," Murdock explained. "We had a cold snap and Heather came close to freezing to death, and hasn't felt warm since."

"Well, get her into the spa so she'll get warmed up."

Murdock left to go to the small cave with the spa. Heather caught up to him inside the rolling rock door. The air was damp, and cold at the door.

"Get in the spa," Murdock said.

He waited until he heard her get into the hot water before he entered the darkened room.

"Now, then, you had your say, and I will have mine. I asked for your help because I need it. Not for any other reason. I think my kids could benefit from your presence in our cabin. "That being said, you raised a few issues that dealt mainly with your perceptions and lack of education. From my perspective, that was nonsense. You're smarter than you think you are. You have innate intelligence—a common sense, if you will—that I want my kids to be exposed to. Next, I've never thought of you as a hooker or a bimbo. Anyone else who thinks that way, can stick it. If I hear it, they in it deep. Declan and Emily will just have to get over themselves if they don't like the situation at my house. It is *my* house and *my* kids, and by definition, none of *their* business.

At this point, I've lost two wives, both of whom I loved. After so many years, I don't know who I am anymore. I know who I used to be, and he wasn't all that pleasant to be around. I may not be much better now, but it's better than I used to be. I'm to the point where I refuse to put up with anyone else's bullshit. I've never been one to start a fight, but I've never failed to end one. Now it feels like I need to resolve things quicker and more definitively. Now I've had my say. Any questions?"

"No, sir," Heather whispered.

"For now, you get warmed through and through, you hear? I'll expect you to be ready to travel upriver in two days if you're accepting the offer."

"Yes, sir."

"Are you accepting the offer?"

"Yes, sir!"

Murdock gathered the kids together for a family meeting.

"First of all, this is not a discussion. This is to let you know that Heather will be going home with us."

"We don't need another mother," Chun Hua said.

"Good. 'Cause you're not getting one. She is here to help me ride herd on you three. She is not Aunt Heather or anything like that. She'll let you know how to refer to her. Second, she's aware of how things should be. She'll be dealing with you the same way I would. If you have any questions, feel free to ask, but make sure you're willing to hear the answer."

"I won't call her Mother," Rosa piped in somewhat defiantly.

"Andy, who was your mother?" Murdock said.

"Rose bore me, but Mei Lee was there whenever I needed something. She was my mother."

"Chunnie?"

"You already know Mei Lee was my and Rosa's mother."

"And you'll never have another. No one else will ever fill that part inside of you quite the same way. Someday, someone may come close, and you may want to call her mother, but that will be your choice. Heather isn't asking to be considered your mother. She's there to talk to you, to help educate you, to answer questions she feels are appropriate. Everything else is referred to me. If you try to force her away, you're in for a rude awakening. You'll find her to be stubborn, and you'll answer to me for it. Same thing if you're cruel or disrespectful. I expect you to make her feel welcome in our home and in our life. If you can't for some reason, then tell me. I'll want to know why. Be advised. I will not have you running to me only, for everything. None of you are babies, so don't act like it. I know Mei Lee did a lot to train you in your fighting skills. Heather lacks those skills, so that training will fall to me. If I'm not there, then try to train her. You'll be better for it. I expect to hear *yes, ma'am'* and *no, ma'am* whenever you answer her. A good general rule will be if you wouldn't talk to your mother that way, then you better not talk to Heather that way. Do you all understand?"

"Yes, Father," all three said, in unison.

———

Murdock was pulling the cart, with Chun Hua and Andrew inside it, and Heather rode Batibat, with Rosa sitting nearly in her lap when they passed Declan's house. Emily was outside with her three children, and smiled and waved as they rode past. The entire Murdock household returned the wave, but didn't stop until they reached Murdock's cabin.

As Murdock went in, he saw Declan inside trying to tidy up.

"Sorry. Wanted to be done before you arrived home." He shook Murdock's hand.

"It's appreciated, Declan," Murdock said, as the rest of the household entered.

"Hey, kids." Declan flashed a broad smile.

"Hi, Uncle Declan," all three kids said, in unison.

"Hello, Heather, and welcome."

"Nice to see ya, Declan."

"Kids, it's been a long trip, so bathing is a priority before eating," Murdock said.

"Yes, sir!" they replied.

"Declan, if you'll excuse us," Murdock said.

"Of course, sorry." Declan was grinning, shyly. "I'll get out of your hair."

"Bring the family over in a couple days. That'll give Heather a chance to settle in, okay?"

"Um… yeah, sure. Em would like that."

When they were alone in the main room, Heather looked at Murdock.

"Well, that wasn't weird, was it?" she said.

"Positively scary." Murdock shook his head at the closed door.

What does it take to break someone? At what point does he stop being human? At what point does he lose that...spark?

— KEVIN MURDOCK, COLLECTED SAYING

S

A n all too familiar communication flashed to Murdock from Beron.

"'Tis time."

"Time? For what?" Murdock responded.

"Spring gather."

"Heather, have you ever been to a spring gathering of the Oomah?" Murdock was sitting at the table.

All three kids were eating without fighting, for once.

"No, sir, I have not," Heather replied, speaking carefully.

Getting her to slow her mind and to concentrate on the words has helped the way she speaks. That and being around people who speak correctly probably helps, too.

"Would you *like* to go?" Murdock asked.

"Oh, Oh, Oh! Can we go, too, Father?"

"If Heather wants to go, then we all go. If not, then..." Murdock looked sad and shook his head.

"Well, I don't know, sir," Heather shook her head.

"Oh, please, please, please, Miss Heather! It's so much fun." The kids were bouncing around.

"I don't know what to wear. Maybe it would be better if you took the children alone this time."

Murdock stood and clapped to get the children's attention. "You have chores to get done, so get to it."

As soon as the kids had gone outside, Kevin led Heather to the table and sat her down.

"You should really come with us, Heather. It's important to me and the kids that you go. I won't insist, but it will be something they'll be talking about for days afterward."

"Are you...certain...I won't be in the way?"

"If you're in the way, then so am I." Murdock smiled at her.

"All right, I'll accompany you and the children."

Murdock patted her hand and smiled.

"*When is it?*" Murdock flashed.

"*Now,*" Beron replied.

"*Wait, we aren't quite ready yet. I'll let you know when we are.*"

Murdock took Heather's hand and led her into the yard. The kids gathered around their father's feet. As he looked over, he saw Declan, Emily, and their brood standing in their yard.

"*We're ready,*" Murdock flashed.

The children squealed with laughter as they all rose into the air. Heather, not being used to traveling this way, gripped Murdock's arm. It took minutes—too soon for the kids— for it to be over, and Heather relaxed.

Murdock offered Heather his arm, and she took it. The two strolled around the Oomah, the humans being the only ones making noise. Soon enough, everyone became quiet.

"*Keev an Mur dook of who man,*" Beron flashed to everyone.

"*This, my tribe,*" Murdock motioned for Declan's family and his own household to stand and present themselves. *"Some unable to come, but these who come."*

"Regrets for mate, from all Oomah," Beron flashed. *"Missed she is."*

All the Oomah dipped their heads.

"New mate?" Beron flashed.

"No. Friend and watcher of young ones. Tribe member."

"Name?"

"Heather Stevens."

Beron bowed to Murdock, and then looked to Declan. Murdock resumed his place with Heather, and she took his arm as before. Murdock was paying attention to the goings on during the presentations, and then he looked down at his arm. Heather was caressing it while she looked around.

Does she realize what she's doing. It does feel nice, natural. Murdock looked up and saw her looking at him, and she started to pull her hand away. He clamped down on her arm with his arm to prevent her from removing her hand. When she relaxed, so did he.

"Do you know everyone here?" Heather whispered near his ear.

"Most of them. It has taken many years, though," Murdock answered.

"And how many humans owe their being here to you?"

"Every member of our tribe is welcomed here."

"So all of them."

"Much to the chagrin of the Oomah. Before humans came, these were quiet and dignified gatherings."

"Yeah, now look at it."

They both laughed.

When the presentations where finished, the young ones gathered to rough-house with the Oomah cubs. Heather kept a grip on Murdock's arm and an eye on her three charges.

"How are you ...*fitting* in?" Emily asked, as she and Declan came over to Heather and Murdock.

Emily was carrying Gordon, while Declan carried Roslynn. Maureen stood close to her parents. Emily glanced at Heather's arm entwined in Murdock's, and a scowl flashed across her face, but didn't remain.

"Fine," Heather replied. "It's all new and wonderful to me." She smiled broadly.

"You do know Kevin has vouched for every human here?" Emily said, with an underlying catty tone.

"No, I didn't know," Heather said concerned.

"It's true. All it would take is for a human to...offend an Oomah..." Emily shook her head.

"From what I know of the Oomah," Murdock said, "they're understanding and hard to offend." He grinned at Emily and patted Heather's hand. "I'm sure that if someone put their mind to it, they could accomplish it. But they'd have to work hard at it."

Emily got a concerned look on her face and guided her brood away from Heather.

"*We need to talk about this later,*" Heather flashed to Murdock.

"*No, we don't.*" He patted her hand. "*I told you before, how I saw things. Did you think I didn't mean it? Trust me.*"

"*I do trust you. It's everyone else I keep my eye on.*"

At nightfall, Murdock, Heather, and the kids were back at their cabin.

Heather shooed the children into the spa, and then made something to eat.

"Did you enjoy yourself?" Murdock sat at the table.

"Yes, I did. Thank you for talking me into it. I wasn't sure, but now I'm glad I went." Heather smiled at him.

"My compliments on keeping your cool with Emily. As sweet as she can be, she can also go the *other* way."

"She was trying to make me feel like I didn't belong, but she failed."

"Good. As I said, if I take you somewhere, you belong. If you don't, then I don't either, and I'm not afraid to say so." Murdock grinned at her.

"Shut up and eat," she flashed a smile, blushing.

———

The kids were asleep in bed. Murdock was lounging in the spa.

"Can I join you?" Heather whispered.

"Certainly." He shifted to the other side of the spa to allow her entry.

It was dark, the only light from the stars. Once Heather was in the water, Murdock stretched his arms back out on the edge of the spa, outside the water. His head was tilted back and resting on the edge.

"Can I ask you something?" Heather whispered.

"You just did." Murdock chuckled.

"Did it bother you …today…when I took your arm?"

"I offered it as moral support in an unfamiliar situation."

"But did it bother you?"

Murdock thought for a second. "Yes, it did."

"Sorry, I didn't mean for it to bother you."

Murdock chuckled. "Yes, you did. You've been here quite some time, and I've noticed that you enjoy *bothering* me."

"I guess I'm not using the correct word."

"Sure you are. Do I find you *distracting*? Very. Did your caressing my arm make me *tingle* all over today? Yes. So did you bother me? Of course. And it was intentional. I know it and so do you."

"You said if I needed something, I should ask you."

"Yes, I said that. Is there something I can do for you?"

"You did it earlier today."

"And what was that?"

"You offered me your arm. It made me feel...accepted. When you prevented me from retracting my arm when you caught me caressing it, it made me feel...wanted. I appreciate those feelings very much. But now...can you hold me like you did when I almost froze?"

Murdock grinned. "Of course."

Heather came over to him and curled up into his shoulder and chest as his arms went around her bare, wet shoulders.

"Better?"

"Much," Heather purred.

Murdock and Heather were lying on a deer skin in front of the hearth, covered with another deerskin. She was snuggled into him, her back to him as she faced the fire.

Murdock was caressing her shoulder.

"Does this make you uncomfortable?" Heather said.

"I don't know. Why don't you ask me in the morning?" Murdock chuckled.

"Meaning?" she said, over her shoulder.

"Meaning, stay here all night and let me cuddle with you, and I'll let you know in the morning if I'm uncomfortable."

Heather giggled. "Wouldn't that be a little late? I mean, the last thing I want to do is make you uncomfortable."

"I *am* a little uncomfortable."

Heather started to move, and Murdock extended his arm and pushed her back down onto it. He then snuggled deeper into her, holding her closer.

"There, that's much better," he said.

"When did you know?" Heather said.

She and Murdock had been strolling upriver from the cabin, taking in the new growth peeking out in the early summer sunshine.

"When you started to remove your hand from my arm at the gathering," Murdock replied.

Their arms were entwined, as they were whenever the couple went for a stroll.

"I felt it moving away, and it saddened me. I didn't want it going anywhere."

They took a few steps in silence.

"How about you?" Murdock said.

"I really don't know." Heather looked down.

"Unfair! You asked, and I answered honestly. So spill it."

Heather thought for a long time.

"Seriously, I can't put my finger on it."

"Okay, I won't pry," Murdock murmured.

"I will say it's one of the reasons I left to be with Alvin, though."

"What?" Murdock asked in shock.

"You see, I was jealous of Mei Lee, which was silly. So I left. I didn't want to cause any problems for anyone."

"I had no clue," Murdock whispered.

"You weren't supposed to. No hint was given. I didn't want Mei Lee to suspect. I never told anyone. It was just something I held close, hidden away."

"But didn't that affect your relationship with Alvin?"

"Relationship? What relationship? He didn't have to sleep alone and had someone to talk to. And I got to survive. Sounds like a strong relationship there!" Heather said sarcastically.

"But... how did you prevent pregnancy?"

Heather chuckled. "Luckily, Alvin's... um, ... predilections bent toward the things that would prevent it. The very things that are... anti-survival."

Murdock was silent for some time. "So you're saying..."

STEPHEN DRAKE

"Me lovey you long time," Heather said, nasally, and both laughed.

When they stopped laughing, they were again serious.

"Sorry, I probably shouldn't joke about it," Heather said.

"So what about what you said when I asked you to come here? You said you had no interest in me."

Heather's face turned bright red. "Um... I lied?" She chewed on the inside of her cheek. "I knew you'd withdraw the offer if I didn't lie. That would imply that I had an agenda. I didn't. I was on my way to quiet hermitude, and content with that possibility."

"Did you hear that Annie had her baby?" Murdock asked, changing the subject.

"What did she have?"

"A girl. She named her Grace Irene."

"It's obvious who *she's* named after," Heather added sadly.

"You wanna get hitched?" Murdock blurted.

"Well, sur, I do declare. Yoa quite a for'ard and brash young man."

They both started laughing.

"Well? Do you?"

Heather touched her fingertips to the top of her sternum. "Oh, my! It's just so... sudden" She batted her eyes at him and blushed. "Next thing you'll be saying is you want me to have your babies."

"Well, there is that." Murdock chuckled.

Heather inhaled deeply and let it out slowly. "If I say no, you'll probably be all sad and mopey and hound me for years until I eventually capitulate...so, yes."

The air was hot and no hint of a breeze marred the late summer air.

Kevin Murdock, Andrew, Rosa, Declan, Emily, carrying

Gordon, Maureen, Roslynn, who was fidgeting, Irene Harris, and Annie Cooper, carrying Grace, all stood before Zeke. Kevin and Andrew stood facing Zeke, who was facing everyone else, when Heather walked the path upriver from Murdock's cabin, with Chun Hua following close behind.

Kevin thought Heather looked stunning with her long, braided, golden, platinum blonde hair, in her new golden buckskin dress, complete with leggings and moccasins. Her dress decorated with images of heather flowers of purple, yellow, and red.

Chun Hua also had a new dress, and Murdock noticed she was starting to favor her mother.

When Heather reached Murdock, the couple looked solemn as Zeke cleared his throat.

"We have gathered here to witness the joining of Kevin Murdock to Heather Stevens...and to party hardy, when it's all said and done. I have personally counseled these two and can publicly state that they're both crazy..." Zeke paused appeared to check his non-existent notes, "... about each other."

The crowd chuckled.

"So without further ado..." Zeke turned to Murdock. "Do you?"

"Absolutely."

Zeke nodded and turned to Heather. "Do you?"

"Unequivocally."

"Then by the power of Grayskull, I pronounce... you uns is hitched."

Everyone laughed heartily.

"Are you going to be okay today?" Murdock said. "I need to hunt, and I was planning on taking Andy with me."

"Where are you going?" Heather said. "Hopefully, you won't be too far from home."

"I was thinking, in the field across the river. We do need another deer for winter, as well as porkers and fish."

"The girls and I can help out with the fish part," Heather came over to her husband, who placed his hand on her swollen belly.

"If you think you can. I don't want you doing too much. Don't want any...um...issues."

"I was just examined by Irene, and she said everything is fine." Heather ran her fingers through some stray strands of his hair. "Sometimes you worry too much."

"Yeah? Go figure. Would you rather I didn't?"

"Nope." She kissed his forehead.

"Mother, is this okay?" Rosa handed Heather some vegetables she was helping Chun Hua harvest.

Heather examined it. "Yes, dear, it's fine. Just listen to Chunnie. She knows what to do."

"Okay. I will, Mother." Rosa left the cabin and returned to the garden.

"How long has that been going on?" Murdock said.

"How long has *what* been going on?"

"Mother?"

"Oh, *that*. Well, Rosa started shortly after we were married. Chunnie started shortly after Rosa. Andrew hasn't yet."

"Are you okay with it?"

Heather put her hands on either side of her swollen belly. "It's a little late if I'm not. By the end of winter, there'll be a little one that will call me that whether I like it or not."

"But did she ask you first, or did she just start calling you that?"

"Does it matter? I know Chunnie asked, but I don't remember if Rosa did."

"Have you talked to Annie lately?" Murdock asked.

"Yes. Grace is fine, but she's having trouble with Dirk and Melanie."

"What now?"

"Dirk The Jerk is insisting on seeing his daughter."

"That's understandable." Murdock nodded.

"Maybe. But Melanie is being a bitch about it. She's been bad-mouthing Annie to her own daughter, with Annie sitting there holding her. I know Grace isn't old enough to understand yet, but that's messed up, no matter how you look at it."

"So Dirk and Melanie are together?" Murdock asked, confused.

Heather laughed. "Nope. She likes to think they're an item, but they're not, according to Annie."

Murdock rubbed his forehead. "Dealing with...this... gives me a headache. Do I need to go down there?"

"Not yet. Annie will let us know if that becomes necessary. She did say she saw Alvin."

"Really? Where and when was that?" Murdock glared.

"She was at Benteen's camp and saw him heading downriver. No, I don't want you to go have a chat with him. Leave it alone, Kevin. He had his chance."

"With you? That isn't why I'm thinking about visiting him. He's one of the few survivors of the attack on the medical facility. I wish to rectify that."

Chris Gundersen stretched his back as he exited the roundhouse he and Benson had built. It was intentionally built closer to the plateau edge than the rest of the roundhouses.

The last house on the last plateau. At least, the last plateau that humans want to live on, for now. Chris gathered his materials and continued working on his bow. *Lucky for us, Al Jones has been around a few times since the end of the first winter. Without his help, and his bow, we'd all be in a bad way.* He brushed the dust off his buckskins. *Without the means to kill a deer at a distance, we would've all starved. As it is, I need to get this bow finished and get a few arrows made.* He'd already spent most of the summer working on it.

"How you doin', big guy?" Jones rode up on his mount.

"Doin'. Or tryin' ta. How's Tricks?"

"Eh… you know." Jones shrugged.

"What's news upriver?"

"Nothin' worth mentionin' "

"I forget where I heard it, but I guess somethin' went down some-ers near a mine? I don't rec'llect the details, though," Gundersen said.

Jones felt the blood drain from his face. *Is Murdock on the prowl again. I wish this hick could remember details. Do I need to go back into hiding?*

He'd just come from spending seven days with the hermit Jeff Carter. He was somewhat safe there. Carter had no idea who Jones was or what he did elsewhere. He preferred to keep his cards close to his vest.

"Ya hear anythin' resemblin' when?" Jones said.

"Afore first snow? After first snow? Some-ers in there, I think." Gundersen started laughing. "Purdy bad when a body livin' out here in the middle of nowheres hears things afore you."

Jones chuckled. "M'kay, Mister Info, what else ya hear?"

"Nothin' "

"I heard that Benson has troubles galore."

"Who's Troubles Galore? Sounds like a stripper ta me." Gundersen shook his head.

"I needs ta git," Jones said. "I be back 'round these parts again real soon."

Jones reined up his mount and headed for Benteen's camp. He needed more information on Murdock and his whereabouts.

They might be able to give me the information I need, if I ask the right questions of the right people.

Five days after seeing Gundersen, Jones was in a bed of soft branches and hides—Melanie Burton's bed.

"What do you hear? Can you tell me about something concerning a mine?" Jones said, while Melanie was servicing him.

"Don't know about a mine," she caught her breath, "but had heard something about Murdock getting re-married."

"Really? When was that?"

"Close to the end of summer, I think. Those in the medical facility know the details as they all went."

"No one else?"

"Not that I know of."

"What do you know about Murdock? Anything?"

"Just what everyone knows. And that he's a badass motherfu—"

"Who told you that?" Jones growled, and pulled Melanie's hair.

"Well," she shrugged, "it's what everyone says. He came here to talk to Dirk Benson a while back."

"Who is Dirk Benson, and what did he have to talk to him about?"

"Dirk Benson. You know… the one I have fun with when you're not around? He's another outdoorsman, like Murdock. Sort of, anyway. He has a place upriver a piece, and one downriver. Gundersen lives at the one downriver."

Jones nodded. "Yeah, I know Gundersen. What a dumbass. What if I wanted to talk to Benson?"

"I suppose you can if he's at his place."

"I'll stop over and talk to him right after you finish."

Jones knocked on a rough-hewn wooden door.

"Who is it?" a man called from inside.

Jones waited. After a bit, he knocked again. This time, he heard someone swearing and coming toward the door.

"Whadda ya want!" The man said angrily as he swung the door open.

"You Benson?" Jones said.

"Yeah. Who are you?" Benson asked warily.

"I'd like to have a discussion with you if you're not busy."

Benson rubbed the edge of his hand under his nose as he eyed Jones. "I 'spose," he said, after giving the man a long once-over and standing aside.

Jones stepped in and closed the door. *All that's missing is the wife-beater and the sweatpants. What a derelict!*

"Okay." Benson sat close to the fire. "Now you're inside, so talk. Who are ya?"

"For now, call me Jones. What do you know about Murdock?"

Benson narrowed his eyes. "Why you wanna know?"

"The *why* is not for *you* to know. It's enough that *I want* to know."

Benson shrugged. "I know what everybody knows. No big secret there."

Jones stared at Benson, stone-faced. "What did he want when he came here the last time?"

"Personal business," Benson said stoically. "None of yours."

Jones chuckled. "I think you're spyin' for Murdock."

"Good luck provin' that. Now get the hell out. You've officially worn out yer welcome."

"Okay, if you say so. You want me to say hi to those at the medical facility? That's my next stop."

"I've a question for ya. Who told ya I met with Murdock here?"

"I *ask* questions, *not* answer them." Jones scoffed.

Nels Osterlund hadn't given any thought at all to his old boss or the other flunkies, of which he was one. So far, no one knew he'd been one of those that helped Palmer rape Doctor Harris. He had figured that since Palmer was dead and everyone who suspected was also either dead or far away, why bring it up to anyone.

Osterlund wasn't married, or even monogamous. Luckily, way back when, when he'd first joined the farmers' group, he'd convinced Lantz to eliminate monogamy within their group.

"What happens if a couple marries and then one of them gets killed or maimed or cheats? Isn't that setting up lawyers to steal everything with wrongful death suits and divorces? Why do we want to do that? Besides, isn't marriage ownership? Do you want to be owned?"

Lantz, having heard the argument and remembering his own slavery due to indebtedness, had banned or refused to acknowledge all marriages, and with marriages, the responsibility that may occur when men got with women.

"Isn't childrearing something the entire community should do? Doesn't it take a village? Or was Saint Hillary wrong?"

Osterlund knew that, at the time of their departure, Hillary hadn't yet been canonized, but it didn't affect his argument.

His life had been calm and predictable. Some would call it boring. All that changed when he answered the knock on his door. He stood at the opened door, staring at the person on the other side of the threshold.

He looks oddly familiar, but I can't place him.

"Don't you recognize your old friend?" the stranger said.

He felt that the voice should've triggered a memory, but it didn't.

"Sorry, but no, I don't."

"How *was* Doc Harris back in the day?" the stranger smirked.

Osterlund frowned. "What the hell do you want? I'm too busy to buy into your fantasies."

"But it's night, and you appear to be doing nothing."

"Like I said, I'm too busy." Osterlund started to close the door.

The stranger pushed his way into the house.

"You're not welcome here. Leave, or I'll throw you out."

"I doubt it." The stranger gave another smirk. "If you do that, I may have to let it slip that you helped rape Doc Harris."

Osterlund was shocked and said nothing.

"But I'm *sure* no one would ever believe you capable of such a thing." The stranger smiled.

Osterlund closed the door. "Who the hell *are* you?"

"I'm shocked you fail to remember your old friend Alvin Jones."

"Al?" Osterlund's recognition showed in the smile and the attitude change. He grabbed Jones' hand and started pumping it. "How the hell you been? Seems like forever since I seen ya. You nearly gave me a coronary with that talk of Harris."

"Been fine." Jones shook Osterlund's hand.

"Sit, sit," Osterlund said. "What brings you here?"

"Right now, looking for information. What do you know about Murdock and the medical facility?" Jones looked around at the interior of the hovel. *Reminds me of mine and Heather's.* He shivered mentally.

"Just what everyone else knows. Harris runs the medical facility. Never been there, myself. Annie Cooper is the *traveling* nurse." Osterlund paused and rubbed his chin in thought. "I know Murdock protects them and spends his time sticking his nose into everyone else's business. Why?"

"Some time ago, I heard something …about the mine…"

"Wagner? You heard something about Wagner? I haven't seen him in a coon's age."

Jones smiled. "Wagner and me hit the medical facility some time ago, but he blew it. He disappeared at that time. He's under a death mark by Murdock. And so am I. I haven't heard anything lately, so I'm asking, what do you know?"

Osterlund shrugged. "That's more info than I've heard in a while. What did you hear from Hornsby? Anything?"

"Nothing." Jones shook his head.

"So now what?"

"Want to make a trip?" Jones asked.

"Road trip!"

Both men laughed.

Jones was looking at the entry that had been dug under the block wall. It wasn't quite dark yet, but it soon would be. With him were Osterlund and Hornsby.

"I don't see nothin' movin' over there," Hornsby said loud enough for the other men to hear.

"Now what?" Osterlund said.

"Let's go." Jones got to his feet and led the way. "We can just walk in. If someone asks, we'll say we're friends with Wagner."

All three men lined up and crept into the entryway. They saw no one. As they slid toward the mine entrance, it was starting to snow.

"Let's get inside," Osterlund said. "It's cold out here."

"Have you seen anything?" Jones said.

"Just something that looks like blood around some of the skeletons," Hornsby said, as each man was searching all corners, looking for someone alive.

"Wonder what happen'd here?" Hornsby said.

Jones shook his head. "Let's keep going. It's getting warmer, at least. That's a plus."

All three men found a room with more than just a skeleton, but not much more. Jones went over and turned the body, and then jumped back.

"Who are you? What do you want? Please don't hurt me!" the body said.

"Who the hell is that?" Osterlund said.

"I don't know," Jones said. "Let's see if we can find some water or food. Then we can see if we can clean this guy up and see who it is."

"Did you see his eyes?" Hornsby said. "He's bat-shit crazy!"

As it turned out, the three men waited until the crazy man got hungry or thirsty and followed him to the pool that was used for catching the bland fish. On their way through the mine, they found the potable water and the hot springs.

"I don't know who this guy is, but his constant maniacal laughter is scaring me," Hornsby said.

"It's not constant," Jones said. "It is often, but not constant. Quit exaggerating."

"Well, it seems like it. And the last time I was looking some-wheres else, it scared me. Who is this guy?"

"Yeah, and where is Wagner?" Osterlund said.

"Wagner?" the crazy man said. "Are you Wagner?" he asked Osterlund. "I'm Wagner, too. Are you Wagner?" the man asked Hornsby. "We're all Wagner. *Ha-ha-ha-ha-ha-ha!*"

"Wait a minute," Jones went to the crazed man and pushed the tangled mess of hair off his face. "Get him bathed and shaved. Knock him out if you have to, but get it done."

"Why?" Hornsby said. "Where's Wagner?"

Jones pointed to the crazed individual in front of them. "I think he's under all that mass of hair."

Everyone turned to the crazy man, their mouths agape.

"Oh, hell no," Osterlund said.

Jones was at the mine entrance, watching the snow pile up outside. Once in a while, a stray gust of wind would blow a few huge flakes inside the cave.

"It took us a while, but we got him cleaned up for now," Hornsby said. "You was right. It's Wagner."

"I thought it would be," Jones said. "Has he said what happened to him? And where everyone else is?"

"He keeps sayin' shit like, *Murdock did it*, and *Murdock killed me*." Hornsby shook his head. "Sad. And cruel. Murdock shoulda just put the dumb bastard out of his misery."

"Be glad he didn't. Now we can get some answers. I want all of us to talk to him, one at a time, which seems to be the most productive. Then we'll get together and compare notes."

Hornsby nodded and turned to go.

What happened here? And what would it take to make someone go around the bend like Wagner has? Why would Murdock—who told me Wagner is a dead man walking—leave him alive? Will he leave me alive as well? When I look at Wagner, am I looking into a mirror of my future?

25

If all you have is speculation, you have nothing. Without facts, all you have is smoke and mirrors.

— KEVIN MURDOCK, COLLECTED SAYINGS

Heather was lying on her back on the sturdy table Mei Lee had built, sweat running down her face.

"H-o-l-y shit! That one hurt!"

"Just take it easy, Heather," Doctor Harris said soothingly. "The first kid is always the hardest. Try to relax, as best you can. And breathe." She lifted a deer hide and peeked under it and probed with her fingers.

"Everything okay, Doc?" Murdock said.

"Don't kibitz, Kevin, or I'll insist you leave." She looked at his concerned face.

"Can I just step out for a bit, too?" Heather said, between spasms, her beautiful hair plastered to her forehead with sweat.

"You stay put, young lady. I can't have my patients walking out in the middle of procedures. It would give people the idea that I don't know what I'm doing."

"Can't have that, Doc," Murdock said.

404

He saw his wife tense as another contraction started.

"Breathe, dear." He started breathing into her face.

Heather started to mock his breathing as the pain built, hung there for a bit, and then released.

"What I wouldn't give for a cold washcloth about now." Her breathing settled down.

"I know it's unpleasant, but you're right on schedule. Soon, you'll be holding a bee-yut-tiful baby...um..." Harris looked to Murdock questioningly.

"Boy," Heather said.

"Girl," Murdock said.

"A beautiful baby for me to spoil and coo over."

"Unpleasant? Is this what you call unpleasant?" Heather said. "Unpleasant is a broken leg compared to this. This is like being hit by a truck."

"Now, dear, Irene is trying to make it as painless as possible."

"You wanna know what it's like? Grab your bottom lip and pull it over your head. That's what it feels like to me."

"I've never had a baby myself, but I'm told that that is pretty accurate," Irene said.

Another contraction hit Heather. Murdock breathed into her face again.

"Don't push until I tell you, okay?" Irene said.

"The next time I deliver, no fish and onions for you." Heather said to Murdock. "I'm about to puke."

Several contractions later.

"Okay, Kevin," Irene said, "climb up onto the table, at your wife's head. I want you to hold her legs behind the knees, with her head in your belly. Pull her legs wide as I have her push. We're almost done. With the hard part, anyway."

Murdock complied and prepared himself.

"Okay, Heather, you ready to do this?" Irene said.

"No! Stop the bus. I wanna get off!" Heather yelled.

"It's a little late for that now. Ready? Ready? Push! Come on! Push!"

It wasn't long until a perfect baby boy, Aryan Jaxxon Murdock, arrived to his sweating and grinning parents.

"Is he okay?" Heather panted. "I know you wanted a girl..."

"He's perfect. All I wanted was a healthy baby, and you gave me that." Murdock stroked his wife's head.

"Here you go." Irene handed the newest member of the Murdock household to Heather, wrapped in a piece of deer hide.

"Thanks, Irene," Heather said, tears streaming.

She unwrapped the baby and counted all the appendages.

Andrew, Chun Hua, and Rosa came into the cabin, having been at Declan's while Heather delivered.

"This is your brother Aryan Jaxxon," Kevin said.

"Hey, Jax." Andy wore a smile as he waved at the baby.

"He's so cute." Chun Hua scrunched down to be small like he was. "Cute little Airy." She touched his dimpled cheeks.

"He's your baby brother, Chunnie, not a puppy," Irene said.

"What's a puppy?" Chun Hua said.

Rosa looked at her older brother and sister. "I was never that small."

"You were smaller, squirt." Chun Hua chuckled. "I remember."

"And so do I," Andy said to Rosa.

After the kids left the room, at Harris' insistence, Zeke, Declan, and Emily filed in.

"Congratulations, son." Zeke shook Murdock's hand.

"Hey, congrats, bro." Declan pumped Murdock's hand.

"Thanks, but I didn't do anything. Heather did all the cooking."

Emily looked over at the baby. "Well, he's cute and everything, but he has a ways to go to be the beauty my Gordon is." She smiled at Heather and clasped her hand. "Not too bad for a couple of amateurs."

Everyone laughed.

Murdock was lying with his wife and newborn son.

"Happy?" he said.

"Sore, but yes, happy and content." Heather smiled. "You?"

"Yes. Happy and in love with my wife." Murdock smiled.

"You better be. After all I just went through?"

"He is a cutie."

"Takes after his father," Heather whispered.

"Been called lots of things in my life, but I don't think I was ever called cute."

"More's the pity. Is Harris staying with Declan and Em?"

"No, she's with Rosa and Chunnie, here. She'll be here at least a week. She says to keep an eye on you and Aryan. It's just my luck to have kids on the coldest, snowiest day of the year."

Annie Cooper was sitting in the pool. Her eyes were closed as she watched through Irene's eyes, the birth of baby Aryan. Her own daughter was in her cradle just a few feet away.

"*He is a cute little bugger,*" Annie flashed to Irene.

"*That he is. Healthy, too. Gonna take after his older brother.*"

"*Andy is going to be a handsome lad in a few years.*"

"*That may be true, but Heather has added a little more to the natural Murdock line.*"

"*So when are you heading home?*"

"*I want to stick close to Heather for a few more days.*"

"*Issues?*"

"*Oh, no. It was hard for her, being her first baby, but I just prefer to err on the side of caution, and I want to spoil the other three before heading home. How's Gracie?*"

"*She's fine. It is a little scary staying here alone sometimes. My hat's off to Em and Mei Lee. They used to stay home alone with babies all the time.*"

"*You're in the residence cave with Gracie and food?*"

"*Yes.*"

"With the stone in place, no one knows where you are, or how to get to you if they did. You're as safe there as you would be anywhere."

"But I would be around family there. Not nearly as lonely."

"We discussed this. Gracie is just too young for a hard journey in the bitter cold. I need to talk to Murdock about addressing that issue. Maybe he can come up with something so you can get up here after we get home. You'll want to make the trip, too. Aryan is just too cute."

Alvin Jones, Jackson Hornsby, and Nels Osterlund were sitting and eating a bland fish.

"So what have we learned up to this point of Wagner's trials?" Jones said.

"We know that, somehow, Murdock can get into someone's head and give them nightmares," Osterlund said.

"We know that Murdock killed everyone here," Hornsby said. "He murdered every single person who had taken refuge here."

"I don't know if it's a fact or not," Jones said, "but apparently, Murdock controls a huge bear."

Hornsby and Osterlund chuckled.

"I know. I don't think I believe that one, either. But from the constant nightmares, Wagner has lost all connection to reality, in my opinion."

"Do we know why Murdock has gone off the rails?" Hornsby said. "I mean, I didn't care for him, but he seemed to be stable and not prone to violence. Not without provocation, anyway."

"I asked Wagner about that," Jones said. "He was vague, and I'm not sure what's real from his perspective. He said something about a hunting accident and Murdock's wife being killed."

The other two men grumbled.

"I know," Jones said. "Like I said, it's hard to tell what's real and what's imagined. This, however, is probably true. I'd heard from one of my sources that Murdock recently got remarried. So that would fit if his wife died, although the reasons are still up in the air."

"Setting Wagner's insanity aside, what are we going to do, and with what?" Hornsby said. "I've been into every chamber and have found absolutely no weapons of any kind. Like you, I know they made weapons here. So where did they go?"

"We have limited weaponry," Hornsby said. "All we have is what we have with us right now. How many arrows do we have? Two dozen? Maybe less? Is that enough for anything? I think it's not enough just for hunting game, let alone a war."

"I'm not planning on doing anything with our limited resources," Jones said. "I think we need to lay low. Plan, recruit, gather resources and intelligence, and most important of all, don't draw attention to ourselves. Wagner screwed up by attacking the medical facility. I had no idea why he was attacking it, except out of a vicious hatred for Murdock and anything he'd built. Have any of you seen that facility up close? It's a damn castle. In some ways, it's better able to withstand an attack, especially given the weapons Wagner's men could manufacture. And what do we know from that attack? That less than six people successfully stood off more than twice their numbers. Most of the time, Wagner was just shooting over the walls for something to do."

"So we hide and cower?" Hornsby said.

"Hardly. I think we need to travel far and wide and tell the tale, once we agree to the narrative, of the bravery of Wagner standing alone against the tyranny of Murdock and his followers."

"But that's not exactly accurate," Osterlund said.

"Does it matter? Histories are often told in a way that is beneficial to the person presenting the history, and seldom has any resemblance to what actually happened. Personally, I think Wagner brought all this on himself. After seeing him in action, I think he and his men came upon Murdock's wife and murdered her. Murdock lost his shit and heaped his vengeance and wrath onto Wagner. As far as the rest, they probably tried to defend themselves against a vengeful Murdock, and lost. But that's just my take, knowing the players involved. What I think we need to do to survive and try to gain back what was lost, is to spin our own epic story with Wagner, a truly pathetic...um, sympathetic person, as the hero. It should gain us followers, and, thus, resources. But we *need* to control the *narrative*."

"So, you're saying we should lie, cheat, steal, whatever it takes?" Osterlund said.

"Of course." Jones said. "Great empires have been started with no more than a good story and a self-serving interpretation of the facts."

Murdock, having being summoned to the springtime Oomah gathering, stood in front of all the gathered Oomah.

"This my tribe, my people." He motioned for the humans to rise.

Declan, Emily, their three kids, Annie Cooper, holding Grace, Doctor Harris, Zeke, Andrew, Chun Hua, Rosa, and Heather, holding Aryan, all rose and stood proudly.

"You tribe has brought distinction and earned honor to themself and are true friends of Oomah," Beron flashed to all in attendance. *"You, Kee van, have alone passed test of recognition. Increase require more pass test. We delay greatly due to you."*

"I understand," Murdock responded.

"I'm glad *you* do. 'Cause I don't," Declan said.

"We'll discuss it later," Murdock replied.

"Only Dee clan, Andiroo, E zek eye al allowed presently," Beron said. *"Before leave, must submit single."*

"I need to have Zeke, Declan, and Andrew over here," Murdock announced.

"What are they saying?" Zeke said. "I understood that there

is a test of some kind, which makes sense. Most cultures have a test of manhood."

"Me and Zeke are a little old for a test of manhood," Declan said.

"Quiet down," Murdock said. "Soon after I landed here, I killed a monster snake and ate it. I had no clue it was the Oomah's test of recognition. At the time, I didn't understand or know there was such a thing as Oomah. Recently, I found out that that act was a test. If I'd not passed it, the Oomah would've never contacted us or helped us. They never would've gotten to know humans. Presently, the Oomah will not recognize any more humans without more humans passing the test."

"So we all have to pass it now?" Declan asked nervously.

"Not all. Only one, for now. Because of me, you all have been given a pass, sort of. They have recognized you because you're under my *grace*, so to speak. The time has come for someone else to do the same. Otherwise, the Oomah won't recognize any other humans."

"I'll do it," Andrew mumbled.

"But that's ridiculous," Declan said. "None of us have ever done anything *to* the Oomah. We have done what we can *for* them."

"It doesn't matter, Declan," Zeke said. "It's their society, their planet, their rules."

"I'll do it," Andrew repeated, louder.

"We have little to say about it," Zeke said. "Screaming the unfairness won't solve the problem."

"I said, I'll do it," Andrew repeated even louder.

Declan and Zeke became silent.

"Are you sure?" Murdock said. "It's dangerous, and there's no need for you to do it at this time. You'll have to eventually, though."

"You, Father, have been training me for this for years, whether you knew it or not.

"What?" Declan said. "He has?"

Murdock closed his eyes. "Yes, I have. Beron has been asking me if Andy was old enough yet, for many years."

"And you didn't think to include us in that?" Declan asked snippily.

"I didn't know it was something open to any male adult. I thought it was just my son—my sons, now—that the Oomah required to be tested."

"So you thought it was a testing of only your kids," Zeke said. "Similar to the testing of a genetic leader?"

"Yes. Only lately, on the relative scale, have I been told of the requirements of all male humans."

"Why is it only for males?" Annie said.

She had eavesdropped without being noticed.

"Women are just as capable as men."

"In some respects, Annie, I'd agree with you," Murdock said. "But not on this one. It's my understanding that the Oomah view females as far more valuable than males. Females are capable of delivering the next generation. Males, however, are the providers, the warriors, and the expendable. So as such, have to be recognized as worthy by other males. It's one of the reasons females are not included in discussions with males, and why females don't communicate with general males, only specific ones. It'll make sense if you look at it from their perspective."

"But women are equal to men," Annie said.

"Really? So-called female equality diminishes females and their value. Besides, it isn't up to me. It's up to the Oomah. Their planet, their society, their rules."

"So you will allow *your* son to do this test?" Declan said. "How dangerous is it?"

"It's dangerous enough. I've done it. I could lose my son. Is that dangerous enough for you?" Murdock spat. "Besides, he volunteered. It isn't something I've asked of him, or anyone else."

"It can't be that dangerous. You'd never risk your own son." Declan sneered as he walked away.

Murdock was standing looking out over the plateau below his own, in the early summer sunshine.

"So you're going to go through with it?" Declan said.

"I'm not going through anything. My son is."

"How can you do this and be so calm about it? I thought you cared about your son. It's becoming obvious to me that either this test isn't really dangerous, or you choose to sacrifice your son."

Murdock turned on Declan. "The last thing I am is calm! I didn't choose anything. Yes, it's dangerous, but I didn't choose it. The Oomah require it. My son volunteered, but I chose nothing."

"You could stop it if you really wanted to."

Murdock glared at Declan. "You're afraid."

"*Phah!* I'm not afraid."

"You're afraid that it's all true and that I'm right. Afraid that Gordon, in the fullness of his time, will have to do the same. Not to mention yourself and any other sons you have. You're afraid they won't survive the test. You know it's dangerous. Otherwise, why bother? My son didn't consult me, didn't require my acceptance or my permission." Murdock looked away from Declan. "You know, the Oomah could've waited and caught everyone unawares. They could've had one of those snakes attack you at a time you didn't expect. I know I wasn't ready for mine. If you know, you can prepare to a point. The unknown is worse."

"Do you know when this test is?"

"It happens when the Oomah say it is to happen. They aren't going to tell me or anyone else." Murdock looked at Declan. "The rules of this test are simple. Without outside interference, Andrew has to dispatch a large snake and survive. The snake will hunt him and attack him. There's no way I can prevent it. There's nowhere on this planet that anyone can hide from the Oomah." He exhaled loudly. "If I could do this for him, I would.

But I can't. You want to fight the Oomah on this, then you're a better man than I, Gunga Din. Now leave me alone."

Murdock walked off, leaving Declan to stare after him.

"How old Andiroo," Beron flashed to Murdock.

It was mid-summer.

"He just turned eleven, as best we can gage it," Murdock replied. *"For my kind, still immature."*

"For my kind, well past testing. More than twice."

"Can I observe?" Murdock asked.

"'Course, but restrained."

"I'd hope I wouldn't need to be, but there is comfort in knowing I could do nothing."

"We un'stand difficult. We not cruel. You, Kee van, closer to Oomah than any other. You wrong. Not fail if die. Failing if not offering."

It was close to the end of summer, as Murdock calculated. He was floating twenty to thirty feet off the grassy plain. From what he could see, it was close to the same spot he had killed the snake sent for him, may years before. He was now looking on as Andy was wandering in the tall grass.

After the Gathering, and Andrew's volunteering, Murdock had presented his son with his birth mother's machetes, knives, and hatchet. Andrew accepted them with pride.

Now Murdock was looking on. Beron was levitating himself and Murdock. In addition, Murdock found he was being restrained. His telepathic abilities had been dampened to the point that he could only communicate with Beron.

Murdock watched Andrew stop and listen. Murdock could see the grass waving as the snake approached, first slow and testing, then faster, more direct. Murdock's heart was pounding, partly from memory of his own test, partly a panic for what was coming toward his son.

As the snake prepared to strike, Andrew drew his eighteen-inch machete. In a practiced maneuver, he made a single circular motion with the machete, and ended in a powerful single stroke that resulted in the beheading of the reptile. Andrew danced around the thrashing body.

A dance of death. Murdock's heartbeat slowed. *He's done it!*

"*Not doubted by Oomah,*" Beron flashed.

"*I didn't doubt my son's abilities, but I know luck has its place as much as skill. Things don't always go the way we think they will.*"

It was then that Murdock noticed the size of the reptile. It was small compared to his memory of the one that came for him. He wasn't sure if it was actually smaller.

"*You growed. Yours growed. Size comparable,*" Beron flashed.

"*So when it comes time for Declan and Zeke...*"

"*They growed. Theirs growed. Wait no help.*"

"*What penalty for avoiding?*"

"*Communicate easier with Oomah help. Avoid test, no Oomah help. We not force.*"

"*Humans fall in esteem with Oomah. Humans not kicked off Oomah planet?*"

"*Kicked off? Explain.*"

Murdock did.

"*Oh, no, not kicked off planet,*" Beron flashed to Murdock. "*Eliminate. Not send elsewhere. To Oomah, either growing to equal or food or other purposes. All others end.*"

"*Other purposes? Like destroyers?*"

Beron flashed an affirmative.

"*Andiroo not require escort. Earn right to go at will.*"

Murdock was released, and his abilities restored. He dropped next to Andrew.

"Where did you come from?" he said.

"I was observing, but Beron was hampering my abilities."

"He was also hiding you somewhere. I saw neither of you. So can I go home now?"

"You can. But before we do, I must say I used to call you Andy, but now you will be Andrew. You earned it."

"I don't care what you call me, as long as it isn't *late for dinner*." Andrew laughed.

"He passed and is fine!" Murdock flashed to all humans that could hear his thoughts.

Everyone responded positively as Murdock picked up his son's prize, and they strolled home.

"As far as the Oomah are concerned," Murdock said to his son, "you're now responsible for your actions. If you vouch for someone else to the Oomah, then you will be held responsible for them."

"And how do you view it?"

"You are still my son. I was there when you were born, but you're no longer a little boy. You've passed your first test on the road to manhood, but that just allows you on the road. You haven't arrived yet. You still have a lot to learn."

"And who will teach me?" Andrew asked.

"Everyone will. You watch. You listen. If you're aware, everyone will teach you."

"But will you? And Mother? Will you continue to teach me?"

"Mother?"

"Heather. She is my mother now, too, isn't she?"

"I don't know. Have you asked her?"

"Not yet. Should I?"

"Do you want her to be your mother? Rose bore you, and Mei Lee raised you up. Both are gone now, but not forgotten. If you respect her, then you need to ask Heather."

"But will she?"

"I have no idea. There are times that you need to take a chance and ask without knowing what the answer will be. I could make a guess, but I'm not going to. You need to ask her for permission to refer to her as Mother. It's the respectful thing to do.

"So it wasn't so bad after all." Declan helped to prepare the snake.

Murdock frowned at him.

"What?"

"I was restrained and had my abilities dampened while I watched my firstborn put his life on the line. I can tell you, it took a fair amount of inner strength to watch helplessly. You'll see soon enough."

"Will I?"

"Let me put it to you this way. If you don't go through the testing and let Gordon go through it, humans will drop in the esteem of the Oomah. That drop in esteem will affect if humans will continue here. The individual who doesn't take part will not have access to the things the Oomah can help to accomplish. In your case, you'd lose the ability to levitate and communicate telepathically at a distance. You wouldn't be able to attend the Spring Gathering, not even if someone sponsors you."

"I could live with all that," Declan said seriously.

"Really? You better check with your wife before that comes up. I'm sure she'll have something to say about it."

"Did you consult your wife before your test?"

"Nope."

"See? Not a big deal."

"Declan, stop talking. Your ignorance is showing."

"What's that supposed to mean?"

"I didn't have a wife until after my test."

"Oh."

"And I was informed it's not about living or dying. It's about the offer, the sacrifice."

"Heather, can I talk to you privately?" Andrew said.

"Certainly." She led the way to her and Murdock's room.

Andrew followed, and she shut the door behind him.

"What did you want?" she said.

"Would you mind if I called you Mother?" He looked down.

"Did your father put you up to this?" Heather asked gruffly.

"No. I asked him if I should call you that, and he said I should ask you myself. So would you be offended?"

Heather smiled. "Not at all. And what should I call you?"

"Anything you want." Andrew chuckled.

"Anything I like? Hmmm... how about... son? Would that be okay?"

"Yes, ma'am, that would be fine."

Heather saw a tear start, and held out her arms. "Come give your mother a hug."

Andrew rushed to her.

"You wouldn't dare!" Declan said to Murdock, as Heather came out to join the rest of the family.

Heather said nothing, and acted as if she weren't paying any attention.

"You'd really be that vindictive?" Declan said.

"It isn't about vindictiveness, Declan."

"What's going on, Kevin?" Heather said.

Chun Hua brought Aryan to her, and she was bouncing him on her hip.

"*Your* husband is evicting us!" Declan said to Heather.

Aryan started frowned, which turned into a cry.

"Calm yourself, Declan. Yelling at my wife isn't going to help, and scaring my baby is gonna get you plenty of trouble," Murdock warned. "Besides, I didn't say you were evicted."

"Your *wife*. Ha! You don't know the half of it!"

Murdock frowned. Heather knew this wasn't a good sign.

"Careful," Murdock said.

"What 'cha gonna do? Beat my ass? You ain't got the gu—"

Heather closed her eyes... and then opened one when she heard someone hit the ground.

"Do you want me to beat your stupid ass?" Murdock held Declan by the front of his leather shirt. "Make one more comment about my wife! Go on. Make just one more"

"Kevin, stop it," Heather said. "Declan is like a brother to you, so stop it."

Murdock looked at her and inhaled deeply. "Sorry, Declan. Didn't mean to hurt you." He helped him to his feet.

Declan was almost standing, when he swung at Murdock's face. Murdock jabbed him in the solar plexus. Declan gasped.

"Told you I was sorry," Murdock said. "If you just would've let it go—"

"What did you do to my husband!" Emily charged toward Murdock.

Heather turned away, sheltering her baby, and started for the cabin.

"Get back here, you dumb bitch!" Emily said. "I know you started all this You never shoulda come here."

Murdock restrained her, and she fell to the ground as if she were wrapped in ropes.

"You two have really done it now," Murdock said, through clenched teeth. "When I release you, Emily, you will collect your husband, and your kids, and return to your house. If you don't apologize to Heather tout suite, you could find yourselves off this plateau."

Murdock released Emily, and then went into the cabin with Heather.

Murdock went into his and Heather's room and found her crying.

"I told you my coming here was a mistake. I knew I should've stayed clear of here."

"You want to move? We can always go to the caves."

"Permanently or temporarily?"

"Any way you want it. You are my wife. I'll take you anywhere you'll be happy, if I can." He caressed her shoulders.

"What started all this? I just don't understand."

"It started when Declan was arguing with me about his duty to the Oomah, for what they've given him and his family."

"What duty?"

"Beron told me that the Oomah don't force anyone, but they do require that males participate in their testing. If they don't, then they lose levitation and telepathy."

"That's not so bad."

"Maybe not. But to live up here, you have to be able to pass the blocks that the Oomah have in place. In other words, you have to belong here. Without telepathy and levitation, you don't really belong, and the Oomah stop those that don't belong. With them, either you're in or you're out. There are no half-measures. It was similar with you, the first time. You didn't know about the Oomah. You may have suspected, but you didn't know. You were asked to join us, and you passed on it at that time." Murdock shook his head and put his hands up. "I'm not blaming, just being factual. Consequently, you left this plateau, and you wouldn't have been allowed back here without joining or being here at the invitation of someone already welcomed. You joined our tribe, and that made you automatically accepted by the Oomah. We fell in love and married. You make me happy, and that's something the Oomah would always approve of. Apparently, that isn't enough for Declan and Emily. Declan is saying he won't submit to the Oomah's test and he won't allow his son, when he gets old enough, to be tested. He thinks they ask too much. I don't know. Maybe they do. But it is their planet.

They can do what they want. If enough humans refuse the test, they could terminate every human already here and every human who comes here. There's a lot more at stake than just one or two lives." Murdock started to break down. "I was restrained and had to watch ...my first-born son... offer himself as a sacrifice. He faced his test ...and dealt with it. Now Declan has jeopardized everyone's continuation. That is what started it all, and when you calmed me down, I felt bad for Declan. He started in on you to hurt me. That's the only reason he said anything, and the only reason for Emily to say anything. If there is another, I don't know what it is."

"So now what?" Heather said.

"They better be apologizing to you, PDQ."

"PDQ?"

"Pretty damn quick!"

"And if they don't?" Heather asked.

"I don't know. We'll have to see. If I have to, I'll talk to Beron."

Everyone asks me if I was scared for my son. Of course I was. The Oomah's test isn't just about sacrifice or survival. The Oomah know that life means standing and fighting. Their test is like asking, Will you stand and fight? Will you fight, even if the odds are against you?

— KEVIN MURDOCK, COLLECTED SAYINGS

Murdock and Declan were standing on the plateau edge, looking over the plateau below. With them were Emily, carrying Gordon, Maureen, and Roslynn.

"Are you certain you won't change your mind?" Murdock said to Declan.

"You've been after me for most of a year. I haven't changed my views and I haven't apologized to your ...wife...so, no. I haven't relented."

Murdock nodded. "As you wish, then. You will not be allowed on this plateau."

Declan shrugged. "Don't want to be."

Murdock frowned. "Your telepathic abilities will no longer be amplified."

"No problem. Take it away completely. I don't care."

"Your ability to levitate will be dampened."

"You act like you're taking something valuable away. You aren't."

Murdock extended his arm toward the plateau below. Declan started the climb down, with the two girls following him.

"You know, you killed Mei Lee." Emily glared at Murdock. "You blamed her for the death of Huo Jin and her unborn child and she knew it."

"No, I didn't."

"She told me that several times. She said she felt you blamed her. Did you do that to drive her to suicide so you could marry your whore?" Emily's eyes flashed the hatred in her heart.

Murdock said nothing.

"It must be true. You have nothing to say about it or in your own defense."

Emily followed the girls and her husband.

"Are they gone?" Heather said.

"Yes." Murdock entered the cabin and sat at the table. "They're off this plateau."

"They knew the price a year ago. You've given them every chance. We even moved to the caves for the winter. Where are they going?"

Murdock exhaled loudly. "They said something about going to Reyes's camp. That area, anyway. They didn't want to be more specific, and I didn't ask them to be."

"What's wrong? I know something is bothering you, so talk." Heather sat at the table.

"I was told that Mei Lee thought I blamed her for the deaths of our two children, and that I drove her to suicide so I could marry you."

Heather was tense and glaring. "I can guess where you heard that. Anything else I should know?"

Murdock shook his head.

"Let me guess, I was called a whore as well?"

Murdock gave no facial indication.

"I was there, or shortly afterwards. I saw the two of you. From what I know of your character, you blamed yourself for failing to protect them adequately. Mei Lee, being who she was, did the same. Blamed herself, not you. I did notice a… cooling, I guess you'd call it, between you two. I'm guessing you blamed yourself to the point that communications broke down? And maybe she did the same?"

"But did I drive her to suicide?" Murdock asked.

"I don't know, did you?"

"I don't think I did."

"I noticed that since the arrival of the most recent newcomers, Mei Lee had become more …reckless. She'd throw herself into dangerous situations."

"I did notice some of that."

"You were concerned with wrangling the newcomers, and she was busy proving she could defend herself against anyone, if I know the two of you. As far as me being a whore, that's just hurting someone else because they hurt you. I was never what anyone would call a whore. When I arrived here, I was young and overly concerned with acceptance and popularity, so I fell in with Phylicia and Kimberly. It allowed me to feel superior, privileged, special. When Palmer took over from Phylicia, he and his men tortured and raped all three of us as often as they could. Here is a secret most don't know. Palmer and his cronies, all had the …um…non-survival predilections. The mentioning of possible pregnancy, by me anyway, was a means to an end to get away from Phylicia. I was never pregnant because no one managed to… um, gain entrance …until you did, after we were married. And that is all I'm going to say about it. Ever. To anyone."

Murdock was shocked.

"I'd suggest you talk to Beron and Bridget about the issues

with you and Mei Lee. In my opinion, the only thing you may have done is blame yourself for something you had no control over. But drive her to suicide? I don't believe it and never will."

"*So you all know,*" Murdock flashed to everyone in his tribe, "*Declan and Emily have decided to leave the tribe. It was their choice.*"

There was silence for some time.

"*Where did they go?*" Irene said.

"*From what they said, they went to Reyes' camp area.*"

"*Are we still free to associate with them?*" Annie said.

"*I've never forced or banned associations with anyone. The Oomah has removed the telepathic amplification available to Declan and Emily. So long-distance connections aren't possible. If you want to associate with them, you can.*"

"*What about the testing?*" Zeke asked, privately.

"*What about it?*" Murdock replied, in kind.

"*I'm willing and am requesting you to witness, as you did for Andrew. If something happens, Irene would rather hear it from you.*"

"*I can do that. And I offer my machetes for you to use. They have been proven.*"

"*I don't know how to let Beron know my wishes. Maybe you can bring it up? Also, you need to train me, if you have the time.*"

"*From my understanding, Because of Andrew's voluntary act, you have some time, maybe a year?*"

By the end of the third year that the two thousand newcomers had endured, the landing pod area had consolidated to the point that few had died after the first winter, but few remained. A large portion of those who survived were distributed between the farmers, Benson's camp, Benteen's camp, and Gundersen's camp. About thirty people joined with Alvin Jones at the mine.

Over the next two years, they managed to make a few metal items, pots and kettles mostly, for trade and to give them a reason to travel about recruiting.

In the middle of the fourth year, Wagner was found hanging in a tree. Jones assumed it was suicide, as Wagner had never gotten over the unrelenting nightmares.

Another group showed itself halfway to the farmers, downriver, and the medical facility, upriver. This group was led by Dirk Benson. He'd decided to start the group so he could be closer to his daughter, and if things worked out that way, he'd be in a position to help the next batch of newcomers, should any land close to the last group's pods.

During the fourth year, Benson had given some thought to re-purposing the landing pods. He'd thought, with the proper tools to dismantle them, the pod's upper half could be used as roofs, but the idea never came to fruition.

Melanie, at the end of the third year, married Benteen and gave him a son a short time later. The boy favored Jones rather than Benteen, but he didn't mind. Gundersen and Mackenzie married and produced a son in the spring of the fourth year.

By the end of the fourth year, Declan and Emily had increased their family by two, both boys. The couple would never apologize to Murdock or Heather, and any accidental meetings were strained at best. Curtis and Angelica had made their way back upriver and lived close to Declan.

Heather gave Murdock another daughter in the fourth year. Little Cassandra Eileen.

At the Oomah's Spring Gathering in the spring of the fifth year since the two thousand had arrived, Murdock found that he missed Declan's and Emily's presence more than he thought he would. He'd heard they had two more sons, but he didn't know their names.

When Murdock stood to give his announcements, he handed Aryan off to Andrew, who took his little brother's hand, keeping a close eye on him. Heather carried little Cassie when it was time to present Murdock's brood. As he looked at everyone, he realized how blessed he was. He had a beautiful wife and five kids, even though one was not technically his, but that didn't matter to him. Andrew was growing into a proud, handsome man. Chun Hua was growing into the image of her mother. Rosa was going to be a heartbreaker when she got older. Aryan and Cassie were both beautiful, but they had a lot of growing to do yet.

"Are you okay?" Heather asked her husband.

"I'm Fine. Just admiring our little family."

"Little? The last thing this brood is, is little. I have figured out why you enjoy these gatherings with the Oomah so much."

He looked at her, puzzled.

"You like to show off your kids. You like all the attention you get because of them."

"And you." Murdock kissed her. "I like showing off my beautiful wife. I hope that meets with your approval?"

"Let me think about it. I'll get back to ya on that." She gave a flirtatious grin.

"Have you seen Annie or Irene? Zeke is missing, too." Murdock looked around for the rest of his tribe.

"They said they'd be here." Heather helped search.

When he'd located them, Murdock did his best to herd his brood toward Zeke and Irene. When the adults had gotten close, Murdock stopped, his mouth agape.

"Irene? Are you—"

"You just keep a civil tongue in your head, Kevin!" Irene Harris snapped. "You need to respect your elders and not draw attention to things that don't concern you."

Heather placed a hand over her mouth as she tried to refrain from laughing.

"Yup! She is," Zeke said. "Who'd a thunk an old codger like me still had it in him?"

"You shoulda kept it in ya, too," Irene said. "What made you think I wanted it? I'm too old." She shook her head.

"You're not old, Irene." Murdock smiled as he bent to hug her. "You look good pregnant."

She slapped his arm. "You go on, ya! I'll not be accepting any of your blarney. Now I suppose I have to get married. Hey, old man," she said to Zeke, "you gonna make an honest woman of me?"

"If you'll have me, and if Kevin will officiate?"

"Of course. I'd love to pay you back for mine and Heather's."

"Oops! Maybe I went a little too far with that one," Zeke said.

"Are you ready, Zeke?" Murdock asked his old friend. "From what I hear, you're close to going through your test."

Zeke became somber. "I dunno. Am I ready?"

Murdock looked at him and smiled. "You're as ready as I can get you. You'll do fine."

"Annie!" Heather said, when she saw her friend coming toward them.

"Hello, everyone." Annie led Grace by the hand.

"Gracie!" Murdock picked up the little girl and snuggled her while Heather and Annie hugged. "You're such a big girl."

The child grinned and nodded.

"How have you been, Annie?" Murdock set Grace back down.

"I've been fine. Been busy chasing after the munchkin here." Annie stroked her daughter's head.

"*Ahem.*" Andrew cleared his throat.

"Yes, son?" Zeke said.

"Since the tribe is here, I would like to call a tribal meeting," Andrew said.

"Uh-oh!" Murdock said. "Sounds serious." He chuckled at his son.

"Could be," Irene said. "Who are you inviting?"

"Everyone. Well, all the adults, anyway."

"That leaves quite a bit to interpretation," Murdock said.

"Okay, everyone older than Rosa. Is that better?"

"Easy, boy, I was just joshing you," Murdock said.

"Sorry. It may not be important to all of you, but it is to me. Besides, I need everyone's expertise."

"Is it something we can discuss here?" Heather said.

"No, Mother. I'd prefer to discuss it at the Common House."

"The Common House?" Annie said.

"It's what we call Declan's old house," Heather replied. "It's empty most of the time, so we use it for a common meeting area."

"Okay, so I guess we're all going to Kevin's from here," Irene said.

Kevin started a small fire in the large fireplace of the Common House.

"Well, son, you called this shindig, what's on your mind?" Murdock sat on a bench.

Andrew got to his feet and cleared his throat. "As some of you know, I turned fourteen this past winter. Because I'm gaining on adulthood, have any of you, as the leaders of our tribe, come up with any procedures for declaring intentions?"

"Speaks well, don't he?" Murdock said to Zeke, who nodded.

"By the way, congratulations on your birthday," Annie said. "What do you mean by intentions?"

"After the instruction given by Zeke, I was thinking—" Andrew started.

"That's always a good thing," Zeke said. "Thinking, I mean."

Everyone nodded.

"So what have you been thinking about, son?" Murdock said. "Spit it out."

"Yes, get to the point," Irene said. "I got a weddin' to get prepared for."

Everybody laughed.

"What?" Irene said. "I don't want tongues waggin' if I choose to wear white. And I ain't getting any younger."

"I was thinking," Andrew said, louder, "I should declare my intentions as to courting."

Everyone sat silent, mouths agape.

"Damn, son, I said get to the point, but...damn!" Murdock commented.

"I agree with Kevin," Heather said.

"And when is this...courting...going to start?" Irene said.

"Not for some time yet. I brought it up so you can come up with some procedures for us youngsters to follow, like they had in Victorian times."

"I don't think we have a need for balls and cotillions," Zeke said, "but I understand your point."

"You do?" Murdock said. "Mind explaining it to me?"

"Excuse me, Andrew," Zeke said, "but I think what this well-spoken young man is saying is that he's wondering what rituals we expect him to follow, if he should wish to declare his intentions to court someone. I mean, are we going to say he can't court someone unless he has her weight in gold? Or would that be something the prospective father-in-law would provide? If it's something that would take years to accomplish, he wants to know it up front." He sat.

"Is that what you mean, Andrew?" Murdock said.

"Not exactly. Let's say, for the sake of argument, I know someone who I would like to court. How do I go about announcing to others that that is my intention? I wouldn't want someone else to be interloping on my intended, and I wouldn't want myself to be that person."

Murdock looked confused.

Heather, seeing her husband's confusion, chuckled. "He doesn't want anyone to jump his claim, and he doesn't want to be the claim-jumper."

"Exactly! Thanks, Mother."

"The young man brings up a valid point" Zeke rose. "Has anyone thought of how they want to determine viable suitors?"

"Hold on a sec," Murdock said. "Andrew, do you have someone in mind already? Someone you want to start courting?"

Andrew turned a few shades of red around his ears and neck. "*Ahem*. Yes, sir."

"And as your tribal leaders and parents," Murdock said, slowly, "may we know who this prospective female is?"

Andrew looked at the floor and tried to remain calm.

"Well, son, who is she?" Zeke said.

"Yes, Andrew, fill us in." Annie grinned.

"Out with it, boy!" Irene bellowed. "Speak up. Tell us."

"Yes, Andrew, tell us," Murdock said coaxingly, "I'm sure your mother and I will be thrilled as hell to know who it is. Wouldn't you, dear?" Murdock asked Heather.

"I must admit, he has intrigued me." Heather focused on Andrew.

Andrew squirmed a little longer, with everyone staring at him.

"It's me!" Chun Hua said. "Now leave him alone."

The adults were all silent, and stayed that way for some time.

"*Ahem*. I think we need to consider this privately," Murdock said.

"*Ahem*. Yes, I agree," Heather said.

"Oh, come off it," Irene said. "They may have been raised as brother and sister, but they aren't genetically related. They're about as related as you are, Kevin and Heather, or me and Zeke, or Annie and… whoever."

"That may be true, Irene," Murdock said, "but…"

"Exactly." Heather shook her head.

"Can I make a suggestion?" Annie said.

"I really wish you would," Kevin pleaded.

"Okay, I think Andrew has dropped a number of bombs on his tribe and his parents, all of which have exploded nicely, thank you very much. I suggest that we consider his request. We sleep on it, for now."

"Agreed," Murdock said quickly. "I move that we adjourn."

"Agreed," Heather said quickly.

"So I guess we're done. For now, anyway" Zeke chuckled. "Nice going, Andrew. Impressive."

Zeke chuckled the rest of the night, every time he thought of it.

"Well?" Kevin asked his wife.

"I'm just as flabbergasted as you are, dear. We always knew Andrew and Chunnie would grow up."

"I know, but come on. No one expected this."

Heather shook her head. "He sure knows how to shock everyone. Is that something you excel at?"

"Why would you think he got that from me?"

"Because I didn't know his mother. I only have his father for reference.

"Can I ask why?" Murdock said.

Andrew fidgeted and looked at Chun Hua. She wiped her hands on her leather dress and looked at Heather.

"I'd like to know how?" she said.

"Can I ask you something first? Andrew said to his father.

"Sure, you can ask."

"Did you trust Rose?"

"Yes, with my life, several times."

"And Mei Lee? Did you trust her, too?"

"Of course I did. You both know that. You grew up seeing it."

"And how about Heather? Do you also trust her?"

"Silly question. If I didn't, do you think I'd let her within a hundred miles of you kids?"

"Well, since the incident with Phylicia," Chun Hua said, "Andy is the only person I trust, maybe even more than you."

"More than me?" Kevin questioned.

"Yes. I'm not trying to hurt you, but Phylicia was here because you brought her. I blamed you a long time for that. Andy has never done anything to hurt me, and he has protected me for a number of years. I wish that protection to continue. Besides, I'm not sure I could begin to trust anyone more than I do Andy."

"Okay. And you? Do you blame me as well?" Murdock asked Andrew.

"No. I know you always do the best you can. Most of the time, it's enough. Only once did you… slip. Chunnie is all I can think of when there's trouble. I worry about her and want to protect her. Always."

Kevin nodded.

Heather said, "Have you two been—"

"Intimate?" Chun Hua interrupted. "No. And neither of us are thinking about that changing anytime soon. It's just that Andy is the best friend anyone can have. I plan on keeping that all to myself."

"Then why?" Kevin said.

"For today? I wanted it known that Chunnie is not available. I didn't want you marrying her off to some stranger."

"Well, you two are old enough to know what happens when intimacy overwhelms you," Kevin said. "So just know I don't have a problem with you two marrying. I know that genetically, you aren't related. Others may not be as understanding, so be mindful of that."

"You know, you could've asked us about this at any time," Heather said.

"I didn't want to take the chance without Irene being there to explain the genetics to you, should you become …intractable,"

Andrew explained. "It wasn't intended to embarrass you, or anyone."

Shortly after Andrew's meeting with the tribe, Murdock announced that, should any of the tribe not approve of Andrew and Chun Hua seeing each other, that it was immaterial, as he had no issue with it. All challenges to his parental authority on the issue would be referred to Irene for a complete explanation on the genetics involved.

Before everyone left for their respective homes, Kevin officiated over Irene and Zeke's wedding. It was respectful and not any more solemn than it had to be.

A few days later, Murdock witnessed Zeke's trial. It went as Murdock had expected. Zeke didn't do anything fancy. It was all strictly business. The Oomah were pleased.

"What about Dee clan?" Beron flashed, in a sad manner.

"He made his choice," Murdock replied. *"I do miss him, though."*

It was a warm night. Summer was close at hand, and Murdock was sitting on the ground close to the plateau's edge, on the first step to Mount Oomah. He had a small fire cooking fish, and he was sitting on a deer hide.

"Contemplating your navel?" Heather said, from behind him.

"No, Heather, I'm not. I'm contemplating my place in the universe."

"Oh, well, that's an easy one," she whispered in his ear. "I can tell you that," she said, seductively.

"I take it the kids are taken care of?" he said, as she pulled him onto his back.

Heather kissed him, an intense, toe-curling one that makes

you forget where you are. The kind of kiss that forces you to focus only on the present moment.

Heather broke contact with his lips. "Damn! For an old married man, you still got it."

"Got what?" Murdock stroked her long hair.

"Every single time I kiss you, my toes curl and my head spins, and you know exactly what to do to excite me."

Heather, through long practice, expertly disrobed him even as he did the same to her.

As he covered her neck with soft kisses, she whispered, "The fish may burn."

"I don't care. If I don't continue, my soul will burn," he whispered, between kisses.

After she mounted him, she leaned back, tossing her head skyward. He caressed every inch of her body. On her third orgasm, she opened her eyes.

"Oh, look. A meteor shower. Spectacular!"

"It's not as spectacular as you." He pulled her down to him.

"More landing pods on way," Beron flashed to Murdock, as he kissed his wife. *"Many times many."*

"I really don't care about that right this minute." Murdock asked his wife, "How did you know?"

"Know what?" Heather collapsed onto her back, on the hide, panting.

"How did you know that you making love with me out here would start the next invasion?"

"Did it? I didn't really notice."

He could hear her smile in her voice. "Personally, for me, the planet moved and nothing else seemed to matter."

Dear reader,

We hope you enjoyed reading *Resolutions*. Please take a moment to leave a review, even if it's a short one. Your opinion is important to us.

Discover more books by Stephen Drake at
https://www.nextchapter.pub/authors/stephen-drake

Want to know when one of our books is free or discounted? Join the newsletter at
http://eepurl.com/bqqB3H

Best regards,

Stephen Drake and the Next Chapter Team

You might also like:
Blackwing by Stephen Drake

To read the first chapter for free, head to:
https://www.nextchapter.pub/books/blackwing

ABOUT THE AUTHOR

Stephen Drake, a retired computer programmer of twenty-plus years, is an American fantasy / sci-fi author. He is an avid Harley Davidson Motorcycle enthusiast, and versed in many survival skills such as martial arts and bow hunting. He is also an avid reader of sci-fi especially that by R.A. Heinlein and John Scalzi, and is a supporter of other independent authors.

Although he has been a long-time resident of Washington State, he was born in Iowa and has lived in Wisconsin, Nebraska, Iowa, Montana, and Virginia

He draws on his experiences to create gripping and believable stories.

OTHER BOOKS BY THIS AUTHOR

THE DISPLACED SERIES:

Displaced (Book 1)

Civilization (Book 2)

Resolutions (Book 3)

BLACKWING

Jessica Strange (Book 2 in the Blackwing Saga) (W.I.P.)

Resolutions
ISBN: 978-4-86747-055-8

Published by
Next Chapter
1-60-20 Minami-Otsuka
170-0005 Toshima-Ku, Tokyo
+818035793528

25th October 2021